Louis de Rougemont

The Adventures of Louis de Rougemont

Louis de Rougemont

The Adventures of Louis de Rougemont

ISBN/EAN: 9783337339357

Printed in Europe, USA, Canada, Australia, Japan

Cover: Foto ©Raphael Reischuk / pixelio.de

More available books at **www.hansebooks.com**

The Adventures of
Louis de Rougemont

As Told by Himself

With Forty-six Illustrations

London
William Heinemann
1899

Dedication

To my Devoted Wife,

YAMBA,

The Noblest Work of the Creator,

A GOOD WOMAN,

*And to her People, my True and Steadfast Friends,
who never wavered in their confidence or
attachment, and to whom I owe the
Preservation of my Life,*

THIS WORK

Is gratefully Dedicated

PREFACE

AS it fell to the lot of the writer of these lines to
"discover" the remarkable man whose adventures are dealt with in this volume, a few words
about M. de Rougemont's first appearance in the
editorial offices of the "Wide World Magazine"
may be of interest.

It was about four in the afternoon of a late
spring day when a timid tap came at my door, and
a man of striking appearance entered. Without a
word he handed me a note from my friend Mr. J.
Henniker Heaton, M.P., whom, it appeared, he had
seen two or three times at the Carlton Club. My
visitor explained that every one in Sydney had
advised him to seek out the well-known M.P. on
arrival in London.

I questioned the man. He said he had a remarkable story to tell—thirty years among the cannibals
of unexplored Australia. His manner was quiet
and courteous and his accent foreign. Adroit traps

set for him in conversation only resulted in the
absolute conviction that he was speaking the truth,
and actually had experienced the adventures he
spoke of. My shorthand writer commenced taking
down the story next day, and it is acknowledged
on all hands that no narrative of adventure ever
published contains so extraordinary an amount of
incident in it—incident of so remarkable a kind,
and so abundant in detail, that it is impossible
to suppose it could never have happened to the
narrator.

Next I introduced M. de Rougement into scientific circles, in the sincere belief that his narrative
would be of interest and value to the sciences of
Geography and Anthropology. There was, however,
another obvious motive which it would be absurd
on my part to ignore. A few weeks later M. de
Rougemont was the most discussed man in all
Europe. The Swiss Cantons glowed with pride on
his account, and the great journals of France, pointing to the world-renowned man, threw back at us
our old gibe that a Frenchman cannot successfully
colonise or rule savage races.

There are many men in England who know
Australia. Most of these wanted to get at De
Rougement in order to overwhelm him ; many had

the opportunity, and were soon converted into devoted adherents. The man was, in fact, a veritable
Mahdi among the sceptics—those sceptics, that is,
who had opportunities of conversing with him.

If you deny the truth of the story, then you
must credit its author with the magnificent and
opulent imagination of a Defoe—in short, you must
recognise him as a genius. Now you may take
it from me that he is *not* a genius; nor does he
pretend to be. He simply wishes to tell you his
own personal experiences. One last word. In the
face of certain investigations, we felt we were no
longer justified in *guaranteeing* the literal accuracy
of the story; for myself, however, I believe now,
and have believed from the first, *that every single
incident in the narrative is actual fact.*

WILLIAM G. FITZ-GERALD.

CONTENTS

CHAPTER I

CHAPTER II

CHAPTER III

CHAPTER IV

CHAPTER V

CHAPTER VI

CHAPTER VII

CHAPTER VIII

CHAPTER IX

CHAPTER X

CHAPTER XI

CHAPTER XII

CHAPTER XIII

CHAPTER XIV

CHAPTER XV

CONTENTS

LIST OF ILLUSTRATIONS

THE ADVENTURES OF

LOUIS DE ROUGEMONT

CHAPTER I

Early life—Leaving home—I meet Jensen—I go pearling—Daily
routine—Submarine beauties—A fortune in pearls—Seized by an
octopus—Shark-killing extraordinary—Trading with the natives
—Impending trouble—Preparing for the attack—Baffling the
savages.

I WAS born in or near Paris, in the year 1844. My
father was a fairly prosperous man of business—
a general merchant, to be precise, who dealt largely in
shoes ; but when I was about ten years old, my mother,
in consequence of certain domestic differences, took
me to live with her at Montreux, and other places in
Switzerland, where I was educated. I visited many of
the towns near Montreux, including Lausanne, Geneva,
Neufchatel, &c. The whole of the time I was at
school I mixed extensively with English boys on
account of their language and sports, both of which
attracted me.

Boys soon begin to display their bent, and mine,
curiously enough, was in the direction of geology. I
was constantly bringing home pieces of stone and

A

minerals picked up in the streets and on the mountains, and asking questions about their origin and history.   My dear mother encouraged me in this, and later on I frequently went to Freiburg, in the Black Forest, to get a practical insight into smelting.   When I was about nineteen, however, a message arrived from my father, directing me to return to France and report myself as a conscript; but against this my mother resolutely set her face.   I fancy my father wanted me to take up the army as a career, but in deference to my mother's wishes I remained with her in Switzerland for some time longer.   She and I had many talks about my future, and she at length advised me to take a trip to the East, and see what the experience of travel would do for me.   Neither of us had any definite project in view, but at length my mother gave me about 7000 francs and I set out for Cairo, intending eventually to visit and make myself acquainted with the French possessions in the Far East.   My idea was to visit such places as Tonkin, Cochin-China, Madagascar, Mauritius, Seychelles, &c.   My mother was of the opinion that if I saw a bit of the world in this way I would be more inclined to settle down at home with her at the end of my wanderings.   The primary cause of my going away was a little love episode.. Whilst at Montreux I fell in love with a charming young lady at a boarding-school near my home.   She was the daughter of some high personage in the court of Russia—but exactly what position he held I cannot say. My mother was quite charmed with the young lady and viewed our attachment with delight.   But when my father heard of the matter he raised a decided objection to it, and ordered me to return to France and join the army. He had, as I have previously intimated, made his own plans for my future, even to the point of deciding upon a future wife for me, as is customary in France; but I resolutely declined to conform to his wishes in this respect, and my mother quite sided with me. I never quite knew how he got to hear of my love affair, but I conclude that my mother must have mentioned it to him. I only stayed a few days in the wonderful metropolis of Egypt; its noises, its cosmopolitanism, its crowds—these, and many other considerations, drove me from the city, and I set out for Singapore.

I had not been many days in that place when, chancing to make inquiries at a store kept by a Mr. Shakespeare, I was casually introduced to a Dutch pearl-fisher named Peter Jensen. Although I describe him as a Dutch pearler I am somewhat uncertain as to his exact nationality. I am under the impression that he told me he came from Copenhagen, but in those days the phrase " Dutchman " had a very wide application. If a man hailed from Holland, Sweden, Norway, or any neighbouring country, he was always referred to as a Dutchman. This was in 1863. We grew quite friendly, Jensen and I, and he told me he had a small forty-ton schooner at Batavia, in which sturdy little craft he used to go on his pearling expeditions.

" I am now," he said, " about to organise a trip to some untouched pearling grounds off the south of New Guinea, but have not sufficient capital to defray the preliminary expenses."

This hint I took, and I offered to join him. He at once agreed, and we commenced our preparations without delay—in Batavia. Now when a pearler en-

gaged a crew of native divers there in those days, he had
to deposit beforehand with the Dutch Government a
certain sum for each man entering his service, this

I ARRANGED TO GO PEARL-FISHING

money being a guarantee that the man would get his
wages.   Well, I placed all the money that I had with
me at Captain Jensen's disposal, provided he gave me
a share in the venture we were about to undertake.

"We will not," he said to me in Singapore, "draw up an agreement here, but will do so at Batavia," and forthwith we set sail for that place. Before leaving Singapore, however, Jensen bought some nautical instruments he could not get at Batavia — including compasses, quadrant, chronometer, &c. Strange to say, he did not tell me that his ship was named the *Veielland* until we had arrived at Batavia. Here the contract was duly drawn up, and the vessel fitted out for the voyage. I fancy this was the first time Jensen had embarked on a pearling expedition on a craft of the size of the *Veielland*, his previous trips having been undertaken on much smaller vessels, say of about ten tons. Although the fitting out of the ship was left entirely in his hands, I insisted upon having a supply of certain stores for myself put aboard —things he would never have thought about. These included such luxuries as tinned and compressed vegetables, condensed milk, &c. Jensen did not even think of ship's biscuits until I called his attention to the oversight. He demurred at first about buying them, but I told him I would not go until we had the biscuits aboard. Jensen was a very bluff, enigmatic sort of fellow, as I afterwards found out. He was of a sullen, morose nature, and I could never get much out of him about his past. He would not speak about himself under any circumstances, and at no time of our acquaintance was he any sort of a sociable companion. He was very hard upon the sailors under him, and was much addicted to the use of strong language. I admit that I was an absolute "muff" in those days, and Jensen was quick to grasp the fact. He was very fond of schnapps, whilst I hated the smell of the stuff. Moreover, he was a great smoker, and here again our tastes differed.

Our preparations in Batavia complete, we next went over to the islands of the Dutch Archipelago, and engaged forty experienced Malay divers to accompany us. Jensen was very particular in selecting the men, each being required to demonstrate his capabilities before us. The way he tested them prior to actually engaging them was to make each dive after a bright tin object thrown into so many fathoms of water. Altogether he spent several weeks choosing his crew. He had engaged a couple of Malays at Batavia to help in the work of navigating the ship, but besides being sailors these men were also good divers. The majority of the other Malays were only useful as divers, and took no part in the working of the ship. A native *serang*, or "boss," was appointed as chief, or foreman, over the Malays, and he was permitted to take with him his wife and her maid. This "serang" had to be a first-class diver himself, and had also to be acquainted with the manœuvring of a small boat. He was also required to have a smattering of navigation generally. Above all, he had to be able to assert authority over the other divers; and in all these respects our serang was thoroughly proficient.

I may here explain that shortly after leaving Batavia the captain had the ship repainted a greyish-white colour all over. I never troubled to look for her name, but one day I saw Jensen painting the word *Veielland* on her. There was a totally different name on the lifeboat, but I cannot remember it. What Jensen's motive was in sailing the ship under another name I never understood; certainly it was a very suspicious circumstance. Perhaps the ship as originally named had a bad name, and if such were the case—mind you, I don't say that it had—the Malays could never have been induced to go aboard. Once out at sea, however, they would be absolutely at the mercy of the captain, and he could treat them just as he pleased. The first thing they did before coming aboard was to look at the name for themselves. No doubt they knew the reputation of every pearler. Jensen did on one occasion exercise his authority to the extent of transferring some of his own Malay divers to another ship when we were out at sea.

At last everything was ready, and when we sailed for the pearling grounds, our crew numbered forty-four all told, not including a fine dog that belonged to the captain. This dog, which played so important—nay, so vitally important—a part in my strange after-life, was given to Jensen at Batavia by a Captain Cadell, a well-known Australian seaman, who had gained some notoriety by navigating the Murray River for the first time. Cadell, who was a great friend of Jensen, was himself a pearler. But he met with a sad end. He was in a pearling expedition in the neighbourhood of Thursday Island, and among his crew were some of the very Australian Blacks who in after years proved so friendly to me. Cadell treated these men very badly, keeping them at work long after the time for their return home had expired, and one day they mutinied and murdered him whilst he was asleep. The blackfellow who called himself "Captain Jack Davies," of whom I shall have more to say hereafter, was amongst the crew at the time. I obtained this information in Sydney from Captain Tucker, a well-known Torres Straits pearler. Bruno, Jensen's dog, was something of a greyhound in build, only that his hind-quarters were heavier.

As you may suppose, my knowledge of seamanship was very limited indeed, but Jensen interested himself in me, so that I soon began to pick up a good deal of useful knowledge. He taught me how to take the sun, I using his old instruments; but I could never grasp the taking of the lunars. On our voyage out I had no duties to perform on board, but I found much to interest myself in the beautiful tropical islands among which we threaded our way; and I took quite a childish delight in everything I saw. It was really a grand time for me. I constantly wrote home to my mother, the last letter I forwarded to her being from Koopang. Occasionally we landed on one of the islands to buy fresh provisions, in the shape of fowls, pigs, fruit, &c. We then set sail for the coast of New Guinea. The voyage thence was accomplished without the slightest hitch, the divers spending most of their time in singing and playing like little children,—all in the best of good spirits. Their favourite form of amusement was to sit round a large fire, either telling stories of the girls they had left behind, or singing love melodies. When the weather was at all cold, they would make a fire in a rather shallow tub, the sides of which were lined with a layer of sand. They were a wonderfully light-hearted lot of fellows, and I greatly enjoyed listening to their chants and yarns. I was more often with them than in Jensen's company, and it did not take me long to pick up bits of their language.

The *Veielland* only drew between seven feet and

eight feet of water, so that we were able to venture very close in-shore whenever it was necessary. At length, about a month after starting, we reached a likely spot where the captain thought that the precious shells might be found; here we anchored, and the divers quickly got to work. I ought to have mentioned that we carried a large whale-boat, and about half-a-dozen frail little "shell" boats for the use of the divers.

The comings and goings of the various pearling expeditions were of course regulated by the weather and the state of the tide. The captain himself went out first of all in the whale-boat, and from it prospected for shells at the bottom of the crystal sea. The water was marvellously transparent, and leaning over the side of the boat, Jensen peered eagerly into his sea-telescope, which is simply a metal cylinder with a lens of ordinary glass at the bottom. Some of the sea-telescopes would even be without this lens, being simply a metal cylinder open at both ends. Although they did not bring the objects looked at nearer the vision, yet they enabled the prospector to see below the ruffled surface of the water.

The big whale-boat was followed at a respectful distance by the flotilla of smaller boats, each containing from four to six Malays. When Jensen discerned a likely spot through his peculiar telescope, he gave the signal for a halt, and before you could realise what was going to happen, the native divers had tumbled out of their boats, and were *swimming* in a weird way down to the bottom of the translucent sea. As a rule, one man was left in each little boat to follow the movements of the divers as they returned to the surface. Not only did these divers wear no mechanical "dress," but they used no stimulants or palliatives of any kind to aid them in their work. All they carried was a small sheath-knife hung from the waist by a piece of string. The water for the most part was only two or three fathoms deep, but sometimes it would be as much as eight fathoms,— which was the greatest depth to which the men cared to go. When he reached the bottom, the diver would grope about for shells, and generally return to the surface with a couple, held in his left hand and hugged against his breast; the right hand was kept free and directed his movements in swimming. Each diver seldom remained under water more than one minute, and on coming to the surface he would take a "spell" of perhaps a quarter of an hour before going down again.

As fast as each man brought his shells into the boat, they were put into a separate little pile, which was respected absolutely, and always recognised as belonging to its owner. The bed of the sea at these pearling grounds is usually coral, with innumerable holes of different depths and sizes dotted all over it. It was in these recesses that the best shells were mostly found.

The marine vegetation down in these seas was always of extreme beauty; there were stately "trees" that waved backwards and forwards, as though under the influence of a gentle breeze; there were high, luxuriant grasses, and innumerable plants of endless variety and colour. The coral rocks, too, were of gorgeous hues—yellow, blue, red, and white; but a peculiar thing was that the moment you brought a piece of this rock up to the surface, the lovely colour it possessed whilst in the water gradually faded away.

Some of the coral I saw had curious little shoots hanging from its numerous projections bearing a striking resemblance to bluebells.

The illusion of a submarine forest was further heightened by the droves of gaily-coloured fish that flitted in and out among the branches. Perhaps the most beautiful of all were the little dolphins. The diving expeditions went away from the ship with the ebb tide, and returned with the flow. Sometimes their search would take them long distances away, and on one occasion they were working fully ten miles from the *Veielland.* When the water suddenly became rough, rendering the divers unable to paddle their own little skiffs back to the ship, they made their way to the whale-boat, clambered aboard, and returned in her, trailing their own craft at the stern. The boats, however, were not always brought back to the ship at night; as a rule they were buoyed near the pearling beds, whilst the divers returned to their quarters aboard. I might here explain that the sleeping accommodation for the Malays was both ample and comfortable. A large room in which the casks of fresh water were stored was set apart for their use. These casks were turned on end and a deck of planks placed over them, on which the Malays laid their sleeping mats and little wooden pillows. They ranged themselves twenty a side. But you may be asking, what was *I* doing during these pearling expeditions? Well, I was intrusted with the important duty of receiving the shells from the men, and crediting each with the number he delivered. Thus I was nearly always left alone on the ship—save for the dog; because even the two Malay women frequently went out diving, and they were credited for work done precisely as the men were.

If I had no shells to open whilst the divers were absent, I filled in my time by sewing sails, which Jensen himself would cut to the required shape—and reading, &c. My library consisted of only five books —a copy of the Bible, and a four-volume medical work in English by Bell, which I had purchased at Singapore. I made quite a study of the contents of this work, and acquired much valuable information, which I was able to put to good use in after years, more particularly during my sojourn amongst the Blacks. Bruno generally sat by my side on deck when I was alone,—in fact he was nearly always with me. He took to me more than to Jensen from the first. Jensen rarely tried to bully me, though of course I was now very much in his power, as he emphatically illustrated one day. A Malay diver had very much annoyed him, and in his fury he picked up a heavy broom with a stick fully four feet long, and felled the poor fellow senseless to the deck with it. I was shocked at such awful brutality, and ventured to protest against it. "Captain," I said, "don't do anything like that again whilst I am aboard." Turning round in a great passion he ordered me to keep my own counsel, otherwise he would have me put in irons. But for all that Jensen never again let his temper get the better of him to such an extent in my presence. He was always very gruff in his manner, and looked upon me as the " darndest fool he had ever met."

These divers, by the way, never seemed to trouble about the value of the treasure they were constantly bringing to the surface. They thought themselves

well paid if they were given plenty of rice and fish,
turtles' eggs and fowls, in addition to such luxuries
as spices, coffee, and "Brummagem" jewellery, of a
kind which is too well known to need description. At
the same time it must be admitted that in addition to
their wages, which were paid them when they were
discharged from the ship, the Malays had practically
no opportunity of being dishonest, even though they
might have been inclined that way. They never came
into actual contact with the pearls; they were rewarded according to the number of shells brought to
the surface, and not the value of the pearls they
might contain. All the shells were opened by me. A
healthy spirit of rivalry was maintained among the
divers, and the man who had the best record of shells
each week was rewarded with an extra allowance of
rum or tobacco ; a choice of some article of jewellery,
or anything else he fancied from among the stock we
had on board. A bottle of chutney or pickles was
considered a specially valuable delicacy. No money
was ever given to the divers as wages whilst at sea, re-
muneration in kind being always given instead. Each
expedition would be absent perhaps six hours, and on
its return each diver generally had between twenty
and forty shells to hand over to me. These I arranged
in long rows on the deck, and allowed them to remain
there all night. Next day I cleaned them by scraping
off the coral from the shells, and then opened them with
an ordinary dinner-knife. Of course, every oyster did
not produce a pearl; in fact, I have opened as many
as a hundred consecutive shells without finding a
single pearl. The gems are hidden away in the fleshy
part of the oyster, and have to be removed by pressure

of the thumb. The empty shells are then thrown in a heap on one side, and afterwards carefully stowed away in the hold, as they constitute a valuable cargo in themselves, being worth—at that time, at any rate (1864)—from £200 to £250, and even £350 a ton. All the pearls I found I placed in a walnut jewel-case, measuring about fourteen inches by eight inches by six inches. The value of the treasure increased day by day, until it amounted to many thousands of pounds; but of this more hereafter. I did not know much of the value of pearls then—how could I, having had no previous experience?

Captain Jensen, however, assured me at the end of the season that we had something like £50,000 worth of pearls aboard, to say nothing about the value of the shells, of which we had about thirty tons. It must be clearly understood that this is Captain Jensen's estimate—I am utterly unable to give one. The oysters themselves we found very poor eating, and no one on board cared about them. Some of the shells contained one pearl, others two, three, and even four. One magnificent specimen I came across produced no fewer than a dozen fine pearls, but that of course was very exceptional. The largest gem I ever found was shaped just like a big cube, more than an inch square. It was, however, comparatively worthless. Actually the finest specimen that passed through my hands was about the size of a pigeon's egg, and of exquisite colour and shape. Some of the pearls were of a beautiful rose colour, others yellow; but most were pure white.

The greatest enemy the divers had to fear in those waters was the dreaded octopus, whose presence occasioned far greater panic than the appearance of a mere shark.

These loathsome monsters—call them squids, or devil-fish, or what you will—would sometimes come and throw their horrible tentacles over the side of the frail craft from which the divers were working, and actually fasten on to the men themselves, dragging them out into the water. At other times octopuses have been known to attack the divers down below, and hold them relentlessly under water until life was extinct. One of our own men had a terribly narrow escape from one of these fearful creatures. I must explain, however, that occasionally when the divers returned from pearl-fishing, they used to rope all their little skiffs together and let them lie astern of the schooner. Well, one night the wind rose and rain fell heavily, with the result that next morning all the little boats were found more or less water-logged. Some of the Malays were told off to go and bale them out. Whilst they were at work one of the men saw a mysterious-looking black object in the sea, which so attracted his curiosity that he dived overboard to find out what it was. He had barely reached the water, however, when an immense octopus rose into view, and at once made for the terrified man, who instantly saw his danger, and with great presence of mind promptly turned and scrambled back into the boat.

The terrible creature was after him, however, and to the horror of the onlookers it extended its great flexible tentacles, enveloped the entire boat, man and all, and then dragged the whole down into the clear depths. The diver's horrified comrades rushed to his assistance, and an attempt was made to kill the octopus with a harpoon, but without success.   Several of his more resourceful companions then dived into the water with

THE OCTOPUS AND THE BOAT

a big net made of stout twine, which they took right underneath the octopus, entangling the creature and its still living prey.   The next step was to drag up both man and octopus into the whale-boat, and this done, the unfortunate Malay was at length seized by his legs, and dragged by sheer force out of the frightful embrace, more dead than alive, as you may suppose. However, we soon revived him by putting him into a very hot bath, the water being at such a temperature as actually to blister his skin. It is most remarkable that the man was not altogether drowned, as he had been held under water by the tentacles of the octopus for rather more than two minutes. But, like all the Malays of our party, this man carried a knife, which he used to very good purpose on the monster's body when first it dragged him under the water. These repeated stabs caused the creature to keep rolling about on the surface, and the unhappy man was in this way enabled to get an occasional breath of air; otherwise he must infallibly have been drowned. It was a horrible-looking creature, with a slimy body, and a hideous cavity of a mouth. It is the tentacles of the creature that are so dreaded, on account of the immense sucking power which they possess.

After this incident the divers always took a tomahawk with them on their expeditions, in order to lop off the tentacles of any octopus that might try to attack them in the boats. And, by the way, we saw many extraordinary creatures during our cruise. I myself had a serious fright one day whilst indulging in a swim.

We had anchored in about five fathoms, and as I was proceeding leisurely away from the vessel at a slow breast stroke, a monstrous fish, fully twenty feet long, with an enormous hairy head and fierce, fantastic moustaches, suddenly reared up out of the water, high

B

into the air.   I must say that the sight absolutely
unmanned me for the moment, and when this extraordinary creature opened his enormous mouth in my
direction, I gave myself up for lost.   It did not molest
me, however, and I got back to the ship safely, but it
was some little time before I recovered from the terrible
fright.

Occasionally too we were troubled with sharks, but
the Malays did not appear to be very much afraid of
them.   Their great dread was the ground shark, which
lay motionless at the bottom of the sea, and gave
no indication of his presence.   The result was that
occasionally the divers would sink down to their
work quite unknowingly almost by the side of one of
these fearful creatures, and in such cases the diver
rarely escaped without injury of some kind.   With
regard to the ordinary shark, however, our divers
actually sought them.   Their method of capturing them
was almost incredible in its simplicity and daring.
Three or four of our divers would go out in a boat and
allow themselves to drift into a big school of sharks.
Then one man, possessed of more nerve than the rest,
would bend over the side and smartly prick the first one
he came across with a spear taken out for the purpose.
The moment he had succeeded in this the other
occupants of the boat would commence yelling and
howling at the top of their voices, at the same time
beating the water with their paddles, in order to
frighten away the sharks.   This invariably succeeded,
but, amazing to relate, the shark that had been pricked
always came back alone a few minutes later to see
what it was that had pricked him.   Care has to be
taken not to inflict a very severe wound, because the

moment the other sharks taste the blood of a wounded companion, they will immediately turn upon him and eat him. When the inquisitive shark is seen coming in the direction of the boat, the Malay who has accosted him in this way quietly jumps overboard, armed only with his small knife and a short stick of hard wood, exactly like a butcher's skewer, about five inches in length, and pointed at each end.

The man floats stationary on the surface of the sea, and, naturally, the shark makes for him. As the creature rolls over to bite, the wily Malay glides out of his way with a few deft strokes of the left hand, whilst with the right he deliberately plants the pointed skewer in an upright position between the open jaws of the expectant monster. The result is simple, but surprising. The shark is, of course, unable to close its mouth, and the water just rushes down his throat and chokes him, in consequence of the gills being forced back so tightly as to prevent the escape of water through them in the natural way. Needless to remark, it requires the greatest possible coolness and nerve to kill a shark in this way, but the Malays look upon it as a favourite recreation and an exciting sport. When the monster is dead its slayer dexterously climbs on to its back, and then, digging his knife into the shark's head to serve as a support and means of balance, the conqueror is towed back to the ship astride his victim by means of a rope hauled by his companions in their boats.

After many adventures and much luck in the way of getting pearls, our food and water supply began to give out. This induced Captain Jensen to make for the New Guinea main in order to replenish his stores. We soon reached a likely spot on the coast, and obtained all that we wanted from the natives by means of barter.

We gave them tomahawks, knives, hoop-iron, beads, turtles, and bright-coloured cloth. Indeed, so friendly did our intercourse become that parties of our divers often went ashore and joined the Papuans in their sports and games. On one of these occasions I came across a curious animal that bore a striking resemblance to a kangaroo, and yet was not more than two feet high. It could climb trees like an opossum and was of the marsupial family. The pigeons, too, which were very plentiful in these parts, were as large as a big fowl. The headman, or chief, took quite an interest in me, and never seemed tired of conversing with me, and pointing out the beauties of the country. He even showed me a certain boundary which he advised us not to pass, as the natives beyond were not under his control. One day, however, a party of our Malays, accompanied by myself, imprudently ventured into the forbidden country, and soon came to a native village, at which we halted. The people here were suspicious of us from the first, and when one of my men indiscreetly offended a native, half the village rose against us, and we had to beat a retreat. We were making the best of our way to the coast again, when the friendly chief came and met us. He interceded with the indignant tribesmen on our behalf, and succeeded in pacifying them. On reaching the ship, which was anchored within a mile of the coast, Jensen complained to me ominously that he was getting fairly swamped with natives, who persisted in coming on board with fruit and vegetables for barter. He said he was getting quite nervous about

the crowds that swarmed over the vessel, the natives
going up and down as though they had a perfect right
to do so.

"I don't like it," said the captain, "and shall have
to put my foot down."

Next morning, when the usual batch of native
canoes came alongside, we declined to allow a single
man on board. While we were explaining this to them,
our friend the chief himself arrived, accompanied by
half-a-dozen notables, most of whom I knew, together with the now friendly dignitary whose wrath
we had aroused the previous day. They were all full
of dignity and anticipation. Captain Jensen, however, was obdurate, and refused permission to any
one to come aboard. That was enough for the chiefs.
They went away in high dudgeon, followed immediately
by all the other canoes and their occupants. When
all had disappeared, a curious stillness came over the
ship, the sea, and the tropical coast, and a strange
sense of impending danger seemed to oppress all
of us. We knew that we had offended the natives,
and as we could not see a single one of them on the
beach, it was pretty evident that they were brooding
over their grievance. We might have weighed anchor
and made for the open sea, only unfortunately there
was a perfect calm, and our sails, which were set
in readiness for a hasty departure, hung limp and
motionless. Suddenly, as we stood looking out
anxiously over the side in the direction of the shore,
we were amazed to see at least twenty fully-equipped
war-canoes, each carrying from thirty to forty warriors,
rounding the headland, some little distance away, and
making straight for our ship. Now my shrewd Dutch

partner had anticipated a possible attack, and had
accordingly armed all the Malays with tomahawks, in
readiness for any attempt that might be made to board
the schooner.   We had also taken off the hatches, and
made a sort of fortification with them round the wheel.

Jensen and I armed ourselves with guns, loaded our
little cannon, and prepared to make a desperate fight
for our lives against the overwhelming odds.   In spite
of the danger of our position, I could not help being
struck with the magnificence of the spectacle presented
by the great fleet of boats now fast advancing towards
us.   The warriors had all assumed their fighting de-
corations, with white stripes painted round their dusky
bodies to strike terror into the beholder.   Their head-
dress consisted of many-coloured feathers projecting
from the hair, which they had matted and caused
to stand bolt upright from the head.   Each boat
had a prow about three feet high, surmounted by a
grotesquely carved figure-head.   The war-canoes were
propelled by twelve men, paddling on either side.
When the first came within hailing distance I called
out and made signs that they were not to advance
unless their intentions were peaceful.   By way of
reply, they merely brandished their bows and arrows
at us.   There was no mistaking their mission.

It was now quite evident that we should have to
make a fight for it, and the natives were coming to
the attack in such numbers as easily to overwhelm
us if they once got on board.   Our position was
rendered still more awkward by the fact that all
round the ship ropes were hanging down to the
water, up which our divers used to climb on their
return from the day's pearling.   These ropes were

attached to a sort of hawser running round the outside bulwarks of the ship. We had not even time to haul these up, and the enemy would certainly have found them very useful for boarding purposes had they been allowed to get near enough. It was therefore very necessary that some decisive step should be taken at once. While we were debating what was best to be done, we were suddenly greeted by a shower of arrows from the leading war-canoe. Without waiting any longer I fired at the leader, who was standing in the prow, and bowled him over. The bullet went right through his body, and then bored a hole low down in the side of the canoe. The amazement of the warriors on hearing the report and seeing the mysterious damage done is quite beyond description; and before they could recover from their astonishment, Jensen sent a charge of grape-shot right into their midst, which shattered several of the canoes and caused a general halt in the advance.

Again I made signs to them not to come nearer, and they seemed undecided what to do. Jabbering consultations were held, but while they were thus hesitating ten more canoes swung round the headland, and their appearance seemed to give the advance-guard fresh courage.

Once more they made for our ship, but I was ready for them with the little cannon we had on board; it had been reloaded with grape after the first discharge. With a roar the gun belched forth a second deadly hail against the advancing savages, and the effect was to demoralise them completely. One of the canoes was shattered to pieces, and nearly all the men in it more or less seriously wounded; whilst the occupants of several other canoes received injuries.

Quite a panic now ensued, and the fleet of canoes got inextricably mixed. Several showers of arrows, however, descended on our deck, and some of them penetrated the sails, but no one was injured. The natives were too much afraid to advance any farther, and as a wind had now sprung up we deemed it time to make a dash for liberty. We therefore quietly slipped our anchor and, heading the ship for the open sea, glided swiftly past the enemy's fleet, whose gaily decked, though sorely bewildered, warriors greeted us with a Parthian flight of arrows as we raced by. In another half-hour we were well out to sea, and able to breathe freely once more.

CHAPTER II

The three black pearls—The fatal morning—Jensen and his flotilla
drift away—Alone on the ship—"Oil on the troubled waters"—
A substitute for a rudder—Smoke signals—The whirlpool—The
savages attack—I escape from the blacks—A strange monster—
The *Veielland* strikes a reef—Stone deaf through the big wave—
I leap into the sea—How Bruno helped me ashore—The dreary
island—My raft—A horrible discovery.

THIS adventure made our Malay crew very anxious
to leave these regions. They had not forgotten
the octopus incident either, and they now appointed
their serang to wait upon the captain—a kind of "one-
man" deputation—to persuade him, if possible, to sail
for fresh fishing-grounds. At first Jensen tried to persuade them to remain in the same latitudes, which is
not to be wondered at, seeing the harvest he had
secured; but they would not listen to this, and at last
he was compelled to direct his ship towards some other
quarter. Where he took us to I cannot say, but in
the course of another week we dropped anchor in some
practically unexplored pearling grounds, and got to
work once more. Our luck was still with us, and we
continued increasing every day the value of our already
substantial treasure. In these new grounds we found
a particularly small shell very rich in pearls, which
required no diving for at all. They were secured by
means of a trawl or scoop dragged from the stern of

the lifeboat; and when the tide was low the men jumped into the shallow water and picked them up at their ease.

One morning, as I was opening the shells as usual, out from one dropped three magnificent black pearls. I gazed at them, fascinated—why, I know not.   Ah! those terrible three black pearls; would to God they had never been found!   When I showed them to the captain he became very excited, and said that, as they were worth nearly all the others put together, it would be well worth our while trying to find more like them. Now, this meant stopping at sea longer than was either customary or advisable.   The pearling season was practically at an end, and the yearly cyclonic changes were actually due, but the captain had got the "pearl fever" very badly and flatly refused to leave. Already we had made an enormous haul, and in addition to the stock in my charge Jensen had rows of pickle bottles full of pearls in his cabin, which he would sit and gloat over for hours like a miser with his gold.   He kept on saying that there *must* be more of these black pearls to be obtained; the three we had found could not possibly be isolated specimens and so on.   Accordingly, we kept our divers at work day after day as usual.   Of course, I did not know much about the awful dangers to which we were exposing ourselves by remaining out in such uncertain seas when the cyclones were due; and I did not, I confess, see any great reason why we should *not* continue pearling.   I was inexperienced, you see.

The pearl-fishing season, as I afterwards learned, extends from November to May.   Well, May came and went, and we were still hard at work, hoping that

each day would bring another haul of black pearls to
our store of treasure; in this, however, we were disappointed. And yet the captain became more determined than ever to find some. He continued to take
charge of the whale-boat whenever the divers went
out to work, and he personally superintended their
operations. He knew very well that he had already
kept them at work longer than he ought to have
done, and it was only by a judicious distribution of
more jewellery, pieces of cloth, &c., that he withheld
them from openly rebelling against the extended stay.
The serang told him that if the men did once go on
strike, nothing would induce them to resume work,
they would simply sulk, he said; and die out of sheer
disappointment and pettishness. So the captain was
compelled to treat them more amiably than usual. At
the very outside their contract would only be for nine
months. Sometimes when he showed signs of being
in a cantankerous mood because the haul of shells did
not please him, the serang would say to him defiantly,
"Come on; take it out of me if you are not satisfied."
But Jensen never accepted the challenge. As the days
passed, I thought the weather showed indications of
a change; for one thing, the aneroid began jumping
about in a very uneasy manner. I called Jensen's
attention to the matter, but he was too much interested
in his hunt for black pearls to listen to me.

And now I pass to the fatal day that made me an
outcast from civilisation for so many weary years.
Early one morning in July 1864, Jensen went off as
usual with the whole of his crew, leaving me absolutely
alone in charge of the ship. The women had often
accompanied the divers on their expeditions, and did

so on this occasion, being rather expert at the work, which they looked upon as sport.

Whenever I look back upon the events of that dreadful day, I am filled with astonishment that the captain should have been so mad as to leave the ship at all. Only an hour before he left, a tidal wave broke over the stern, and flooded the cabins with a perfect deluge. Both Jensen and I were down below at the time, and came in for an awful drenching. This in itself was a clear and ominous indication of atmospheric disturbance; but all that poor Jensen did was to have the pumps set to work, and after the cabins were comparatively dry he proceeded once more to the pearl banks that fascinated him so, and on which he probably sleeps to this day. The tide was favourable when he left, and I watched the fleet of little boats following in the wake of the whale-boat, until they were some three miles distant from the ship, when they stopped for preparations to be made for the work of diving. I had no presentiment whatever of the catastrophe that awaited them and me.

A cool, refreshing breeze had been blowing up to his time, but the wind now developed a sudden violence, and the sea was lashed into huge waves that quickly swamped nearly every one of the little cockleshell boats. Fortunately, they could not sink, and as I watched I saw that the Malays who were thus thrown into the water clung to the sides of the little boats, and made the best of their way to the big craft in charge of Captain Jensen. Every moment the sea became more and more turbulent as the wind quickened to a hurricane. When all the Malays had scrambled into the whale-boat, they attempted to pull back to the ship, but I could see that they were unable to make the slightest headway against the tremendous sea that was running, although they worked frantically at the oars.

On the contrary, I was horrified to see that they were gradually drifting *away from me*, and being carried farther and farther out across the illimitable sea. I was nearly distracted at the sight, and I racked my brains to devise some means of helping them, but could think of nothing feasible. I thought first of all of trying to slip the anchor and let the ship drift in their direction, but I was by no means sure that she would actually do this. Besides, I reflected, she might strike on some of the insidious coral reefs that abound in those fair but terribly dangerous seas. So I came to the conclusion that it would be better to let her remain where she was—at least, for the time being. Moreover, I felt sure that the captain, with his knowledge of those regions, would know of some island or convenient sandbank, perhaps not very far distant, on which he might run his boat for safety until the storm had passed.

The boats receded farther and farther from view, until, about nine in the morning, I lost sight of them altogether. They had started out soon after sunrise. It then occurred to me that I ought to put the ship into some sort of condition to enable her to weather the storm, which was increasing instead of abating. This was not the first storm I had experienced on board the *Veielland*, so I knew pretty well what to do. First of all, then, I battened down the hatches; this done, I made every movable thing on deck as secure as I possibly could. Fortunately all the sails were

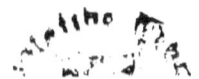

furled at the time, so I had no trouble with them.   By
mid-day it was blowing so hard that I positively could
not stand upright, but had to crawl about on my hands
and knees, otherwise I should have been hurled overboard.   I also attached myself to a long rope, and
fastened the other end to one of the masts, so that in
the event of my being washed into the raging sea, I
could pull myself on board again.

Blinding rain had been falling most of the time, and
the waves came dashing over the deck as though longing to engulf the little ship; but she rode them all in
splendid style.   The climax was reached about two
o'clock, when a perfect cyclone was raging, and the
end seemed very near for me.   It made me shudder
to listen to the wind screaming and moaning round
the bare poles of the sturdy little vessel, which
rose on veritable mountains of water and crashed as
suddenly into seething abysses that made my heart
stand still.   Then the weather suddenly became calm
once more—a change that was as unexpected as the
advent of the storm itself.   The sky, however, continued very black and threatening, and the sea was
still somewhat boisterous; but both wind and rain had
practically subsided, and I could now look around me
without feeling that if I stirred I was a doomed man.
I clambered up the lower portion of the main rigging,
but only saw black, turbulent waters, hissing and
heaving, and raging on every side, and seemingly
stretching away into infinity.   With terrible force
the utter awfulness and hopelessness of my position
dawned upon me, yet I did not despair.   I next
thought it advisable to try and slip my anchor, and
let the ship drift, for I still half-fancied that perhaps

I might come across my companions somewhere.
Before I could free the vessel, however, the wind
veered completely round, and, to my horror and despair, sent a veritable mountain of water on board, that
carried away nearly all the bulwarks, the galley, the
top of the companion-way, and, worst of all, completely
wrenched off the wheel. Compasses and charts were
all stored in the companion-way, and were therefore
lost for ever. Then, indeed, I felt the end was near.
Fortunately, I was for'ard at the time, or I must inevitably have been swept into the appalling waste of
whirling, mountainous waters. This lashing of myself
to the mast, by the way, was the means of saving my
life time after time. Soon after the big sea—which I
had hoped was a final effort of the terrible storm—the
gale returned and blew in the opposite direction with
even greater fury than before. I spent an awful time
of it the whole night long, without a soul to speak to
or help me, and every moment I thought the ship must
go down in that fearful sea. The only living thing on
board beside myself was the captain's dog, which I
could occasionally hear howling dismally in the cabin
below, where I had shut him in when the cyclone first
burst upon me.

Among the articles carried overboard by the big sea
that smashed the wheel was a large cask full of oil,
made from turtle fat, in which we always kept a
supply of fresh meats, consisting mainly of pork and
fowls. This cask contained perhaps twenty gallons,
and when it overturned, the oil flowed all over the
decks and trickled into the sea. The effect was
simply magical. Almost immediately the storm-tossed
waves in the vicinity of the ship, which hitherto had

been raging mountains high, quieted down in a way
that filled me with astonishment.   This tranquillity
prevailed as long as the oil lasted ; but as soon as the
supply was exhausted the giant waves became as
turbulent and mountainous as ever.

All night long the gale blew the ship blindly hither
and thither, and it was not until just before daybreak
that the storm showed any signs of abating.   By six
o'clock, however, only a slight wind was blowing, and
the sea no longer threatened to engulf me and my
little vessel.   I was now able to look about me, and
see what damage had been done ; and you may imagine
my relief when I found that the ship was still sound
and water-tight, although the bulwarks were all gone,
and she had all the appearance of a derelict.   One of
the first things I did was to go down and unloose the
dog—poor Bruno.   The delight of the poor creature
knew no bounds, and he rushed madly up on deck,
barking frantically for his absent master.   He seemed
very much surprised to find no one aboard besides
myself.

Alas ! I never saw Peter Jensen again, nor the forty
Malays and the two women.   Jensen *may* have escaped; he may even have lived to read these lines;
God only knows what was the fate of the unfortunate
fleet of pearl-fishers.   Priggish and uncharitable people
may ejaculate : " The reward of cupidity ! "   But I say,
" Judge not, lest ye also be judged."

As the morning had now become beautifully fine, I
thought I might attempt to get out some spare sails.
I obtained what I wanted from the fo'c'sle, and after a
good deal of work managed to " bend " a mainsail and
staysail.   Being without compass or chart, however, I

knew not where I was, nor could I decide what course
to take in order to reach land. I had a vague idea
that the seas in those regions were studded with
innumerable little islands and sandbanks known only
to the pearl-fishers, and it seemed inevitable that I
must run aground somewhere or get stranded upon a
coral reef after I had slipped the cable.

However, I did not see what advantage was to be
gained by remaining where I was, so I fixed from the
stern a couple of long sweeps, or steering oars, twenty-
six feet long, and made them answer the purpose of a
rudder. These arrangements occupied me two or
three days, and then, when everything was completed
to my satisfaction, and the ship was in sailing trim, I
gave the *Veielland* her freedom. This I managed
as follows: The moment the chain was at its tautest
—at its greatest tension—I gave it a violent blow
with a big axe, and it parted. I steered due west,
taking my observations by the sun and my own
shadow at morning, noon, and evening. For I had
been taught to reckon the degree of latitude from the
number of inches of my shadow. After a time I
altered my course to west by south, hoping that I
might come upon one of the islands of the Dutch
Indies,—Timorland, for instance, but day after day
passed without land coming in sight.

Imagine the situation, if you can: alone on a dis-
abled ship in the limitless ocean,—tortured with doubts
and fears about the fate of my comrades, and filled
with horror and despair at my own miserable prospects
for the future.

I did not sail the ship at night, but got out a sea-
anchor (using a float and a long coir rope), and lay-to

while I turned in for a sleep. I would be up at daybreak next morning, and as the weather continued
beautifully fine, I had no difficulty in getting under
way again. At last the expected happened. One
afternoon, without any warning whatsoever, the vessel
struck heavily on a reef. I hurriedly constructed a
raft out of the hatches and spare spars, and put biscuits
and water aboard, after which I landed on the rocks.
When the tide reached its lowest point the stern of
the *Veielland* was left fully *twenty feet out of water*,
securely jammed between two high pinnacles of coral
rock. The sight was remarkable in the extreme. The
sails were still set, and the stiff breeze that was blowing dead against them caused them to belly out just as
though the craft were afloat, and practically helped to
keep the vessel in position. The bows were much
higher than the stern, the line of the decks being
at an angle of about forty-five degrees. In this
remarkable situation she remained secure until the
turning of the tide. My only hope was that she
would not suffer from the tremendous strain to which
she was necessarily being subjected. It seemed to
me every minute that she would free herself from
her singular position between the rocks, and glide
down bows foremost into the sea to disappear for
ever. But the sails kept her back. How earnestly
I watched the rising of the waters; and night
came on as I waited. Slowly and surely they crept
up the bows, and the ship gradually assumed her
natural level until at length the stanch little craft
floated safe and sound once more, apparently very
little the worse for her strange experience. And then
away I went on my way—by this time almost schooled

to indifference.   Had she gone down I must inevitably
have succumbed on those coral reefs, for the stock of
biscuits and water I had been able to put aboard the
raft would only have lasted a very few days.

For nearly a fortnight after the day of the great
storm I kept on the same course without experiencing
any unpleasant incident or check, always excepting the
curious threatened wreck which I have just mentioned.

Just before dusk on the evening of the thirteenth
day, I caught sight of an island in the distance—
Melville Island I now know it to be; and I was
greatly puzzled to see smoke floating upwards apparently from many fires kindled on the beach.   I
knew that they were signals of some kind, and at
first I fancied that it must be one of the friendly
Malay islands that I was approaching.   A closer
scrutiny of the smoke signals, however, soon convinced me that I was mistaken.   As I drew nearer, I
saw a number of natives, perfectly nude, running
wildly about on the beach and brandishing their spears
in my direction.

I did not like the look of things at all, but when I
tried to turn the head of the ship to skirt the island
instead of heading straight on, I found to my vexa-
tion that I was being carried forward by a strong tide
or current straight into what appeared to be a large
bay or inlet.   I had no alternative but to let myself
drift, and soon afterwards found myself in a sort of
natural harbour three or four miles wide, with very
threatening coral reefs showing above the surface.
Still the current drew me helplessly onward, and in
a few minutes the ship was caught in a dangerous
whirlpool, round which she was carried several times

before I managed to extricate her. Next we were
drawn close in to some rocks, and I had to stand
resolutely by with an oar in order to keep the vessel's
head from striking. It was a time of most trying
excitement for me, and I wonder to this day how it
was that the *Veielland* did not strike and founder then
and there, considering, firstly, that she was virtually a
derelict, and secondly, that there was no living creature
on board to navigate her save myself.

I was beginning to despair of ever pulling the
vessel through, when we suddenly entered a narrow
strait. I knew that I was in a waterway between
two islands — Apsley Strait, dividing Melville and
Bathurst Islands, as I have since learned.

The warlike and threatening natives had now been
left behind long ago, and I never thought of meeting
any other hostile people, when just as I had reached
the narrowest part of the waterway, I was startled by
the appearance of a great horde of naked blacks—
giants, every one of them—on the rocks above me.

They were tremendously excited, and greeted me
first of all with a shower of spears. Fortunately, on
encountering the first lot of threatening blacks, I had
prepared a shelter for myself on deck by means of the
hatches reared up endwise against the stanchions, and
so the spears fell harmlessly around me. Next, the
natives sent a volley of boomerangs on board, but without any result. Some of these curious weapons hit the
sails and fell impotently on the deck, whilst some returned to their throwers, who were standing on the
rocks about fifty yards away, near the edge of the
water. I afterwards secured the boomerangs that
came on board, and found that they were about

twenty-four inches in length, shaped like the blade
of a sickle, and measured three or four inches across
at the widest part.
They were made
of extremely hard
wood, and were

ATTACKED BY SAVAGES

undoubtedly capable of doing considerable injury when
dexterously and accurately thrown. The blacks kept
up a terrific hubbub on shore, yelling like madmen,

and hurling at me showers of barbed spears. The fact that they had boomerangs convinced me that I must be nearing the Australian mainland. All this time the current was carrying the *Vcielland* rapidly along, and I had soon left the natives jabbering furiously far behind me.

At last I could see the open sea once more, and at the mouth of the strait was a little low, wooded island, where I thought I might venture to land. As I was approaching it, however, yet another crowd of blacks, all armed, came rushing down to the beach; they jumped into their catamarans, or "floats," and paddled out towards me.

After my previous experience I deemed it advisable not to let them get too near, so I hoisted the mainsail again and stood for the open sea. There was a good supply of guns and ammunition on board, and it would have been an easy matter for me to have sunk one or two of the native catamarans, which are mere primitive rafts or floats, and so cooled their enthusiasm a bit; but I refrained, on reflecting that I should not gain anything by this action.

By this time I had abandoned all hope of ever coming up with my friends, but, of course, I did not despair of reaching land—although I hardly knew in what direction I ought to shape my course. Still, I thought that if I kept due west, I should eventually sight Timor or some other island of the Dutch Indies, and so, for the next three or four days, I sailed steadily on without further incident.

About a week after meeting with the hostile blacks, half a gale sprang up, and I busied myself in putting the ship into trim to weather the storm, which I knew was inevitable. I happened to be looking over the stern watching the clouds gathering in dark, black masses, when a strange upheaval of the waters took place almost at my feet, and a huge black fish, like an exaggerated porpoise, leaped into the air close to the stern of my little vessel.

It was a monstrous, ungainly looking creature, nearly the size of a small whale. The strange way it disported itself alongside the ship filled me with all manner of doubtings, and I was heartily thankful when it suddenly disappeared from sight. The weather then became more boisterous, and as the day advanced I strove my utmost to keep the ship's head well before the wind; it was very exhausting work. I was unable to keep anything like an adequate look-out ahead, and had to trust to Providence to pull me through safely.

All this time I did not want for food. Certainly I could not cook anything, but there was any quantity of tinned provisions. And I fed Bruno, too. I conversed with him almost hourly, and derived much encouragement and sympathy therefrom. One morning sometime between the fifteenth and twentieth day, I was scanning the horizon with my customary eagerness, when suddenly, on looking ahead, I found the sea white with the foam of crashing breakers; I knew I must be in the vicinity of a sunken reef. I tried to get the ship round, but it was too late. I couldn't make the slightest impression upon her, and she forged stolidly forward to her doom.

A few minutes later her keel came into violent contact with a coral reef, and as she grated slowly over it, the poor thing seemed to shiver from stem to

stern.   The shock was so severe that I was thrown
heavily to the deck.   Bruno could make nothing whatever of it, so he found relief in doleful howls.   While
the vessel remained stuck on the rocks, I was looking
out anxiously from the rigging, when, without a
moment's warning, a gigantic wave came toppling and
crashing overboard from the stern, overwhelming me
in the general destruction that followed.   I was dashed
with tremendous force on to the deck, and when I
picked myself up, bruised and bleeding, the first thing
I was conscious of was a deathly stillness, which filled
me with vague amazement, considering that but a few
moments before my ears had been filled with the roar
and crash of the breakers.   And I could see that the
storm was still raging with great fury, although not a
sound reached my ears.

Gradually the horrible truth dawned upon me—*I
was stone deaf!*   The blow on the head from the great
wave had completely deprived me of all sense of
hearing.   How depressed I felt when I realised this
awful fact no one can imagine.   Nevertheless, things
were not altogether hopeless, for next morning I felt
a sudden crack in my left ear, and immediately afterwards I heard once more the dull roar of the surf,
the whistling of the wind, and the barking of my
affectionate dog.   My right ear, however, was perma-
nently injured, and to this day I am decidedly deaf
in that organ.   I was just beginning to think that we
had passed over the most serious part of the danger,
when to my utter despair I again heard that hideous
grating sound, and knew she had struck upon another
reef.   She stuck there for a time, but was again forced
on, and presently floated in deep water.   The pitiless

reefs were now plainly visible on all sides, and some distance away I could see what appeared to be nothing more than a little sandbank rising a few feet above the waters of the lagoon.

While I was watching and waiting for developments the deck of the vessel suddenly started, and she began rapidly to settle down by the stern. Fortunately, however, at that point the water was not excessively deep. When I saw that nothing could save the ship, and that her deck was all but flush with the water, I loosened several of the fittings, as well as some spars, casks, and chests, in the hope that they might drift to land and perhaps be of service to me afterwards. I remained on board as long as I possibly could, trying to build a raft with which to get some things ashore, but I hadn't time to finish it.

Up and up came the inexorable water, and at last, signalling to Bruno to follow me, I leaped into the sea and commenced to swim towards the sandbank. Of course, all the boats had been lost when the pearling fleet disappeared. The sea was still very rough, and as the tide was against us, I found it extremely exhausting work. The dog seemed to understand that I was finding it a dreadful strain, for he swam immediately in front of me, and kept turning round again and again as though to see if I were following safely.

By dint of tremendous struggling I managed to get close up to the shore, but found it utterly impossible to climb up and land. Every time I essayed to plant my legs on the beach, the irresistible backwash swept me down, rolling me head over heels, and in my exhausted condition this filled me with despair. On one occasion this backwash sent me spinning into deep water again, and I am sure I should have been drowned had not my brave dog come to my rescue and seized me by my hair—which, I should have explained, I had always worn long from the days of my childhood. Well, my dog tugged and tugged at

HOW BRUNO HELPED ME

me until he had got me half-way through the breakers, nor did this exertion seem to cause him much trouble in swimming.

I then exerted myself sufficiently to allow of his letting go my hair, whilst I took the end of his tail between my teeth, and let him help me ashore in this peculiar way. He was a remarkably strong and saga-

cious brute—an Australian dog—and he seemed to
enjoy the task. At length I found myself on my legs
upon the beach, though hardly able to move from
exhaustion of mind and body. When at length I had
recovered sufficiently to walk about, I made a hasty
survey of the little island or sandbank upon which I
found myself. Thank God, I did not realise at that
moment that I was doomed to spend a soul-killing *two
and a half years* on that desolate, microscopical strip
of·sand! Had I done so I must have gone raving
mad. It was an appalling, dreary-looking spot, without
one single tree or bush growing upon it to relieve the
terrible monotony. I tell you, words can never describe
the horror of the agonising months as they crawled by.
"My island" was nothing but a little sand-spit, with
here and there a few tufts of grass struggling through
its parched surface. As a matter of fact the sand was
only four or five inches deep in most places, and underneath was solid coral rock.

Think of it, ye who have envied the fate of the castaway on a gorgeous and fertile tropical island perhaps
miles in extent! It was *barely a hundred yards in
length, ten yards wide, and only eight feet above sea-
level at high water!* There was no sign of animal life
upon it, but birds were plentiful enough—particularly
pelicans. My tour of the island occupied perhaps ten
minutes; and you may perhaps form some conception
of my utter dismay on failing to come across any trace
of fresh water.

With what eager eyes did I look towards the ship
then! So long as she did not break up I was safe
because there were water and provisions in plenty on
board. And how I thanked my God for the adamant

bulwarks of coral that protected my ark from the fury of the treacherous seas! As the weather became calmer, and a brilliant moon had risen, I decided to swim back to the ship, and bring some food and clothing ashore from her.

I reached the wreck without much trouble, and clambered on board, but could do very little in the way of saving goods, as the decks were still below water. However, I dived, or rather ducked, for the depth of water was only four or five feet, into the cabin and secured some blankets, but I could not lay my hands on any food.

After infinite trouble I managed to make some sort of a raft out of pieces of wood I found lying loose and floating about, and upon this platform I placed the blankets, an oak chest, and one or two other articles I proposed taking ashore. In the oak chest were a number of flags, some clothing and medicine together with my case of pearls and the four medical books. But after I had launched it, I found that the tide was still running out, and it was impossible for me to get anything ashore that night. The weather was beautifully fine, however, and as the forepart of the ship was well out of water, I decided to remain on board and get an hour or two's sleep, which I needed badly. The night passed without incident, and I was astir a little before dawn.

As the tide was now favourable, I loosed my raft and swam it ashore. When I gained the island, I made another survey of it, to find the most suitable spot for pitching my camp, and in the course of my wanderings I made a discovery that filled me with horror and the anguish of blackest despair. My curiosity was first attracted by a human skull that lay near a large circular depression in the sand about two feet deep. I commenced scratching with my fingers at one side, and had only gone a few inches down, when I came upon a quantity of human remains.

The sight struck terror to my heart, and filled me with the most dismal forebodings. "My own bones," I thought, "will soon be added to the pile." So great was my agony of mind that I had to leave the spot, and interest myself in other things; but some time afterwards, when I had got over my nervousness, I renewed my digging operations, and in an hour or so had unearthed no fewer than sixteen complete skeletons —fourteen adults, and two younger people, possibly women! They lay alongside one another, covered by sand that had been blown over them by the wind.

CHAPTER III

THAT morning I made my breakfast off raw sea-
gulls' eggs, but was unable to get anything to
drink. Between nine and ten o'clock, as the tide was
then very low, I was delighted to find that it was
possible to reach the wreck by walking along the rocks.
So, scrambling aboard, I collected as many things as I
could possibly transfer ashore. I had to take dangerous
headers into the cabin, as the whole ship's interior
was now full of water, but all I could manage to secure
were a tomahawk and my bow and arrows, which had
been given me by the Papuans. I had always taken a
keen interest in archery, by the way, and had made
quite a name for myself in this direction long before I
left Switzerland. I also took out a cooking-kettle.
All these seemingly unimportant finds were of vital
importance in the most literal sense of the phrase,
particularly the tomahawk and the bow, which were in
after years my very salvation time after time.

48

I was very delighted when I secured my bow and arrows, for I knew that with them I could always be certain of killing sea-fowl for food. There was a stock of gunpowder on board and a number of rifles and shot-guns, but as the former was hopelessly spoiled, I did not trouble about either. With my tomahawk I cut away some of the ship's woodwork, which I threw overboard and let drift to land to serve as fuel. When I did eventually return to my little island, I unravelled a piece of rope, and then tried to produce fire by rubbing two pieces of wood smartly together amidst the inflammable material. It was a hopeless business, however; a full half-hour's friction only made the sticks hot, and rub as hard as I would I could not produce the faintest suspicion of a spark. I sat down helplessly, and wondered how the savages I had read of ever got fire in this way.

Up to this time I had not built myself a shelter of any kind. At night I simply slept in the open air on the sand, with only my blankets round me. One morning I was able to get out of the vessel some kegs of precious water, a small barrel of flour, and a quantity of tinned foods. All these, together with some sails, spars, and ropes, I got safely ashore, and in the afternoon I rigged myself up a sort of canvas awning as a sleeping-place, using only some sails and spars.

Among the things I brought from the ship on a subsequent visit were a stiletto that had originally been given to me by my mother. It was an old family relic with a black ebony handle and a finely tempered steel blade four or five inches in length. I also got a stone tomahawk—a mere curio, obtained from the Papuans; and a quantity of a special kind of wood, also taken on board at New Guinea. This wood possessed the peculiar property of smouldering for hours when once ignited, without actually bursting into flame. We took it on board because it made such good fuel.

As the most urgent matter was to kindle a fire, I began experiments with my two weapons, striking the steel tomahawk against the stone one over a heap of fluffy material made by unravelling and teasing out a piece of blanket. Success attended my patient efforts this time, and to my inexpressible relief and joy I soon had a cheerful fire blazing alongside my improvised shelter—and, what is more, I took good care *never to let it go out during the whole time I remained a prisoner on the island*. The fire was always my first thought, and night and day it was kept at least smouldering by means of the New Guinea wood I have already mentioned, and of which I found a large stock on board. The ship itself, I should mention, provided me with all the fuel that was required in the ordinary way, and, moreover, I was constantly finding pieces of wreckage along the shore that had been gathered in by the restless waves. Often—oh! often—I reflected with a shudder what my fate would have been had the ship gone down in deep water, leaving me safe, but deprived of all the stores she contained. The long, lingering agony, the starvation, the madness of thirst, and finally a horrible death on that far-away strip of sand, and another skeleton added to that grisly pile!

The days passed slowly by. In what part of the world I was located I had not the remotest idea. I felt that I was altogether out of the beaten track of ships because of the reefs that studded these seas, and therefore the prospect of my being rescued was very

remote indeed—a thought that often caused me a kind
of dull agony, more terrible than any mere physical
pain.

However, I fixed up a flagstaff on the highest point
of the island—(poor "island,"—*that* was not many
inches)—and floated an ensign *upside down* from it,
in the hope that this signal of distress might be
sighted by some stray vessel, and indicate the presence
of a castaway to those on board. Every morning I
made my way to the flagstaff, and scanned the horizon
for a possible sail, but I always had to come away
disappointed. This became a habit; yet, so eternal
is hope, that day by day, week by week, and month
by month the bitter disappointment was always a
keen torture. By the way, the very reefs that made
those seas so dangerous served completely to protect
my little island in stormy weather. The fury of the
billows lost itself upon them, so that even the surf very
rarely reached me. I was usually astir about sunrise.
I knew that the sun rose about 6 A.M. in those tropical
seas and set at 6 P.M.; there was very little variation
all the year round. A heavy dew descended at night,
which made the air delightfully cool; but in the day it
was so frightfully hot that I could not bear the weight
of ordinary clothes upon my person, so I took to
wearing a silk shawl instead, hung loosely round my
waist.

Another reason why I abandoned clothes was because
I found that when a rent appeared the sun blazed down
through it and raised a painful blister. On the other
hand, by merely wearing a waist-cloth, and taking
constant sea baths, I suffered scarcely at all from the
scorching tropical sun. I now devoted all my energies

to the wreck of the *Veielland*, lest anything should happen to it, and worked with feverish energy to get everything I possibly could out of the ship. It took me some months to accomplish this, but eventually I had removed everything—even the greater part of the cargo of pearl shells. The work was rendered particularly arduous in consequence of the decks being so frequently under water; and I found it was only at the full and new moons that I could actually *walk* round on the rocks to the wreck. In course of time the ship began to break up, and I materially assisted the operation with an axe. I wanted her timbers to build a boat in which to escape.

The casks of flour I floated ashore were very little the worse for their immersion; in fact, the water had only soaked through to the depth of a couple of inches, forming a kind of protecting wet crust, and leaving the inner part perfectly dry and good. Much of this flour, however, was afterwards spoiled by weevils; nor did my spreading out the precious grain in the sunlight on tarpaulins and sails save it from at least partial destruction. I also brought ashore bags of beans, rice, and maize; cases of preserved milk and vegetables, and innumerable other articles of food, besides some small casks of oil and rum. In fact, I stripped the ship's interior of everything, and at the end of nine months very little remained of her on the rocks but the bare skeleton of the hull. I moved all the things out day by day according to the tides.

In a large chest that came ashore from the captain's cabin I found a stock of all kinds of seeds, and I resolved to see whether I could grow a little corn. Jensen himself had put the seeds aboard in order to

plant them on some of the islands near which we might
be compelled to anchor for some length of time.
Another object was to grow plants on board for the
amusement of the Malays.   The seeds included
vegetables, flowers, and Indian corn, the last named
· being in the cob.   The Malays are very fond of
flowers, and the captain told them that they might
try and cultivate some in boxes on board ; but when
he saw that this would mean an additional drain
upon his supply of fresh water he withdrew the permission.   I knew that salt water would not nourish
plants, and I was equally certain I could not spare
fresh water from my own stock for this purpose.

Nevertheless, I set my wits to work, and at length
decided upon an interesting experiment.   I filled a
large turtle shell with sand and a little clay, and
thoroughly wetted the mixture with turtle's blood,
then stirring the mass into a puddle and planting
corn in it.

The grain quickly sprouted, and flourished so rapidly,
that within a very short time I was able to transplant
it—always, however, nourishing it with the blood of
turtles.   This most satisfactory result induced me to
extend my operation, and I soon had quaint little
crops of maize and wheat growing in huge turtle
shells ; the wheat-plants, however, did not reach
maturity.

For a long time I was content with the simple
awning I have described as a place of shelter, but
when I began to recover the pearl shells from the
ship, it occurred to me that I might use them as
material with which to build some kind of a hut.
Altogether there were about thirty tons of pearl shells

on board, and at first I took to diving for them merely as a sort of pastime.

I spent many weeks getting enough shells ashore to build a couple of parallel walls, each about seven feet high, three feet thick, and ten feet in length. The breeze blew gratefully through them. I filled

BUILDING MY HOUSE

the interstices of these walls with a puddle of clayey sand and water, covered in the top with canvas, and made quite a comfortable living-place out of it. The walls at any rate had a high commercial value! When the wet season set in I built a third wall at one end, and erected a sort of double awning in front, under which I always kept my fire burning. I also put a straw thatch over the hut, proudly using my own straw which I had grown with blood.

In course of time I made myself crude articles of furniture, including a table, some chairs, a bed, &c. My bedding at first consisted of sails, but afterwards I was able to have a mattress filled with straw from my corn patch. The kettle I had saved from the wreck was for a long time my only cooking utensil, so when I had anything to prepare I generally made an oven in the sand, after the manner of the natives I had met on the New Guinea main. I could always catch plenty of fish— principally mullet; and as for sea-fowls, all that I had to do was walk over to that part of the island where they were feeding and breeding, and knock them over with a stick. I made dough-cakes from the flour whilst it lasted; and I had deputies to fish for me— I mean the hundreds of pelicans. The birds who had little ones to feed went out in the morning, and returned in the afternoon, with from three to ten pounds of delicious fresh fish in their curious pouches.

On alighting on the island they emptied their pouches on the sand—too often, I must confess, solely for my benefit. Selfish bachelor birds on returning with full pouches jerked their catch into the air, and so swallowed it. It used to amuse me, however, to watch a robber gull, perched on their back, cleverly and neatly intercepting the fish as it ascended. These fish, with broiled turtle meat and tinned fruits, made quite a sumptuous repast.

After breakfast I would have a swim when the tide was low and there was no likelihood of sharks being about. A run along the beach in the sun until I was dry followed, and then I returned to my awning and read aloud to myself in English, from my medical books and my English-French Testament, simply for the pleasure of hearing my own voice. I was a very good linguist in those days, and spoke English particularly well long before I left Switzerland. After breakfast, my dog and I would go out to catch a peculiar sort of fish called the "sting-rae." These curious creatures have a sharp bony spike about two inches in length near the tail, and this I found admirably adapted for arrow-heads. The body of the fish resembled a huge flounder, but the tail was long and tapering. They would come close in-shore, and I would spear them from the rocks with a Papuan fishing-spear. The smallest I ever caught weighed fifteen pounds, and I could never carry home more than a couple of average weight. They have the power of stinging, I believe, electrically, hence their name. At all events, I was once stung by one of these fish, and it was an experience I shall never forget. It fortunately happened at a time when some friendly blacks were at hand, otherwise I question very much whether I should be alive to-day.

I was wading slowly along the beach in rather deep water, when I suddenly felt a most excruciating pain in my left ankle. It seemed as though I had just received a paralysing shock from a powerful battery, and down I fell in a state of absolute collapse, unable to stir a finger to save myself, although I knew I was rapidly drowning. Fortunately the blacks who were with me came and pulled me ashore, where I slowly recovered. There was only a slight scratch on my ankle, but for a long time my whole body was racked with pain, and when the natives got to know

of the symptoms they told me that I had been attacked
by a "sting-rae." The spike or sting measures from
two to six inches in length according to the size of the
fish.

But to return to my solitary life on the island.
The flesh of the sting-rae was not pleasant to eat,
being rather tough and tasteless, so I used it as a
bait for sharks. Turtles visited the island in great
numbers, and deposited their eggs in holes made in
the sand above high-water mark. They only came
on land during the night, at high tide; and whenever
I wanted a special delicacy, I turned one over on its
back till morning, when I despatched it leisurely with
my tomahawk. The creatures' shells I always devoted
to the extension of my garden, which became very
large, and eventually covered fully two-thirds of the
island. The maize and cob-corn flourished remarkably well, and I generally managed to get three
crops in the course of a year. The straw came in
useful for bedding purposes, but as I found the
sand-flies and other insects becoming more and more
troublesome whilst I lay on the ground, I decided to
try a hammock. I made one out of shark's hide,
and slung it in my hut, when I found that it answered
my purpose splendidly.

The great thing was to ward off the dull agony, the
killing depression, and manias generally. Fortunately
I was of a very active disposition, and as a pastime I
took to gymnastics, even as I had at Montreux. I
became a most proficient tumbler and acrobat, and
could turn two or three somersaults on dashing down
from the sloping roof of my pearl-shell hut; besides,
I became a splendid high jumper, with and without

the pole. Another thing I interested myself in was the construction of a sun-dial.

Indeed, I spent many hours devising some means whereby I could fashion a reliable "clock," and at last I worked out the principle of the sun-dial on the sand. I fixed a long stick perfectly upright in the ground, and then marked off certain spaces round it by means of pegs and pearl shells. I calculated the hours according to the length of the shadows cast by the sun.

But, in spite of all that I could do to interest or amuse myself, I was frequently overwhelmed with fits of depression and despair, and more than once I feared I should lose my mental balance and become a maniac. A religious craze took possession of me, and, strive as I might, I could not keep my mind from dwelling upon certain apparent discrepancies in the various apostles' versions of the Gospel!

I found myself constantly brooding over statements made in one form by St. Matthew, and in another by St. Luke; and I conjured up endless theological arguments and theories, until I was driven nearly frantic. Much as I regretted it, I was compelled at last to give up reading my New Testament, and by the exercise of a strong will I forced myself to think about something totally different.

It took me a long time to overcome this religious melancholia, but I mastered it in the long run, and was greatly delighted when I found I could once more read without being hypercritical and doubtful of everything. Had I been cast on a luxuriant island, growing fruits and flowers, and inhabited at least by animals —how different would it have been!. But here there was nothing to save the mind from madness—merely a tiny strip of sand, invisible a few hundred yards out at sea.

When the fits of depression came upon me I invariably concluded that life was unbearable, and would actually rush into the sea, with the deliberate object of putting an end to myself. At these times my agony of mind was far more dreadful that any degree of physical suffering could have been, and death seemed to have a fascination for me that I could not resist. Yet when I found myself up to my neck in water, a sudden revulsion of feeling would come over me, and instead of drowning myself I would indulge in a swim or a ride on a turtle's back by way of diverting my thoughts into different channels.

Bruno always seemed to understand when I had an attack of melancholia, and he would watch my every movement. When he saw me rushing into the water, he would follow at my side barking and yelling like a mad thing, until he actually made me forget the dreadful object I had in view. And we would perhaps conclude by having a swimming race. These fits of depression always came upon me towards evening, and generally about the same hour.

In spite of the apparent hopelessness of my position, I never relinquished the idea of escaping from the island some day, and accordingly I started building a boat within a month of my shipwreck.

Not that I knew anything whatever about boat-building; but I was convinced that I could at least make a craft of some sort that would float. I set to work with a light heart, but later on paid dearly for my ignorance in bitter, bitter disappointment and impotent

regrets. For one thing, I made the keel too heavy;
then, again, I used planks that were absurdly thick for
the shell, though, of course, I was not aware of these
things at the time. The wreck, of course, provided
me with all the woodwork I required. In order to
make the staves pliable, I soaked them in water for a
week, and then heated them over a fire, afterwards
bending them to the required shape. At the end of
nine months of unremitting labour, to which, latterly,
considerable anxiety—glorious hopes and sickening
fears—was added, I had built what I considered a
substantial and sea-worthy sailing boat, fully fifteen
feet long by four feet wide. It was a heavy ungainly
looking object when finished, and it required much
ingenuity on my part to launch it. This I eventually
managed, however, by means of rollers and levers;
but the boat was frightfully low in the water at the
stern. It was quite watertight though, having an
outer covering of sharks' green hide, well smeared with
Stockholm tar, and an inside lining of stout canvas.
I also rigged up a mast, and made a sail. When my
boat floated I fairly screamed aloud with wild delight,
and sympathetic Bruno jumped and yelped in unison.

But when all my preparations were complete, and I
had rowed out a little way, I made a discovery that
nearly drove me crazy. I found I had launched the
boat in a sort of lagoon several miles in extent, barred
by a crescent of coral rocks, over which *I could not
possibly drag my craft into the open sea.* Although
the water covered the reefs at high tide it was never
of sufficient depth to allow me to sail the boat over
them. I tried every possible opening, but was always
arrested at some point or other. After the first acute

paroxysm of despair — beating my head with my
clenched fists—I consoled myself with the thought that
when the high tides came, they would perhaps lift the
boat over that terrible barrier. I waited, and waited,
and waited, but alas! only to be disappointed. My nine weary months of arduous

WILD DELIGHT

travail and half-frantic anticipation were cruelly wasted.
At no time could I get the boat out into the open sea
in consequence of the rocks, and it was equally impossible for me unaided to drag her back up the steep
slope again and across the island, where she could be
launched opposite an opening in the encircling reefs.

So there my darling boat lay idly in the lagoon—a useless thing, whose sight filled me with heartache and despair. And yet, in this very lagoon I soon found amusement and pleasure. When I had in some measure got over the disappointment about the boat, I took to sailing her about in the lagoon. I also played the part of Neptune in the very extraordinary way I have already indicated. I used to wade out to where the turtles were, and on catching a big six-hundred-pounder, I would calmly sit astride on his back.

Away would swim the startled creature, mostly a foot or so below the surface. When he dived deeper I simply sat far back on the shell, and then he was forced to come up. I steered my queer steeds in a curious way. When I wanted my turtle to turn to the left, I simply thrust my foot into his right eye, and *vice versa* for the contrary direction. My two big toes placed simultaneously over both his optics caused a halt so abrupt as almost to unseat me. Sometimes I would go fully a mile out to sea on one of these strange steeds. It always frightened them to have me astride, and in their terror they swam at a tremendous pace until compelled to desist through sheer exhaustion.

Before the wet season commenced I put a straw thatch on the roof of my hut, as before stated, and made my quarters as snug as possible. And it was a very necessary precaution, too, for sometimes it rained for days at a stretch. The rain never kept me indoors, however, and I took exercise just the same, as I didn't bother about clothes, and rather enjoyed the shower bath. I was always devising means of making life more tolerable, and amongst other things I made a sort of swing, which I found extremely useful in beguiling time. I would also practise jumping with long poles. One day I captured a young pelican, and trained him to accompany me in my walks and assist me in my fishing operations. He also acted as a decoy. Frequently I would hide myself in some grass, whilst my pet bird walked a few yards away to attract

RIDING ON A TURTLE

his fellows. Presently he would be joined by a whole flock, many of which I lassoed, or shot with my bow and arrows.

But for my dog—my almost human Bruno—I think I must have died. I used to talk to him precisely as though he were a human being. We were absolutely inseparable. I preached long sermons to him from

Gospel texts.   I told him in a loud voice all about my
early life and school-days at Montreux; I recounted
to him all my adventures, from the fatal meeting with
poor Peter Jensen in Singapore, right up to the present;
I sang little *chansons* to him, and among these he
had his favourites as well as those he disliked cordially.
If he did not care for a song, he would set up a pitiful
howl.   I feel convinced that this constant communing
aloud with my dog saved my reason.   Bruno seemed
always to be in such good spirits that I never dreamed
of anything happening to him; and his quiet, sympathetic companionship was one of the greatest bless-
ings I knew throughout many weird and terrible years.
As I talked to him he would sit at my feet, looking
so intelligently at me that I fancied he understood
every word of what I was saying.

When the religious mania was upon me, I talked
over all sorts of theological subjects with my Bruno,
and it seemed to relieve me, even though I never received any enlightenment from him upon the knotty
point that would be puzzling me at that particular
time.   What delighted him most of all was for me to
tell him that I loved him very dearly, and that he
was even more valuable to me than the famous dogs
of St. Bernard were to benighted travellers in the
snow.

I knew very little about musical instruments, but as
I had often longed for something to make a noise with,
if only to drown the maddening crash of the eternal surf,
I fashioned a drum out of a small barrel, with sharks'
skin stretched tightly over the open ends.   This I beat
with a couple of sticks as an accompaniment to my
singing, and as Bruno occasionally joined in with a

howl of disapproval or a yell of joy, the effect must have been picturesque if not musical. I was ready to do almost anything to drown that ceaseless cr-ash, cr-ash of the breakers on the beach, from whose melancholy and monotonous roar I could never escape for a single moment throughout the whole of the long day. However, I escaped its sound when I lay down to sleep at night by a very simple plan. As I was stone-deaf in the right ear I always slept on the left side.

Seven weary months had passed away, when one morning, on scanning the horizon, I suddenly leaped into the air and screamed : " My God ! A sail ! A sail !" I nearly became delirious with excitement, but, alas ! the ship was too far out to sea to notice my frantic signals. My island lay very low, and all that I could make out of the vessel in the distance was her sails. She must have been fully five miles away, yet, in my excitement, I ran up and down the miserable beach, shouting in a frenzy and waving my arms in the hope of attracting the attention of some one on board ; but it was all in vain. The ship, which I concluded was a pearler, kept steadily on her way, and eventually disappeared below the horizon.

Never can I hope to describe the gnawing pain at my heart as, hoarse and half mad, I sank exhausted on the sand, watching the last vestige of the ship disappearing. Altogether, I saw five ships pass in this way during my sojourn on the island, but they were always too far out at sea to notice my signals. One of these vessels I knew to be a man-o'-war flying the British ensign. I tried to rig up a longer flag-staff, as I thought the original one not high enough

E

for its purpose.   Accordingly I spliced a couple of
long poles together, but to my disappointment found
them too heavy to raise in the air. Bruno always
joined in my enthusiasm when a sail was in sight ;
in fact, he was generally the first to detect it, and
he would bark and drag at me until he had drawn
my attention to the new hope.   And I loved him
for his tender sympathy in my paroxysms of regret
and disappointment.   The hairy head would rub
coaxingly against my arm, the warm tongue licking
my hand, and the faithful brown eyes gazing at
me with a knowledge and sympathy that were
more than human — these I feel sure saved me
again and again.   I might mention that, although
my boat was absolutely useless for the purpose of
escape, I did not neglect her altogether, but sailed
her about the enclosed lagoon by way of practice in
the handling of her sails.   This was also a welcome
recreation.

I never feared a lack of fresh water, for when, in
the dry season, the ship's stock and my reserve from
the wet season were exhausted, I busied myself with
the condensing of sea water in my kettle, adding to
my store literally drop by drop.   Water was the only
liquid I drank, all the tea and coffee carried on board
having been rendered utterly useless.

The powerful winged birds that abounded on the
island one day gave me an idea : Why not hang a
message around their necks and send them forth into
the unknown ?   Possibly they might bring help—who
knows ?   And with me to conceive was to act.   I
got a number of empty condensed-milk tins, and, by
means of fire, separated from the cylinder the tin disc

that formed the bottom. On this disc I scratched a message with a sharp nail. In a few words I conveyed information about the wreck and my deplorable condition. I also gave the approximate bearings—latitude fifteen to thirteen degrees, not far from the Australian main.

These discs—I prepared several in English, French, bad Dutch, German, and Italian—I then fastened round the necks of the pelicans, by means of fish-gut, and away across the ocean sped the affrighted birds, so scared by the mysterious encumbrance that *they never returned to the island*.

I may say here that more than twenty years later, when I returned to civilisation, I chanced to mention the story about my messenger-birds to some old inhabitants at Fremantle, Western Australia, when, to my amazement, they told me that a pelican carrying a tin disc round its neck, bearing a message in French from a castaway, *had* been found many years previously by an old boatman on the beach near the mouth of the Swan River. But it was not mine.

So appalling was the monotony, and so limited my resources, that I welcomed with childish glee any trifling little incident that happened. For example, one lovely night in June I was amazed to hear a tremendous commotion outside, and on getting up to see what was the matter, I beheld dimly countless thousands of birds—Java sparrows I believe them to be. I went back to bed again, and in the morning was a little dismayed to find that my pretty visitors had eaten up nearly all my green corn. And the birds were still there when I went forth in the morning.

They made the air ring with their lively chatter, but the uproar they made was as music to me. The majority of them had greyish-yellow bodies, with yellow beaks and pink ruffs, and they were not at all afraid of me. I moved about freely among them, and did not attempt to drive them out of my corn patch, being only too grateful to see so much life about me. They rose, however, in great clouds the next day, much to my regret, and as they soared heavenwards I could not help envying them their blessed freedom.

I kept count of the long days by means of pearl shells, for I had not used up the whole cargo in the walls of my hut. I put shells side by side in a row, one for each day, until the number reached seven, and then I transferred one shell to another place, representing the weeks. Another pile of shells represented the months; and as for the years, I kept count of those by making notches on my bow. My peculiar calendar was always checked by the moon.

Now, I am not a superstitious man, so I relate the following extraordinary occurrence merely as it happened, and without advancing any theory of my own to account for it. I had been many, many months —perhaps more than a year—on that terrible little sand-spit, and on the night I am describing I went to bed as usual, feeling very despondent. As I lay asleep in my hammock, I dreamed a beautiful dream. Some spiritual being seemed to come and bend over me, smiling pityingly. So extraordinarily vivid was the apparition, that I suddenly woke, tumbled out of my hammock, and went outside on a vague search. In a

few minutes, however, I laughed at my own folly and
turned in again.

I lay there for some little time longer, thinking about
the past—for I dared not dwell on the future—when
suddenly the intense stillness of the night was broken
by a strangely familiar voice, which said, distinctly
and encouragingly, "*Je suis avec toi. Soit sans peur.
Tu reviendras.*" I can never hope to describe my feelings at that moment.

It was not the voice of my father nor of my mother,
yet it was certainly the voice of some one I knew and
loved, yet was unable to identify. The night was
strangely calm, and so startling was this mysterious
message that instinctively I leaped out of my hammock
again, went outside and called out several times, but,
of course, nothing happened. From that night, however, I never absolutely despaired, even when things
looked their very worst.

Two interminable years had passed away, when
one day the weather suddenly changed, and a terrible
gale commenced to blow, which threatened almost to
wreck my little hut. One morning, a few days later,
when the storm had abated somewhat, I heard Bruno
barking wildly on the beach. A few seconds afterwards he came rushing into the hut, and would not
rest until I prepared to follow him outside. Before
doing so, however, I picked up an oar—I knew not
why. I then followed my dog down to the beach,
wondering what could possibly have caused him to
make such a fuss. The sea was somewhat agitated,
and as it was not yet very light, I could not clearly
distinguish things in the distance.

On peering seawards for the third or fourth time,

however, I fancied I could make out a long, black object, which I concluded must be some kind of a boat, tossing up and down on the billows. Then I must confess I began to share Bruno's excitement,— particularly when a few minutes later I discerned a well-made catamaran, *with several human figures lying prostrate upon it !*

CHAPTER IV

MY state of mind was perfectly indescribable. Here, I thought, are some poor shipwrecked creatures like myself; and I prayed to God that I might be the means of saving them. The prospect of having at length some one to converse with filled me with unutterable joy, and I could hardly restrain myself from rushing into the water and swimming out to the catamaran, which was still several hundred yards away from me. Would it *never* draw near? I thought, wild with impatience. And then, to my horror, I saw that it was closely followed by a number of sharks, which swam round and round it expectantly. Seeing this, I could contain myself no longer. Sternly commanding my dog not to follow me, I waded into the waves and then swam boldly out to the catamaran, taking good care, however, to make a great noise as I swam, by shouting and splashing in order to frighten away the sharks. When eventually I did come up to the floating platform of logs, I found that there were four blacks upon it—a man, a woman, and two boys. All were lying quite

71

prostrate through exhaustion, apparently more dead than alive. The sharks still hung on persistently, but at length I drove them away by beating the water with my oar, with which I then proceeded to paddle the catamaran ashore. You see, the oar I grasped when Bruno came to give the alarm proved of inestimable value; and so all through my marvellous years of sojourn among the cannibals an undeniable Providence guided my every action. But this will be seen from my narrative in a hundred amazing instances. I climbed aboard the catamaran and paddled it into shallow water; and then, jumping overboard again I pulled it right up on to the beach, and carried the four blacks one by one into my hut. They were in a most pitiable state of collapse. Their tongues were swollen and protruding out of their mouths, and for a long time I could get nothing down their throats. First of all I tried to revive them with cold water, but found they could not swallow.

Then I remembered the rum I had saved from the wreck all this time, and procuring some I rubbed their bodies with it, tied wet bandages round their necks, and rolled them about in wet sails, in the hope that in this way their bodies might absorb the necessary liquid. You see I had an idea that they were dying from want of water. All four were terribly emaciated, and in the last stages of exhaustion. After two or three hours' treatment, the two boys recovered consciousness, and some little time later the man also showed signs of reviving, but the woman did not come to until the afternoon. None of them, of course, were able to walk; and in the meantime they did nothing but drink water. They seemed not to realise what had happened or where they were until the following day, and then their surprise—mainly at the sight of me—was beyond all description. Their first symptom was one of extreme terror, and in spite of every kind action I could think of, they held out for a long time against my advances—although I signed to them that I was their friend, patting them on the shoulders to inspire confidence, and trying to make them understand that I had saved them from a terrible death. I fancy they all thought they had died and were now in the presence of the mysterious Great Spirit! At any rate, it was not until they began to eat freely that they grew in some measure accustomed to me. Then an ungovernable curiosity manifested itself. From gazing at me unceasingly, they took to feeling me and patting my skin. They made queer, guttural sounds with their mouths, evidently expressive of amazement; they slapped their thighs, and cracked their fingers.

Next, my belongings came in for inspection, and everything excited wonderment and delight to such a degree, that I blessed Providence for sending me so much entertaining society. My hut, with its curious thatched roof, excited vast interest; and it was amusing to see the two boys, aged respectively about twelve and fourteen, following their parents about, jabbering incessantly, and giving me sly, half-terrified glances as they examined my implements and utensils. The woman was the first to get over her fear of me, and she soon grew to trust me implicitly; whereas her husband never ceased to view me with inexplicable suspicion until we regained his own country. He was a big, repulsive-looking savage, with a morose and sullen temper; and although he never showed signs

of open antagonism, yet I never trusted him for a
moment during the six long months he was my
"guest" on the little sand-bank! It seems I un-
wittingly offended him, and infringed the courtesy
common among his people by declining to take advantage of a certain embarrassing offer which he made
me soon after his recovery.

It may not be anticipating too much to say here that
the woman was destined to play a vitally important
part in the whole of my life, and with her I went
through adventures and saw sights more weird and
wonderful than anything I had ever read of, even in
the wildest extravagances of sensational fiction. But
the ruling passion was very strong, and one of the
first things I did was to take my black friends down
to the beach and show them my precious boat floating
idly in the lagoon. Oddly enough, I had in the meantime always taken the greatest care of the boat, keeping
her bottom clean and generally furbishing her up—
having, however, no particular object in view in doing
this, except perhaps that it gave me something to do.
The poor little "home-made" boat threw the blacks
into a perfect frenzy of astonishment, and they concluded that I must have come from a very distant part
of the world in so enormous a "catamaran." As a
matter of fact, from that moment they looked upon me
as most certainly a kind of Supreme Spirit from another
world; they may have had doubts before. Next I
showed them the wreck, which was now only a bare
skeleton of rotting woodwork, but still plainly discernible among the coral rocks. I tried to explain to
them that it was in the larger boat that I had come,
but they failed to understand me.

On returning to the hut I put on my clothes for
their benefit, whereupon their amazement was so great
that I seriously contemplated discontinuing my list of

MY SECONDARY SKIN

wonders, lest they should become absolutely afraid to
remain with me. The clothes they considered part of
myself—in fact, a kind of secondary skin ! They were

terribly frightened and distressed, and not one of the four dared approach me.

The blacks did not build themselves any place of shelter, but merely slept in the open air at night, under the lee of my hut, with a large fire always burning at their feet. I offered them both blankets and sails by way of covering, but they refused them, preferring to lie huddled close together for warmth. In the morning the woman would prepare breakfast for them, consisting of fish (mainly mullet), birds' and turtles' eggs, and sea-fowl; to which would perhaps be added some little luxury from my own stock. They only had two meals a day—one in the morning and the other in the afternoon. Their favourite food was turtle, of which they could eat enormous quantities, especially the fat. Bruno was a long time before he took kindly to the new arrivals, probably because they manifested such extraordinary emotion whenever he lifted up his voice and barked.

I think the only thing that roused the father of the family from his sullen moods was my extraordinary acrobatic performances, which also threw the two little nigger boys into hysterics of delight. Father, mother, and children tried to imitate my somersaults, "wheels," and contortions, but came to grief so desperately (once the morose man nearly broke his neck) that they soon gave it up. The man would sit and watch our gambols for hours without moving a muscle. I was never actually afraid of him, but took good care not to let him get possession of any of my weapons; and as I had also taken the precaution to break up and throw into the sea the spears he had brought with him on his catamaran, I felt pretty sure he could not do much mischief even if he were so disposed. After seeing me bring down birds with my bow and arrow he began to hold me in absolute fear, probably because he had some idea that his own skin might be jeopardised if he did not accommodate himself to circumstances. I repeatedly told him that with my boat I might perhaps some day help him to get back to his own country, and I must say that this suggestion roused him somewhat from his lethargy, and he appeared profoundly grateful.

Gradually I acquired a slight acquaintance with the extraordinary language of the blacks, and had many a chat with the woman, who also picked up a few words of comical English from me. She was a woman of average height, lithe and supple, with an intelligent face and sparkling eyes. She was a very interesting companion, and as I grew more proficient in her queer language of signs, and slaps, and clicks, I learnt from her many wonderful things about the habits and customs of the Australian aborigines, which proved extremely useful to me in after years. Yamba—for that was her name—told me that when I rescued them they had been blown miles and miles out of their course and away from their own country by the terrible gale that had been raging about a fortnight previously. It seems that they had originally started out on an expedition to catch turtles on a little island between Cambridge Gulf and Queen's Channel, but the storm carried them out to sea. They drifted about for many days, until at length they reached my little island. The only food they had during the whole of this time was turtle, but they were entirely without water. One would think that they must inevitably have died of thirst, but the blacks are wonderful people for going

without water for prolonged periods.   Moreover, they
find a mouthful of salt water occasionally quite sustaining.

One of my most amusing experiences with the blacks
was one day when, quite accidentally, Yamba caught
sight of herself for the first time in the little oval
looking-glass I had hanging up in the hut near my
hammock.   She thoughtlessly took it down and held
it close up to her face.   She trembled, felt the surface
of the glass, and then looked hurriedly on the back.
One long, last, lingering look she gave, and then flew
screaming out of the hut.

Oddly enough, she overcame her fears later, and,
woman-like, would come and look in the mirror for an
hour at a stretch, smacking her lips all the while in
wonderment, and making most comical grimaces and
contortions to try various effects.   Her husband, however (Gunda, as I called him), was very differently
affected, for the moment his wife showed him his own
reflection in the glass he gave a terrific yell and bolted
to the other end of the little island, in a state of the
most abject terror.   He never quite overcame his terror
and distrust of the mirror, which he evidently considered possessed of life, and in reality a kind of spirit
to be feared and avoided.

But, of course, the two boys found the glass a
never-ending source of amazement and wonder, and
were not in the least afraid of it after the first natural
shock of surprise.   Altogether, I thanked God for
sending me my new companions ; and, as you may
suppose, they afforded me as much entertainment and
gratification as I and my belongings did them.

Every evening, before retiring to rest, the family

squatted round the fire and indulged in a mournful kind of chant—singing, as I afterwards learnt, the wonders they had seen on the white man's island; my mirror coming in for special mention. This was the only approach to a "religious service" I ever saw, and was partly intended to propitiate or frighten away the spirits of the departed, of whom the Australian blacks have a great horror.

The blacks had been with me two or three weeks, when one evening the man approached and intimated in unmistakable terms that he wanted to get away from the island and return to his own land. He said he thought he and his family could easily return to their friends on the mainland by means of the catamaran that had brought them.

And Yamba, that devoted and mysterious creature, solemnly pointed out to me a glowing star far away on the horizon. There, she said, lay the home of her people. After this I was convinced that the mainland could not be more than a couple of hundred miles or so away, and I determined to accompany them on the journey thither, in the hope that this might form one of the stepping-stones to civilisation and my own kind. We lost no time. One glorious morning we three—Yamba, her husband, and myself—repaired to the fatal lagoon that hemmed in my precious boat, and without more ado dragged it up the steep bank by means of rollers run on planks across the sand-spit, and then finally, with a tremendous splash and an excited hurrah from myself, it glided out into the water, a thing of meaning, of escape, and of freedom. The boat, notwithstanding its long period of uselessness, was perfectly water-tight and thoroughly seaworthy,

although still unpleasantly low at the stern. Gunda
was impatient to be off, but I pointed out to him that,
as the wind persistently blew in the wrong direction day
after day, we should be compelled perforce to delay our
departure perhaps for some months. You see, Gunda
was not a man who required to make much preparation:
he thought all we should have to do was to tumble into
the boat and set sail across the sunlit sea. "I can
paddle my catamaran against both wind and tide; why
cannot you do the same?" he would say. He did not
understand the advantage or uses of sails. He had
lost his own paddles in the storm, otherwise he would
in all probability have left the island on his own
account. He was like a fish out of water when the
novelty of his situation wore off. On the other hand,
I thought of water, provisions, and other equally
vital necessaries. So Gunda had to rest content for
a time, and he grew, if possible, more morose and
sullen than ever.

During this period of impatient waiting, we made
many experimental voyages out to sea, and generally
got the boat into capital trim for the great and eventful
journey. I saw to it that she was thoroughly well
provisioned with tinned stuffs—long put on one side
for the purpose; and I may say here that at the last
moment before starting I placed on board three large live
turtles, which supplied us with meat until we reached
the Australian main. I also took a plentiful supply
of water, in bags made from the intestines of birds
and fishes; also a small cask containing about ten
gallons of the precious fluid, which was placed near the
mast. In short, as far I was able, I provided everything
that was necessary for this most important journey.

But consider for a moment the horrible doubts and fears that racked me. I *fancied* the mainland was not very far away, but you must remember I was not at all certain how long it would take us to reach it; nor could I be sure, therefore, whether I had taken a sufficient supply of food and water. Our provisions, which included tinned meats, corn in the cob and loose, turtles' flesh and intestines, flour, rice, beans, &c., would, however, on a fairly liberal allowance, last a little over three weeks. We also carried some blankets, nails, tar, and other requisites. Of my books I only took my Bible with me. This I wrapped up in parchment made from pelican skin, together with four photographs of a certain young lady which I carried about with me throughout the whole of my wanderings. The propulsive power was, of course, the big lug-sail, which was always held loosely in the hand, and never made fast, for fear of a sudden capsize.

Six months had passed away since the advent of my visitors, when one morning we all marched out from the hut and down to the beach; the two boys fairly yelling with joy, and waving bunches of green corn plucked from my garden. Their mother skipped gaily hither and thither, and I myself was hardly able to control my transports of excitement and exhilaration. Even Gunda beamed upon the preparations for our release. I did not demolish my hut of pearl shells, but left it standing exactly as it had been during the past two and a half years. Nor must I omit to mention that I buried my treasure of pearls deep in the sand at one end of the island, and in all human probability it is there at this moment, for I have never returned for them, as I fondly hoped to be able to do

F

so at some future date.   It is, of course, possible that
the precious box has been washed away in a storm,
but more probably the contrary is the case, and still
deeper layers of sand have been silted over this great
treasure.   I dared not carry anything oversea that
was not vitally necessary, and what good were pearls
to me on my fearful journey, convoying four other
people out into the unknown in a crazy, home-made

GREAT EXCITEMENT

boat?   Even masses of virgin gold were of very little
use to me in the years that followed; but of this more
anon.   My condition, by the way, at this time was
one of robust health; indeed, I was getting quite
stout owing to the quantity of turtle I had been
eating, whilst Yamba's husband was positively corpu-
lent from the same reason.

   That glorious morning in the last week of May

1866 will ever be graven in my memory. As I cast off from that saving but cruel shore, I thanked my Maker for having preserved me so long and brought me through such awful perils, as well as for the good health I had always enjoyed. As the boat began to ripple through the inclosed waters of the lagoon, the spirits of the four blacks rose so high that I was afraid they would capsize the little craft in their excitement.

There was a strong, warm breeze blowing in our favour, and soon my island home was receding swiftly from our view. The last thing to remain in sight was the shell hut, but this, too, disappeared before we had covered three miles. It would have been visible from a big ship at a much greater distance, but no one would ever imagine what it really was. Yamba sat near me in the stern, but her husband curled himself up at the opposite end of the boat; and from the time we reached the open sea practically until we gained the main, he did not relax his attitude of reserve and dogged silence. He ate and drank enormously, however. You would have thought we were in a land flowing with milk and honey, instead of an open boat with limited provisions and an unknown journey in front of us. He did exert himself sufficiently on one occasion, however, to dive overboard and capture a turtle. He was sitting moodily in the prow of the boat as usual one afternoon, when suddenly he jumped up, and with a yell took a header overboard, almost capsizing our heavily laden boat. At first I thought he must have gone mad, but on heaving to, I saw him some little distance away in the water struggling with a turtle. He managed to get it on its back after a time, and though I felt annoyed at his recklessness, I could not help laughing at his antics and the comical efforts made by the turtle to escape. The turtle was duly hauled aboard, and we then continued our voyage without delay. I was dreadfully afraid of being caught in a storm. Our boat must inevitably have foundered had the seas been at all rough.

Fortunately never once did the wind change, so that we were able to sail on steadily and safely night and day, without deviating in the least from our course. We travelled fully four knots an hour, the wind and current being nearly always in our favour. It was, however, a painfully monotonous and trying experience to sit thus in the boat, cramped up as we were, day after day and night after night. About the fifth day we sighted a small island—probably Barker Island, in the vicinity of Admiralty Gulf—and landed upon it at once solely for the purpose of stretching our aching limbs. This little island was uninhabited, and covered to the very water's edge with dense tropical vegetation. It was a perfectly exhilarating experience to walk about on real earth once more. We cooked some turtle meat and stayed a few hours on the island, after which we entered the boat and put off on our journey again. Just before leaving I stored a quantity of corn, cobs, seeds, &c., in a little cairn in case we might be compelled to return. I always steered, keeping east by north, but Yamba relieved me for a few hours each evening—generally between six and nine o'clock, when I enjoyed a brief but sound sleep. Gunda never offered to take a spell, and I did not think it worth while to trouble him.

Thus night and day we sailed steadily on, occasion-

ally sighting sharks and even whales.   We passed a
great number of islands, some of them wooded and
covered with beautiful jungle growths, whilst others
were nothing but rock and sand.   None of them
seemed to be inhabited.   The sea was smooth all
the time, but occasionally the currents carried us out
of our course among the islands, and then we had
to land and wait till the tide turned.   No matter
how the wind was, if the tide was not also in
our favour we had to land.   We cruised in and out
among the islands for ten days or more, when we
rounded Cape Londonderry and then steered S. by E.
The current, however, carried us straight for Cambridge Gulf.   One little island I sighted between
Cambridge Gulf and Queen's Channel had a curious
house-like structure built in one of the trees on the
coast.   The trunk of this tree was very large and
tapering, and the platform arrangement was built
amongst the branches at the top, after the manner
adopted by the natives of New Guinea.

You may imagine my feelings when, early one
morning, Yamba suddenly gripped my arm and mur-
mured, "We are nearing my home at last."   I leaped
to my feet, and a few minutes afterwards the mainland
came hazily into view.   Instead of heading straight
for it, however, we made for a beautiful island that
stood in the mouth of a large bay, and here we landed
to recuperate for a day or so.   Immediately on our
arrival, Yamba and her husband lit some fires, and
made what were apparently smoke-signals to their
friends on the main.   They first cut down a quantity
of green wood with my tomahawk and arranged it in
the form of a pyramid.   Next they obtained fire by

rubbing together two pieces of a certain kind of wood ; and as the smoke ascended we saw answering smoke-signals from the opposite shore. The smoke was allowed to ascend in puffs which were regulated by the manipulation of boughs. Not long after this curious exchange of signals (and the practice is virtually universal throughout the whole of aboriginal Australia), we saw three catamarans, or floats, each carrying a man, shooting across towards our island. These catamarans merely consisted of a broad plank with a stick placed transversely at the prow, on which the black placed his feet. He squatted down on the plank and then paddled forward. I viewed their approach with mixed sensations of alarm and hope. I was in the power of these people, I thought. They could tear me limb from limb, torture me, kill and eat me, if they so pleased ; I was absolutely helpless. These fears, however, were but momentary, and back upon my mind rushed the calm assurances I had obtained from my clear-eyed mentor, Yamba, to say nothing about the mysterious message of hope and consolation that had startled the solemn stillness of that tropical night. I knew these people to be cannibals, for, during the long talks we used to have on the island, Yamba had described to me their horrid feasts after a successful war. Nevertheless, I awaited the arrival of the little flotilla with all the complacency I could muster, but at the same time I was careful to let Yamba's husband be the first to receive them.

And he advanced to meet them. The new-comers, having landed, squatted down some little distance away from the man they had come to meet, and then Gunda and they gradually edged forwards towards one another, until at length each placed his nose upon the other's shoulder. This was apparently the native method of embracing. Later Gunda brought his friends to be introduced to me, and to the best of my ability I went through the same ridiculous ceremony. I must say my new friends evinced an almost uncontrollable terror at the sight of me. Gunda, however, made it clear that I was *not* a returned spirit, but a man like themselves—a great man certainly, and a mysterious man, but a man all the same. Although by this time my skin had become tanned and dark, there was seemingly no end to the amazement it caused the blacks. They timidly touched and felt my body, legs, and arms, and were vastly anxious to know what the covering was I had round my body. In due time, however, the excitement subsided somewhat, and then the new-comers prepared more smoke-signals to their friends on the mainland—this time building five separate fires in the form of a circle.

It was interesting to watch this remarkable method of communication. Each fire was set smoking fiercely a few seconds after its neighbour had started. Finally, the columns of smoke united, and ascended together in the form of a huge pyramid, going up a tremendous height into the still, hot air. The meaning of these signals was explained to me. They indicated to the people on the mainland that the advance guard had found Gunda and his family; that they had a great man with them; and that, furthermore, they might expect us to return all together almost immediately. By this time, thanks to Yamba's able and intelligent lessons, I was able to speak the queer language of the blacks with some show of fluency, and I could understand them well enough when they did not jabber too quickly.

The next phase of our arrival was that "smokes" were ascending in all directions on the mainland, evidently calling the tribes from far and near. How these smoke-signals gave an idea of the white man and his wonders I am utterly at a loss to imagine. In the meantime Yamba had prepared a great feast for the visitors, the principal dish being our remaining big turtle, of which the blacks ate a prodigious quantity. I afterwards told them that I was in need of a prolonged rest, my long journey having wearied me, and after this explanation I retired, and slung my hammock in a shady nook, where I slept undisturbed from shortly before noon until late in the day, when my ever-faithful Yamba, who had been keeping a careful watch, woke me and said that the festivities prior to our departure were about to take place.

Much refreshed, I rejoined the blacks, and, to their unbounded delight and amazement, entertained them for a few minutes with some of my acrobatic tricks and contortions. Some of the more emulous among them tried to imitate my feats of agility, but always came dismally to grief—a performance that created even more frantic merriment than my own. After a little while the blacks disappeared, only to come forth a few minutes later with their bodies gorgeously decorated with stripes of yellow ochre and red and white pigments. These startling preparations preceded a great *corroboree* in honour of my arrival, and in this embarrassing function I was, of course, expected to join. The ceremony was kept up with extraordinary vigour the whole night long, but all I was required to do was to sit beating sticks together, and join in the general uproar. This was all very well for a little while, but the monotony of the affair was terrible, and I withdrew to my hammock before midnight.

In the morning I saw a great fleet of catamarans putting off from the mainland, and in a very short time between fifty and sixty natives joined our party on the island. Then followed the usual greetings and comical expressions of amazement—of course, at the sight of me, my boat, and everything in it. A few hours later the whole crowd left the island, led by me in the big boat—which, by the way, attracted as much interest as I did myself. The natives forced their catamarans through the water at great speed, using only one paddle, which was dipped first on one side and then on the other in rapid succession, without, however, causing the apparently frail craft to swerve in the slightest degree.

As we approached the new country, I beheld a vast surging crowd of excited blacks—men, women, and children, all perfectly naked—standing on the beach. The moment we landed there was a most extraordinary rush for my boat, and everything on board her was there and then subjected to the closest scrutiny.

The people seemed to be divided into clans, and when one clan was busy inspecting my implements and utensils, another was patiently waiting its turn to examine the white man's wonders. I sat in the boat for some time, fairly bewildered and deafened by the uproarious jabberings and shrill, excited cries of amazement and wonder that filled the air all round me. At last, however, the blacks who had come out to meet us on the island came to my rescue, and escorted me through the crowd, with visible pride, to an eminence overlooking the native camping-ground.   I then learnt that the news of my coming had been smoke-signalled in every direction for many miles; hence the enormous gathering of clans on the beach.

The camping-ground I now found myself upon consisted of about thirty primitive shelters, built of

APPROACHING THE NEW COUNTRY

boughs in the most flimsy manner, and only intended to break the force of the wind. These shelters, or "break-winds," were crescent-shaped, had no roof, and were not in any way closed in in front. There were, however, two or three grass huts of beehive shape, about seven feet high and ten feet in diameter, with a queer little hole at the base through which the occupier had to crawl. The inside was perfectly dark.

I was told I could have either a break-wind of boughs or a beehive hut, and on consideration I chose the latter. It would, I reflected, ensure something approaching privacy. My indefatigable Yamba and a few of her women friends set to work then and there, and positively in less than an hour the grass hut was ready for occupation! I did not, however, stay to witness the completion of the building operations, but went off with some self-appointed cicerones to see the different camps; everywhere I was received with the greatest enthusiasm and manifestations of respect and friendship. My simple loin-cloth of crimson Japanese silk occasioned much astonishment among the blacks, but curiously enough the men were far more astonished at my *footprints* than any other attribute I possessed. It seems that when they themselves walk they turn their feet sideways, so that they only make a half impression, so to speak, instead of a full footprint. On the other hand, I of course planted my feet squarely down, and this imprint in the sand was followed by a crowd of blacks, who gravely peered at every footprint, slapping themselves and clicking in amazement at the wonderful thing!

CHAPTER V

I SAW very little of Gunda from the moment of landing. I feel sure that the fact of his having seen so
much of the world, and travelled such a long distance
—to say nothing about bringing back so wonderful
a creature as myself—had rendered him a very great
man indeed in the estimation of his friends; and in
consequence of this so much honour was paid him
that he became puffed up with pride, and neglected
his faithful wife.

Everywhere I went the natives were absolutely overwhelming in their hospitality, and presents of food of
all kinds were fairly showered upon me, including such
delicacies as kangaroo and opossum meat, rats, snakes,
tree-worms, fish, &c., which were always left outside
my hut. Baked snake, I ought to mention, was a very
pleasant dish indeed, but as there was no salt forthcoming, and the flesh was very tasteless, I cannot say
I enjoyed this particular native dainty. The snakes
were invariably baked whole in their skins, and the
meat was very tender and juicy, though a little insipid

as to flavour. The native method of cooking is to scoop out a hole in the sand with the hands, and then place the article to be cooked at the bottom. Some loose stones would then be thrown over the "joint." Next would come a layer of sand, and the fire was built on the top of all. Rats were always plentiful—often so much so as to become a serious nuisance. They were of the large brown variety, and were not at all bad eating. I may say here that the women-folk were responsible for the catching of the rats, the method usually adopted being to poke in their holes with sticks, and then kill them as they rushed out. The women, by the way, were responsible for a good many things. They were their masters' dressers, so to speak, in that they were required to carry supplies of the greasy clay or earth with which the blacks anoint their bodies to ward off the sun's rays and insect bites ; and beside this, woe betide the wives if *corroboree* time found them without an ample supply of coloured pigments for the decoration of their masters' bodies. One of the principal duties of the women-folk, however, was the provision of roots for the family's dinner. The most important among these necessaries—besides fine yams—were the root and bud of a kind of water-lily, which when roasted tasted not unlike a sweet potato.

There was usually a good water supply in the neighbourhood of these camps, and if it failed (as it very frequently did), the whole tribe simply moved its quarters elsewhere—perhaps a hundred miles off.

The instinct of these people for finding water, how-ever, was nothing short of miraculous. No one would think of going down to the seashore to look for fresh water, yet they often showed me the purest and most refreshing of liquids oozing up out of the sand on the beach after the tide had receded.

All this time, and for many months afterwards, my boat and everything it contained were saved from molestation and theft by a curious device on the part of Yamba. She simply placed a couple of crossed sticks on the sand near the bows, this being evidently a kind of Masonic sign to all beholders that they were to respect the property of the stranger among them; and I verily believe that the boat and its contents might have remained there until they fell to pieces before any one of those cannibal blacks would have dreamed of touching anything that belonged to me.

After a time the natives began pointedly to suggest that I should stay with them. They had probably heard from Yamba about the strange things I possessed, and the occult powers I was supposed to be gifted with. A day or two after my landing, a curious thing happened—nothing more or less than the celebration of my marriage! I was standing near my boat, still full of thoughts of escape, when two magnificent naked chiefs, decked with gaudy pigments and feather head-dresses, advanced towards me, leading between them a young, dusky maiden of comparatively pleasing appearance.

The three were followed by an immense crowd of natives, and were within a few feet of me, when they halted suddenly. One of the chiefs then stepped out and offered me a murderous-looking club, with a big knob at one end, which ugly weapon was known as a "waddy." As he presented this club the chief made signs that I was to knock the maiden on the head with it. Now, on this I confess I was struck

with horror and dismay at my position, for, instantly
recalling what Yamba had told me, I concluded *that a
cannibal feast was about to be given in my honour,* and
that—worst horror of all—I might have to lead off
with the first mouthful of that smiling girl.   Of course,
I reflected they had brought the helpless victim to me,
the distinguished stranger, to kill with my own hands.
At that critical moment, however, I resolved to be
absolutely firm, even if it cost me my life.

While I hesitated, the chief remained absolutely
motionless, holding out the murderous-looking club,
and looking at me interrogatively, as though unable to
understand why I did not avail myself of his offer.
Still more extraordinary, the crowd behind observed a
solemn and disconcerting silence.   I looked at the girl;
to my amazement she appeared delighted with things
generally—a poor, merry little creature, not more than
fifteen or sixteen years of age.   I decided to harangue
the chiefs, and as a preliminary I gave them the universal
sign to sit down and parley.   They did so, but did
not seem pleased at what they doubtless considered
an unlooked-for hitch in an interesting ceremony.

Then in hesitating signs, slaps, clicks, and guttural
utterances, I gave them to understand that it was
against my faith to have anything whatever to do
with the horrid orgy they contemplated.   The Great
Spirit they dreaded so much yet so vaguely, I went
on to say, had revealed to me that it was wrong to kill
any one in cold blood, and still more loathsome and
horrible to eat the flesh of a murdered fellow-creature.
I was very much in earnest, and I waited with nervous
trepidation to see the effect of my peroration.   Under
the circumstances, you may judge of my astonishment

when not only the chiefs, but the whole "nation" assembled, suddenly burst into roars of eerie laughter.

Then came Yamba to the rescue. Ah! noble and
devoted creature! The bare mention of her name
stirs every fibre of my being with love and wonder.
Greater love than hers no creature ever knew, and not
once but a thousand times did she save my wretched
life at the risk of her own.

Well, Yamba, I say, came up and whispered to me.
She had been studying my face quietly and eagerly,
and had gradually come to see what was passing in
my mind. She whispered that the chiefs, far from
desiring me to kill the girl for a cannibal feast, were
offering her to me as a wife, and that I was merely
expected to tap her on the head with the stick, in
token of her subjection to her new spouse! In short,
this blow on the head was the legal marriage ceremony
tout simple. I maintained my dignity as far as possible,
and proceeded to carry out my part of the curious
ceremony.

I tapped the bright-eyed girl on the head, and she
immediately fell prostrate at my feet, in token of her
wifely submission. I then raised her up gently, and
all the people came dancing round us, uttering weird
cries of satisfaction and delight. Oddly enough,
Yamba, far from manifesting any jealousy, seemed to
take as much interest as any one in the proceedings,
and after everything was over she led my new wife
away to the little "humpy," or hut, that had been
built for me by the women. That night an indescrib-
ably weird *corroboree* was held in my honour, and I
thought it advisable, since so much was being made
of me, to remain there all night and acknowledge the

impromptu songs that were composed and sung in my honour by the native bards. I am afraid I felt utterly lost without Yamba, who was, in the most literal sense, my right hand.

By this time she could speak a little English, and was so marvellously intelligent that she seemed to discover things by sheer intuition or instinct. I think she never let a day go by without favourably impressing the chiefs concerning me, my prowess and my powers; and without her help I simply could not have lived through the long and weary years, nor should I ever have returned to civilisation.

The very next day after my "marriage," having been still further enlightened as to the manners and customs of the natives, I waited upon Gunda, and calmly made to him the proposition that we should exchange wives. This suggestion he received with a kind of subdued satisfaction, or holy joy, and very few further negotiations were needed to make the transaction complete; and, be it said, it was an every-day transaction, perfectly legal and recognised by all the clans. Yamba was full of vigour and resource, while the only phrase that fitly describes her bush lore is absolutely miraculous. This will be evinced in a hundred extraordinary instances in this narrative.

But you may be asking, What of my dog, Bruno? Well, I am thankful to say, he was still with me, but it took him a long time to accustom himself to his new surroundings; he particularly objected to associating with the miserable pariah curs that prowled about the encampment. They would take sly bites out of him when he was not looking, but on the whole, he was

G

well able to hold his own, being much more powerful than they.

I settled down to my new life in the course of a few days, but I need hardly remark I did not propose staying in that forlorn spot longer than I could help. This was my plan. I would, first of all, make myself acquainted with the habits and customs of the blacks, and pick up as much bushmanship and knowledge of the country as it was possible to acquire, in case I should have to travel inland in search of civilisation instead of oversea. I knew that it would be folly on my part to attempt to leave those hospitable regions without knowing more of the geography of the country and its people. There was always, however, the hope that some day I might be able either to get away by sea in my boat, or else hail some passing vessel. The blacks told me they had seen many pass at a distance.

Every morning I was astir by sunrise, and—hope springing eternal—at once searched for the faintest indication of a passing sail. Next I would bathe in a lagoon protected from sharks, drying myself by a run on the beach. Meanwhile Yamba would have gone out searching for roots for breakfast, and she seldom returned without a supply of my favourite water-lily buds already mentioned. Often, in the years that followed, did that heroic creature *tramp on foot a hundred miles* to get me a few sprigs of saline herbs. She had heard me say I wanted salt, which commodity, strange to say, was never used by the natives; and even when I gave them some as an experiment they did not seem to care about it. She would also bring in, by way of seasoning, a kind of small onion, known

as the *nelga*, which, when roasted, made a very ac-
ceptable addition to our limited fare. The natives
themselves had but two meals a day — breakfast,
between eight and nine o'clock, and then an enormous
feast in the late afternoon. Their ordinary food consisted of kangaroo, emu, snakes, rats, and fish; an
especial dainty being a worm found in the black ava
tree, or in any decaying trunk.

These worms were generally grilled on hot stones,
and eaten several at a time like small whitebait. I
often ate them myself, and found them most palatable.
After breakfast the women of the tribe would go out
hunting roots and snaring small game for the afternoon meal, while the men went off on their war and
hunting expeditions, or amused themselves with feats
of arms. The children were generally left to their
own devices in the camp, and the principal amusement
of the boys appeared to be the hurling of reed spears
at one another. The women brought home the roots
(which they dug up with yam sticks, generally about
four feet long) in nets made out of the stringy parts of
the grass tree; stringy bark, or strong pliable reeds,
slung on their all-enduring backs. They generally
returned heavily laden between two and three in the
afternoon. I always knew the time pretty accurately
by the sun, but I lost count of the days. The months,
however, I always reckoned by the moon, and for each
year I made a notch on the inside of my bow.

My own food was usually wrapped in palm leaves
before being placed in the sand oven. Of course the
leaves always burned, but they kept the meat free
from sand; and my indefatigable wife was always
exercising her ingenuity to provide me with fresh

dainties. In addition to the ordinary fare of the natives, I frequently had wild ducks and turkeys, and —what was perhaps the greatest luxury of all—eggs, which the natives sent for specially on my account to distant parts of the surrounding country, and also to the islands of the coast where white cockatoos reared their young in rocky cliffs.

At the time of my shipwreck I had little or no knowledge of Australian geography, so that I was utterly at a loss as to my position. I afterwards learnt, however, that Yamba's home was on Cambridge Gulf, on the NNW. coast of the Australian continent, and that the central point of our camping ground at this time was near the mouth of the Victoria River, which flows into Queen's Channel.

Almost every evening the blacks would hold a stately *corroboree*, singing and chanting; the burden of their song being almost invariably myself, my belongings, and my prowess—which latter, I fear, was magnified in the most extravagant manner. Besides the *corroboree* they also would assemble for what might not inaptly be termed evening prayers, which consisted of a poetical recital of the events of the day. I ought to mention that at first I did not accompany the men on their excursions abroad, because I was far from perfect in their language; and furthermore, I was not skilled in hunting or in bush lore. Therefore, fearful of exciting ridicule, I decided to remain behind in the camp until I was thoroughly grounded in everything there was to be learned. Supposing, for example, I had gone out with the blacks, and had to confess myself tired after tramping several miles. Well, this kind of thing would certainly have engendered contempt; and once the mysterious white stranger was found to be full of the frailties of the ordinary man, his prestige would be gone, and then life would probably become intolerable.

Thus everything I did I had to excel in, and it was absolutely necessary that I should be perpetually "astonishing the natives," in the most literal sense of the phrase. Accordingly, for the next few weeks, I used to accompany the women on their root-hunting and rat-catching expeditions, and from them I picked up much valuable information.

The *corroboree* was, perhaps, the greatest institution known to the blacks, who, obliged to do no real work, as we understand it, simply had to pass the time somehow; and there can be no doubt that, were it not for the constant feuds and consequent incessant wars, the race would greatly deteriorate. The *corroboree* after a successful battle commenced with a cannibal feast off the bodies of fallen foes, and it would be kept up for several days on end, the braves lying down to sleep near the fire towards morning, and renewing the festivities about noon next day. The chiefs on these occasions decked themselves with gorgeous cockatoo feathers, and painted their bodies with red and yellow ochre and other glaring pigments, each tribe having its own distinguishing marks. A couple of hours were generally spent in dressing and preparing for the ceremony, and then the gaily-decorated fighting-men would dance or squat round the fires and chant monotonous songs, telling of all their own achievements and valour, and the extraordinary sights they had seen in their travels.

The words of the songs were usually composed by

the clan's own poet, who made a living solely by his
profession, and even sold his effusions to other tribes.
As there was no written language the purchaser would
simply be coached orally by the vendor poet; and as
the blacks were gifted with most marvellous memories,
they would transmit and resell the songs throughout

THE FEAST

vast stretches of country. These men of the north-west
were of magnificent stature, and possessed great personal strength. They were able to walk extraordinary
distances, and their carriage was the most graceful I
have ever seen. Many of them were over six feet
high, well made in proportion and with high broad
foreheads—altogether a very different race from the

inhabitants of Central Australia. One of their favourite tests of strength was to take a short stick of very hard wood and bend it in their hands, using the thumbs as levers, till it snapped. Strange to say, I failed to bend the stick more than a quarter of an inch. The women are not very prepossessing, and not nearly so graceful in their bearing and gait as the men. Poor creatures! they did all the hard work of the camp— building, food-hunting, waiting, and serving. Occasionally, however, the men did condescend to go out fishing, and they would also organise *battues* when a big supply of food was wanted. These great hunting-parties, by the way, were arranged on an immense scale, and fire figured largely in them. The usual routine was to set fire to the bush, and then as the terrified animals and reptiles rushed out in thousands into the open, each party of blacks speared every living thing that came its way within a certain sphere. The roar of the fast-spreading fire, the thousands of kangaroos, opossums, rats, snakes, iguanas, and birds that dashed hither and thither, to the accompaniment of bewildering shouts from the men and shrill screeches from the women, who occasionally assisted, flitting hither and thither like eerie witches amidst the dense pall of black smoke—all these made up a picture which is indelibly imprinted on my mind.

As a rule, hosts of hawks and eagles are to be seen flying over the black man's camp, but on the occasion of a bush fire they follow its train, well knowing that they will obtain prey in abundance. With regard to the fishing parties, these went out either early in the morning, soon after sunrise, or in the evening, when it was quite dark. On the latter occasions, the men carried big torches, which they held high in the air with one hand, while they waded out into the water with their spears poised, in readiness to impale the first big fish they came across.

When the spearmen *did* strike, their aim was unerring, and the struggling fish would be hurled on to the beach to the patient women-folk, who were there waiting for them, with their big nets of grass slung over their backs. Sometimes a hundred men would be in the shallow water at once, all carrying blazing torches, and the effect as the fishermen plunged and splashed this way and that, with shouts of triumph or disappointment, may be better imagined than described. In the daytime a rather different method was adopted. Some acres of the shallow lagoon would be staked out at low water in the shape of an inverted V, an opening being left for the fish to pass through.

The high tide brought the fish in vast shoals, and then the opening would be closed. When the tide receded, the staked enclosure became, in effect, a gigantic net, filled with floundering fish, big and little. The natives then waded into the inclosure, and leisurely despatched the fish with their spears.

Nothing was more interesting than to watch one of these children of the bush stalking a kangaroo. The man made not the slightest noise in walking, and he would stealthily follow the kangaroo's track for miles (the tracks were absolutely invisible to the uninitiated). Should at length the kangaroo sniff a tainted wind, or be startled by an incautious movement, his pursuer would suddenly become as rigid as a bronze figure, and he could remain in this position for hours. Finally, when within thirty or forty yards of the animal, he launched his spear, and in all the years I was among these people I never knew a man to miss his aim. Two distinct kinds of spears were used by the natives, one for hunting and the other for war purposes. The former averaged from eight to ten feet, whilst the latter varied from ten to fourteen feet in length ; the blade in each case, however, consisting either of bone or stone, with a shaft of some light hard wood. Metals were, of course, perfectly unknown as workable materials. The war-spear was not hurled javelin-fashion like the hunting-spear, but propelled by means of a wommerah, which, in reality, was a kind of sling, perhaps twenty-four inches long, with a hook at one end to fix on the shaft of the spear. In camp the men mainly occupied their time in making spears and mending their weapons. They hacked a tree down and split it into long sections by means of wedges, in order to get suitable wood for their spear-shafts.

To catch emus the hunters would construct little shelters of grass at a spot overlooking the water-hole frequented by these birds, and they were then speared as they came down for water. The largest emu I ever saw, by the way, was more than six feet high, whilst the biggest kangaroo I came across was even taller than this. Snakes were always killed with sticks, whilst birds were brought down with the wonderful boomerang.

As a rule, only sufficient food was obtained to last from day to day ; but on the occasion of one of the big *battues* I have described there would be food in abundance for a week or more, when there would be a horrid orgy of gorging and one long continuous *corroboree*, until supplies gave out.

The sport which I myself took up was dugong hunting; for I ought to have mentioned that I brought a harpoon with me in the boat, and this most useful article attracted as much attention as anything I had. The natives would occasionally put their hands on my tomahawk or harpoon, and never ceased to wonder why the metal was so cold.

Whenever I went out after dugong, accompanied by Yamba (she was ever with me), the blacks invariably came down in crowds to watch the operation from the beach.

But, you will ask, what did I want with dugong, when I had so much other food at hand? Well, my idea was to lay in a great store of dried provisions against the time when I should be ready to start for civilisation in my boat. I built a special shed of boughs, in which I conducted my curing operations; my own living-place being only a few yards away. It was built quite in European fashion, with a sloping roof. The interior was perhaps twenty feet square and ten feet high, with a small porch in which my fire was kept constantly burning. When we had captured a dugong the blacks would come rushing into the sea to meet us and drag our craft ashore, delighted at the prospect of a great feast. The only part of the dugong I preserved was the belly, which I cut up into strips and dried.

The blacks never allowed their fires to go out, and whenever they moved their camping-ground, the women-folk always took with them their smouldering fire-sticks, with which they can kindle a blaze in a few minutes. Very rarely, indeed, did the women allow their fire-sticks to go out altogether, for this would entail a cruel and severe punishment. A fire-stick would keep alight in a smouldering state for days. All that the women did when they wanted to make it glow was to whirl it round in the air. The wives bore ill-usage with the most extraordinary equanimity, and never attempted to parry even the most savage blow. They would remain meek and motionless under a shower of brutal blows from a thick stick, and would then walk quietly away and treat their bleeding wounds with a kind of earth. No matter how cruelly the women might be treated by their husbands, they hated sympathy, so their women friends always left them alone. It often surprised me how quickly the blacks' most terrible wounds healed; and yet they were only treated with a kind of clay and leaves of the wild rose.

I am here reminded of the native doctor. This functionary was called a *rui*, and he effected most of his cures with a little shell, with which he rubbed assiduously upon the affected part. Thus it will be seen that the medical treatment was a form of massage, the rubbing being done first in a downward direction and then crosswise. I must say, however, that the blacks were very rarely troubled with illness, their most frequent disorder being usually the result of excessive gorging when a particularly ample supply of food was forthcoming—say, after a big *battue* over a tribal preserve.

In an ordinary case of overfeeding, the medicine man would rub his patient's stomach with such vigour as often to draw blood. He would also give the sufferer a kind of grass to eat, and this herb, besides clearing the system, also acted as a most marvellous appetiser. The capacity of some of my blacks was almost beyond belief. One giant I have in my mind ate a whole kangaroo by himself. I saw him do it. Certainly it was not an excessively big animal, but, still, it was a meal large enough for three or four stalwart men.

In a case of fever the natives resorted to charms to drive away the evil spirit that was supposed to be troubling the patient. The universal superstition about all maladies is that they are caused by the " evil eye," directed against the sufferer by some enemy. Should one member of a tribe be stricken down with a disease, his friends at once come to the conclusion that he has been " pointed at " by a member of another tribe who owed him a grudge; he has, in short, been bewitched, and an expedition is promptly organised to seek out and punish the individual in question and all his tribe. From this it is obvious that war is of pretty frequent occurrence. And not only so, but every death is likewise the signal for a tribal war. There is no verdict of " Death from natural causes." Punitive expeditions are not organised in the event of slight fevers or even serious illness—only when the patient dies. A tribe I once came across some miles inland were visited by a plague of what I now feel sure must have been smallpox. The disease, they said, had been brought down from the coast, and although numbers of the blacks died, war was not declared against any particular tribe. As a rule, the body of the dead brave is placed upon a platform erected in the forks of trees, and his weapons neatly arranged below. Then, as decay set in, and the body began to crumble away, the friends and chiefs would come and

THE ENGAGEMENT BECAME GENERAL.

observe certain mystic signs, which were supposed to give information as to what tribe or individual had caused the death of the deceased.

It must have been within a month of my landing on Yamba's country, in Cambridge Gulf, that I witnessed my first cannibal feast. One of the fighting-men had died in our camp, and after the usual observations had been taken, it was decided that he had been pointed at, and his death brought about, by a member of another tribe living some distance away. An expedition of some hundreds of warriors was at once fitted out. The enemy was apparently only too ready for the fray, because the armies promptly met in an open plain, and I had an opportunity of witnessing the extraordinary method by which the Australian blacks wage war. One of the most redoubtable of our chiefs stepped forward, and explained the reason of his people's visit in comparatively calm tones. An opposing chief replied to him, and gradually a heated altercation arose, the abuse rising on a crescendo scale for ten or fifteen minutes. These two then retired, and another couple of champion abusers stepped forward to "discuss" the matter. This kind of thing went on for a considerable time, the abuse being of the most appalling description, and directed mainly against the organs of the enemy's body (heart, liver, &c.), his ancestors, "his ox, his ass, and everything that was his." At length, when every conceivable thing had been said that it was possible to say, the warriors drew near, and at last some one threw a spear. This, of course, was the signal for real action, and in a few minutes the engagement became general. There was no strategy or tactics of any kind, every man fighting single-handed.

But to return to the battle I was describing. After a very few minutes' fighting the enemy were utterly routed, and promptly turned tail and fled from the scene of the encounter, leaving behind them—after all the uproar and the flood of vilification—only three of their warriors, and these not dead, but only more or less badly wounded. Quarter being neither given nor expected in these battles, the three prostrate blacks were promptly despatched by the leader of my tribe, the *coup de grâce* being given with a waddy, or knobbed stick. The three bodies were then placed on litters made out of spears and grass, and in due time carried into our own camp.

There were so many unmistakable signs to presage what was coming that I *knew* a cannibal feast was about to take place. But for obvious reasons I did not protest against it, nor did I take any notice whatever. The women (who do all the real work) fell on their knees, and with their fingers scraped three long trenches in the sand, each about seven feet long and three deep. Into each of these ovens was placed one of the bodies of the fallen warriors, and then the trench was filled up —firstly with stones, and then with sand. On top of all a huge fire was built, and maintained with great fierceness for about two hours. There was great rejoicing during this period of cooking, and apparently much pleasurable anticipation among the triumphant blacks. In due time the signal was given, and the ovens laid open once more. I looked in and saw that the bodies were very much burnt. The skin was cracked in places and liquid fat was issuing forth. . . . But, perhaps, the less said about this horrible spectacle the better. With a yell, several warriors leaped into each trench and stuck spears through the big "joints." And the moment the roasted carcasses were taken out of the trenches the whole tribe literally fell upon them and tore them limb from limb. I saw mothers with a leg or an arm surrounded by plaintive children, who were crying for their portion of the fearsome dainty.

Others, who were considered to have taken more than their share, were likewise fallen upon and their "joint" subdivided and hacked to pieces with knives made from shells. The bodies were not cooked all through, so that the condition of some of the revellers, both during and after the orgy, may best be left to the imagination. A more appalling, more ghastly, or more truly sickening spectacle it is impossible for the mind of man to conceive. A great *corroboree* was held after the feast, but, with my gorge rising and my brain reeling, I crept to my own humpy and tried to shut out from my mind the shocking inferno I had just been compelled to witness.

But let us leave so fearful a subject and consider something more interesting and amusing.

H

CHAPTER VI

THE women of the tribe lived amicably enough together as a rule, but of course they had their differences. They would quarrel about the merits and demerits of their own families and countries; but the greatest source of heartburning and trouble was the importation of a new wife — especially if she chanced to be better looking than the others. In such cases, woe to the comparatively pretty wife. The women certainly had a novel way of settling their differences. The two combatants would retire to some little distance, armed with *one stick between them*. They would then stand face to face, and one would bend forward meekly, whilst the other dealt her a truly terrific blow between the shoulders or on the head— not with a cane or a light stick, be it remembered, but a really formidable club. The blow (which would be enough to kill an ordinary white woman) would be borne with wonderful fortitude, and then the aggressor would hand the club to the woman she had just struck. The latter would then take a turn; and so it would go on, turn and turn about, until one of the unfortunate, stoical creatures fell bleeding and half-senseless to the earth. The thing was magnificently simple. The woman who kept her senses longest, and remained on her legs to the end,

SETTLING A QUARREL

was the victor. There was no kind of ill-feeling after these extraordinary combats, and the women would even dress one another's wounds.

I now come to an event of very great importance
in my life. Elsewhere I have spoken of my *penchant*
for dugong hunting. Well, one day this sport effec-
tually put an end to all my prospects of reaching
civilisation across the sea. I went forth one morning,
accompanied by my ever-faithful Yamba and the
usual admiring crowd of blacks. In a few minutes
we two were speeding over the sunlit waters, my
only weapon being the steel harpoon I had brought
with me from the island, and about forty or fifty
feet of manilla rope. When we were some miles from
land I noticed a dark-looking object on the surface
of the water a little way ahead. Feeling certain it
was a dugong feeding on the well-known "grass," I
rose and hurled my harpoon at it with all the force
I could muster. Next moment, to my amazement,
the head of a calf whale was thrust agonisingly into
the air, and not until then did I realise what manner
of creature it was I had struck. This baby whale was
about fifteen feet long, and it "sounded" immediately
on receiving my harpoon. As I had enough rope, or
what I considered enough, I did not cut him adrift.
He came up again presently, lashing the water with
his tail, and creating a tremendous uproar, considering his size. He then darted off madly, dashing
through the water like an arrow, and dragging our
boat at such a tremendous pace as almost to swamp
us in the foaming wash, the bow wave forming a
kind of wall on each side.

Up to this time I had no thought of danger, but
just as the baby whale halted I looked round, and
saw to my horror that its colossal mother had joined
her offspring, and was swimming round and round

it like lightning, apparently greatly disturbed by its sufferings. Before I could even cut the line or attempt
to get out of the way, the enormous creature caught
sight of our little craft, and bore down upon us like
a fair-sized island rushing through the sea with the
speed of an express train. I shouted to Yamba,
and we both threw ourselves over the side into the
now raging waters, and commenced to swim away
with long strokes, in order to get as far as possible
from the boat before the catastrophe came which we
knew was at hand. We had not got many yards
before I heard a terrific crash, and, looking back, I
saw the enormous tail of the great whale towering
high out of the water, and my precious boat descending in fragments upon it from a height of from fifteen
feet to twenty feet above the agitated waters. Oddly
enough, the fore-part of the boat remained fixed to
the rope of the harpoon in the calf. My first
thought, even at so terrible a moment, and in so
serious a situation, was one of bitter regret for the
loss of what I considered the only means of reaching civilisation. Like a flash it came back to me
how many weary months of toil and hope and ex-
pectancy I had spent over that darling craft; and
I remembered, too, the delirious joy of launching it,
and the appalling dismay that struck me when I
realised that it was worse than useless to me in
the inclosed lagoon. These thoughts passed through
my mind in a few seconds.

At this time we had a swim of some *ten miles* before
us, but fortunately our predicament was observed from
the land, and a crowd of blacks put out in their
catamarans to help us. Some of the blacks, as I hinted

before, always accompanied me down to the shore on
these trips. They never tired, I think, of seeing me
handle my giant "catamaran" and the (to them)
mysterious harpoon.

After the mother whale had wreaked its vengeance
upon my unfortunate boat it rejoined its little one,
and still continued to swim round and round it at
prodigious speed, evidently in a perfect agony of con-
cern. Fortunately the tide was in our favour, and we
were rapidly swept inshore, even when we floated
listlessly on the surface of the water. The sea was
quite calm, and we had no fear of sharks, being well
aware that we would keep them away by splashing in
the water.

Before long, the catamarans came up with us, but
although deeply grateful for Yamba's and my own
safety, I was still greatly distressed at the loss of
my boat. Never once did this thought leave my
mind. I remembered, too, with a pang, that I had
now no tools with which to build another; and to
venture out into the open sea on a catamaran, probably
for weeks, simply meant courting certain destruction.
I was a greater prisoner than ever.

My harpoon had evidently inflicted a mortal wound
on the calf whale, because as we looked we saw it
lying exhausted on the surface of the water, and
being gradually swept nearer and nearer the shore
by the swift-flowing tide. The mother refused to
leave her little one however, and still continued to
wheel round it continuously, even when it had reached
dangerously shallow water.

The result was that when the tide turned, both the
mother and her calf were left stranded high and dry

on the beach, to the unbounded delight and amazement of the natives, who swarmed round the leviathans,
and set up such a terrific uproar, that I verily believe
they frightened the mother to death.   In her dying
struggle she lashed the water into a perfect fury with
her tail, and even made attempts to lift herself bodily
up.   Furious smoke-signals were at once sent up to
summon all the tribes in the surrounding country—
enemies as well as friends.   Next day the carcasses
were washed farther still inshore—a thing for which
the blacks gave me additional credit.

I ought to mention here that the loss of my boat
was in some measure compensated for by the enormous
amount of prestige which accrued to me through this
whale episode.   To cut a long story short, the natives
fully believed that *I had killed single-handed and
brought ashore both whales!*   And in the *corroborees*
that ensued, the poets almost went delirious in trying
to find suitable eulogiums to bestow upon the mighty
white hunter.   The mother whale surpassed in size
any I had ever seen or read about.   I measured her
length by pacing, and I judged it to be nearly 150 feet.
My measurements may not have been absolutely accurate, but still the whale was, I imagine, of record
size.   As she lay there on the beach her head towered
above me to a height of nearly fifteen feet.   Never
can I forget the scene that followed, when the blacks
from the surrounding country responded to the smoke-
signals announcing the capture of the "great fish."
From hundreds of miles south came the natives,
literally in their thousands—every man provided with
his stone tomahawk and a whole armoury of shell
knives.   They simply swarmed over the carcasses

like vermin, and I saw many of them staggering away under solid lumps of flesh weighing between thirty and forty pounds.   The children also took part in the general feasting, and they too swarmed about the whales like a plague of ants.

A particularly enterprising party of blacks cut an enormous hole in the head of the big whale, and in the bath of oil that was inside they simply wallowed for hours at a time, only to emerge in a condition that filled me with disgust.   There was no question of priority or disputing as to whom the tit-bits of the whale should go.   Even the visitors were quite at liberty to take whatever portion they could secure. For about a fortnight this cutting-up and gorging went on, but long before this the stench from the decompos-ing carcasses was so horrible as to be painfully notice-able at my camp, over a mile away.   Some of the flesh was cooked, but most of it was eaten absolutely raw. The spectacle witnessed on the beach would have been intensely comical were it not so revolting.   Many of the savages, both men and women, had gorged themselves to such an extent as to be absolutely un-able to walk ; and they rolled about on the sand, tearing at the ground in agony, their stomachs distended in the most extraordinary and disgusting manner.   It may amuse you to know that smoke-signals were at once sent up for all the "doctors" in the country, and these ministering angels could presently be seen with their massage shells, rubbing the distended stomachs of the sufferers as they lay on the beach.   I saw some men fairly howling with agony, but yet still devouring enormous quantities of oil and blubber !   Besides the massage treatment (with the thumbs as well as shells), the "doctors" administered a kind of pill, or pellet, of some green leaf, which they first chewed in their own mouth and then placed in that of the patient. So magical was this potent herb in its action, that I feel sure it would make the fortune of an enterprising syndicate. Other patients, who had obtained temporary relief through the kind offices of the medicine-men, returned to the whales again, and had another enormous gorge. In fact, the blacks behaved more like wild beasts of the lowest order than men, and in a very short time—considering the enormous bulk of the whales—nothing remained except the immense bones.

On the other hand, the orgie had its uses from my point of view, because I took advantage of the arrival of so many strange tribes to make myself acquainted with their chiefs, their languages, and their manners and customs, in the hope that these people might be useful to me some day when I commenced my journey overland to civilisation. For, of course, all hope of escape by sea had now to be abandoned, since my boat was destroyed. Several days elapsed, however, before I was able to remain in their presence without a feeling of utter disgust. To be precise, I could not talk to them before they ate, because they were so anxious to get at the food; and after the feast they were too gorged with fat to be able to talk rationally. In all my wanderings amongst the blacks I never came across anything that interested them so much as a whale.

Soon after the loss of the boat, Yamba made me a small bark canoe about fifteen feet long, but not more than fourteen inches wide, and in this we undertook various little excursions together to the various islands that studded the bay. The construction of this little canoe was very interesting. Yamba, first of all, heated the bark, and then turned the rough part underneath in order that the interior might be perfectly smooth. She then *sewed* up the ends, finally giving the little craft a coat of resin, obtained by making incisions in the gum-trees. Of course, I missed my own substantial boat, and it was some little time before I grew accustomed to the frail canoe, which necessitated the greatest possible care in handling, and also on the part of the passengers generally.

One day I decided to go and explore one of the islands that studded Cambridge Gulf, in search of a kind of shell mud-fish which I was very partial to. I also wanted to make the acquaintance of the bats or flying foxes I had seen rising in clouds every evening at sunset. I required the skins of these curious creatures for sandals. This would perhaps be a year after my advent amongst the blacks. As usual, Yamba was my only companion, and we soon reached a likely island. As I could find no suitable place for landing, I turned the canoe up a small creek. From this course, however, my companion strongly dissuaded me. Into the creek, nevertheless, we went, and when I saw it was a hopeless *impasse*, I scrambled ashore and waded through five inches or six inches of mud. The little island was densely covered with luxuriant tropical vegetation, the mangroves coming right down to the water's edge; so that I had actually to force my way through them to gain the top of the bank. I then entered a very narrow track through the forest, the bush on both sides being so dense as to

resemble an impenetrable wall or dense hedge. It is
necessary to bear this in mind to realise what followed.
I had not gone many yards along this track, when I
was horrified to see, right in front of me, an enormous
alligator! This great reptile was shuffling along down
the path towards me, evidently making for the water,
and it not only blocked my advance, but also necessitated my immediate retreat. The moment the brute
caught sight of me he stopped, and began snapping his
jaws viciously. I confess I was quite nonplussed for the
moment as to how best to commence the attack upon
this unexpected visitor. It was impossible for me to
get round him in any way, on account of the dense
bush on either side of the narrow forest track. I
decided, however, to make a bold dash for victory,
having always in mind the prestige that was so necessary to my existence among the blacks. I therefore
walked straight up to the evil-looking monster ; then,
taking a short run, I leaped high into the air, shot over
his head, and landed on his scaly back, at the same
time giving a tremendous yell in order to attract
Yamba, whom I had left in charge of the boat.

The moment I landed on his back I struck the alligator with all my force with my tomahawk, on what
I considered the most vulnerable part of his head. So
powerful was my stroke, that I found to my dismay
that I could not get the weapon out of his head again.
While I was in this extraordinary situation—standing
on the back of an enormous alligator, and tugging at
my tomahawk, embedded in its head—Yamba came
rushing up the path, carrying one of the paddles,
which, without a moment's hesitation, she thrust down
the alligator's throat as he turned to snap at her. She

immediately let go her hold and retreated. The alligator tried to follow her, but the shaft of the paddle caught among some tree trunks and stuck.   In this way the monster was prevented from moving his head, either backwards or forwards, and then, drawing my stiletto, I blinded him in both eyes, afterwards finishing him leisurely with my tomahawk, when at length I managed to release it.   Yamba was immensely proud of me after this achievement, and when we returned to the mainland she gave her tribesmen a graphic account of my gallantry and bravery.   But she always did this.   She was my advance agent and bill-poster, so to say.   I found in going into a new country that my fame had preceded me; and I must say this was most convenient and useful in obtaining hospitality, concessions, and assistance generally.   The part I had played in connection with the death of the two whales had already earned for me the admiration of the blacks —not only in my own tribe, but all over the adjacent country.   And after this encounter with the alligator, they looked upon me as a very great and powerful personage indeed.   We did not bring the dead monster back with us, but next day a number of the blacks went over with their catamarans, and towed the reptile back to the mainland, where it was viewed with open-mouthed amazement by crowds of admiring natives. So great was the estimation in which my prowess was held, that little scraps of the dead alligator were distributed (as relics, presumably) among the tribes throughout the whole of the surrounding country. Singularly enough this last achievement of mine was considered much more commendable than the killing of the whale, for the simple reason that it sometimes

happened they caught a whale themselves stranded
on the beach; whereas the killing of an alligator with
their primitive weapons was a feat never attempted.
They chanted praises in my honour at night, and
wherever I moved, my performances with the whales
and alligator were always the first things to be sung.
Nor did I attempt to depreciate my achievements; on
the contrary, I exaggerated the facts as much as I possibly could. I described to them how I had fought and
killed the whale with my stiletto in spite of the fact
that the monster had smashed my boat. I told them
that I was not afraid of facing anything single-handed,
and I even went so far as to allege that I was good
enough to go out against a nation! My whole object
was to impress these people with my imaginary greatness, and I constantly made them marvel at my prowess
with the bow and arrow. The fact of my being able
to bring down a bird on the wing was nothing more
nor less than a miracle to them. I was given the
name of "Winnimah" by these people, because my
arrows sped like lightning. Six of the alligator's teeth
I took for myself, and made them into a circlet which
I wore round my head.

Some little time after this incident I decided to
remove my dwelling-place to the top of a headland
on the other side of the bay, some twenty miles away,
where I thought I could more readily discern any sail
passing by out at sea. The blacks themselves, who
were well aware of my hopes of getting back to my
own people, had themselves suggested that I might
find this a more likely place for the purpose than the
low-lying coast on which their tribe was then encamped. They also pointed out to me, however, that

I should find it cold living in so exposed a position. But the hope of seeing passing sails decided me, and one morning I took my departure, the whole nation of blacks coming out in full force to bid us adieu. I think the last thing they impressed upon me, in their peculiar native way, was that they would always be delighted and honoured to welcome me back among them. Yamba, of course, accompanied me, as also did my dog, and we were escorted across the bay by a host of my native friends in their catamarans. I pitched upon a fine bold spot for our dwelling-place, but the blacks assured me that we would find it uncomfortably cold and windy, to say nothing about the loneliness, which I could not but feel after so much intercourse with the friendly natives. I persisted, however, and we at length pitched our encampment on the bleak headland, which I now know to be Cape Londonderry, the highest northern point of Western Australia. Occasionally some of our black friends would pay us a visit, but we could never induce them to locate their village near us.

Day after day, day after day, I gazed wistfully over the sea for hours at a time, without ever seeing a sail, and at last I began to grow somewhat despondent, and sighed for the companionship of my black friends once more. Yamba was unremitting in her endeavours to make life pleasant for me and keep me well supplied with the best of food; but I could see that she, too, did not like living on this exposed and desolate spot. So, after a few weeks' experience of life there, I decided to return to my bay home, and later on make preparations for a journey overland to a point on the Australian coast, where I learned ships quite frequently passed. The point in question was Somerset Point, at the extreme north of the Cape York peninsula; and I had learnt of its existence from Jensen when we were pearl-fishing. The blacks were delighted to see me on my return, and I remained with them several months before attempting my next journey. They were keenly anxious that I should join them in their fighting expeditions, but I always declined, on the ground that I was not a fighting man. The fact of the matter was, that I could never hope to throw a spear with anything like the dexterity they themselves possessed; and as spears were the principal weapons used in warfare, I was afraid I would not show up well at a critical moment. Moreover, the warriors defended themselves so dexterously with shields as to be all but invulnerable, whereas I had not the slightest idea of how to handle a shield. And for the sake of my ever-indispensable prestige, I could not afford to make myself ridiculous in their eyes. I always took good care to let the blacks see me performing only those feats which I felt morally certain I could accomplish, and accomplish to their amazement.

So far I had won laurels enough with my mysterious arrows or "flying spears," as the natives considered them, and my prowess with the harpoon and tomahawk was sung in many tribes. And not the least awkward thing about my position was that I dared not even attempt a little quiet practice in spear-throwing, for fear the blacks should come upon me suddenly, when I would most certainly lose caste. I had several narrow escapes from this serious calamity, but most of them cannot be published here. I must tell you, though, that the blacks, when drinking at a river or water-hole, invariably scoop up the water with their hands, and never put their mouths right down close to the surface of the water.   Well, one day I was guilty of this solecism.   I had been out on a hunting expedition, and

BURNING THIRST

reached the water-hole with an intense burning thirst. My mentor was not with me.   I fell on my knees and fairly buried my face in the life-giving fluid.   Suddenly I heard murmurs behind me.   I turned presently and saw a party of my blacks regarding me with horror.

They said I drank like a kangaroo. But Yamba soon came to the rescue, and explained away the dreadful breach of etiquette, by telling them that I was not drinking, but simply cooling my face; when we were alone she solemnly cautioned me never to do it again.

The months passed slowly away, and I was still living the same monotonous life among my blacks—accompanying them upon their hunting expeditions, joining in their sports, and making periodical trips inland with Yamba, in preparation for the great journey I proposed to make overland to Cape York. When I spoke to my devoted companion about my plans, she told me she was ready to accompany me wherever I went—to leave her people and to be for ever by my side. Right well I knew that she would unhesitatingly do these things. Her dog-like fidelity to me never wavered, and I know she would have laid down her life for me at any time.

Often I told her of my own home beyond the seas, and when I asked her whether she would come with me, she would reply, "Your people are my people, and your God (spirit) my God." I will go with you wherever you take me."

At length everything was ready, and I paid a final farewell, as I thought, to my black friends in Cambridge Gulf, after a little over eighteen months' residence among them. They knew I was venturing on a long journey overland to another part of the country many moons distant, in the hope of being able to get into touch with my own people; and though they realised they should never see me again, they thought my departure a very natural thing. The night before

I

we left, a great *corroboree* was held in my honour.
We had a very affectionate leave-taking, and a body of
the natives escorted us for the first 100 miles or so of
our trip.   At last, however, Yamba, myself, and the
faithful dog were left to continue our wanderings alone.
The reliance I placed upon this woman by the way
was absolute and unquestioning.   I knew that alone I
could not live a day in the awful wilderness through
which we were to pass; nor could any solitary white
man.   By this time, however, I had had innumerable
demonstrations of Yamba's almost miraculous powers
in the way of providing food and water when, to the
ordinary eye, neither was forthcoming.   I should have
mentioned that before leaving my black people I
had provided myself with what I may term a native
passport—a kind of Masonic mystic stick, inscribed
with certain cabalistic characters.   Every chief carried
one of these sticks.   I carried mine in my long,
luxuriant hair, which I wore "bun" fashion, held in a
net of opossum hair.   This passport stick proved
invaluable as a means of putting us on good terms
with the different tribes we encountered.   The chiefs
of the blacks never ventured out of their own country
without one of these mysterious sticks, neither did the
native message-bearers.   I am sure I should not have
been able to travel far without mine.

Whenever I encountered a strange tribe I always
asked to be taken before the chief, and when in his
presence I presented my little stick, he would at once
manifest the greatest friendliness, and offer us food
and drink.   Then, before I took my departure, he
also would inscribe his sign upon the message stick,
handing it back to me and probably sending me on

to another tribe with an escort. It often happened, however, that I was personally introduced to another tribe whose "frontier" joined that of my late hosts, and in such cases my passport was unnecessary.

At first the country through which our wanderings led us was hilly and well wooded, the trees being particularly fine, many of them towering up to a height of 150 feet or 200 feet. Our principal food consisted of roots, rats, snakes, opossum, and kangaroo. The physical conditions of the country were constantly changing as we moved farther eastward, and Yamba's ingenuity was often sorely taxed to detect the whereabouts of the various roots necessary for food. It was obviously unfair to expect her to be familiar with the flora and fauna of every part of the great Australian Continent. Sometimes she was absolutely nonplused, and had to stay a few days with a tribe until the women initiated her into the best methods of cooking the roots of the country. And often we could not understand the language. In such cases, though, when spoken words were unlike those uttered in Yamba's country, we resorted to a wonderful sign-language which appears to be general among the Australian blacks. All that Yamba carried was a basket made of bark, slung over her shoulder, and containing a variety of useful things, including some needles made out of the bones of birds and fish ; a couple of light grinding-stones for crushing out of its shell a very sustaining kind of nut found on the palm trees, &c. Day after day we walked steadily on in an easterly direction, guiding ourselves in the daytime by the sun, and in the evening by opossum scratches on trees and the positions of the ant-hills, which are always built facing the east. We crossed many creeks and rivers, sometimes wading and at others time swimming.

Gradually we left the hilly country behind, and after about five or six weeks' tramping got into an extraordinary desert of red sand, which gave off a dust from our very tracks that nearly suffocated us. Each water-hole we came across now began to contain less and less of the precious liquid, and our daily *menu* grew more and more scanty, until at length we were compelled to live on practically nothing but a few roots and stray rats. Still we plodded on, finally striking a terrible spinifex country, which was inconceivably worse than anything we had hitherto encountered. In order to make our way through this spinifex (the terrible "porcupine grass" of the Australian interior), we were bound to follow the tracks made by kangaroos or natives, otherwise we should have made no progress whatever. These tracks at times wandered about zigzag fashion, and led us considerable distances out of our course, but, all the same, we dare not leave them. Not only was water all but unobtainable here, but our skin was torn with thorns at almost every step. Yamba was terribly troubled when she found she could no longer provide for my wants. Fortunately the dew fell heavily at night, and a sufficient quantity would collect on the foliage to refresh me somewhat in the morning. How eagerly would I lick the precious drops from the leaves! Curiously enough, Yamba herself up to this time did not seem distressed from lack of water; but nothing about this marvellous woman surprised me. It took us about ten days to pass through the awful spinifex desert, and for at least eight days of that period we were virtually without water, tramping through never-ending tracts of scrub, prickly grass, and undulating sand-hills of a reddish colour.   Often and often I blamed myself bitterly for ever going into that frightful country at all.   Had I known beforehand that it was totally un-inhabited I certainly should not have ventured into it.   We were still going due east, but in consequence of the lack of water-holes, my heroic guide thought it advisable to strike a little more north.

CHAPTER VII

BY this time I began to feel quite delirious; I
fear I was like a baby in Yamba's hands. She
knew that all I wanted was water, and became almost
distracted when she could not find any for me. Of
herself she never thought. And yet she was full of
strange resources and devices. When I moaned aloud
in an agony of thirst, she would give me some kind
of grass to chew; and although this possessed no real
moisture, yet it promoted the flow of saliva, and thus
slightly relieved me.

Things grew worse and worse, however, and the
delirium increased. Hour after hour through the
endless nights would that devoted creature sit by my
side, moistening my lips with the dew that collected
on the grass. On the fifth day without water I
suffered the most shocking agonies, and in my lucid
moments gave myself up for lost. I could neither
stand nor walk, speak nor swallow. My throat seemed
to be almost closed up, and when I opened my eyes
everything appeared to be going round and round in

the most dizzy and sickening manner. My heart beat with choking violence, and my head ached, so that I thought I was going mad. My bloodshot eyes (so Yamba subsequently told me) projected from their sockets in the most terrifying manner, and a horrible indescribable longing possessed me to kill my faithful Bruno, in order to drink his blood. My poor Bruno! As I write these humble lines, so lacking in literary grace, I fancy I can see him lying by my side in that glaring, illimitable wilderness, his poor, dry tongue lolling out, and his piteous brown eyes fixed upon me with an expression of mute appeal that added to my agony. The only thing that kept him from collapsing altogether was the blood of some animal which Yamba might succeed in killing.

Gradually I grew weaker and weaker, and at last feeling the end was near, I crawled under the first tree I came across—never for a moment giving a thought as to its species,—and prepared to meet the death I now fervently desired. Had Yamba, too, given up, these lines would never have been written. Amazing to relate, she kept comparatively well and active, though without water; and in my most violent paroxysm she would pounce upon a lizard or a rat, and give me its warm blood to drink, while yet it lived. Then she would masticate a piece of iguana flesh and give it to me in my mouth, but I was quite unable to swallow it, greatly to her disappointment. She must have seen that I was slowly sinking, for at last she stooped down and whispered earnestly in my ear that she would leave me for a little while, and go off in search of water. Like a dream it comes back to me how she explained that she had seen some birds passing overhead, and that if she followed in the same direction she was almost certain to reach water sooner or later.

I could not reply; but I felt it was a truly hopeless enterprise on her part. And as I did not want her to leave me, I remember I held out my tomahawk feebly towards her, and signed to her to come and strike me on the head with it, and so put an end to my dreadful agonies. The heroic creature only smiled and shook her head emphatically. She took the proffered weapon, however, and after putting some distinguishing marks on my tree with it, she hurled it some distance away from me. She then stooped and propped me against the trunk of the tree; and then leaving my poor suffering dog to keep me company, she set out on her lonely search with long, loping strides of amazing vigour.

It was late in the afternoon when she took her departure; and I lay there hour after hour, sometimes frantically delirious, and at others in a state of semi-consciousness, fancying she was by my side with shells brimming over with delicious water. I would rouse myself with a start from time to time, but, alas! my Yamba was not near me. During the long and deathly stillness of the night, the dew came down heavily, and as it enveloped my bed, I fell into a sound sleep, from which I was awakened some hours later by the same clear and ringing voice that had addressed me on that still night on my island sand-spit. Out upon the impressive stillness of the air rang the earnest words: "*Coupe l'arbre! Coupe l'arbre!*"

I was quite conscious, and much refreshed by my

sleep, but the message puzzled me a great deal. At
first I thought it must have been Yamba's voice, but
I remembered that she did not know a word of French ;
and when I looked round there was no one to be seen.
The mysterious message still rang in my ears, but I
was far too weak to attempt to cut the tree myself, I
lay there in a state of inert drowsiness until, rousing
myself a little before dawn, I heard the familiar footsteps of Yamba approaching the spot where I lay.
Her face expressed anxiety, earnestness, and joy.

In her trembling hands she bore a big lily leaf containing two or three ounces of life-giving water. This
I drank with gasping eagerness, as you may suppose.
My delirium had now entirely left me, although I was
still unable to speak. I signed to her to cut the tree,
as the voice in my dream had directed me. Without
a word of question Yamba picked up the tomahawk
from where she had hurled it, and then cut vigorously
into the trunk, making a hole three or four inches deep.
It may seem astonishing to you, but it surprised me
in no wise when out from the hole there *trickled a
clear, uncertain stream of water*, under which Yamba
promptly held my fevered head. This had a wonderfully refreshing effect upon me, and in a short time I
was able to speak feebly but rationally, greatly to the
delight of my faithful companion. As, however, I was
still too weak to move, I indulged in another and far
sounder sleep. I do not know the scientific name of
that wonderful Australian tree which saved my life,
but believe it is well known to naturalists. I have
heard it called the "bottle tree," from the shape of
the trunk. All through that terrible night, while
Yamba was far away searching for water, Bruno had

never left my side, looking into my face wistfully, and occasionally licking my body sympathetically with his poor, parched tongue. Whilst I was asleep the second time, Yamba went off with the dog in search of food, and returned with a young opossum, which was soon frizzling in an appetising way on a tripod of sticks over a blazing fire. I was able to eat a little of the flesh, and we obtained all the water we wanted from our wonderful tree. Of course, Yamba was unacquainted with the fact that water was stored in its interior. As a rule, her instinct might be depended upon implicitly; and even after years of her companionship I used to be filled with wonder at the way in which she would track down game and find honey. She would glance at a tree casually, and discern on the bark certain minute scratches, which were quite invisible to me, even when pointed out. She would then climb up like a monkey, and return to the ground with a good-sized opossum, which would be roasted in its skin, with many different varieties of delicious roots.

When I had quite recovered, Yamba told me she had walked many miles during the night, and had finally discovered a water-hole in a new country, for which she said we must make as soon as I was sufficiently strong. Fortunately this did not take very long, and on reaching the brink of the water-hole we camped beside it for several days, in order to recuperate. I must say that the water we found here did not look very inviting—it was, in fact, very slimy and green in colour; but by the time we took our departure there was not a drop left. Yamba had a method of filtration which excited my admiration. She dug another hole alongside the one containing the water, leaving a few inches of earth between them, through which the water would percolate, and collect in the second hole perfectly filtered.

At other times, when no ordinary human being could detect the presence of water, she would point out to me a little knob of clay on the ground in an old dried-up water-hole. This, she told me, denoted the presence of a frog, and she would at once thrust down a reed about eighteen inches long, and invite me to suck the upper end, with the result that I imbibed copious draughts of delicious water.

At the water-hole just described birds were rather plentiful, and when they came down to drink, Yamba knocked them over without difficulty. They made a very welcome addition to our daily bill of fare. Her mode of capturing the birds was simplicity itself. She made herself a long covering of grass that completely enveloped her, and, shrouded in this, waited at the edge of the water-hole for the birds to come and drink. Then she knocked over with a stick as many as she required. In this way we had a very pleasant spell of rest for four or five days. Continuing our journey once more, we pushed on till in about three weeks we came to a well-wooded country, where the eucalyptus flourished mightily and water was plentiful; but yet, strange to say, there was very little game in this region. Soon after this, I noticed that Yamba grew a little anxious, and she explained that as we had not come across any kangaroos lately, nor any blacks, it was evident that the wet season was coming on. We therefore decided to steer for higher ground, and accordingly went almost due north for the next few days, until we reached the banks of a big river—the Roper River, as I afterwards found out—where we thought it advisable to camp. This would probably be sometime in the month of December.

One day I saw a number of small snakes swarming round the foot of a tree, and was just about to knock some of them over with my stick, when Yamba called out to me excitedly not to molest them. They then began to climb the tree, and she explained that this clearly indicated the advent of the wet season. "I did not wish you to kill the snakes," she said, "because I wanted to see if they would take refuge in the trees from the coming floods."

Up to this time, however, there had not been the slightest indication of any great change in the weather. Many months must have elapsed since rain had fallen in these regions, for the river was extremely low between its extraordinarily high banks, and the country all round was dry and parched; but even as we walked, a remarkable phenomenon occurred, which told of impending changes. I was oppressed with a sense of coming evil. I listened intently when Yamba requested me to do so, but at first all I could hear was a curious rumbling sound, far away in the distance. This noise gradually increased in volume, and came nearer and nearer, but still I was utterly unable to account for it. I also noticed that the river was becoming strangely agitated, and was swirling along at ever-increasing speed. Suddenly an enormous mass of water came rushing down with a frightful roar, in one solid wave, and then it dawned upon me that it must have already commenced raining in the hills, and the tributaries of the river were now sending down their floods into the main stream, which was rising with astonishing rapidity. In the course of a couple of hours it had risen between thirty and forty feet. Yamba seemed a little anxious, and suggested that we had better build a hut on some high ground and remain secure in that locality, without attempting to continue our march while the rains lasted; and it was evident they were now upon us.

We therefore set to work to construct a comfortable little shelter of bark, fastened to a framework of poles by means of creepers and climbing plants. Thus, by the time the deluge was fairly upon us, we were quite snugly ensconced. We did not, however, remain in-doors throughout the whole of the day, but went in and out, hunting for food and catching game just as usual; the torrential rain which beat down upon our naked bodies being rather a pleasant experience than otherwise. At this time we had a welcome addition to our food in the form of cabbage-palms and wild honey. We also started building a catamaran, with which to navigate the river when the floods had subsided. Yamba procured a few trunks of very light timber, and these we fastened together with long pins of hardwood, and then bound them still more firmly together with strips of kangaroo hide. We also collected a stock of provisions to take with us—kangaroo and opossum meat, of course; but principally wild honey, cabbage-palm, and roots of various kinds. These preparations took us several days, and by the time we had arranged everything for our journey the weather had become settled once more. Yamba remarked to me that if we simply drifted down the Roper River we should be carried to the open sea; nor would we be very long, since the swollen current was now running like a mill-race. Our catamaran, of course, afforded no shelter of any kind, but we carried some sheets of bark to form seats for ourselves and the dog.

At length we pushed off on our eventful voyage, and no sooner had we got fairly into the current than we were carried along with prodigious rapidity, and without the least exertion on our part, except in the matter of steering. This was done by means of paddles from the side of the craft. We made such rapid progress that I felt inclined to go on all night, but shortly after dusk Yamba persuaded me to pull in-shore and camp on the bank until morning, because of the danger of travelling at night among the logs and other wreckage that floated about on the surface of the water.

We passed any number of submerged trees, and on several of these found snakes coiled among the branches. Some of these reptiles we caught and ate. About the middle of the second day we heard a tremendous roar ahead, as though there were rapids in the bed of the river. It was now impossible to pull the catamaran out of its course, no matter how hard we might have striven, the current being absolutely irresistible. The banks narrowed as the rapids were reached, with the result that the water in the middle actually became *convex*, so tremendous was the rush in that narrow gorge. Yamba cried out to me to lie flat on the catamaran, and hold on as tightly as I could until we reached smooth water again. This she did herself, seizing hold of the dog also.

Nearer and nearer we were swept to the great seething caldron of boiling and foaming waters, and at last, with a tremendous splash we entered the terrify-

ing commotion. We went right under, and so great
was the force of the water, that had I not been clinging
tenaciously to the catamaran I must infallibly have
been swept away to certain death. Presently, however, we shot into less troubled waters and then continued our course, very little the worse for having
braved these terrible rapids. Had our craft been a
dug-out boat, as I originally intended it to be,
we must inevitably have been swamped. Again we
camped on shore that night, and were off at an early
hour next morning. As we glided swiftly on, I noticed
that the river seemed to be growing tremendously
wide. Yamba explained that we were now getting
into very flat country, and therefore the great stretch
of water was a mere flood. She also prophesied a
rather bad time for us, as we should not be able to go
ashore at night and replenish our stock of provisions.
Fortunately we had a sufficient supply with us on the
catamaran to last at least two or three days longer.
The last time we landed Yamba had stocked an
additional quantity of edible roots and smoked meats,
and although we lost a considerable portion of these
in shooting the rapids, there still remained enough for
a few days' supply.

In consequence of the ever-increasing width of the
river, I found it a difficult matter to keep in the
channel where the current was, so I gave up the
steering paddle to Yamba, who seemed instinctively
to know what course to take.

On and on we went, until at length the whole
country as far as the eye could reach was one vast
sea, extending virtually to the horizon; its sluggish
surface only broken by the tops of the submerged

trees. One day we sighted a number of little islets some distance ahead, and then we felt we must be nearing the mouth of the river. The last day or two had been full of anxiety and inconvenience for us, for we had been simply drifting aimlessly on, without being able to land and stretch our cramped limbs or indulge in a comfortable sleep. Thus the sight of the islands was a great relief to us, and my ever-faithful and considerate companion remarked that as we had nothing to fear now, and I was weary with my vigil of the previous night, I had better try and get a little sleep. Accordingly I lay down on the catamaran, and had barely extended my limbs when I fell fast asleep. I awoke two or three hours later, at mid-day, and was surprised to find that our catamaran was not moving. I raised myself up, only to find that we had apparently drifted among the tops of a ring of trees rising from a submerged island. "Halloa!" I said to Yamba, "are we stuck?" "No," she replied quietly, "but look round."

You may judge of my horror and amazement when I saw outside the curious ring of tree-tops, scores of huge alligators peering at us with horrid stolidity through the branches, some of them snapping their capacious jaws with a viciousness that left no doubt as to its meaning. Yamba explained to me that she had been obliged to take refuge in this peculiar but convenient shelter, because the alligators seemed to be swarming in vast numbers in that part of the river. She had easily forced a way for the catamaran through the branches, and once past, had drawn them together again. The ferocious monsters could certainly have forced their way into the inclosure after us, but they didn't seem to realise that such a thing was possible, apparently being quite content to remain outside. Judge, then, our position for yourself—with a scanty food supply, on a frail platform of logs, floating among the tree-tops, and literally besieged by crowds of loathsome alligators! Nor did

ALLIGATORS PEERING AT US

we know how long our imprisonment was likely to last. Our poor dog, too, was terribly frightened, and sat whining and trembling in a most pitiable way in spite of reassuring words and caresses from Yamba and myself. I confess that I was very much alarmed, for the monsters would occasionally emit a most peculiar and terrifying sound—not unlike the roar of a

K

lion. Hour after hour we sat there on the swaying
catamaran, praying fervently that the hideous reptiles
might leave us, and let us continue our journey in peace.
As darkness began to descend upon the vast waste of
waters, it occurred to me to make a bold dash through
the serried ranks of our besiegers, but Yamba restrained
me, telling me it meant certain death to attempt to run
the gantlet under such fearsome circumstances.

Night came on. How can I describe its horrors?
Even as I write, I seem to hear the ceaseless roars
of those horrible creatures, and the weird but gentle
lappings of the limitless waste that extended as far
as the eye could reach. Often I was tempted to give
up in despair, feeling that there was no hope whatever
for us. Towards morning, however, the alligators
apparently got on the scent of some floating carcasses
brought down by the floods, and one and all left us.
Some little time after the last ugly head had gone
under, the catamaran was sweeping swiftly and noiselessly down the stream again.

We made straight for a little island some distance
ahead of us, and found it uninhabited. Black and
white birds, not quite so large as pigeons, were very
plentiful, as also were eggs. Soon my Yamba had
a nice meal ready for me, and then we lay down for
a much-needed rest. After this we steered for a large
island some nine or ten miles distant, and as we approached we could see that this one *was* inhabited,
from the smoke-signals the natives sent up the moment
they caught sight of us.

As we came nearer we could see the blacks as-
sembling on the beach to meet us, but, far from showing any friendliness, they held their spears poised

threateningly, and would no doubt have thrown them had I not suddenly jumped to my feet and made signs that I wished to sit down with them—to parley with them. They then lowered their spears, and we landed; but to my great disappointment neither Yamba nor I could understand one word of their language, which was totally different from the dialect of Yamba's country. Our first meeting was conducted in the usual way—squatting down on our haunches, and then drawing nearer and nearer until we were able to rub noses on one another's shoulders. I then explained by means of signs that I wanted to stay with them a few days, and I was inexpressibly relieved to find that my little passport stick (which never left my possession for a moment), was recognised at once, and proved most efficacious generally. After this I became more friendly with my hosts, and told them by signs that I was looking for white people like myself, whereupon they replied I should have to go still farther south to find them. They took us to their camp, and provided us with food, consisting mainly of fish, shell-fish, and roots. So far as I could ascertain, there were no kangaroo or opossum on the island. After two or three days, I thought it time to be continuing our journey; but feeling convinced that I must be in the vicinity of the Cape York Peninsula—instead of being on the west coast of the Gulf of Carpentaria—I decided not to go south at all, but to strike due north, where I felt certain Somerset Point lay; and I also resolved to travel by sea this time, the blacks having presented me with a very unsubstantial "dug-out" canoe. Leaving behind us the catamaran that had brought us so many hundreds of miles, we set out on our travels once more—taking care, however, never to lose sight of the coast-line on account of our frail craft. We passed several beautiful islands, big and little, and on one that we landed I came across some native chalk drawings on the face of the rock. They depicted rude figures of men—I don't remember any animals—but were not nearly so well done as the drawings I had seen in caves up in the Cape Londonderry district.

We also landed from time to time on the mainland, and spoke with the chiefs of various tribes. They were all hostile at first. On one occasion we actually met one or two blacks who spoke a few words of English. They had evidently been out with pearlers at some time in their lives, but had returned to their native wilds many years before our visit. I asked them if they knew where white men were to be found, and they pointed east (Cape York), and also indicated that the whites were many moons' journey away from us. I was sorely puzzled. A glance at a map of Australia will enable the reader to realise my great blunder. Ignorant almost of Australian geography I fancied, on reaching the western shores of the Gulf of Carpentaria, that I had struck the Coral Sea, and that all I had to do was to strike north to reach Somerset, the white settlement I had heard about from the pearlers. I felt so confident Cape York lay immediately to the north, that I continued my course in that direction, paddling all day and running in-shore to camp at night. We lived mainly on shell-fish and sea-birds' eggs at this time, and altogether life became terribly wearisome and monotonous. This, however, was mainly owing to my anxiety.

About a fortnight after leaving the mouth of the Roper River we came to a place which I now know to be Point Dale. We then steered south into a beautiful landlocked passage which lies between the mainland and Elcho Island, and which at the time I took to be the little strait running between Albany Island and Cape York. I steered south-west in consequence; and after a time, as I did not sight the points I was on the look-out for, I felt completely nonplused. We landed on Elcho Island and spent a day or two there. Being still under the impression that Cape York was higher up, I steered west, and soon found myself in a very unpleasant region. We explored almost every bay and inlet we came across, but of course always with the same disheartening result. Sometimes we would come near being stranded on a sandbank, and would have to jump overboard and push our craft into deeper water. At others, she would be almost swamped in a rough sea, but still we stuck to our task, and after passing Goulbourn Island we followed the coast. Then we struck north until we got among a group of islands, and came to Croker Island, which goes direct north and south. Day after day we kept doggedly on, hugging the shore very closely, going in and out of every bay, and visiting almost every island, yet never seeing a single human being. We were apparently still many hundreds of miles away from our destination. To add to the wretchedness of the situation, my poor Yamba, who had been so devoted, so hardy, and so contented, at length began to manifest symptoms of illness, and complained gently of the weariness of it all. "You are looking," she would say, "for a place that does not exist. You are looking for friends of whose very existence you are unaware." I would not give in, however, and persuaded her that all would be well in time, if only she would continue to bear with me. Both of us were terribly cramped in the boat; and by way of exercise one or the other would occasionally jump overboard and have a long swim. Whenever we could we landed at night.

One morning, shortly after we had begun our usual trip for the day, and were rounding a headland, I was almost stupefied to behold in front of me the masts of a boat (which I afterwards found to be a Malay proa), close in-shore. The situation, in reality, was between Croker's Island and the main, but at the time I thought that I had at length reached Somerset. I sprang to my feet in a state of the greatest excitement: "Thank God! thank God!" I shouted to Yamba; "we are saved at last!—saved—saved—saved!" As I shouted, I pulled the canoe round and made for the vessel with all possible despatch. We very soon came up with her, and found her almost stranded, in consequence of the lowness of the tide. I promptly clambered aboard, but failed to find a soul. I thought this rather strange, but as I could see a hut not very far away, close to the beach, I steered towards it. This little dwelling, too, was uninhabited, though I found a number of trays of fish lying about, which afterwards I found to be *bêche-de-mer* being dried and smoked. Suddenly, while Yamba and I were investigating the interior of the hut, a number of Malays unexpectedly appeared on the scene, and I then realised I had had the good fortune to come across a Malay *bêche-de-mer* expedition.

The fishermen were exceedingly surprised at seeing

Yamba and me; but when they found I could speak
their language a little they evinced every sign of delight, and forthwith entertained us most hospitably on
board their craft, which was a boat of ten or fifteen tons.
They told me they had come from the Dutch islands
south of Timor, and promptly made me an offer that
set my heart beating wildly. They said they were
prepared to take me back to Kopang, if I wished; and
I, on my part, offered to give them all the pearl shells
left on my little island in the Sea of Timor—the latitude of which I took good care not to divulge—on
condition that they called there. They even offered
Yamba a passage along with me; but, to my amazement
and bitter disappointment, she said she did not wish to
go with them. She trembled as though with fear. She
was afraid that when once we were on board, the
Malays would kill me and keep her.

One other reason for this fear I knew, but it in no
way mitigated my acute grief at being obliged to
decline what would probably be my only chance of
returning to civilisation. For this I had pined day and
night for four or five years, and now that escape was
within my grasp I was obliged to throw it away. For
let me emphatically state, that even if civilisation had
been but a mile away, I would not have gone a yard
towards it without that devoted creature who had been
my salvation, not on one occasion only, but practically
every moment of my existence.

With passionate eagerness I tried to persuade Yamba
to change her mind, but she remained firm in her de-
cision; and so, almost choking with bitter regret, and
in a state of utter collapse, I had to decline the offer
of the Malays. We stayed with them, however, a few

weeks longer, and at length they accompanied me to a camp of black fellows near some lagoons, a little way farther south of their own camp.   Before they left, they presented me with a quantity of *bêche-de-mer*, or sea-slugs, which make most excellent soup.   At the place indicated by the Malays, which was in Raffles Bay, the chief spoke quite excellent English.   One of his wives could even say the Lord's Prayer in English, though, of course, she did not know what she was talking about.   " Captain Jack Davis," as he called himself, had been for some little time on one of her Majesty's ships, and he told me that not many marches away there was an old European settlement ; he even offered to guide me there, if I cared to go.   He first led me to an old white settlement in Raffles Bay, called, I think, Fort Wellington, where I found some large fruit-trees, including ripe yellow mangoes.   There were, besides, raspberries, strawberries, and Cape gooseberries. Needless to remark, all this made me very happy and contented, for I felt I must now be getting near the home of some white men.   I thought that, after all, perhaps Yamba's refusal to go with the Malays was for the best, and with high hopes I set out with Captain Davis for another settlement he spoke of. This turned out to be Port Essington, which we reached in two or three days.   Another cruel blow was dealt me here.

You can perhaps form some idea of my poignant dismay and disappointment on finding that this dreary-looking place of swamps and marshes was quite deserted, although there were still a number of ruined brick houses, gardens, and orchards there.   The blacks told me that at one time it had been one of the most important penal settlements in Australia, but had to be abandoned on account of the prevalence of malarial fever arising from the swamps in the neighbour-hood. I came across a number of graves, which were evidently those of the exiled settlers; and one of the wooden headstones bore the name of Captain Hill

CATCHING WATER-FOWL.

(I think that was the name). I have an idea that the fence round this old cemetery still remained. There was food in abundance at this place — raspberries, bananas, and mangoes grew in profusion; whilst the marshes were inhabited by vast flocks of geese, ducks, white ibis, and other wild-fowl. Indeed in the swamps the birds rose in such prodigious numbers as actually to obscure the face of the sun. Here for the first time I saw web-footed birds perched in trees.

The blacks had a very peculiar method of catching water-fowl. They would simply wade through the reeds into the water almost up to their necks, and then cover their heads with a handful of reeds. Remaining perfectly still, they would imitate the cry of different wild-fowl. Then at a convenient opportunity, they would simply seize a goose or a duck by the leg, and drag it down under the water until it was drowned. The number of water-fowl caught in this way by a single black fellow was truly astonishing.

After having remained a fortnight at Port Essington itself, we returned to Raffles Bay, where Yamba and I made a camp among the blacks and took up our residence among them; for Captain Davis had told me that ships called there occasionally, and it was possible that one might call soon from Port Darwin. The vessels, he added, came for buffalo meat—of which more hereafter. I had decided to remain among these people some little time, because they knew so much about Europeans, and I felt sure of picking up knowledge which would prove useful to me.

CHAPTER VIII

I HAD not been established in this camp many days,
however, before I was struck down, for the first
time, with a terrible attack of malarial fever, probably
produced by the many hours I had spent wading in
the swamps at Port Essington. There were the usual
symptoms—quick flushings and fever heats, followed
by violent fits of shivering, which no amount of natural
warmth could mitigate. My faithful Yamba was terribly distressed at my condition, and waited upon me
with most tender devotion ; but in spite of all that
could be done for me, I grew gradually weaker, until
in the course of a few days I became wildly delirious.
The blacks, too, were very good to me, and doctored
me, in their quaint native way, with certain leaves and
powders. All to no purpose, however; and for several
days I was even unable to recognise my Yamba. Then
the fever subsided somewhat, and I was left as weak
and helpless as a little child.

It was some time before I quite recovered from the

fever; and I was frequently seized with distressing fits
of shivering. I also experienced an overwhelming
desire for a drink of milk; why, I am unable to say.
Therefore, when some of the blacks told me that wild
buffalo were to be found in the neighbourhood—beasts
which had formerly belonged to settlers, but were now
run wild—I resolved, when sufficiently strong, to try
and capture one of the cows for the sake of its milk.
Captain Davis ridiculed the idea, and assured me that
it was only possible to slay one with a rifle; but I
determined to see what I could do.

Yamba, of course, accompanied me on my expedition, and her bushmanship was altogether quite
indispensable. We came upon buffalo tracks near a
large water-hole, and here we each climbed a gum-tree
and awaited the arrival of our prey. We waited a
long time, but were at length rewarded by seeing a
big cow buffalo and her calf wandering leisurely in
our direction. My only weapons were a lasso made
out of green kangaroo hide, fixed to the end of a long
pole; and my bow and arrows. I slid down the tree
a little way, and when the calf was near enough, I
gently slipped the noose over its neck, and promptly
made it a prisoner under the very nose of its
astonished mother, who bellowed mournfully. My
success so elated Yamba that she, too, slid down from
her hiding-place, and was making her way over to me
and the calf, when suddenly an enormous bull, which we
had not previously seen, rushed at her at full speed.
Yamba instantly realised her danger, and swarmed up a
tree again like lightning, just as the great brute was
upon her. I called out to her to attract the attention of
the old bull whilst I attended to the mother and calf. I

dropped my pole to which the lasso was attached, and allowed the little one to walk quickly away with it; but, as I anticipated, the trailing shaft soon caught between the stumps of some trees, and made the calf a more secure prisoner than ever. It was a curious repetition of the story of the two whales. The mother walked round and round, and appeared to be in the greatest distress. She never left her little one's side, but continued to bellow loudly, and lick the calf to coax it away. Quietly sliding down my tree, I made my way to where Yamba was still holding the attention of the bull—a fiery brute who was pawing the ground with rage at the foot of her tree. I had fitted an arrow to my bow, and was preparing to shoot, when, unfortunately, the bull detected the noise of my approach, and rushed straight at me. I confess it was rather a trying moment, but I never lost my head, feeling confident of my skill with the bow—which I had practised off and on ever since I had left school at Montreux. I actually waited until the charging monster was within a few paces, and then I let fly. So close was he that not much credit is due to me for accurate aim. The arrow fairly transfixed his right eye, causing him to pull up on his haunches, and roar with pain.

Yamba, full of anxiety, hurried down her tree; but she had scarcely reached the ground when the baffled bull wheeled and charged her, with more fury than ever. She simply glided behind a tree, and then I showed myself and induced the bull to charge me once more. Again I waited until he was almost upon me, and then I sent another arrow into his other eye, blinding him completely. On this, the poor brute brought up sharp, and commenced to back in an

uncertain way, bellowing with pain. I forgot all my
fever in the excitement, and rushing upon the beast
with my tomahawk, I dealt him a blow on the side
of the head that made him stagger. I brought him to
the earth with two or three more blows, and a few
minutes later had administered the *coup-de-grâce*. No
sooner was the big bull dead than I determined to test
the efficacy of a very popular native remedy for fever
—for shivering fits still continued to come upon me
at most awkward times, usually late in the day. No
matter how much grass poor Yamba brought me as
covering, I never could get warm, and so now I
thought I would try some animal heat.

Scarce had life left the body of the prostrate bull
before I ripped open the carcass between the fore and
hind legs ; and after remarking to Yamba, " I am going
to have heat this time," I crawled into the interior. My
head, however, was protruding from the buffalo's chest.
Yamba understood perfectly well what I was doing;
and when I told her I was going to indulge in a long
sleep in my curious resting-place, she said she would
keep watch and see that I was not disturbed. I remained buried in the bull's interior for the rest of the
day and all through the night. Next morning, to my
amazement, I found I was a prisoner, the carcass
having got cold and rigid, so that I had literally to
be dug out. As I emerged I presented a most ghastly
and horrifying spectacle. My body was covered with
congealed blood, and even my long hair was all matted
and stiffened with it. But never can I forget the
feeling of exhilaration and strength that took possession of me as I stood there looking at my faithful
companion. *I was absolutely cured*—a new man, a

giant of strength! I make a present of the cure to
the medical profession.

Without delay I made my way down to the lagoon
and washed myself thoroughly, scrubbing myself with
a kind of soapy clay, and afterwards taking a run in
order to get dry. This extraordinary system of apply-
ing the carcass of a freshly killed animal is invariably
resorted to by the natives in case of serious illness, and
they look upon it as an all but infallible cure. Certainly
it was surprisingly efficacious in my own case.

Next day we directed our attention to the capture
of the cow, which was still wandering around her im-
prisoned little one, and only leaving it for a few minutes
at a time in order to get food. I constructed a small
fence or inclosure of sticks, and into this we managed
to drive the cow. We then kept her for two days
without food and water, in order to tame her, and did
not even let her little calf come near her. We then
approached her, and found her perfectly subdued, and
willing to take food and water from us precisely as
though she were the gentlest Alderney.

I found I was even able to milk her; and I can
assure you that I never tasted anything more delicious
in my life than the copious draughts of fresh milk I
indulged in on that eventful morning. In fact, I practically lived on nothing else for the next few days, and
it pulled me round in a most surprising way. The
flesh of the dead buffalo I did not touch myself, but
handed it over to the blacks, who were vastly impressed
by my prowess as a mighty hunter. They themselves
had often tried to kill buffalo with their spears, but had
never succeeded. I removed the bull's hide, and made
a big rug out of it, which I found very serviceable

indeed in subsequent wet seasons.   It was as hard as a board, and nearly half an inch thick.

When I returned to "Captain Davis" and the rest of my friends at Raffles Bay, I was quite well and strong once more, and I stayed with them three or four months, hunting almost every day (there were even wild ponies and English cattle—of course, relics of the old settlement), and picking up all the information I could.   I had many conversations with Davis himself, and he told me that I should probably find white men at Port Darwin, which he said was between three and four hundred miles away.   The tribe at Port Essington, I may mention, only numbered about fifty souls. This was about the year 1868.   Captain Davis—who was passionately fond of tobacco, and would travel almost any distance to obtain an ounce or two from the Malay *bêche-de-mer* fishers—pointed out to me a blazed tree near his camp on which the following inscription was cut :—

LUDWIG LEICHHARDT,
Overland from Sydney,
1847.

It was therefore evident that this district had already been visited by a white man; and the fact that he had come overland filled me with hopes that some day I, too, might return to civilisation in the same way.   The English-speaking black chief assured me that his father had acted as guide to Leichhardt, but whether the latter got back safely to Sydney again he never knew.   The white traveller, he said, left Port Essington in a ship.

Having considered all things, I decided to attempt

to reach Port Darwin by boat, in the hope of finding
Europeans living there. At first I thought of going
overland, but in discussing my plans with "Captain
Davis," he told me that I would have to cross swamps,
fords, creeks, and rivers, some of which were alive
with alligators. He advised me to go by water, and
also told me to be careful not to be drawn into a
certain large bay I should come across, because of the
alligators that swarmed on its shores. The bay that
he warned me against was, I think, Van Dieman's Gulf.
He told me to keep straight across the bay, and then
pass between Melville Island and the main. He fitted
me out with a good stock of provisions, including a
quantity of *bêche-de-mer*, cabbage-palm, fruit, &c. I
arranged my buffalo skin over my provisions as a protection, turtle-back fashion. Our preparations completed, Yamba and I and the dog pushed out into the
unknown sea in our frail canoe, which was only about
fifteen feet long and fourteen inches wide. Of course,
we kept close in-shore all the time, and made pretty
good progress until we passed Apsley Strait, avoiding
the huge Van Dieman's Gulf, with its alligator-infested
rivers and creeks. We must have been close to Port
Darwin when, with little or no warning, a terrific storm
arose, and quickly carried us out to sea in a south-
westerly direction. In a moment our frail little craft
was partially swamped, and Yamba and I were compelled to jump overboard and hang on to the gunwale
on either side to prevent it from being overwhelmed
altogether. This was about a fortnight after I left
Captain Davis. We knew that if we were swamped,
all our belongings, including my poor Bruno, my
live geese, water, and other provisions, would be lost

L

in the raging sea. The night that followed was perhaps one of the most appalling experiences that ever
befell me; but I had by this time become so inured
to terrible trials that I merely took it as a matter
of course.

Imagine for yourself the scene. The giant waves
are rolling mountains high; the darkness of night is
gathering round us fast, and I and my heroic wife are
immersed in the tremendous sea, hanging on for dear
life to a little dug-out canoe only fourteen inches wide.
Although we were soon thoroughly exhausted with
our immersion in the water, we dared not climb
aboard. Will it be believed that *all night long* we
were compelled to remain in the sea, clinging to the
canoe, half drowned, and tossed about like the insig-
nificant atoms we were in the midst of the stupendous
waves, which were literally ablaze with phosphor-
escent light? Often as those terrible hours crawled
by, I would have let go my hold and given up altogether were it not for Yamba's cheery and encouraging
voice, which I heard above the terrific roar of the
storm, pointing out to me how much we had been
through already, and how many fearful dangers we
had safely encountered together. It seemed to me
like the end of everything. I thought of a certain
poem relating to a man in a desperate situation,
written, I believe, by an American, whose name I
could not remember. It described the heart-breaking
efforts made by a slave to obtain his freedom. How
bloodhounds were put upon his track; how he is at
last cornered in a swamp, and as he looks helplessly
up at the stars he asks himself, "Is it life, or is it
death?" As I hung on to the little dug-out, chilled

to the very marrow, and more than half drowned
by the enormous seas, I recalled the whole poem and
applied the slave's remarks to myself.   "Can it be
possible," I said, "after all the struggles I have made
against varying fortune, that I am to meet death
now?"   I was in absolute despair.   Towards the
early hours of the morning Yamba advised me to
get into the canoe for a spell, but she herself remained
hanging on to the gunwale, trying to keep the head
of the little canoe before the immense waves that were
still running. _I was very cold and stiff, and found it
difficult to climb aboard.   As the morning advanced,
the sea began to abate somewhat, and presently Yamba
joined me in the canoe.   We were, however, unable
to shape our course for any set quarter, since by this
time we were out of sight of land altogether, and had
not even the slightest idea as to our position.

All that day we drifted aimlessly about, and then,
towards evening, a perfect calm settled on the sea.
When we were somewhat rested we paddled on in
a direction where we concluded land must lie (we
steered south-east for the main); and in the course of
a few hours we had the satisfaction of seeing a little
rocky island, which we promptly made for and landed
upon.   Here we obtained food in plenty in the form
of birds; but drinking-water was not to be found
anywhere, so we had to fall back on the small stock
we always carried in skins.   Judging from the appearance of the rocks, and the smell that pervaded
the place, I imagined that this must be a guano island.
I now knew that we were near Port Darwin, *but as a
fact we had passed it in the great storm, while we
were fighting for our lives.*   We slept on the island

that night, and felt very much better next morning
when we started out on our voyage once more, visiting
every bay and inlet. Hope, too, began to reassert
itself, and I thought that after all we might be able
to reach Port Darwin in spite of the distance we must
have been driven out of our course. Several islands
studded the sea through which we were now steadily
threading our way, and that evening we landed on one
of these and camped for the night. Next day we were
off again, and as the weather continued beautifully fine
we made splendid progress.

One evening a few days after the storm, as we were
placidly paddling away, I saw Yamba's face suddenly
brighten with a look I had never seen on it before,
and I felt sure this presaged some extraordinary
announcement. She would gaze up into the heavens
with a quick, sudden motion, and then her intelligent
eyes would sparkle like the stars above. I questioned
her, but she maintained an unusual reserve, and, as
I concluded that she knew instinctively we were approaching Port Darwin, I, too, felt full of joy and
pleasure that the object of our great journey was at
length about to be achieved. Alas! what awaited me
was only the greatest of all the astounding series of
disappointments—one indeed so stunning as to plunge
me into the very blackest depths of despair.

Yamba still continued to gaze up at the stars, and
when at length she had apparently satisfied herself
upon a certain point, she turned to me with a shout
of excited laughter and delight, pointing frantically at
a certain glowing star. Seeing that I was still puzzled
by her merriment, she cried, "That star is one you
remember well." I reflected for a moment, and then

the whole thing came to me like a flash of lightning. *Yamba was approaching her own home once more—the very point from which we had both started eighteen months previously!* In the storm, as I have already said, we had passed Port Darwin altogether, having been driven out to sea.

I tell you, my heart nearly burst when I recalled the awful privations and hardships we had both experienced so recently; and when I realised that all these things had been absolutely in vain, and that once more my trembling hopes were to be dashed to the ground in the most appalling manner, I fell back into the canoe, utterly crushed with horror and impotent disappointment. Was there ever so terrible an experience? Take a map of Australia, and see for yourself my frightful blunder—mistaking the west coast of the Gulf of Carpentaria for the eastern waters of the Cape York Peninsula, and then blindly groping northward and westward in search of the settlement of Somerset, which in reality lay hundreds of miles north-east of me. I was unaware of the very existence of the great Gulf of Carpentaria. But were it not for having had to steer north to get out of the waterless plains, I might possibly have reached the north-eastern coast of the continent in due time, avoiding the Roper River altogether.

Yamba knelt by my side and tried to comfort me in her own sweet, quaint way, and she pictured to me—scant consolation—how glad her people would be to have us both back amongst them once more. She also urged what a great man I might be among her people if only I would stay and make my home with them. Even her voice, however, fell dully on my ears, for I was

fairly mad with rage and despair—with myself, for
not having gone overland to Port Darwin from Port
Essington, as, indeed, I should most certainly have
done were it not that Davis had assured me the
greater part of the journey lay through deadly swamps
and creeks, and great waters swarming with alligators.
I had even had in my mind the idea of attempting *to
reach Sydney overland!* but thought I would first of
all see what facilities in the way of reaching civilisation Port Darwin had to offer. Now, however, I was
back again in Cambridge Gulf,—in the very spot I had
left a year and a half ago, and where I had landed
with my four blacks from the island sand-spit. But
you, my readers, shall judge of my feelings.

We landed on an island at the mouth of the gulf,
and Yamba made smoke-signals to her friends on the
mainland, telling them of our return. We resolved it
would never do to confess we had been *driven* back.
No, we had roamed about and had come back to our
dear friends of our own free-will, feeling there was no
place like home! Just think what a *rôle* this was for
me to play,—with my whole being thrilling with an
agony of helpless rage and bitter disappointment.

This time, however, we did not wait for the blacks
to come out and meet us, but paddled straight for the
beach, where the chiefs and all the tribe were assembled in readiness to receive us. The first poignant
anguish being passed, and the warmth of welcome
being so cordial and excessive (they cried with joy), I
began to feel a little easier in my mind and more resigned to inexorable fate. The usual ceremony of
nose-rubbing on shoulders was gone through, and
almost every native present expressed his or her

individual delight at seeing us again. Then they
besieged us with questions, for we were now great
travellers. A spacious "humpy" or hut was built
without delay, and the blacks vied with one another
in bringing me things which I sorely needed, such as
fish, turtles, roots, and eggs.

That evening a *corroboree* on a gigantic scale was
held in my honour; and on every side the blacks manifested great rejoicing at my return,—which, of course,
they never dreamed was involuntary. Human nature
is, as I found, the same the world over, and one
reason for my warm welcome was, that my blacks had
just been severely thrashed by a neighbouring tribe,
and were convinced that if I would help them to
retaliate, they could not fail to inflict tremendous
punishment upon their enemies. By this time, having
become, as I said before, somewhat resigned to my
fate, I consented to lead them in their next battle, on
condition that two shield-bearers were provided to
protect me from the enemy's spears. This being the
first time I had ever undertaken war operations with
my friends, I determined that the experiment should
run no risk of failure, and that my dignity should in
no way suffer. I declared, first of all, that I would
choose as my shield-bearers the two most expert men
in the tribe. There was much competition for these
honoured posts, and many warriors demonstrated their
skill before me.

At length I chose two stalwart fellows, named
respectively Warriga and Bommera, and every day for
a week they conducted some trial manœuvres with
their friends. There would be a kind of ambush prepared, and flights of spears would be hurled at me,

only to be warded off with astonishing dexterity by my alert attendants. All I was provided with was my steel tomahawk and bow and arrows. I never really became expert with the spear and shield, and I knew only too well that if I handled these clumsily I should immediately lose prestige among the blacks.

After a week or two of practice and sham combats, I felt myself pretty safe with my two protectors, and I then began organising an army to lead against the enemy. Altogether I collected about 100 fighting men, each armed with a bundle of throwing spears, a shield made of light wood, and a short, heavy waddy or club for use at close quarters. When everything was in readiness, I marched off at the head of my "army" and invaded the enemy's country. We were followed by the usual crowd of women-folk, who saw to the commissariat department and did the transport themselves. On the first day out, we had to ford a large stream—a branch of the Victoria River, I think —and at length reached a suitable place in which to engage the enemy. It is difficult for me to fix the exact locality, but I should judge it to be between Murchison and Newcastle ranges. The country in which the operations took place was a fine open grassy plain, thinly skirted with trees and with mountains almost encircling it in the distance.

I ought here to describe my personal appearance on this important day, when, for the first time, I posed as a great chief, and led my people into battle, filled with the same enthusiasm that animated them. My hair was built up on strips of whalebone to a height of nearly two feet from my head, and was decorated with black and white cockatoo feathers. My face, which had now

become very dark from exposure to the sun, was decorated in four colours—yellow, white, black, and red.

There were two black-and-white arched stripes
across the forehead, and a yellow curving line across
each cheek under the eye.   I also wore a fairly long
beard, moustache, and side-whiskers.   There were
four different-coloured stripes on each arm, whilst on
the body were four vari-coloured stripes, two on each
side ; and a long, yellow, curving stripe extended across
the stomach, belt-wise.   Around my middle I wore a
kind of double apron of emu skin, with feathers.
There were other stripes of different-coloured ochres
on my legs, so that altogether you may imagine I
presented a terrifying appearance.   Of this, however,
I soon grew quite oblivious—a fact which I afterwards
had occasion bitterly to regret.   It were, indeed, well
for me that I had on subsequent occasions realised
better the bizarre nature of my appearance, for had I
done so I would probably have reached civilisation
years before I did.

At this period, then, you find me a fully equipped
war chief of the cannibal blacks, leading them on to
battle attired as one of their own chiefs in every
respect, and with nearly all their tribal marks on my
body.   When we reached the battle-ground, my men
sent up smoke-signals of defiance, announcing the fact
of our invasion, and challenging the enemy to come
down from the mountains and fight us.   This challenge
was promptly responded to by other smoke-signals,
but as at least a day must elapse before our antagonists
could arrive I spent the interval in devising a plan of
battle—oddly enough, on the lines of a famous historic
Swiss encounter at Grandson five or six centuries ago.

I arranged that fifty or sixty men, under the leadership of a chief, should occupy some high ground in our rear, to form a kind of ambush.

They were also to act as a reserve, and were instructed to come rushing to our assistance when I signalled for them, yelling out their weird war-cry of "Warra-hoo-oo,—warra-hoo-oo!" I concluded that this in itself would strike terror into the hearts of our opponents, who were accustomed to see the whole force engaged at one time, and knew nothing about troops held in reserve, or tactics of any kind whatsoever. The native method of procedure, as, I think, I have already remarked, was usually to dash pell-mell at one another after the abuse and fight, until one side or the other drew blood, without which no victory could be gained.

Just before the battle commenced I had a real inspiration which practically decided the affair without any fighting at all. It occurred to me that if I mounted myself on stilts, some eighteen inches high, and shot an arrow or two from my bow, the enemy would turn tail and bolt. And so it turned out. As the armies approached one another in full battle array they presented quite an imposing appearance, and when a suitable distance separated them they halted for the inevitable abusive parley. Into the undignified abuse, needless to remark, I did not enter, but kept well in the background. The spokesman of my tribe accused the enemy of being without pluck—said that they were cowards, and would soon have their livers eaten by the invaders. There was any amount of spear-brandishing, yelling, and gesticulating. For these blacks apparently find it impossible to come up to

THE ENEMY TURNED AND FLED

actual fighting pitch without first being worked up to an extraordinary degree of excitement.

When at length the abuse had got perfectly delirious, and the first spear was about to be thrown, I dashed to the front on my stilts. Several spears were launched at me, but my shield-bearers turned them on one side. I then shot half-a-dozen arrows into the enemy's ranks in almost as many seconds. The consternation produced by this flight of "invisible spears" was perfectly indescribable. With a series of appalling yells the enemy turned and fled pell-mell. My men gave chase, and wounded many of them. In the midst of the rout (the ruling thought being always uppermost), it occurred to me that it might be a useful stroke of business to make friends with this vanquished tribe, since they might possibly be of service to me in that journey to civilisation, the idea of which I never really abandoned from the day I was cast upon my little sand-spit. Furthermore, it flashed across my mind that if I made these nomadic tribes interested in me and my powers, news of my isolation might travel enormous distances inland —perhaps even to the borders of civilisation itself.

I communicated my ideas to my men, and they promptly entered into my views. They consented to help me with great readiness. While I was speaking with them, the vanquished warriors had re-formed into position some three or four hundred yards away, and were watching our movements with much curiosity. I now abandoned my stilts and my bow and arrows, and marched off with my chiefs in the direction of our late opponents.

As we approached, with branches in our hands as flags of truce, I signed to the startled men that we wished to be friendly; and when we halted, several chiefs came forward unarmed from the ranks of the enemy to confer with us. At first they were much surprised at my overtures, but I soon convinced them of my sincerity, and they at length consented to accept my offers of friendship. They acknowledged at once my superiority and that of my men, and presently all the chiefs came forward voluntarily and squatted at my feet in token of subjection. The two armies then united, and we all returned to a great encampment, where the women prepared a truly colossal feast for conquerors and conquered alike, and the greatest harmony prevailed. It was magnificent, but I am sure it was not war. The braves of both sides decorated themselves with many pigments in the evening, and the two tribes united in one gigantic *corroboree*, which was kept up all night, and for several days afterwards. We remained encamped in this district for about a week, holding continuous *corroboree*, and each day becoming more and more friendly with our late enemies. The country abounded in game, and as the rivers were also well stocked with fish the supply of food was abundant. At the end of the week, however, we retired to our respective homes, but, strangely enough, I felt I could no longer settle down to the old life among my friendly blacks.

The old desire for wandering came over me, and I resolved that some day in the near future I would make yet another attempt to reach civilisation, this time striking directly south. For a time, however, I forced myself to remain content, accompanying the men on their hunting expeditions and going out fishing with my devoted Yamba.

CHAPTER IX

I WAS much interested in the children of the blacks,
and observed all their interesting ways. It is not
too much to say in the case of both boys and girls that
they can swim as soon as they can walk. There is no
squeamishness whatever on the part of the mothers,
who leave their little ones to tumble into rivers, and
remain out naked in torrential rains, and generally
shift for themselves. From the time the boys are
three years old they commence throwing toy spears at
one another as a pastime. For this purpose, long dry
reeds, obtained from the swamps, are used, and the
little fellows practise throwing them at one another
from various distances, the only shields allowed being
the palms of their own little hands. They never seem
to tire of the sport, and acquire amazing dexterity at it.
At the age of nine or ten they abandon the reeds and
adopt a heavier spear, with a wooden shaft and a point
of hard wood or bone. All kinds of interesting competitions are constantly organised to test the boys' skill,

the most valued prizes being the approbation of parents and elders.

A small ring of hide, or creeper, is suspended from the branch of a tree, and the competitors have to throw their spears clean through it at a distance of twenty paces. All the chiefs and fighting men of the tribe assemble to witness these competitions, and occasionally some little award is made in the shape of anklets and bangles of small shells, strung together with human hair. The boys are initiated into the ranks of the "men and warriors" when they reach the age of about seventeen.

This initiation ceremony, by the way, is of a very extraordinary character. Many of the details cannot be published here. As a rule, it takes place in the spring, when the mimosa is in bloom, and other tribes come from all parts to eat the nuts and gum. We will say that there are, perhaps, twenty youths to undergo the ordeal, which is conducted far from all camps and quite out of the sight of women and children. The candidate prepares himself by much fasting, giving up meat altogether for at least a week before the initiation ceremony commences. In some cases candidates are despatched on a tramp extending over many days; and such implicit faith is placed in their honour that judges are not even sent with them to see that everything is carried out fairly. They must accomplish this task within a given period, and without partaking of either food or water during the whole time. No matter how great the temptation may be on the route, they conform strictly to the rules of the test, and would as soon think of running themselves through with a spear, as of seeking a water-hole. The inspectors who judge at this amazing examination are, of course, the old and experienced chiefs.

After the fasting comes the ordeal proper. The unfortunate candidate presents himself before one of the examiners, and settles his face into a perfectly stoical expression. He is then stabbed repeatedly on the outside of the thighs and in the arms (never once is an artery cut) ; and if he remains absolutely statuesque at each stab, he comes through the most trying part of the ordeal with flying colours. A motion of the lips, however, or a mutter—these are altogether fatal. Not even a toe must move in mute agony ; nor may even a muscle of the eyelid give an uneasy and involuntary twitch. If the candidate fails in a minor degree, he is promptly put back, to come up again for the next examination ; but in the event of his being unable to stand the torture, he is contemptuously told to go and herd with the women—than which there is no more humiliating expression.

While yet the candidate's wounds are streaming with blood, he is required to run with lightning speed for two or three miles and fetch back from a given spot a kind of toy lance planted in the ground. Then, having successfully passed the triple ordeals of fasting, stabbing, and running against time, and without food and water, the candidate, under the eyes of his admiring father, is at length received into the ranks of the bravest warriors, and is allowed to take a wife. At the close of the ceremony, the flow of blood from the candidate's really serious flesh-wounds is stopped by means of spiders' webs, powdered charcoal, and dry clay powder.

With regard to the girls, I am afraid they received but scant consideration.

M

Judged by our standard, the women were far from handsome. They had very bright eyes, broad, flat noses, low, narrow foreheads, and heavy chins. But there are comely exceptions. And yet at big *corroborees* on the occasion of a marriage, the men always chanted praises to the virtue and beauty of the bride!

The girl who possessed an exceptionally large and flat nose was considered a great beauty. Talking about noses, it was to me a remarkable fact, that the blacks consider a warrior with a big nose and large distended nostrils a man possessed of great staying power. For one thing, they consider his breathing apparatus exceptionally perfect.

As a general rule (there are exceptions in the case of a very "beautiful" woman), when a woman dies she is not even buried; she simply lies where she has fallen dead, and the camp moves on to another place and never returns to the unholy spot. And it may be mentioned here that the blacks never allude to a dead person by name, as they have a great horror of departed spirits. And so childish and suspicious are they, that they sometimes even cut off the feet of a dead man to prevent his running about and frightening them at inconvenient moments. I used to play upon their fears, going out into the bush after dark, and pretending to commune with the evil spirits. The voice of these latter was produced by means of reed whistles. Once I made myself a huge, hideous mask out of a kangaroo skin, with holes slit in it for the nose, mouth, and eyes. I would don this strange garb in the evenings, and prowl about the vicinity of the camp, holding blazing torches behind the mask, and emitting strange noises—sometimes howling like a wolf and at others shouting aloud in my natural voice. On these occasions the blacks thought I was in my natural element as a spirit. But they never ventured to follow me or attempted to satisfy themselves that I was not fooling them all the while. Yamba, of course, knew the joke, and as a rule helped me to dress for the farce, but she took good care never to tell any one the secret. No doubt had the blacks ever learned that it was all done for effect on my part, the result would have been very serious ; but I knew I was pretty secure because of the abnormal superstition prevalent among them.

The women, as I have before hinted, are treated in a horribly cruel manner, judged from our standpoint ; but in reality they know not what cruelty is, because they are absolutely ignorant of kindness. They are the beasts of burden, to be felled to the earth with a bludgeon when they err in some trivial respect ; and when camp is moved each woman carries virtually the whole household and the entire worldly belongings of the family. Thus it is a common sight to see a woman carrying a load consisting of one or two children and a quantity of miscellaneous implements, such as heavy grindstones, stone hatchets, sewing-bones, yam-sticks, &c. During the shifting of the camp the braves themselves stalk along practically unencumbered, save only for their elaborate shield, three spears (never more), and a stone tomahawk stuck in their belt of woven opossum hair. The men do not smoke, knowing nothing of tobacco, but their principal recreation and relaxation from the incessant hunting consists in the making of their war weapons, which is a very important part of their daily life. They will even fell a whole tree, as has already been explained, to make a single spear shaft. As to the shield, the elaborate carving upon it corresponds closely with the prowess of the owner; and the more laurels he gains, the more intricate and elaborate becomes the carving on his shield. Honour prevents undue pretence.

But we have wandered away from the consideration of the girl-children. The baby girls play with their brothers and participate in their fights until they are perhaps ten years of age. They are then expected to accompany their mothers on the daily excursions in search of roots. When the little girls are first taken out by their mothers they are instructed in the use of the yam-stick, with which the roots are dug up out of the earth. The stick used by the women is generally three feet or four feet long, but the girl novices use a short one about fifteen inches in length. Each woman, as I have said elsewhere, is also provided with a reed basket or net, in which to hold the roots, this being usually woven out of strings of prepared bark; or, failing that, native flax or palm straw.

But the unfortunate wife occasionally makes the acquaintance of the heavy yam-stick in a very unpleasant, not to say serious, manner. Of course, there are domestic rows. We will suppose that the husband has lately paid a great amount of attention to one of his younger wives—a circumstance which naturally gives great offence to one of the older women. This wife, when she has an opportunity and is alone with her husband, commences to sing or chant a plaint—a little thing of quite her own composing.

Into this song she weaves all the abuse which long experience tells her will lash her husband up to boiling-

point.   The later stanzas complain that the singer has
been taken from her own home among a nation of real
warriors to live among a gang of skulking cowards,

ABUSING THE HUSBAND

whose hearts, livers, and other vital organs are not at
all up to the standard of her people.

The epithets are carefully arranged up a scale until
they reach *bandy-legged* — an utterly unpardonable

insult. But there is, beyond this, one other unpublish-
able remark, which causes the husband to take up the
yam-stick and fell the singer with one tremendous blow,
which is frequently so serious as to disable her for many
days. The other women at once see to their sister, who
has incurred the wrath of her lord, and rub her wounds
with weird medicaments. The whole shocking business is regarded as quite an ordinary affair ; and after
the sufferer is able to get about again she bears her
husband not the slightest ill-feeling. You see, she
has had her say and paid for it.

The girls, as they grow up, are taught to cook
according to the native fashion, and are also required
to build ovens in the earth or sand ; make the fires,
build " break-winds," and generally help their mothers
in preparing meals. When at length the meal is cooked,
the manner of eating it is very peculiar. First of
all, the women retire into the background. The lord
and master goes and picks out the tit-bits for himself, and then sits down to eat them off a small
sheet of bark. More often, however, he simply tears
the meat in pieces with his hands. During his meal,
the wives and children are collected behind at a respectful distance, awaiting their own share. Then, as
the warrior eats, he literally hurls certain oddments
over his shoulder, which are promptly pounced upon
by the wives and children in waiting. It sometimes
happens, however, that a favourite child—a boy invariably, never a girl (it is the girls who are eaten
by the parents whenever there are any superfluous
children to be got rid of)—will approach his father
and be fed with choice morsels from the great man's
" plate."

Each tribe has its own particular country over which it roams at pleasure, and the boundaries are defined by trees, hillocks, mountains, rocks, creeks, and water-holes. And from these natural features the tribes occasionally get their names. Outside the tribal boundary—which often incloses a vast area—the blacks never go, except on a friendly visit to a neighbouring camp. Poaching is one of the things punishable with death, and even if any woman is caught hunting for food in another country she is seized and punished. I will tell you later on how even Yamba "put her foot" in it in this way.

The blacks are marvellously clever at tracking a man by his footprints, and a poacher from a neighbouring tribe never escapes their vigilance, even though he succeeds in returning to his own people without being actually captured. So assiduously do these blacks study the footprints of people they know and are friendly with, that they can tell at once whether the trespasser is an enemy or not; and if it be a stranger, a punitive expedition is at once organised against his tribe.

Gradually I came to think that each man's track must have an individuality about it quite as remarkable as the finger-prints investigated by Galton and Bertillon. The blacks could even tell a man's name and many other things about him, solely from his tracks—how, it is of course impossible for me to say. I have often known my blacks to follow a man's track *over hard rocks*, where even a disturbed leaf proved an infallible clue, yielding a perfectly miraculous amount of information. They will know whether a leaf has been turned over by the wind or by human agency!

But to continue my narrative. Yamba was very anxious that I should stay and make my home among her people, and so, with the assistance of other women, she built me a substantial beehive-shaped hut, fully twenty feet in diameter and ten feet high. She pointed out to me earnestly that I had everything I could possibly wish for, and that I might be a very great man indeed in the country if only I would take a prominent part in the affairs of the tribe. She also mentioned that so great was my prowess and prestige, that if I wished I might take unto myself a whole army of wives!— the number of wives being the sole token of greatness among these people. You see they had to be fed, and that implied many great attributes of skill and strength. Nevertheless, I pined for civilisation, and never let a day go by without scanning the bay and the open sea for a passing sail. The natives told me they had seen ships at various times, and that attempts had even been made to reach them in catamarans, but without success, so far out at sea were the vessels passing.

Gradually, about nine months after my strange return to my Cambridge Gulf home, there came a time when life became so monotonous that I felt I *must* have a change of some sort, or else go mad. I was on the very best of terms with all my blacks, but their mode of living was repulsive to me. I began to loathe the food, and the horrible cruelty to the women frequently sickened me. Whenever I saw one of these poor patient creatures felled, bleeding, to the earth, I felt myself being worked up into a state of dangerous nervous excitement, and I longed to challenge the brutal assailant as a murderous enemy. Each time, however, I sternly compelled myself to restrain my feelings. At length the spirit of unrest grew so strong that I determined to try a short trip inland in a direction I had never hitherto attempted. I intended to cross the big bay in my dug-out, round Cape Londonderry, and then go south among the beautiful islands down past Admiralty Gulf, which I had previously explored during my residence on the Cape, and where I had found food and water abundant; numerous caves, with mural paintings; quiet seas, and gorgeous vegetation. Yamba willingly consented to accompany me, and one day I set off on the sea once more, my faithful wife by my side, carrying her net full of odds and ends, and I with my bow and arrows, tomahawk, and stiletto; the two latter carried in my belt. I hoped to come across a ship down among the islands, for my natives told me that several had passed while I was away.

At length we started off in our dug-out, the sea being perfectly calm—more particularly in the early morning, when the tide was generally with us. After several days' paddling we got into a narrow passage between a long elevated island and the main, and from there found our way into an inlet, at the head of which appeared masses of wild and rugged rocks. These rocks were, in many places, decorated with a number of crude but striking mural paintings, which were protected from the weather. The drawings I found represented men chiefly. My own contributions consisted of life-size sketches of my wife, myself, and Bruno. I emphasised my long hair, and also reproduced my bow and arrow. This queer "art gallery" was well lighted, and the rock smooth. We found the spot a very suitable one for camping;

in fact, there were indications on all sides that the
place was frequently used by the natives as a camping-
ground.   A considerable quantity of bark lay strewn
about the ground in sheets, which material my wife
told me was used by the natives as bedding.   This
was the first time I had known the black-fellows to use
any material in this way.   I also came across traces
of a feast—such as empty oyster shells in very large
heaps, bones of animals, &c.   The waters of the inlet
were exceedingly well stocked with fish ; and here I
saw large crayfish for the first time.   I caught and
roasted some, and found them very good eating.   This
inlet might possibly be in the vicinity of Montague
Sound, a little to the south of Admiralty Gulf.

We stayed a couple of days in this beautiful spot,
and then pushed down south again, always keeping
close under shelter of the islands on account of our
frail craft.   The seas through which we paddled
were studded with innumerable islands, some rocky
and barren, others covered with magnificent foliage
and grass.   We landed on several of these, and on
one—it might have been Bigges Island—I discovered
a high cairn or mound of stones erected on the most
prominent point.   Yamba told me that this structure
was not the work of a native.   She explained that
the stones were laid too regularly.   A closer examination convinced me that the cairn had been built by
some European—possibly a castaway—and that at
one time it had probably been surmounted by a flag-
staff as a signal to passing ships.   Food was very
plentiful on this island, roots and yams being obtainable in great abundance.   Rock wallabies were also
plentiful.   After leaving this island we continued our

PAINTINGS ON THE ROCKS

journey south, paddling only during the day, and always with the tide, and spending the night on land. By the way, whilst among the islands, I came across, at various times, many sad signs of civilisation, in the form of a lower mast of a ship, and a deck-house, a wicker-basket, empty brandy cases, and other flotsam and jetsam, which, I supposed, had come from various wrecks. After having been absent from my home in Cambridge Gulf, two or three months, I found myself in a large bay, which I now know to be King's Sound. I had come across many tribes of natives on my way down. Some I met were on the islands on which we landed, and others on the mainland. Most of these black-fellows knew me both personally and by repute, many having been present at the great whale feast. The natives at King's Sound recognised me, and gave me a hearty invitation to stay with them at their camp. This I consented to do, and my friends then promised to set all the other tribes along the coast on the look-out for passing vessels, so that I might immediately be informed by smoke-signals when one was in sight. Not long after this came an item of news which thrilled me through and through.

One of the chiefs told me quite casually that at another tribe, some days' journey away, the chief had TWO WHITE WIVES. They had, he went on to explain, a skin and hair exactly like my own; but in spite of even this assurance, after the first shock of amazement I felt confident that the captives were Malays. The news of their presence among the tribe in question was a well-known fact all along the coast of King's Sound. My informant had never actually *seen* the white women, but he was absolutely certain of their existence. He added that the captives had been seized after a fight with some white men, who had come to that coast in a "big catamaran." However, I decided to go and see for myself what manner of women they were. The canoe was beached well above the reach of the tides at Cone Bay, and then, accompanied by Yamba only, I set off overland on my quest. The region of the encampment towards which I now directed my steps lies between the Lennard River and the Fitzroy. The exact spot, as near as I can fix it on the chart, is a place called Derby, at the head of King's Sound. As we advanced the country became very rugged and broken, with numerous creeks intersecting it in every direction. Farther on, however, it developed into a rich, low-lying, park-like region, with water in abundance. To the north-west appeared elevated ranges. I came across many fine specimens of the bottle tree. The blacks encamped at Derby were aware of my coming visit, having had the news forwarded to them by means of the universal smoke-signals.

The camp described by my informant I found to be a mere collection of gunyahs, or break-winds, made of boughs, and I at once presented my "card"—the ubiquite passport stick; which never left me for a moment in all my wanderings. This stick was sent to the chief, who immediately manifested tokens of friendship towards me.

Unfortunately, however, he spoke an entirely different dialect from Yamba's; but by means of the sign language I explained to him that I wished to stay with him for a few "sleeps" (hand held to the side of the head, with fingers for numbers), and partake of his hospitality. To this he readily consented.

Now, I knew enough of the customs of the blacks to realise that, being a stranger among them, they would on request provide me with additional wives during my stay,—entirely as a matter of ceremonial etiquette; and it suddenly occurred to me that I might make very good use of this custom by putting in an immediate demand for the two white women—if they existed. You see, I wanted an interview with them, in the first place, to arrange the best means of getting them away. I confess I was consumed with an intense curiosity to learn their history—even to see them. I wondered if they could tell me anything of the great world now so remote in my mind. As a matter of courtesy, however, I spent the greater part of the day with the chief, for any man who manifests a desire for women's society loses caste immediately; and in the evening, when the fact of my presence among the tribe had become more extensively known, and their curiosity aroused by the stories that Yamba had taken care to circulate, I attended a great *corroboree*, which lasted nearly the whole of the night. As I was sitting near a big fire, joining in the chanting and festivities, Yamba noiselessly stole to my side, and whispered in my ear that *she had found the two white women.*

I remember I trembled with excitement at the prospect of meeting them. They were very young, Yamba added, and spoke "my" language—I never said "English," because this word would have conveyed nothing to her; and she also told me that the prisoners were in a dreadful state of misery. It was next explained to me that the girls, according to native custom, were the absolute property of the chief. He was seated not very far away from me, and was certainly one of the most ferocious and repulsive-looking creatures I have ever come across,—even among the blacks. He was over six feet high, and of rather a lighter complexion than his fellows,—almost like a Malay. The top of his head receded in a very curious manner, whilst the mouth and lower part of the face generally protruded like an alligator's, and gave him a truly diabolical appearance. I confess a thrill of horror passed through me, as I realised that two doubtless tenderly reared English girls were in the clutches of this monster. Once I thought I must have been dreaming, and that the memories of some old story-book I had read years ago were filling my mind with some fantastic delusion. For a moment I pictured to myself the feelings of their prosaic British relatives, could they only have known what had become of the long-lost loved ones—a fate more shocking and more fearful than any ever conceived by the writer of fiction. Of course, my readers will understand that much detail about the fate of these poor creatures must be suppressed for obvious reasons. But should any existing relatives turn up, I shall be only too happy to place at their disposal all the information I possess.

Presently, I grasped the whole terrible affair, and realised it as absolute fact ! My first impulse was to leap from the *corroboree* and go and reassure the unhappy victims in person, telling them at the same time that they might count on my assistance to the last. It was not advisable, however, to withdraw suddenly from the festivities, for fear my absence might arouse suspicion.

The only alternative that presented itself was to
send a note or message of some kind to them, and so
I asked Yamba to bring me a large fleshy leaf of a
water-lily, and then, with one of her bone needles, I

AN ORIGINAL LETTER

pricked, in printed English characters, "*A friend is
near; fear not.*" Handing this original letter to Yamba,
I instructed her to give it to the girls and tell them
to hold it up before the fire and read the perforations.
This done, I returned to the *corroboree*, still displaying a

N

feigned enthusiasm for the proceedings, but determined upon a bold and resolute course of action. I must say though, that at that particular moment I was not very sanguine of getting the girls away out of the power of this savage, who had doubtless won them from some of his fellows by more or less fair fighting.

I made my way over to where the chief was squatting, and gazed at him long and steadily. I remember his appearance as though it were but yesterday that we met. I think I have already said he was the most repulsive-looking savage I have ever come across, even among the Australian blacks. The curious raised scars were upon this particular chief both large and numerous. This curious form of decoration, by the way, is a very painful business. The general practice is to make transverse cuts with a sharp shell, or stone knife, on the chest, thighs, and sometimes on the back and shoulders. Ashes and earth are then rubbed into each cut, and the wound is left to close. Next comes an extremely painful gathering and swelling, and a little later the earth that is inside is gradually removed—sometimes with a feather. When the wounds finally heal up, each cicatrice stands out like a raised weal, and of these extraordinary marks the blacks are inordinately proud.

But to return to the chief who owned the girls. I must say that, apart from his awful and obviously stubborn face, he was a magnificently formed savage.

I commenced the conversation with him by saying, I presumed the usual courtesy of providing a wife would be extended to me during my stay. As I anticipated, he readily acquiesced, and I instantly followed up the concession by calmly remarking that I should like to have the two white women who were in the camp sent over to my "little place." To this suggestion he gave a point-blank refusal. I persisted, however, and taunted him with deliberately breaking the inviolable rules of courtesy; and at length he gave me to understand he would think the matter over.

All this time Yamba had been as busy as a showman out West. She had followed with unusual vigour her customary *rôle* of "advance agent," and had spread most ridiculously exaggerated reports of my supernatural prowess and magical attributes. I controlled the denizens of Spiritland, and could call them up in thousands to torment the blacks. I controlled the elements; and was in short all-powerful.

I must admit that this energetic and systematic "puffing" did a great deal of good, and wherever we went I was looked upon as a sort of wizard, entitled to very great respect, and the best of everything that was going.

For a long time the tribal chief persisted in his opposition to my request for the girls; but as most of his warriors were in my favour (I had given many appalling demonstrations in the bush at night), I knew he would submit sooner or later. The big *corroboree* lasted all night, and at length, before we separated on the second day, the great man gave way—with exceedingly bad grace. Of course, I did not disturb the girls at that hour, but next day I told Yamba to go and see them and arrange for an interview. She came back pretty soon, and then undertook to guide me to their "abode." The prospect of meeting white people once more—even these two poor unfortunates—threw me into a strange excitement, in the midst of which I quite forgot my own astonishing appearance, which was far more like that of a gaily decorated and gorgeously painted native chief than a civilised European. For it must be remembered that by this time I had long ago discarded all clothing, except an apron of emu feathers, whilst my skin was extremely dark and my hair hung down my back fully three feet, and was built up in a surprising way in times of war and *corroboree*.

I followed Yamba through the camp, getting more and more excited as we approached the girls' domicile. At length she stopped at the back of a crescent-shaped break-wind of boughs, and a moment later— eager, trembling, and almost speechless — I stood before the two English girls. Looking back now, I remember they presented a truly pitiable spectacle. They were huddled together on the sandy ground, naked, and locked in one another's arms. Before them burned a fire, which was tended by the women. Both looked frightfully emaciated and terrified—so much so, that as I write these words my heart beats faster with horror as I recall the terrible impression they made upon me. As they caught sight of me, they screamed aloud in terror. I retired a little way discomfited, remembering suddenly my own fantastic appearance. Of course, they thought I was another black fellow coming to torture them. All kinds of extraordinary reflections flashed through my mind at that moment. What would people in my beloved France, I wondered—or among my Swiss mountains, or in stately England—think of the fate that had overtaken these girls—a fate that would infallibly read

more like extravagant and even offensive fiction than
real, heart-rending fact?

I went back and stood before the girls, saying,
reassuringly, "Ladies, I am a white man and a friend;
and if you will only trust in me I think I can save
you."

Their amazement at this little speech knew no
bounds, and one of the girls became quite hysterical.
I called Yamba, and introduced her as my wife, and
they then came forward and clasped me by the hand,
crying, shudderingly, "Oh, save us! Take us away
from that fearful brute."

I hastily explained to them that it was solely because
I had resolved to save them that I had ventured into
the camp; but they would have to wait patiently until
circumstances favoured my plans for their escape. I
did not conceal from them that my being able to take
them away at all was extremely problematical; for I
could see that to have raised false hopes would have
ended in real disaster. Gradually they became quieter
and more reasonable—and my position obviously more
embarrassing. I quickly told them that, at any rate,
so long as I remained in the camp, they need not fear
any further visits from the giant chief they dreaded so
much, and with this reassurance I walked swiftly
away, followed by Yamba.

The laws of native hospitality absolutely forbade
any one to interfere with the girls during my stay, so,
easy in my mind, I made straight for the extensive
swamps which I knew lay a few miles from the camp.
In this wild and picturesque place I brought down,
with Yamba's assistance, a great number of cockatoos,
turkeys, and other wild fowl, which birds were promptly

skinned, my wife and I having in view a little amateur
tailoring which should render my future interviews with
the girls a little less embarrassing.   As a matter of fact,
I handed over the bird-skins to Yamba, and she, with
her bone needles and threads of kangaroo sinews, soon
made a couple of extraordinary but most serviceable
garments, which we immediately took back to the poor
girls, who were shivering with cold and neglect.   I at
once saw the reason of most of their suffering.

Their own clothing had apparently been lost or
destroyed, and the native women, jealous of the attention which the chief was bestowing upon the new-
comers, gave them little or no food.   Nor did the
jealous wives instruct the interlopers in the anointing
of their bodies with that peculiar kind of clay which
forms so effective a protection alike against the burning heat of the sun, the treacherous cold of the night-
winds, and the painful attacks of insects.   All the
information I could elicit from the girls that evening
was the fact that they had been shipwrecked, and had
already been captive among the blacks for three and
a half months.   The elder girl further said that they
were not allowed their liberty, because they had on
several occasions tried to put an end to their indescribable sufferings by committing suicide.   Anything more
extraordinary than the costumes we made for the girls
you never saw.   They were not of elaborate design,
being of the shape of a long sack, with holes for the
arms and neck; and they afterwards shrank in the
most absurd way.

CHAPTER X

AT our next interview, thanks to Yamba's good offices,
both girls were looking very much better than
when I first saw them; and then, consumed with
natural curiosity and a great desire to learn something
of the outside world, I begged them to tell me their
story.

The first thing I learnt was that they were two
sisters, named Blanche and Gladys Rogers, their
respective ages being nineteen and seventeen years.
Both girls were extremely pretty, the particular attrac-
tion about Gladys being her lovely violet eyes. It
was Blanche who, with much hysterical emotion, told
me the story of their painful experience, Gladys occasionally prompting her sister with a few interpolated
words.

Here, then, is Blanche Rogers's story, told as nearly
as possible in her own words. Of course it is absurd
to suppose that I can reproduce *verbatim* the fearful
story told by the unfortunate girl.

"My sister and I are the daughters of Captain Rogers, who commanded a 700-ton barque owned by our uncle." [I am not absolutely certain whether the girls were the daughters of the captain or the owner.—L. de R.] "We were always very anxious, even as children, to accompany our dear father on one of his long trips, and at length we induced him to take us with him when he set sail from Sunderland [not certain, this] in the year 1868 [or 1869], with a miscellaneous cargo bound for Batavia [or Singapore]. The voyage out was a very pleasant one, but practically without incident—although, of course, full of interest to us. The ship delivered her freight in due course, but our father failed to obtain a return cargo to take back with him to England. Now, as a cargo of some kind was necessary to clear the expenses of the voyage, father decided to make for Port Louis, in Mauritius, to see what he could do among the sugar-exporters there.

"On the way to Port Louis, we suddenly sighted a ship flying signals of distress. We at once hove to and asked what assistance we could render. A boat presently put off from the distressed vessel, and the captain, who came aboard, explained that he had run short of provisions and wanted a fresh supply—no matter how small—to tide him over his difficulty. He further stated that his vessel was laden with guano, and was also *en route* for Port Louis. The two captains had a long conversation together, in the course of which an arrangement was arrived at between them.

"We said we were in ballast, searching for freight, whereupon our visitor said: 'Why don't you make for the Lacepede Islands, off the north-west Australian coast, and load guano, which you can get there for nothing ?' We said we did not possess the necessary requisites in the shape of shovels, sacks, punts, wheel-barrows, and the like. These were promptly supplied by the other captain in part payment for the provisions we let him have. Thus things were eventually arranged to the entire satisfaction of both parties, and then the *Alexandria* (I think that was the name of the ship) proceeded on her way to Port Louis, whilst we directed our course to the Lacepede Islands.

" In due time we reached a guano islet, and the crew quickly got to work, with the result that in a very short time we had a substantial cargo on board. A day or two before we were due to leave, we went to father and told him we wanted very much to spend an evening on the island to visit the turtle-breeding ground. Poor father, indulgent always, allowed us to go ashore in a boat, under the care of eight men, who were to do a little clearing-up whilst they were waiting for us. We found, as you may suppose, a great deal to interest us on the island, and the time passed all too quickly. The big turtles came up with the full tide, and at once made nests for themselves on the beach by scraping out with their hind-flippers a hole about ten inches deep and five inches in diameter. The creatures then simply lay over these holes and dropped their eggs into them. We learned that the number of eggs laid at one sitting varies from twelve up to forty. We had great fun in collecting the eggs and generally play-ing with the turtles. I am afraid we got out of sight of the men, and did not notice that the weather showed decided signs of a sudden change. When at length the crew found us it was past midnight—though not very dark ; and though we ought to have been making preparations for returning to the ship, it was blowing hard. On account of this, the crew said they did not consider it advisable to launch the boat; and as we had our big cloaks with us, it was decided to remain on the island all night to see if the weather improved by the morning. Our ship was anchored fully three miles away, outside the reefs, and it would have been impossible, in the sea that was running, to pull out to her. There was only one white man among our protectors, and he was a Scotchman. The men made a fire in a more or less sheltered spot, and round this we squatted, the men outside us, so as to afford us greater protection from the storm.

"In this way the whole night passed, principally in telling stories of adventure by sea and land. We all hoped that by morning at any rate the wind would have abated; but at daybreak, as we looked anxiously out over the tempestuous sea, it was blowing as hard as ever; and by ten o'clock the storm had increased to a terrific gale. Our men unanimously declared they dared not attempt to reach the ship in their small boat, although we could see the vessel plainly riding at her old anchorage. What followed Gladys and I gathered afterwards, just before the dreadful thing happened. We were all safe enough on land, but it became evident to the sailors with us that the ship could not weather the storm unless she weighed anchor and stood out to sea. The crew watched with eager eyes to see what my father would do. Manifestly he was in too much distress of mind about us to go right away, and I suppose he preferred to trust to the strength of his cables.

"Shortly after ten o'clock in the morning, however,

the ship began to drag her anchors, and in spite of all
that could be done by my father and his officers, the
shapely little vessel gradually drifted on to the coral
reefs. All this time Gladys and I, quite ignorant of
seamanship and everything pertaining to it, were watching the doomed ship, and from time to time asked
anxiously what was the meaning of all the excitement.
The men returned us evasive answers, like the kind-
hearted fellows they were, and cheered us up in
every possible way. Presently we heard signals of
distress (only we didn't know they were signals of
distress then), and our companions saw that the
captain realised only too well his terribly dangerous
position. It was, however, utterly impossible for them
to have rendered him any assistance. The rain was
now descending in sheets, lashing the giant waves with
a curious hissing sound. The sky was gloomy and
overcast, and altogether the outlook was about as
terrible as it could well be. Presently we became
dreadfully anxious about our father; but when the
sailors saw that the ship was apparently going to pieces,
they induced us to return to the camp fire and sit there
till the end was past. By this time the barque was
being helplessly buffeted about amongst the reefs, a
little less than a mile and a half from shore.

" Suddenly, as we afterwards learnt, she gave a lurch
and completely disappeared beneath the turbulent
waters, without even her mastheads being left standing
to show where she had gone down. She had evidently
torn a huge hole in her side in one of her collisions
with the jagged reefs, for she sank with such rapidity
that not one of the boats could be launched, and not
a single member of the crew escaped—so far as we

knew—save only those who were with us on the island.
The loss of the ship was, of course, a terrible blow
to our valiant protectors, who were now left absolutely
dependent on their own resources to provide food and
means of escape. Thus passed a dreadful day and
night, the men always keeping us ignorant of what
had happened. They resolved to make for Port
Darwin, on the mainland of Australia, which was
believed to be quite near; for we had no water, there
being none on the guano island. The interval was
spent in collecting turtles' eggs and sea-fowl, which
were intended as provisions for the journey. Next
morning the storm had quite abated, and gradually
the stupefying news was communicated to us that our
father and his ship had gone down with all hands in
the night. Indeed, these kind and gentle men told
us the whole story of their hopes and doubts and fears,
together with every detail of the terrible tragedy of
the sea that had left us in such a fearful situation.
No one needs to be told our feelings.

" Shortly before noon next day the sail was hoisted ;
we took our places in the boat, and soon were rippling
pleasantly through the now placid waters, leaving the
guano island far behind. The wind being in our favour,
very satisfactory progress was made for many hours ;
but at length, tortured by thirst, it was decided to land
on the mainland or the first island we sighted, and lay
in a stock of water—if it was obtainable. Gladys and
I welcomed the idea of landing, because by this time
we were in quite a disreputable condition, not having
washed for several days. It was our intention, while
the crews were getting water and food, to retire to the
other side of the island, behind the rocks, and there

have a nice bath. The boat was safely beached, and there being no signs of natives anywhere in the vicinity, the men soon laid in a stock of water without troubling to go very far inland for it. My sister and I at once retired several hundred yards away, and there undressed and went into the water.

"We had scarcely waded out past our waists when, to our unspeakable horror, a crowd of naked blacks, hideously painted and armed with spears, came rushing down the cliffs towards us, yelling and whooping in a way I am never likely to forget. They seemed to rise out of the very rocks themselves; and I really think we imagined we were going mad, and that the whole appalling vision was a fearful dream, induced by the dreadful state of our nerves. My own heart seemed to stand still with terror, and the only description I can give of my sensations was that I felt absolutely paralysed. At length, when the yelling monsters were quite close to us, we realised the actual horror of it all, and screaming frantically, tried to dash out of the water towards the spot where we had left our clothes. But some of the blacks intercepted us, and we saw one man deliberately making off with the whole of our wearing apparel.

"Of course, when the boat's crew heard the uproar they rushed to our assistance, but when they were about twenty yards from our assailants, the blacks sent a volley of spears among them with such amazing effect that every one of the sailors fell prostrate to the earth. The aim of the blacks was wonderfully accurate.

"Some of our men, however, managed to struggle to their feet again, in a heroic but vain endeavour to reach our side; but these poor fellows were at once butchered in the most shocking manner by the natives,

INTERCEPTED BY THE BLACKS

who wielded their big waddies or clubs with the most sickening effect. Indeed, so heart-rending and horrible was the tragedy enacted before our eyes, that for a long time afterwards we scarcely knew what was happening to us, so dazed with horror were we. For myself, I have a faint recollection of being dragged across the island by the natives, headed by the hideous and gigantic chief who afterwards claimed us as his 'wives.' We were next put on board a large cata- maran, our hands and feet having been previously tied with hair cords ; and we were then rowed over to the mainland, which was only a few miles away. We kept on asking by signs that our clothing might be returned to us, but the blacks tore the various garments into long strips before our eyes, and wrapped the rags about their heads by way of ornament. We reached the encampment of the black-fellows late that same evening, and were at once handed over to the charge of the women, who kept us close prisoners and—so far as we could judge—abused us in the most violent manner. Of course, I don't know exactly what their language meant, but I do know that they treated us shamefully, and struck us from time to time. I gathered that they were jealous of the attention shown to us by the big chief.

"We afterwards learnt that the island on which the terrible tragedy took place was not really inhabited, but the blacks on the coast had, it appeared, seen our boat far out at sea, and watched it until we landed for water. They waited a little while in order to lull the crew into a sense of fancied security, and then, without another moment's delay, crossed over to the island and descended upon us.

"We passed a most wretched night. Never—never can I hope to describe our awful feelings. We suffered intensely from the cold, being perfectly naked. We

were not, however, molested by any of our captors.
But horror was to be piled on horror's head, for the
next day a party of the blacks returned to the island
and brought back the dead bodies of all the murdered
sailors.   At first we wondered why they went to this
trouble; and when, at length, it dawned upon us that
a great cannibal feast was in preparation, I think we
fainted away.

"We did not actually see the cooking operations, but
the odour of burning flesh was positively intolerable;
and we saw women pass our little grass shelters carrying some human arms and legs, which were doubtless
their own families' portions.   I thought we should both
have gone mad, but notwithstanding this, we did keep
our reason.   Our position, however, was so revolting
and so ghastly, that we tried to put an end to our lives
by strangling ourselves with a rope made of plaited
grass.   But we were prevented from carrying out
our purpose by the women-folk, who thereafter kept
a strict watch over us.   It seemed to me, so embarrassing were the attentions of the women, that
these pitiable but cruel creatures were warned by the
chief that, if anything befell us, they themselves would
get into dire trouble.   All this time, I could not seem
to think or concentrate my mind on the events that had
happened.   I acted mechanically, and I am absolutely
certain that neither Gladys nor myself realised our
appalling position.

"In the meantime, it seems, a most sanguinary fight
had taken place among four of the principal blacks who
had assisted in the attack upon our sailors, the object
of the fight being to decide who should take possession of us.

"One night we managed to slip out of the camp without attracting the notice of the women, and at once rushed down to the beach, intending to throw ourselves into the water, and so end a life which was far worse than death. We were, unfortunately, missed, and just as we were getting beyond our depth a party of furious blacks rushed down to the shore, waded out into the water and brought as out.

"After this incident our liberty was curtailed altogether, and we were moved away. The women were plainly told—so we gathered—that if anything happened to us, death, and nothing less, would be their portion. Now that we could no longer leave the little break-wind that sheltered us, we spent the whole of our time in prayer—mainly for death to release us from our agonies. I was surprised to see that the women themselves, though nude, were not much affected by the intense cold that prevailed at times, but we afterwards learnt that they anointed their naked bodies with a kind of greasy clay, which formed a complete coating all over their bodies. During the ensuing three months the tribe constantly moved their camp, and we were always taken about by our owner and treated with the most shocking brutality. The native food, which consisted of roots, kangaroo flesh, snakes, caterpillars, and the like, was utterly loathsome to us, and for several days we absolutely refused to touch it, in the hope that we might die of starvation.

"Finally, however, the blacks compelled us to swallow some mysterious-looking meat, under threats of torture from those dreadful fire-sticks. You will not be surprised to learn that, though life became an intolerable burden to us, yet, for the most part, we obeyed our

o

captors submissively. At the same time, I ought to tell you that now and again we disobeyed deliberately, and did our best to lash the savages into a fury, hoping that they would spear us or kill us with their clubs. Our sole shelter was a break-wind of boughs with a fire in front. The days passed agonisingly by; and when I tell you that every hour—nay, every moment—was a crushing torture, you will understand what that phrase means. We grew weaker and weaker, and, I believe, more emaciated. We became delirious and hysterical, and more and more insensible to the cold and hunger. No doubt death would soon have come to our relief had you not arrived in time to save us."

This, then, was the fearful story which the unfortunate Misses Rogers had to tell. The more I thought it over, the more I realised that no Englishwomen had ever lived to tell so dreadful an experience. I compared their story with mine, and felt how different it was. I was a man, and a power in the land from the very first—treated with the greatest consideration and respect by all the tribes. And, poor things, they were terribly despondent when I explained to them that it was impossible for me to take them right away at once. Had I attempted to do so surreptitiously, I should have outraged the sacred laws of hospitality, and brought the whole tribe about my ears and theirs. Besides, I had fixed upon a plan of my own; and, as the very fact of my presence in the camp was sufficient protection for the girls, I implored them to wait patiently and trust in me.

That very night I called Yamba to me and despatched her to a friendly tribe we had encountered in the King Leopold Ranges—perhaps three days' journey away. I instructed her to tell these blacks that I was in great danger, and, therefore, stood in need of a body of warriors, who ought to be sent off immediately to my assistance. They knew me much better than I did them. They had feasted on the whale. As I concluded my message, I looked into Yamba's eyes and told her the case was desperate. Her dear eyes glowed in the firelight, and I saw that she was determined to do or die. I trusted implicitly in her fertility of resource and her extraordinary intelligence.

In a few days she returned, and told me that everything had been arranged, and a body of armed warriors would presently arrive in the vicinity of the camp, ready to place themselves absolutely at my service.

And sure enough, a few days later twenty stalwart warriors made their appearance at the spot indicated by Yamba; but as I did not consider the force quite large enough for my purpose, I sent some of them back with another message asking for reinforcements, and saying that the great white chief was in danger. Finally, when I felt pretty confident of my position, I marched boldly forward into the camp with my warriors, to the unbounded amazement of the whole tribe with whose chief I was sojourning. He taxed me with having deceived him when I said I was alone, and he also accused me of outraging the laws of hospitality by bringing a party of warriors, obviously hostile, into his presence.

I wilfully ignored all these points, and calmly told

him I had been thinking over the way in which
he had acquired the two white girls, and had come
to the conclusion that he had no right to them at
all.   Therefore, I continued airily, it was my intention to take them away forthwith.   I pointed out to
the repulsive giant that he had not obtained the girls
by fair means, and if he objected to my taking them
away, it was open to him, according to custom, to
sustain his claim to ownership by fighting me for
the "property."

Now, these blacks are neither demonstrative nor
intelligent, but I think I never saw any human being
so astonished in the whole of my life.   It dawned
upon him presently, however, that I was not joking,
and then his amazement gave place to the most
furious anger.   He promptly accepted my challenge,
greatly to the delight of all the warriors in his own
tribe, with whom he was by no means popular.   But,
of course, the anticipation of coming sport had something to do with their glee at the acceptance of the
challenge.   The big man was as powerful in build
as he was ugly, and the moment he opened his mouth
I realised that for once Yamba had gone too far in
proclaiming my prodigious valour.   He said he had
heard about my wonderful "flying-spears," and
declined to fight me if I used such preternatural
weapons.   It was therefore arranged *that we should
wrestle*—the one who overthrew the other twice out
of three times to be declared the victor.   I may say
that this was entirely my suggestion, as I had always
loved trick wrestling when at school, and even had a
special tutor for that purpose—M. Viginet, an agile
little Parisian, living in Geneva.   He was a Crimean

veteran. The rank-and-file of the warriors, however, did not look upon this suggestion with much favour, as they thought it was not paying proper respect to my wonderful powers. I assured them I was perfectly satisfied, and begged them to let the contest proceed.

Then followed one of the most extraordinary combats on record. Picture to yourself, if you can, the agony of mind of poor little Blanche and Gladys Rogers during the progress of the fight; and also imagine the painful anxiety with which I went in to win.

A piece of ground about twenty feet square was lightly marked out by the blacks with their waddies, and the idea was that, to accomplish a throw, the wrestler had to hurl his opponent clean outside the boundary. We prepared for the combat by covering our bodies with grease; and I had my long hair securely tied up into a kind of "chignon" at the back of my head. My opponent was a far bigger man than myself, but I felt pretty confident in my ability as a trick wrestler, and did not fear meeting him. What I did fear, however, was that he would dispute the findings of the umpires if they were in my favour, in which case there might be trouble. I had a shrewd suspicion that the chief was something of a coward at heart. He seemed nervous and anxious, and I saw him talking eagerly with his principal supporter. As for myself, I constantly dwelt upon the ghastly plight of the two poor girls. I resolved that, with God's help, I would vanquish my huge enemy and rescue them from their dreadful position. I was in splendid condition, with muscles like steel from incessant walking. At length the warriors squatted down upon the ground in the form of a crescent, the chiefs in the foreground, and every detail of the struggle that followed was observed with the keenest interest.

I was anxious not to lose a single moment. I felt that if I thought the matter over I might lose heart, so I suddenly bounded into the arena. My opponent was there already—looking, I must say, a little undecided.

In a moment his huge arms were about my waist and shoulders. It did not take me very long to find out that the big chief was going to depend more upon his weight than upon any technical skill in wrestling. He possessed none. He first made a great attempt to force me upon my knees and then backwards ; but I wriggled out of his grasp, and a few minutes later an opening presented itself for trying the "cross-buttock" throw. There was not a moment to be lost. Seizing the big man round the thigh I drew him forward, pulled him over on my back, and in the twinkling of an eye—certainly before I myself had time to realise what had happened —he was hurled right over my head outside the enclosure. The spectators—sportsmen all—frantically slapped their thighs, and I knew then that I had gained their sympathies. My opponent, who had alighted on his head and nearly broken his neck, rose to his feet, looking dazed and furious that he should have been so easily thrown. When he faced me for the second time in the square he was much more cautious, and we struggled silently, but forcefully, for some minutes without either gaining any decided advantage. Oddly enough, at the time I was not struck by the dramatic element of the situation ; but now that I have returned to civilisation I *do* see the extraordinary nature of the combat as I look back upon those dreadful days.

Just picture the scene for yourself. The weird, unexplored land stretches away on every side, though one could not see much of it on account of the grassy hillocks. I, a white man, was alone among the blacks in the terrible land of "Never Never,"—as the Australians call their *terra incognita ;* and I was wrestling with a gigantic cannibal chief for the possession of two delicately-reared English girls, who were in his power. Scores of other savages squatted before us, their repulsive faces aglow with interest and excitement. Very fortunately Bruno was not on the spot. I knew what he was of old, and how he made my quarrels his with a strenuous energy and eagerness that frequently got himself as well as his master into serious trouble. Knowing this, I had instructed Yamba to keep him carefully away, and on no account let him run loose.

Fully aware that delays were dangerous, I gripped my opponent once more and tried to throw him over my back, but this time he was too wary, and broke away from me. When we closed again he commenced his old tactics of trying to crush me to the ground by sheer weight, but in this he was not successful. Frankly, I knew his strength was much greater than mine, and that the longer we wrestled the less chance I would have. Therefore, forcing him suddenly sideways, so that he stood on one leg, I tripped him, hurling him violently from me sideways; and his huge form went rolling outside the square, to the accompaniment of delighted yells from his own people.

I cannot describe my own sensations, for I believe I was half mad with triumph and excitement. I must not forget to mention that I, too, fell to the ground, but fortunately well within the square. I was greatly astonished to behold the glee of the spectators—but, then, the keynote of their character is an intense love of deeds of prowess, especially such deeds as provide exciting entertainment.

The vanquished chief sprang to his feet before I did, and ere I could realise what was happening, he dashed at me as I was rising and dealt me a terrible blow in the mouth with his clenched fist. As he was a magnificently muscular savage, the blow broke several of my teeth and filled my mouth with blood. My lips, too, were very badly cut, and altogether I felt half stunned. The effect upon the audience was astounding. The warriors leaped to their feet, highly incensed at the cowardly act, and some of them would actually have speared their chief then and there had I not forestalled them. I was furiously angry, and dexterously drawing my stiletto from its sheath so as not to attract attention, I struck at my opponent with all my force, burying the short, keen blade in his heart. He fell dead at my feet with a low, gurgling groan. As I withdrew the knife, I held it so that the blade extended up my forearm and was quite hidden. This, combined with the fact that the fatal wound bled mainly internally, caused the natives to believe I had struck my enemy dead by some super-natural means. The act was inevitable.

You will observe that by this time I would seize
every opportunity of impressing the blacks by an
almost intuitive instinct ; and as the huge savage lay
dead on the ground, I placed my foot over the

A DEADLY COMBAT

wound, folded my arms, and looked round trium-
phantly upon the enthusiastic crowd, like a gladiator
of old.

According to law and etiquette, however, the nearest

relatives of the dead man had a perfect right to challenge me, but they did not do so, probably because they were disgusted at the unfair act of my opponent. I put the usual question, but no champion came forward ; on the contrary, I was overwhelmed with congratulations, and even offers of the chieftainship. I am certain, so great was the love of fair-play among these natives, that had I not killed the chief with my stiletto, his own people would promptly have speared him. The whole of this strange tragedy passed with surprising swiftness ; and I may mention here that, as I saw the chief rushing at me, I thought he simply wanted to commence another round. His death was actually an occasion for rejoicing in the tribe. The festivities were quickly ended, however, when I told the warriors that I intended leaving the camp with the two girls in the course of another day or so, to return to my friends in the King Leopold Ranges. In reality it was my intention to make for my own home in the Cambridge Gulf district. The body of the chief was not eaten (most likely on account of the cowardice he displayed), but it was disposed of according to native rites. The corpse was first of all half-roasted in front of a huge fire, and then, when properly shrivelled, it was wrapped in bark and laid on a kind of platform built in the fork of a tree.

The girls were kept in ignorance of the fatal termination of the wrestling match, as I was afraid it might give them an unnecessary shock. After twelve or fourteen days in the camp, we quietly took our departure. Our party consisted of the two girls, who were nearly frantic with excitement over their

DISPOSING OF THE CHIEF

escape ; Yamba, and myself — together with the friendly warriors who had so opportunely come to my assistance.

We had not gone far, however, before the girls complained of sore feet. This was not surprising, considering the burning hot sand and the rough country we were traversing, which was quite the worst I had yet seen—at any rate, for the first few days' march after we got out of the level country in the King's Sound region. I, therefore, had to rig up a kind of hammock made of woven grass, and this, slung between two poles, served to carry the girls by turns, the natives acting as bearers. But being totally unused to carrying anything but their own weapons, they proved deplorably inefficient as porters, and after a time, so intolerable to them did the labour become, the work of carrying the girls devolved upon Yamba and myself. Gladys, the younger girl, suffered most, but both were weak and footsore and generally incapable of much exertion. Perhaps a reaction had set in after the terrible excitement of the previous days. Soon our escort left us, to return to their own homes ; and then Yamba and I had to work extremely hard to get the girls over the terribly rough country. Fortunately there was no need for hurry, and so we proceeded in the most leisurely manner possible, camping frequently and erecting grass shelters for our delicate charges. Food was abundant, and the natives friendly.

CHAPTER XI

AT length we came to a stately stream that flowed
in a NNE. direction to Cambridge Gulf. This,
I believe, is the Ord River. Here we constructed a
catamaran, and were able to travel easily and luxu-
riously upon it, always spending the night ashore.
This catamaran was exceptionally large, and long
enough to admit of our standing upright on it with
perfect safety. After crossing the King Leopold
Ranges we struck a level country, covered with rich,
tall grass, and well though not thickly wooded. The
rough granite ranges, by the way, we found rich
in alluvial and reef tin. Gradually the girls grew
stronger and brighter. At this time they were, as
you know, clad in their strange " sack " garments of
bird-skins ; but even before we reached the Ord River
these began to shrink to such an extent that the
wearers were eventually wrapped as in a vice, and
were scarcely able to walk. Yamba then made some
make-shift garments out of opossum skins.

As the girls' spirits rose higher and higher I was assailed by other misgivings. I do not know quite how the idea arose, but somehow they imagined that their protector's home was a more or less civilised settlement, with regular houses, furnished with pianos and other appurtenances of civilised life! So great was their exuberance that I could not find it in my heart to tell them that they were merely going among my own friendly natives, whose admiration and affection for myself only differentiated them from the other cannibal blacks of unknown Australia.

When first I saw these poor girls, in the glow of the firelight, and in their rude shelter of boughs, they looked like old women, so haggard and emaciated were they; but now, as the spacious catamaran glided down the stately Ord, they gradually resumed their youthful looks, and were very comely indeed. The awful look of intolerable anguish that haunted their faces had gone, and they laughed and chatted with perfect freedom. They were like birds just set at liberty. They loved Bruno from the very first; and he loved them. He showed his love, too, in a very practical manner, by going hunting on his own account and bringing home little ducks to his new mistresses. Quite of his own accord, also, he would go through his whole répertoire of tumbling tricks; and whenever the girls returned to camp from their little wanderings, with bare legs bleeding from the prickles, Bruno would lick their wounds and manifest every token of sympathy and affection.

Of course, after leaving the native encampment, it was several weeks before we made the Ord River, and then we glided down that fine stream for many days, spearing fish in the little creeks, and generally amusing ourselves, time being no object. I have, by the way, seen enormous shoals of fish in this river— mainly mullet—which can only be compared to the vast swarms of salmon seen in the rivers of British Columbia.

We came across many isolated hills on our way to the river, and these delayed us very considerably, because we had to go round them. Here, again, there was an abundance of food, but the girls did not take very kindly to the various meats, greatly preferring the roots which Yamba collected. We came upon fields of wild rice, which, apart from any other consideration, lent great beauty to the landscape, covering the country with a pinkish-white blossom. We forced ourselves to get used to the rice, although it was very insipid without either salt or sugar.

Sometimes, during our down-river journey, we were obliged to camp for days and nights without making any progress. This, however, was only after the river became tidal and swept up against us.

When at length we would put off again in a homeward direction, I sang many little *chansons* to my fair companions. The one that pleased them most, having regard to our position, commenced—

> " Filez, filez, mon beau navire,
> Car la bonheur m'attend la bas."

Whenever the girls appeared to be brooding over the terrible misfortunes they had undergone, I would tell them my own story, which deeply affected them. They would often weep with tender sympathy over the series of catastrophes that had befallen me. They sang to me, too—chiefly hymns, however—such as "Rock of Ages," "Nearer, my God, to Thee," "There is a Happy Land," and many others. We were constantly meeting new tribes of natives, and for the most part were very well received. Bruno, however, always evinced an unconquerable aversion for the blacks. He was ever kind to the children, though mostly in disgrace with the men—until they knew him.

When at length we reached my own home in Cambridge Gulf, the natives gave us a welcome so warm that in some measure at least it mitigated the girls' disappointment at the absence of civilisation.

You see, my people were delighted when they saw me bringing home, as they thought, two white wives ; "for now," they said, "the great white chief will certainly remain among us for ever." There were no wars going on just then, and so the whole tribe gave themselves up to festivities.

The blacks were also delighted to see the girls, though of course they did not condescend to greet them, they being mere women, and therefore beneath direct notice.

I ought to mention here, that long before we reached my home we were constantly provided with escorts of natives from the various tribes we met. These people walked along the high banks or disported themselves in the water like amphibians, greatly to the delight of the girls. We found the banks of the Ord very thickly populated, and frequently camped at night with different parties of natives. Among these we actually came across some I had fought against many months previously.

P

As we neared my home, some of our escort sent up smoke-signals to announce our approach—the old and wonderful "Morse code" of long puffs, short puffs, spiral puffs, and the rest; the variations being produced by damping down the fire or fires with green boughs. Yamba also sent up signals. The result was that crowds of my own people came out in their catamarans to meet us. My reception, in fact, was like that accorded a successful Roman General. Needless to say, there was a series of huge *corroborees* held in our honour. The first thing I was told was that my hut had been burnt down in my absence (fires are of quite common occurrence); and so, for the first few days after our arrival, the girls were housed in a temporary grass shelter, pending the construction of a substantial hut built of logs. Now, as logs were very unusual building material, a word of explanation is necessary.

The girls never conquered their fear of the blacks —even *my* blacks; and therefore, in order that they might feel secure from night attack (a purely fanciful idea, of course), I resolved to build a hut which should be thoroughly spear-proof. Bark was also used extensively, and there was a thatch of grass. When finished, our new residence consisted of three fair-sized rooms—one for the girls to sleep in, one for Yamba and myself, and a third as a general "living room,"—though, of course, we lived mainly *en plein air*. I also arranged a kind of veranda in front of the door, and here we frequently sat in the evening, singing, chatting about distant friends; the times that were, and the times that were to be.

Let the truth be told. When these poor young

ladies came to my hut their faces expressed their bitter disappointment, and we all wept together the greater part of the night. Afterwards they said how sorry they were thus to have given way; and they begged me not to think them ungrateful. However, they soon resigned themselves to the inevitable, buoyed up by the inexhaustible optimism of youth; and they settled down to live as comfortably as possible among the blacks until some fortuitous occurrence should enable us all to leave these weird and remote regions. The girls were in constant terror of being left alone—of being stolen, in fact. They had been told how the natives got wives by stealing them; and they would wake up in the dead of the night screaming in the most heart-rending manner, with a vague, nameless terror. Knowing that the ordinary food must be repulsive to my new and delightful companions, I went back to a certain island, where, during my journey from the little sand-spit to the main, I had hidden a quantity of corn beneath a cairn.

This corn I now brought back to my Gulf home, and planted for the use of the girls. They always ate the corn green in the cob, with a kind of vegetable "milk" that exudes from one of the palm-trees. When they became a little more reconciled to their new surroundings, they took a great interest in their home, and would watch me for hours as I tried to fashion rude tables and chairs and other articles of furniture. Yamba acted as cook and waitress, but after a time the work was more than she could cope with unaided. You see, she had to *find* the food as well as cook it. The girls, who were, of course, looked upon as my wives by the tribe (this was their greatest protection), knew nothing about root-hunting, and therefore they did not attempt to accompany Yamba on her daily expeditions. I was in something

MAKING THE CHAIRS

of a dilemma. If I engaged other native women to help Yamba, they also would be recognised as my wives. Finally, I decided there was nothing left for me but to acquire five more helpmates, who were of the greatest assistance to Yamba.

Of course, the constant topic of conversation was our ultimate escape overland; and to this end we made little expeditions to test the girls' powers of endurance. I suggested, during one of our conversations, that we should either make for Port Essington, or else go overland in search of Port Darwin; but the girls were averse to this, owing to their terror of the natives.

Little did I dream, however, that at a place called Cossack, on the coast of the North-West Division of Western Australia, there was a settlement of pearl-fishers; so that, had I only known it, civilisation—more or less—was comparatively near. Cossack, it appears, was the pearling rendezvous on the western side of the continent, much as Somerset was on the north-east, at the extremity of the Cape York Peninsula.

My tongue or pen can never tell what those young ladies were to me in my terrible exile. They would recite passages from Sir Walter Scott's works —the "Tales of a Grandfather" I remember in particular; and so excellent was their memory that they were also able to give me many beautiful passages from Byron and Shakespeare. I had always had a great admiration for Shakespeare, and the girls and myself would frequently act little scenes from "The Tempest," as being the most appropriate to our circumstances. The girls' favourite play, however, was "Pericles, Prince of Tyre." I took the part of the King, and when I called for my robes Yamba would bring some indescribable garments of emu skin, with a gravity that was comical in the extreme. I, on my part, recited passages from the French classics—

particularly the Fables of La Fontaine, in French ; which language the girls knew fairly well.

And we had other amusements. I made some fiddles out of that peculiar Australian wood which splits into thin strips. The strings of the bow we made out of my own hair ; whilst those for the instrument itself were obtained from the dried intestines of the native wild-cat.

We lined the hut with the bark of the paper-tree, which had the appearance of a reddish-brown drapery.

The native women made us mats out of the wild flax ; and the girls themselves decorated their room daily with beautiful flowers, chiefly lilies. They also busied themselves in making garments of various kinds from opossum skins. They even made some sort of costume for me, but I could not wear it on account of the irritation it caused.

The natives would go miles to get fruit for the girls—wild figs, and a kind of nut about the size of a walnut, which, when ripe, was filled with a delicious substance looking and tasting like raspberry jam. There was also a queer kind of apple which grew upon creepers in the sand, and of which we ate only the outer part raw, cooking the large kernel which is found inside. I do not know the scientific name of any of these things.

I often asked the girls whether they had altogether despaired in the clutches of the cannibal chief; and they told me that although they often attempted to take their own lives, yet they had intervals of bright hope—so strong is the optimism of youth. My apparition, they told me, seemed like a dream to them.

The natives, of course, were constantly moving
their camp from place to place, leaving us alone for
weeks at a time ; but we kept pretty stationary, and
were visited by other friendly tribes, whom we entertained (in accordance with my consistent policy) with
songs, plays, recitations, and acrobatic performances.

In these latter Bruno took a great part, and
nothing delighted the blacks more than to see him
put his nose on the ground and go head over heels
time after time with great gravity and persistency.
But the effect of Bruno's many tricks faded into the
veriest insignificance beside that produced by his
bark. You must understand that the native dogs do
not bark at all, but simply give vent to a melancholy
howl, not unlike that of the hyena, I believe. Bruno's
bark, be it said, has even turned the tide of battle, for
he was always in the wars in the most literal sense of
the phrase. These things, combined with his great
abilities as a hunter, often prompted the blacks to put
in a demand that Bruno should be made over to
them altogether. Now, this request was both awkward and inconvenient to answer ; but I got out of
it by telling them—since they believed in a curious
kind of metempsychosis—that Bruno was *my brother*,
whose soul and being he possessed ! His bark, I
pretended, was a perfectly intelligible language, and
this they believed the more readily when they saw
me speak to the dog and ask him to do various things,
such as fetching and carrying ; tumbling, walking on
his hind-legs, &c. &c. But even this argument did
not suffice to overcome the covetousness of some
tribes, and I was then obliged to assure them con-
fidentially that he was a relative of the Sun, and

therefore if I parted with him he would bring all manner of most dreadful curses down upon his new owner or owners. Whenever we went rambling I had to keep Bruno as near me as possible, because we sometimes came across natives whose first impulse, not knowing that he was a dog, was to spear him. Without doubt the many cross-breeds between Bruno and the native dogs will yet be found by Australian explorers.

Our hut was about three-quarters of a mile away from the sea, and in the morning the very first thing the girls and I did was to go down to the beach arm-in-arm and have a delicious swim.

They very soon became expert swimmers, by the way, under my tuition. Frequently I would go out spearing and netting fish, my principal captures being mullet. We nearly always had fish of some sort for breakfast, including shell-fish ; and we would send the women long distances for wild honey. Water was the only liquid we drank at breakfast, and with it Yamba served a very appetising dish of lily-buds and roots. We used to steam the wild rice—which I found growing almost everywhere, but never more than two feet high—in primitive ovens, which were merely adapted ants' nests. The material that formed these nests, we utilised as flooring for our house. We occasionally received quantities of wild figs from the inland natives in exchange for shell and other ornaments which they did not possess. I also discovered a cereal very like barley, which I ground up and made into cakes. The girls never attempted to cook anything, there being no civilised appliances of any kind. Food was never boiled.

From all this you would gather that we were as happy as civilised beings could possibly be under the circumstances. Nevertheless—and my heart aches as I recall those times—we had periodical fits of despondency, which filled us with acute and intolerable agony.

These periods came with curious regularity almost once a week. At such times I at once instituted sports, such as swimming matches, races on the beach, swings, and acrobatic performances on the horizontal bars. Also Shakespearian plays, songs (the girls taught me most of Moore's melodies), and recitations both grave and gay. The fits of despondency were usually most severe when we had been watching the everlasting sea for hours, and had perhaps at last caught sight of a distant sail without being able to attract the attention of those on board. The girls, too, suffered from fits of nervous apprehension lest I should go away from them for any length of time. They never had complete confidence even in my friendly natives. Naturally we were inseparable, we three. We went for long rambles together, and daily inspected our quaint little corn-garden. At first my charming companions evinced the most embarrassing gratitude for what I had done, but I earnestly begged of them never even to mention the word to me. The little I had done, I told them, was my bare and obvious duty, and was no more than any other man, worthy of the name, would have done.

In our more hopeful moments we would speak of the future, and these poor girls would dwell upon the thrill of excitement that would go all through the civilised world, when their story and mine should first be made known to the public.

For they felt certain their adventures were quite unique in the annals of civilisation, and they loved to think they would have an opportunity of "lionising" me when we should return to Europe. They would not hear me when I protested that such a course would, from my point of view, be extremely unpleasant and undignified—even painful.

Every day we kept a good look-out for passing ships; and from twenty to forty catamarans were always stationed on the beach in readiness to take us out to sea should there be any hope of a rescue. As my knowledge of English was at this time not very perfect, the girls took it upon themselves to improve me, and I made rapid progress under their vivacious tuition. They would promptly correct me in the pronunciation of certain vowels when I read aloud from the only book I possessed—the Anglo-French Testament I have already mentioned. They were, by the way, exceedingly interested in the records of my daily life, sensations, &c., which I had written *in blood* in the margins of my little Bible whilst on the island in Timor Sea. About this time I tried to make some ink, having quill pens in plenty from the bodies of the wild geese; but the experiment was a failure.

Both girls, as I have already hinted, had wonderful memories, and could recite numberless passages which they had learnt at school. Blanche, the elder girl, would give her sister and myself lessons in elocution; and I should like to say a word to teachers and children on the enormous utility of *committing something to memory*—whether poems, songs, or passages from historical or classical works. It is, of course, very unlikely that any one who reads these lines will be cast away as we were, but still one never knows what the future has in store ; and I have known pioneers and prospectors who have ventured into the remoter wilds, and emerged therefrom years after, to give striking testimony as to the usefulness of being able to sing or recite in a loud voice.

Sometimes we would have an improvised concert, each of us singing whatever best suited the voice ; or we would all join together in a rollicking glee. One day, I remember, I started off with—-

"À notre heureux séjour,"

but almost immediately I realised how ridiculously inappropriate the words were. Still, I struggled on through the first verse, but to my amazement, before I could start the second, the girls joined in with " God Save the Queen," which has exactly the same air. The incident is one that should appeal to all British people, including even her Most Gracious Majesty herself. As the girls' voices rose, half sobbingly, in the old familiar air, beloved of every English-speaking person, tears fairly ran down their fair but sad young faces, and I could not help being struck with the pathos of the scene.

But all things considered, these were really happy days for all of us, at any rate in comparison with those we had previously experienced. We had by this time quite an orchestra of reed flutes and the fiddles aforesaid, whose strings were of gut procured from the native wild-cat—a very little fellow, by the way, about the size of a fair-sized rat ; I found him everywhere. These cats were great thieves, and only roamed about at night. I trapped them in great numbers by means of an ingenious native arrangement of pointed sticks of wood, which, while providing an easy entrance, yet confronted the out-going cat with a formidable *chevaux-de-frise*. The bait I used was meat in an almost putrid condition.

I could not handle the prisoners in the morning, because they scratched and bit quite savagely; I therefore forked them out with a spear. As regards their own prey, they waged perpetual warfare against the native rats. The skin of these cats was beauti-fully soft, and altogether they were quite leopards in miniature. Best of all, they made excellent eating, the more so in that their flesh was almost the only meat dish that had not the eternal flavour of the eucalyptus leaf, which all our other "joints" possessed. The girls never knew that they were eating cats, to say nothing about rats. In order to save their feel-ings, I told them that both "dishes" were squirrels!

My hair at this time was even longer than the girls' own, so it is no wonder that it provided bows for the fiddles. My companions took great delight in dressing my absurdly long tresses, using combs which I had made out of porcupines' quills.

Our contentment was a great source of joy to Yamba, who was now fully convinced that I would settle down among her people for ever.

The blacks were strangely affected by our singing. Any kind of civilised music or singing was to them anathema. What they liked best was the harsh uproar made by pieces of wood beaten together, or the weird jabbering and chanting that accompanied a big feast. Our singing they likened to the

howling of the dingoes! They were sincere, hardly
complimentary.

DRESSING MY HAIR

Elsewhere I have alluded to the horror the girls
had of being left alone. Whenever I went off with
the men on a hunting expedition I left them in charge

of my other women-folk, who were thoroughly capable
of looking after them.   I also persuaded the natives
to keep some distance away from our dwelling, particularly when they were about to hold a cannibal
feast, so that the girls were never shocked by such
a fearful sight.   Certainly they had known of cannibalism in their old camp, but I told them that my
own people were a superior race of natives, who were
not addicted to this loathsome practice.

Although we had long since lost count of the days,
we always set aside one day in every seven and recognised it as Sunday, when we held a kind of service
in our spacious hut. · Besides the girls, Yamba, and
myself, only our own women-folk were admitted,
because I was careful never to attempt to proselytise
any of the natives, or wean them from their ancient
beliefs.   The girls were religious in the very best
sense of the term, and they knew the Old and New
Testaments almost by heart.   They read the Lessons,
and I confess they taught me a good deal about
religion which I had not known previously.   Blanche
would read aloud the most touching and beautiful
passages from the Bible ; and even as I write I
can recall her pale, earnest face, with its pathetic
expression and her low, musical voice, as she dwelt
upon passages likely to console and strengthen us
in our terrible position.   The quiet little discussions
we had together on theological subjects settled, once
and for all, many questions that had previously vexed
me a great deal.

Both girls were devoted adherents of the Church
of England, and could repeat most of the Church
services entirely from memory.   They wanted to do

a little missionary work among the blacks, but I gently told them I thought this inadvisable, as any rupture in our friendly relations with the natives would have been quite fatal—if not to our lives, at least to our chances of reaching civilisation.   Moreover, my people were not by any means without a kind of religion of their own.   They believed in the omnipotence of a Great Spirit in whose hands their destinies rested ; and him they worshipped with much the same adoration which Christians give to God.   The fundamental difference was that the sentiment animating them was not *love*, but *fear :* propitiation rather than adoration.

We sang the usual old hymns at our Sunday services, and I soon learned to sing them myself. On my part, I taught the girls such simple hymns as the one commencing " *Une nacelle en silence*," which I had learnt at Sunday-school in Switzerland.   It is interesting to note that this was Bruno's favourite air.   Poor Bruno ! he took more or less kindly to all songs—except the Swiss *jödellings*, which he simply detested.   When I started one of these plaintive ditties Bruno would first protest by barking his loudest, and if I persisted, he would simply go away in disgust to some place where he could not hear the hated sounds.   On Sunday evening we generally held a prayer-service in the hut, and at such times offered up most fervent supplications for delivery.

Often I have seen these poor girls lifting up their whole souls in prayer, quite oblivious for the moment of their surroundings, until recalled to a sense of their awful positions by the crash of an unusually large wave on the rocks.

The girls knew no more of Australian geography than I did; and when I mention that I merely had a vague idea that the great cities of the continent— Sydney, Adelaide, Perth, and Melbourne—all lay in a southerly direction, you may imagine how dense was my ignorance of the great island. I am now the strongest possible advocate of a sound geographical training in schools.

On ordinary days we indulged in a variety of games, the principal one being a form of " rounders." I made a ball out of opossum skin, stuffed with the light soft bark of the paper-tree, and stitched with gut. We used a yam-stick to strike it with. My native women attendants often joined in the fun, and our antics provided a vast amount of amusement for the rest of the tribe. The girls taught me cricket, and in due time I tried to induce the blacks to play the British national game, but with little success. We made the necessary bats and stumps out of hard acacia, which I cut down with my tomahawk. The natives themselves, however, made bats much better than mine, simply by whittling flat their waddies; and they soon became expert batsmen. But unfortunately they failed to see why they should run after the ball, especially when they had knocked it a very great distance away. Running about in this manner, they said, was only fit work for women, and was quite beneath their dignity. Yamba and I fielded, but soon found ourselves unequal to the task, owing to the enormous distances we had to travel in search of the ball. Therefore we soon abandoned the cricket, and took up football, which was very much more successful.

We had a nice large football made of soft goose-skin stuffed with the paper bark; and in considering our game you must always bear in mind that boots or footgear of any kind were quite unknown. The great drawback of football, from the native point of view, was that it entailed so much exertion, which could be otherwise expended in a far more profitable and practical manner. They argued that if they put the exertion requisite for a game of football into a hunt for food, they would have enough meat to last them for many days. It was, of course, utterly impossible to bring them round to my view of sports and games. With regard to the abandoned cricket, they delighted in hitting the ball and in catching it —oh! they were wonderfully expert at this—but as to running after the ball, this was quite impossible.

About this time the girls showed me the steps of an Irish jig, which I quickly picked up and soon became quite an adept, much to the delight of the natives, who never tired of watching my gyrations. I kept them in a constant state of wonderment, so that even my very hair—now about three feet long—commanded their respect and admiration!

Sometimes I would waltz with the younger girl, whilst her sister whistled an old familiar air. When I danced, the blacks would squat in a huge circle around me; those in the front rank keeping time by beating drums that I had made and presented to them. The bodies of the drums were made from sections of trees which I found already hollowed out by the ants. These wonderful little insects would bore through and through the core of the trunk, leaving only the outer shell, which soon became light and dry.

I then scraped out with my tomahawk any of the
rough inner part that remained, and stretched over
the ends of each section a pair of the thinnest wallaby
skins I could find; these skins were held taut by
sinews from the tail of a kangaroo. I tried emu-
skins for the drum-heads, but found they were no
good, as they soon became perforated when I scraped
them.

Never a day passed but we eagerly scanned the
glistening sea in the hope of sighting a passing sail.
One vessel actually came right into our bay from the
north, but she suddenly turned right back on the
course she had come. She was a cutter-rigged vessel,
painted a greyish-white, and of about fifty tons
burden. She was probably a Government vessel—
possibly the *Claud Hamilton*, a South Australian
revenue boat stationed at Port Darwin—as she
flew the British ensign at the mast-head; whereas a
pearler would have flown it at the peak. The moment
we caught sight of that ship I am afraid we lost our
heads. We screamed aloud with excitement, and ran
like mad people up and down the beach, waving
branches and yelling like maniacs. I even waved
wildly my long, luxuriant hair. Unfortunately, the
wind was against us, blowing from the WSW.
We were assisted in our frantic demonstration by
quite a crowd of natives with branches; and I think
it possible that, even if we had been seen, the people
on the ship would have mistaken our efforts for a more
hostile demonstration.

When it was too late, and the ship almost out of
sight, I suddenly realised that I had made another
fatal mistake in having the blacks with me. Had I

and the two girls been alone on the beach I feel sure the officers of the ship would have detected our white skins through their glasses.   But, indeed, we may well have escaped notice altogether.

There was a terrible scene when the supposed Government vessel turned back on her course and passed swiftly out of sight.   The girls threw themselves face downwards on the beach, and wept wildly and hysterically in the very depths of violent despair. I can never hope to tell you what a bitter and agonising experience it was—the abrupt change from delirious excitement at seeing a ship steering right into our bay, to the despairing shock of beholding it turn away from us even quicker than it came.

THE weeks gradually grew into months, and still
we were apparently no nearer civilisation than ever.
Again and again we made expeditions to see whether
it were possible for the girls to reach Port Darwin
overland; but, unfortunately, I had painted for them
in such vivid colours the tortures of thirst which I had
undergone on my journey towards Cape York, that
they were always afraid to leave what was now their
home to go forth unprovided into the unknown. Sometimes a fit of depression so acute would come over
them, that they would shut themselves up in their
room and not show themselves for a whole day.

We had a very plentiful supply of food, but one
thing the girls missed very much was milk,—which of
course, was an unheard-of luxury in these regions.
We had a fairly good substitute, however, in a certain
creamy and bitter-tasting juice which we obtained from
a palm-tree. This "milk," when we got used to it,
we found excellent when used with the green corn.
The corn-patch was carefully fenced in from kangaroos,

and otherwise taken care of; and I may here remark
that I made forks and plates of wood for my fair
companions, and also built them a proper elevated bed,
with fragrant eucalyptus leaves and grass for bedding.
For the cold nights there was a covering of skin rugs,
with an overall quilt made from the wild flax.

FASHIONABLE COSTUMES

The girls made themselves sun-bonnets out of palm-
leaves; while their most fashionable costume was composed of the skins of birds and marsupials, cunningly
stitched together by Yamba.   During the cold winter
months of July and August we camped at a more
sheltered spot, a little to the north, where there was
a range of mountains, whose principal peak was shaped
like a sugar-loaf.

I frequently accompanied the warriors on their fighting expeditions, but did not use my stilts, mainly because we never again met so powerful an enemy as we had battled with on that memorable occasion, My people were often victorious, but once or twice we got beaten by reason of the other side having drawn first blood. My natives took their reverses with a very good grace, and were never very depressed or inclined to view me with less favour because of their want of success. We were always the best of friends, and I even ventured gradually to wean them from cannibalism.

I knew they ate human flesh, not because they felt hungry, but because they hoped to acquire the additional valour of the warrior they were eating. I therefore diplomatically pointed out to them that, in the first place, all kinds of dreadful diseases which the dead man might have had would certainly be communicated to them, and in this I was providentially borne out by a strange epidemic. The second consideration I mentioned was that by making anklets, bracelets, and other ornaments out of the dead braves' hair, they could acquire for themselves in a much . more efficacious manner the valour and other estimable qualities of the departed warrior.

Whilst I was on this subject I also advised them strongly and impressively never wantonly to attack white men, but rather to make friendly advances towards them. I often wonder now whether explorers who follow in my track will notice the absence of cannibalism and the friendly overtures of the natives.

Two half painful, half merry years, passed by. We had seen several ships passing out at sea, and on more

than one occasion Yamba and I, taught by previous
lessons, had jumped into our canoe and pulled for
many miles in the direction of the sail, leaving the
girls watching us eagerly from the shore. But it was
always useless, and we were compelled to return without having accomplished our purpose; we merely inflicted additional pain on ourselves.

I now come to what is possibly the most painful
episode of my career, and one which I find it impossible to discuss, or write about, without very real pain.
Even at this distance of time I cannot recall that
tragic day without bitter tears coming into my eyes,
and being afflicted with a gnawing remorse which can
never completely die in my heart. Do not, I beg of
you, in considering my actions, ask me why I did not
do this, or that, or the other. In terrible crises I
believe we become almost mechanical, and are not
responsible for what we do. I have often thought
that, apart from our own volition, each set of nerves
and fibres in our being has a will of its own.

Well, one gloriously fine day we sighted a ship
going very slowly across the gulf, several miles away.
Would to God we had never seen her! We were
thrown, as usual, into a perfect frenzy of wild excitement, and the girls dashed here and there like people
possessed. Of course, I determined to intercept the
vessel if possible, and the girls at once expressed their
intention of coming with me. I attempted earnestly
to dissuade them from this, but they wept pitifully
and implored me to let them come. They were filled
with an ungovernable longing to get away—the same
longing, perhaps, that animates a caged bird who,
although well fed and kindly treated, soars away

without a moment's hesitation when an opportunity occurs. Quite against my better judgment, I let them come. Every second was precious and every argument futile. While Yamba was getting ready the canoe I rushed from one group of natives to the other, coaxing, promising, imploring. I pointed out to them that they could propel their catamarans faster than I could paddle my canoe; and I promised them that if I reached the ship I would send them presents from the white man's land of tomahawks and knives; gaily coloured cloths and gorgeous jewellery. But they were only too ready to help me without any of these inducements; and in an incredibly short time at least twenty catamarans, each containing one or two men, put off from the shore in my wake and made directly towards the ship, whilst I struck off at a tangent so as to head her off. I now see that without doubt we must have presented a very formidable appearance to the people on the vessel as we paddled over the sunlit seas, racing one another, yelling, and gesticulating like madmen. Of course, the people on board quite naturally thought they were being attacked by a savage flotilla. But in the excitement of the moment I never gave this a thought. Had I only left my faithful natives behind all might have been well. Yamba and I kept the canoe well ahead, and we reached the neighbourhood of the ship first.

As we approached, the excitement of the girls was painful to witness. They could scarcely contain themselves for joy; and as I forcibly prevented them from standing up in the frail canoe, they contented themselves with frantically waving their hands and screaming themselves hoarse.

Nearing the vessel I was surprised to see the top-sail being hoisted, but, strange to say, the crew kept well out of sight. This was easy to do, considering the spread of canvas. She was not a Malay vessel, being decidedly of European rig. She was only a small craft, of perhaps ten or fifteen tons, with one mast carrying a main-sail and stay-sail, in addition to the top-sail that had been hoisted as we approached. To us, however, she was a "ship." We were now about one hundred and fifty yards away, and I suddenly leapt to my feet and coo-eed several times. Still no one showed himself, and not a soul was visible on board. My own joyful excitement speedily turned to heart-sickness, alarm, and even terror. By this time the flotilla of catamarans was close behind me; and just as I was about to sit down and take to my paddle again, so as to advance still closer to the vessel, the loud report of a gun was heard; and then—well, what followed next is exceedingly difficult for me to describe accurately. Whether I was wounded by the shot, or whether the girls suddenly stood up, causing me to lose my balance and fall on the side of the canoe and cut my thigh, I do not know.

At any rate, I crashed heavily overboard in spite of Yamba's desperate attempt to save me. The next moment I had forgotten all about the ship, and was only conscious of Yamba swimming close by my side, and occasionally gripping my long hair when she thought I was going under. We righted the canoe and climbed in as quickly as we could. I think I was dazed and incapable of any coherent thought. As I collapsed in the bottom of the canoe, I suddenly realised that Yamba and I were alone; and sitting up, I gasped, "The girls, the girls! Where are they? Oh, where are they? We must save them!"

Alas! they had sunk beneath the smiling waves, and they never rose again. True, they were expert swimmers, but I suppose the terrible excitement, followed by the sudden shock, was too much for them, and as they sank for the first time they probably clung to each other in the embrace of death. God knows best. Perhaps it was better that He should take my loved ones from me than that they should be dragged through the terrible years that followed.

But for a long time I utterly refused to believe that my darlings were lost—they were truly as sisters to me; and Yamba and I and the natives dived for them time after time, searching the sea in every direction. But at length, seeing that I was exhausted, Yamba forcibly detained me, and told me that I myself would inevitably drown if I went into the water again. The wound in my thigh (I am uncertain to this day whether it was the result of the gun-shot or mere collision with the rough gunwale of the canoe) was bleeding freely; and as it was also pointed out to me that there was a very strong and swift current at this spot, I allowed myself to be taken away without any further opposition.

I simply *could* not realise my bereavement. It seemed too terrible and stunning to think, that when God had provided me with these two charming companions, who were all in all to me every moment of my existence, as a consolation for the horrors I had gone through—it seemed impossible, I say, that they should be snatched from me just at the very moment when salvation seemed within our reach. Every detail

of the incident passed before my mental vision, but I
could not grasp it—I could not seem to think it real.
I can never explain it.   These poor girls were more to
me than loving sisters.   They turned the black night
of my desolate existence into sunshine, and they were
perpetually devising some sweet little surprise—some
little thing which would please me and add additional
brightness to our daily lives.   This dreadful thing
happened many years ago, but to this day, and to
the day of my death, I feel sure I shall suffer agonies
of grief and remorse (I blame myself for not having
forbidden them to go in the canoe) for this terrible
catastrophe.

After we returned to the land, I haunted the sea-
shore for hours, hoping to see the bodies rise to the
surface; but I watched in vain.   When at length the
full magnitude of the disaster dawned upon me, despair
—the utter abandonment of despair—filled my soul for
the first time.   Never again would my sweet companions cheer my solitary moments.   Never again
would I see their loved forms, or hear their low,
musical voices.   Never again would we play together
like children on the sand.   Never again would we
build aerial castles about the bright and happy future
that was in store for us, looking back from the bourne
of civilisation on our fantastic adventures.   Never again
should we compare our lot with that of Robinson
Crusoe or the Swiss Family Robinson.

My bright dream had passed away, and with a
sudden revulsion of feeling I realised that the people
around me were repulsive cannibals, among whom I
was apparently doomed to pass the remainder of my
hideous days—a fate infinitely more terrible than that

of joining my darlings beneath the restless waves, that beat for ever on that lonely shore.   I was a long time before I could even bring myself to be thankful

I HAUNTED THE SEA-SHORE FOR HOURS

for Yamba's escape, which was no doubt dreadfully ungrateful of me.   I can only ask your pity and sympathy in my terrible affliction.   What made my

sorrow and remorse the more poignant, was the reflection that if I had retained one atom of my self-posses-
sion I would never have dreamed of approaching the
little European vessel at the head of a whole flotilla
of catamarans, filled with yelling and gesticulating
savages. As to the people on board the vessel, I
exonerated them then, and I exonerate them now,
from all blame. Had you or I been on board, we
should probably have done exactly the same thing
under the circumstances.

Clearly the only reasonable plan of action was to
have gone alone; but then, at critical times, even the
wisest among us is apt to lose his head. God knows
I paid dearly enough for my lack of judgment on this
melancholy occasion.

My wound was not at all serious, and, thanks to
Yamba's care, it quickly healed, and I was able to get
about once more.

But I ought to tell you that when we returned I
could not bear to go into our hut, where every little
bunch of withered flowers, every garment of skin, and
every implement, proclaimed aloud the stunning loss
I had sustained. No, I went back direct to the camp
of the natives, and remained among them until the
moment came for my departure. I think it was in the
soft, still nights that I felt it most. I wept till I was
as weak as a baby. Oh the torments of remorse I
endured—the fierce resentment against an all-wise Providence! "Alone! alone! alone!" I would shriek in an
agony of wretchedness; "Gone! gone! gone! Oh, come
back to me, come back to me, I cannot live here now."

And I soon realised that it was impossible for me
to remain there any longer. There was much weeping

and lamentation among the native women, but I guessed it was not so much on account of the poor girls, as out of sympathy for the loss the great white chief had sustained. I think Yamba went among them, and pointed out the magnitude of the disaster; otherwise they would have failed to grasp it. What was the loss of a woman or two to them? I felt, I say, that I could not settle down in my hut again, and I was consumed with an intense longing to go away into the wilderness and there hide my grief. In making an attempt to reach civilisation, I thought this time of going due south, so that perhaps I might ultimately reach Sydney, or Melbourne, or Adelaide. I argued thus casually to myself, little dreaming of the vast distances—mountain ranges and waterless deserts—that separated me from these great cities, For all I knew, I might have come upon them in a few weeks! All I was certain of was that they lay somewhere to the south. Time was no object to me, and I might as well be walking in the direction of civilisation as remaining in idle misery in my bay home. brooding over the disaster that had clouded my life and made it infinitely more intolerable than it was before the girls came.

Yamba instantly agreed to accompany me, and a few weeks after the loss of the girls we started out once more on our wanderings, accompanied by my ever faithful dog.

Bruno also missed his young mistresses. He would moan and cry pitifully, and run aimlessly up and down the beach looking out to sea. Ah! had I only taken Bruno on that fatal day, he would not have let my dear ones drown!

As I have said, I remained only a few weeks in my bay home, and then departed. The blacks, too, left the spot, for they never stay where the shadow of death lies, fearing the unpleasant attentions of the spirits of the deceased. The parting between me and my people was a most affecting one, the women fairly howling in lamentations, which could be heard a great distance away. They had shown such genuine sympathy with me in my misfortune that our friendship had very materially increased; but in spite of this good feeling, I knew I could never be happy among them again.

So we started off into the unknown, with no more provision or equipment than if we were going for a stroll of a mile or so. Yamba carried her yam-stick and basket, and I had my usual weapons—tomahawk and stiletto in my belt, and bow and arrows in my hand. I never dreamed when we started that to strike due south would take us into the unexplored heart of the continent. Day after day, however, we walked steadily on our course, steering in a very curious manner. We were guided by the ant-hills, which are always built facing the east, whilst the top inclines towards the north; and we knew that the scratches made on trees by the opossums were invariably on the north side.

We often steered by the habits of insects, wasps' nests, and other curious auguries, fixing our position at night by the stars and in the daytime by our own shadows. Yamba always went in front and I followed. The bush teemed with fruits and roots. After leaving our own camp in the Cambridge Gulf region we struck a fine elevated land, excellently well watered; and later on we followed the Victoria River in a south-easterly direction through part of the Northern Terri-tories of South Australia. We at length struck a peculiar country covered with coarse grass ten feet or twelve feet high—not unlike the sugar-cane which I afterwards saw, but much more dense.

It was, of course, impossible for us to pursue our course due south, owing to the forests and ranges which we encountered; we had, as a matter of fact, to follow native and kangaroo tracks wherever they took us—east, west, and even north occasionally, generally to water-holes. The progress of the natives is simply from one water supply to another. But as far as possible we pursued our way south. You will understand that this kind of travelling was very dif-ferent from that which we experienced on the Victoria River—which, by the way, traversed a very fine country. As we ascended it we passed many isolated hills of perhaps a few hundred feet, and nowhere did I see any scrub or spinifex.

After leaving the Victoria we came upon a more elevated plateau covered with rather fine but short grass; the trees were scarcer here, but finer and bigger. There was plenty of water in the native wells and in the hollows, although we frequently had to remove a few stones to get at it. There were plenty of kangaroos and emus about, as well as turkeys; these latter provided us with an unwonted dish, to say nothing of their delicious eggs.

Another reason for our coming round out of our course when we came to forests was because but little food was found in them. Kangaroos and other animals were seldom or never found there: they abounded

usually in the more scrubby country. Our progress
was very leisurely, and, as we met tribe after tribe, we
ingratiated ourselves with them and camped at their
wells. Occasionally we came upon curious rivers and
lagoons that ran into the earth and disappeared in the
most mysterious way, only to reappear some distance
farther on. Of course, I may be mistaken in this, but
such at any rate was my impression.

One day as we were marching steadily along, Yamba
startled me by calling out excitedly, "Up a tree,—
quick! Up a tree!" And so saying she scampered
up the nearest tree herself. Now, by this time I had
become so accustomed to acting upon her advice un-
questioningly, that without waiting to hear any more I
made a dash for the nearest likely tree and climbed
into it as fast as I could. Had she called out to me,
"Leap into the river," I should have done so without
asking a question. When I was safely in the branches,
however, I called out to her (her tree was only a few
yards away), "What is the matter?" She did not
reply, but pointed to a vast stretch of undulating
country over which we had just come; it was fairly
well wooded. It lingers in my mind as a region in
which one was able to see a fairly long way in every
direction—a very unusual feature in the land of "Never
Never"!

I looked, but at first could see nothing. Presently,
however, it seemed to me that the whole country in
the far distance was covered with a black mantle,
which appeared to be made up of living creatures.

Steadily and rapidly this great mysterious wave
swept along towards us; and seeing that I was both
puzzled and alarmed, Yamba gave me to understand

R

that *we should presently be surrounded by myriads of rats*, stretching away in every direction like a living sea.   The phenomenon was evidently known to Yamba, and she went on to explain that these creatures were migrating from the lowlands to the mountains, knowing by instinct that the season of the great floods was at hand.   That weird and extraordinary sight will live in my memory for ever.   I question whether a spectacle so fantastic and awe-inspiring was ever dealt with, even in the pages of quasi-scientific fiction.   It was impossible for me to observe in what order the rats were advancing, on account of the great stretch of country which they covered.   Soon, however, their shrill squeals were distinctly heard, and a few minutes later the edge of that strange tide struck our tree and swept past us with a force impossible to realise.   No living thing was spared.   Snakes, lizards—ay, even the biggest kangaroos—succumbed after an ineffectual struggle.   The rats actually ate those of their fellows who seemed to hesitate or stumble.   The curious thing was that the great army never seemed to stand still. It appeared to me that each rat simply took a bite at whatever prey came his way, and then passed on with the rest.

I am unable to say how long the rats were in passing —it might have been an hour.   Yamba told me that there would have been no help for us had we been overtaken on foot by these migratory rodents.   It is my opinion that no creature in Nature, from the elephant downwards, could have lived in that sea of rats.   I could not see the ground between them, so closely were they packed.   The only creatures that escaped them were birds.   The incessant squealing

and the patter of their little feet made an extraordinary
sound, comparable only to the sighing of the wind or
the beat of a great rain-storm.   I ought to mention,
though, that I was unable accurately to determine the
sound made by the advancing rats owing to my partial
deafness, which you will remember was caused by the
great wave which dashed me on to the deck of the
Veielland, just before landing on the sand-spit in the
Sea of Timor.   I often found this deafness a very
serious drawback, especially when hunting.   I was
sometimes at a loss to hear the "coo-ee" or call of my
natives.   Fortunate men ! *they* did not even understand
what deafness meant.   Lunacy also was unknown
among them, and such a thing as suicide no native can
possibly grasp or understand.   In all my wanderings
I only met one idiot or demented person.   He had
been struck by a falling tree, and was worshipped as
a demi-god !

When the rats had passed by, we watched them
enter a large creek and swim across, after which they
disappeared in the direction of some ranges which
were not very far away.   They never seemed to break
their ranks; even when swimming, one beheld the
same level brownish mass on the surface of the water.
Yamba told me that this migration of rats was not
at all uncommon, but that the creatures rarely moved
about in such vast armies as the one that had just
passed.

I also learned that isolated parties of migrating
rats were responsible for the horrible deaths of many
native children, who had, perhaps, been left behind
in camp by their parents, who had gone in search
of water.

Up to this time we had always found food plentiful. On our southward journey a particularly pleasant
and convenient article of diet turned up (or fell down)
in the form of the *maru*, as it is called, which collects
on the leaves of trees during the night. Both in its
appearance and manner of coming, this curious substance may be likened to the manna that fell in the
wilderness for the benefit of the Israelites. This *maru*

A LIVING BRIDGE

is a whitish substance, not unlike raw cotton in appearance. The natives make bread of it; it is rather tasteless, but is very nutritious, and only obtained at certain
times—for example, it never falls at the time of full
moon, and is peculiar to certain districts.

During this great southward journey many strange
things happened, and we saw a host of curious sights.
I only wish I could trust my memory to place these
in their proper chronological order.

We had several visitations of locusts; and on one occasion, some months after leaving home, they settled upon the country around us so thickly as actually to make a living bridge across a large creek. On several occasions I have had to dig through a living crust of these insects, six or eight inches thick, in order to reach water at a water-hole. These locusts are of a yellowish-brown colour (many are grey), and they range in length from two to four inches.

As they rise in the air they make a strange cracking, snapping sound; and they were often present in such myriads as actually to hide the face of the sun. I found them excellent eating when grilled on red-hot stones.

Yamba, of course, did all the cooking, making a fire with her ever-ready fire-stick, which no native woman is ever without; and while she looked after the supply of roots and opossum meat, I generally provided the snakes, emus, and kangaroos. Our shelter at night consisted merely of a small *gunyah* made of boughs, and we left the fire burning in front of this when we turned in.

When we had been fully three months out, a very extraordinary thing happened, which to many people would be incredible were it not recognised as a well-known Australian phenomenon. We had reached a very dry and open grass country, where there was not a tree to be seen for miles and miles. Suddenly, as Yamba and I were squatting on the ground enjoying a meal, we saw a strange black cloud looming on the horizon, and hailed its advent with the very greatest delight, inasmuch as it presaged rain—which is always so vitally important a visitation in the " Never

Never." We waited in anticipation until the cloud was right over our heads. Then the deluge commenced, and to my unbounded amazement I found that with the rain *live fish as big as whitebait were falling from the clouds!* When this wonderful rain-storm had passed, large pools of water were left on the surface of the ground, and most of these were fairly alive with fish. This surface-water, however, evaporated in the course of a few days, and then, as the blazing sun beat down upon the fish-covered country, we found the region growing quite intolerable on account of the awful stench.

Talking of storms, I have seen it stated that the Australian natives are in a state of high glee whenever they hear thunder. This is perfectly true, but I have never seen any explanation of this joy. It is simple enough. The natives know that thunder presages rain, which is always a blessing of great price in that thirsty country.

I think this was the first time I had actually *seen* it rain fish. But I had often been surprised, to find water-holes, and even the pools in grassy plains, literally alive with fish a few days after a storm. And they grew with astounding rapidity, provided the water did not evaporate. This was in the vicinity of my Cambridge Gulf home.

We remained in the neighbourhood for some time, living on a most welcome fish diet. Very frequently in our wanderings we were provided with another dainty in the shape of a worm, which, when broiled over charcoal, had the flavour of a walnut.

These worms we found in the grass trees, which grow to a height of ten to twenty feet, and have bare trunks surmounted by what looks at a distance like a big bunch of drooping bulrushes. The worms were of a whitish colour, and were always found in the interior of a well-matured or decaying stem; so that all we had to do was to push the tree over with our feet and help ourselves.

In the course of our wanderings we usually went from tribe to tribe, staying a little time with some, and with others merely exchanging greetings. With some tribes we would perhaps travel a little way south, and only part with them when they were about to strike northwards; and as their course was simply from water-hole to water-hole, as I have told you, it was always pretty erratic.

OCCASIONALLY one of the tribes would display hostility towards us at first sight, but I generally managed to ingratiate myself into their good graces by the exercise of a little diplomacy—and acrobatics. Curiously enough, many of these tribes did not display much surprise at seeing a white man, apparently reserving all their amazement for Bruno's bark and the white man's wonderful performances.

I may here remark that, in the event of our coming across a hostile tribe who fought shy of my friendly advances, I would, without ceremony, introduce myself by dashing into their midst and turning a few somersaults or Catherine-wheels such as the London *gamins* display for the benefit of easily-pleased excursionists. This queer entertainment usually created roars of laughter, and set every one at his ease.

I remember once being surprised by the sudden appearance over .the crest of a hillock of about twenty blacks, all well armed and presenting rather a formidable appearance. The moment they caught sight of Yamba and myself they halted, whereupon I advanced and called out to them that I was a friend, at the same time holding out my passport stick. By the way, the efficacy of this talisman varied according to the tribes. Yamba could make neither head nor tail of these people; they jabbered in a language quite unintelligible to either of us. I then reverted to the inevitable sign language, giving them to understand that I wished to sleep with them a night or two; but they still continued to brandish their spears ominously. Yamba presently whispered in my ear that we had better not trouble them any further, as they were evidently inclined to be pugnacious. This was a very exceptional *rencontre*, because I usually induced the natives to sit down and parley with me, and then I would produce my mysterious stick. In the event of this proving of little account, both I and Bruno would without a moment's hesitation plunge into our performance. It always began with a few somersaults. Bruno needed no looking after. He knew his business, and went through his own repertoire with great energy and excitement. The accompanying barks were probably involuntary, but they were a great help in astonishing and impressing the natives.

Even in this instance I was unwilling to retire defeated; so suddenly pulling out one of my little reed whistles capable of producing two notes, I commenced a violent jig to my own "music." The effect on the scowling and ferocious-looking blacks was quite magical. They immediately threw down their spears and laughed uproariously at my vigorous antics. I danced till I was quite tired, but managed to wind up the entertainment with a few somersaults, which impressed them vastly.

I had conquered. When I had finished they

advanced and greeted me most heartily, and from that
moment we were friends. I had completely done away
with their enmity by my simple efforts to amuse them.
For the most part, this was my invariable experience.
The natives were the easiest people in the world to
interest and amuse, and when once I had succeeded
in winning them in this way, they were our warmest
friends. This band of warriors took us back to their
camping-ground, some miles away, and actually gave a
great feast in my honour that evening, chanting the
wonderful things they had seen until far into the night.
The place where I met these blacks was a broken,
stony, and hilly country, which, however, abounded
in roots and snakes—especially snakes. My hosts had
evidently had a recent battue, or fire hunt, for they had
a most extraordinary stock of food. So completely had
I won them over, that I actually hung up my bow and
arrows along with their spears before retiring to rest.
The expression "hung up" may seem curious, so I
hasten to explain that the natives tied up their spears
in bunches and placed them on the scrub bushes.

Next morning I brought down a few hawks on the
wing with my bow and arrows, and then the amazement
of the natives was quite comical to witness. Shooting
arrows in a straight line astonished them somewhat,
but the more bombastic among them would say, "Why
I can do that," and taking his woomerah he would hurl
a spear a long distance. Not one of them, however,
was able *to throw a spear upwards*, so I scored over
even the most redoubtable chiefs. It may be well
to explain, that birds are always to be found hovering
about a native camp; they act as scavengers, and their
presence in the sky is always an indication that an

encampment is somewhere in the vicinity. These birds are especially on the spot when the blacks set fire to the bush and organise a big battue. At such times the rats and lizards rush out into the open, and the hawks reap a fine harvest.

My natives are referred to as "blacks," or "black-fellows," but they are not really *black*, their hue being rather a brown, ranging from a very dark brown, indeed, to almost the lightness of a Malay. I found the coast tribes lightest in hue, while the inland natives were very much darker. Here I may mention that after having been on my way south for some months, I began to notice a total difference between the natives I met and my own people in the Cambridge Gulf district. The tribes I was now encountering daily were inferior in physique, and had inferior war implements; I do not remember that they had any shields.

The blacks I had whistled and jigged before were, perhaps, the ugliest of all the aborigines I had met, which was saying a very great deal. The men were very short, averaging little more than five feet, with low foreheads and hideously repulsive features. I noticed, however, that the animals they had for food seemed very much fatter than similar creatures farther north. One thing I was grateful to these people for was honey, which I urgently required for medicinal purposes. They were very sorry when we left them, and a small band of warriors accompanied us on our first day's march. We were then handed on from tribe to tribe, smoke signals being sent up to inform the next "nation" that friendly strangers were coming.

Nevertheless, I gradually became uneasy. We were evidently getting into a country where the greatest of our wonders could not save us from the hostility of the natives. We presently encountered another tribe, who not only at first refused to accept our friendly overtures, but even threatened to attack us before I had time to consider another plan. I tried the effect of my whistle, but even this failed in its effect; and to my alarm, before I could give them an exhibition of my acrobatic powers they had hurled one or two war spears, which whizzed by unpleasantly close to my head. Without further ado, well knowing that vacillation meant death, I sent half-a-dozen arrows in succession amongst them, taking care, however, to aim very low, so as not unduly to injure my opponents.

The hostile blacks came to a sudden halt, as they found the mysterious spears flying round them, and then watching my opportunity, I dashed forward right among them, and turned over and over in a series of rapid and breathless somersaults.

I had conquered again. Do not blame the natives, for with them every stranger is an enemy until he has proved himself a friend. Hence it is that when white men suddenly appear among these natives they run imminent risk of being promptly speared, unless they can make it quite clear that no harm is intended.

Bruno ran the same risk. Incident after incident of this kind happened almost daily, and although they involved some peril, yet they came as a welcome break when life on the march grew too monotonous. Deliberate treachery was very rare among the natives I came across, but it was by no means altogether absent; and, notwithstanding all my knowledge, my wife and I were sometimes in serious danger of our lives.

One day we came upon a tribe as usual, and after the customary preliminaries were gone through they became apparently quite friendly. I was careful never unduly to exhibit my steel tomahawk, which I always kept in a kind of sheath or covering of opossum-skin, so that it might not arouse envy; a second motive for this was to prevent its chafing my body. I never used either stiletto or tomahawk unless absolutely necessary, reserving both for great emergencies. I knew they could never be replaced, so it behoved me jealously to guard such precious possessions. I never even used my stiletto at meal-times, nor even in cutting up animals for food, lest the blood should rust the blade and eat it away. Many times already had it come in useful at close quarters—notably in the case of the fight with the alligator and the killing of the cannibal chief who owned the white girls.

The chief of the tribe I am discussing saw me using my tomahawk one day, and eagerly asked me to make over the implement to him as a gift. I courteously told him that I could not do so. He seemed somewhat disappointed at my refusal, but did not appear to bear me any ill-feeling in consequence. The blacks, by the way, seldom cut down trees except for spears, and the reason for this is very curious. They imagine the tree to be a thing of life, and when they are forced to cut one down, quite a religious ceremony is held, and profuse apologies made to the tree for taking its life.

They never even take a strip of bark right round, knowing that this will kill the tree; they always leave a little bit of connecting bark.

As some reason for the refusal of my tomahawk was expected, I told the chief that it was part of my life—indeed, part of my very being, which was perfectly true. I also worked on the chief's superstitions, assuring him earnestly that if I parted with the weapon it would so anger the spirits as to bring about a terrible curse in the country. The tomahawk I declared was a direct gift to me from the Sun itself, so how could I part with it? I had thought of offering it, curses and all, but the risk of prompt acceptance was too great.

That night Yamba warned me that trouble was impending. For myself I never knew, and I suppose she read the signs among the men and got certain definite information from the women. We therefore slept some miles away from the encampment in a makeshift gunyah built of boughs, in front of which the usual fire was made. After we had retired to rest, Yamba woke me and said that she detected strange noises. I immediately sprang to my feet and looked all round our little shelter. It was much too dark for me to see anything distinctly, but I fancied I heard retreating footsteps. Utterly at a loss to account for this strange occurrence, and fearing that some danger threatened us, Yamba and I covered in the front of the shelter, and then quietly retired into the bush, where we lay hidden without a fire until morning. When we returned to our shelter it was broad daylight, and, as we half expected, we found three formidable spears buried in the sides of our little hut. Three others were stuck in the ground near the fire, clearly proving that an attempt had been made upon our lives during the night. On examining the spears we found they most certainly belonged to the tribe we had left the previous day. The spear-heads were of a different kind of flint from anything I had previously seen, being dark green in colour; and they were extremely sharp. The individuality of the different tribes is strongly and decidedly marked in the make of their spears. Our treacherous hosts had evidently determined to obtain the coveted tomahawk by force, and when they reached the spot where they supposed we lay (they could not see into the interior from the front), they hurled their spears in the hope of killing us, but did not investigate the result, they being such arrant cowards at night. Remember, they had actually ventured at night into the bush in spite of their inveterate fear of "the spirits."

The precaution adopted on this occasion was always followed by us when we had any real doubt about the natives; that is to say, we built a "dummy" gunyah of boughs, which we were supposed to sleep in; and we covered in the front so as our possible assailants could not easily detect our absence. We would then creep away into the bush or hide behind a tree, and, of course, would light no fire.

Many times was that same tomahawk coveted. You see, the natives would watch me cutting boughs with it, or procuring honey by cutting down branches with an ease that caused them to despise their own rude stone axes.

The case of treachery I have just described was not an isolated one, but I am bound to say such occurrences were rare in the interior—although more or less frequent about the western shores of the

Gulf of Carpentaria. At any rate, this was my experience.

During our journey from my home to the shores of the Gulf, I remember coming across a flat country from which the natives had apparently disappeared altogether. When we did come upon them, however, in the high ground I was probably guilty of some little breach of etiquette, such as *looking* at the women—(for many reasons I always studied the various types in a tribe)—and Yamba and I were often in peril of our lives on this account. As a rule, however, safety lay in the fact that the natives are terribly afraid of darkness, and they believe the spirits of the dead roam abroad in the midnight hours.

Month after month we continued our progress in a southerly direction, although, as I have said before, we often turned north-east and even due west, following the valleys when stopped by the ranges —where, by the way, we usually found turkeys in great numbers. We had water-bags made out of the skins of kangaroos and wallabies, and would camp wherever possible close to a native well, where we knew food was to be found in plenty.

At this period I noticed that the more easterly I went, the more ranges I encountered; whilst the somewhat dreary and mostly waterless lowland lay to the west. We would sometimes fail to obtain water for a couple of days; but this remark does not apply to the mountainous regions. Often the wells were quite dry and food painfully scarce; this would be in a region of sand and spinifex.

When I beheld an oasis of palms and ti-trees

I would make for it, knowing that if no water existed there, it could easily be got by digging. The physical conditions of the country would change suddenly, and my indefatigable wife was frequently at fault in her root-hunting expeditions. Fortunately, animal life was very seldom scarce. On the whole, we were extremely fortunate in the matter of water, —although the natives often told me that the low wastes of sand and spinifex were frequently so dry, that it was impossible even for them to cross. What astonished me greatly was that the line of demarcation between an utter desert and, say, a fine forest was almost as sharply marked as if it had been drawn with a rule. A stretch of delightfully wooded country would follow the dreary wastes, and this in turn would give place to fairly high mountain ranges.

Once, during a temporary stay among one of the tribes, the chief showed me some very interesting caves among the low limestone ranges that were close by. It was altogether a very rugged country. Always on the look-out for something to interest and amuse me, and always filled with a strange, vague feeling that something *might* turn up unexpectedly which would enable me to return to civilisation, I at once determined to explore these caves ; and here I had a very strange and thrilling adventure.

Whilst roaming among the caves I came across a pit measuring perhaps twenty feet in diameter and eight feet or nine feet in depth. It had a sandy bottom ; and as I saw a curious-looking depression in one corner, I jumped down to investigate it, leaving Bruno barking at the edge of the pit, because I knew I should have some trouble in hoisting him up again

s

if I allowed him to accompany me.   I carried a long
stick, much longer than a waddy; perhaps it was a
yam-stick—I cannot remember.   At any rate, just
as I was about to probe a mysterious-looking hole, I
beheld with alarm and amazement the ugly head of
a large black snake suddenly thrust out at me from
a dark mass, which I presently found was the
decayed stump of a tree.   I fell back as far as
possible, and then saw that the reptile had quite
uncoiled itself from the stem, and was coming
straight at me.   I promptly dealt it a violent blow
on the body, just below that point where it raised its
head from the ground.   No sooner had I done this
than another dark and hissing head came charging in
my direction.   Again I struck at the reptile's body
and overpowered it.   Next came a third, and a
fourth, and fifth, and then I realised that the whole
of the dead stump was simply one living mass of
coiled snakes, which were probably hibernating.   One
after another they came at me; of course, had they
all come at once, no power on earth could have
saved me.   I wondered how long this weird contest
would be kept up; and again and again between the
attacks I tried to escape, but had scarcely taken an
upward step when another huge reptile was upon me.

I was aware that Bruno was running backwards
and forwards at the edge of the pit all this time,
barking frantically in a most excited state.   He knew
perfectly well what snakes were, having frequently
been bitten.   I owe my life on this occasion solely
to the fact that the snakes were in a torpid state,
and came at me one at a time instead of altogether.
It was the cold season, about the month of June or

ONE AFTER ANOTHER THEY CAME

July. It is impossible at such moments to take any account of time, so I cannot say how long the battle lasted. At length, however, I was able to count the slain. I did this partly out of curiosity and partly because I wanted to impress the natives—to boast, if you prefer that phrase. Modesty, where modesty is unknown, would have been absurd, if not fatal to my prestige. Well, in all there were *sixty-eight black snakes, averaging about four feet six inches in length.*

I do not remember that I was fatigued ; I think my excitement was too great for any such feeling to have made itself felt. When at length I was able to get away, I and Bruno rushed off to the native camp a few miles away, and brought back the blacks to see what I had done. The spectacle threw them into a state of great amazement, and from that time on I was looked upon with the greatest admiration. The story of how I had killed the snakes soon spread abroad among the various tribes for miles round, and was chanted by many tribes, the means of inter-communication being the universal smoke-signals. One important consequence of this adventure was that I was everywhere received with the very greatest respect.

It may be mentioned here that no matter how unfriendly tribes may be, they always exchange news by means of smoke-signals. I may also say that at *corroborees* and such-like festivities a vast amount of poetic boasting and exaggeration is indulged in, each "hero" being required to give practical demonstrations of the things he has seen, the doughty deeds he has done, &c. He warms up as he goes along, and magnifies its importance in a ridiculous way. It amuses me to this day to recall my own preposterous songs about how I killed the two whales *with my stiletto*, and other droll pretensions. But, ah! I was serious enough then!

In the mountainous region where I encountered the snakes, I also met a native who actually spoke English. He called himself either Peter or Jacky Jacky—I cannot remember which; but in any case it was a name given him by pearlers. He had once lived with some pearlers near the north-west coast of Western Australia—probably on the De Grey River. His story was quite unprecedented among the blacks, and he gave me many terrible instances of the perfidy shown by white adventurers towards the unfortunate natives. The precise locality where I met this man was probably near Mount Farewell, close to the border-line of South Australia and Western Australia. Well, then, Jacky Jacky—to give him the name which lingers most tenaciously in my mind—was persuaded to join in a pearling expedition, together with a number of his companions. They all accepted engagements from the whites, on the distinct understanding that they were to be away about three moons. Instead, they were practically kidnapped by force, and treated— or rather ill-treated—as slaves for several years.

First of all, the poor creatures were taken to an island in the vicinity of North-West Cape, off which the pearling fleet lay. During the voyage to the pearling grounds the water supply on board ran short, and so great was the suffering among the blacks—they were kept on the shortest of short commons, as you may suppose—that they plotted to steal a cask of the precious fluid for their own use. The vessel was quite a small one, and the

water was kept in the hold.   But the two or three
whites who formed the crew forcibly prevented the
black-fellows from carrying out their plan.   This
gave rise to much discontent, and eventually the
blacks, in desperation, openly rose and mutinied.
Arming themselves with heavy pieces of firewood
they proceeded to attack their masters, and some
of them succeeded in getting at the water, in
spite of the whites, by simply knocking the bungs
out of the casks.   The captain thereupon went down
to parley with them, but was met by a shower of
blows from the heavy sticks I have just mentioned.
Half-stunned, he dashed out of the hold, got his
musket, and fired down among the mutineers, hitting
one black-fellow in the throat, and killing him instantly.
Far from infuriating the rest, as would most certainly
have been the case with any other race, this course of
action terrified the blacks, and they barricaded themselves down below.   Eventually the whites again sought
them and made peace, the blacks promising to con-
duct themselves more obediently in the future.   It may
here be said that the ship had called specially at Jacky
Jacky's home on the coast to kidnap the natives.

On arriving at the pearling settlement, the blacks
found themselves among a number of other unfortunate creatures like themselves, and all were compelled
to go out in pearling vessels just as the exigencies of
the industry required.   Jacky Jacky himself was kept
at this work for upwards of three years ; and he told
me many terrible stories of the white man's indescribable cruelty and villainy.   He and his companions
were invariably chained up during the night and
driven about like cattle in the daytime.   Many of his

mates at the pearling settlement had been kidnapped from their homes in a cruel and contemptible manner, and herded off like sheep by men on horseback armed with formidable weapons.

Their sufferings were very great because, of course, they were totally unused to work of any kind. The enforced exile from home and the dreary compulsory labour made the life far worse than death for these primitive children of Nature. Then, again, they were exiled from their wives, who would, of course, be appropriated in their absence — another tormenting thought. They were frequently beaten with sticks, and when they attempted to run away they were speared as enemies by other tribes; whilst, in the event of their escaping altogether, they would not have been recognised even when they returned to their own homes. One day Jacky Jacky's ship came into a little bay on the mainland for water, and then my enterprising friend, watching his opportunity, struck inland for home and liberty, accompanied by several other companions in misery. These latter the coast natives promptly speared, but Jacky Jacky escaped, thanks probably to his knowledge of the white man's wiles. He soon reached the more friendly mountain tribes in the interior, where he was received as a man and a brother. You see, he had stolen a revolver from his late masters, and this mysterious weapon created great terror among his new friends. Altogether he posed as quite a great man, particularly when his story became known. He worked his way from tribe to tribe, until at length he got to the ranges where I met him—quite a vast distance from the coast.

Many parts of the extensive country I traversed on my southward journey, after the death of the girls, were exceedingly rich in minerals, and particularly in gold, both alluvial and in quartz. As I was making my way one day through a granite country along the banks of a creek, I beheld some reddish stones, which I at once pounced upon and found to be beautiful rubies. Having no means of carrying them, however, and as they were of no value whatever to me, I simply threw them away again, and now merely record the fact. I also came across large quantities of alluvial tin, but this, again, was not of the slightest use, any more than it had been when I found it in very large quantities in the King Leopold Ranges. The test I applied to see whether it really *was* tin was to scratch it with my knife. Even when large quantities of native gold lay at my feet, I hardly stooped to pick it up, save as a matter of curiosity. Why should I? What use was it to me? As I have stated over and over again in public, I would have given all the gold for a few ounces of salt, which I needed so sorely. Afterwards, however, I made use of the precious metal in a very practical manner, but of this more hereafter. At one place—probably near the Warburton Ranges in Western Australia— I picked up an immense piece of quartz, which was so rich that it appeared to be one mass of virgin gold ; and when on showing it to Yamba I told her that in my country men were prepared to go to any part of the world, and undergo many terrible hardships to obtain it, she thought at first I was joking. Indeed, the thing amused her ever after, as it did the rest of my people. I might also mention that up

in the then little-known Kimberley district, many of
the natives weighted their spears with pure gold. I
must not omit to mention that natives never poison
their spear-heads. I only found the nuggets, big
and little, near the creeks during and after heavy
rains ; and I might mention that having with some
difficulty interested Yamba in the subject, she was
always on the look-out for the tell-tale specks and
gleams. In some of the ranges, too, I found the
opal in large and small quantities, but soon discovered that the material was too light and brittle
for spear-heads, to which curious use I essayed to
put this beautiful stone. Talking about spear-heads,
in the ranges where I met Jacky Jacky there was a
quarry of that kind of stone which was used for the
making of war and other implements. It was very
much worked, and as you may suppose was a valua-
able possession to the tribe in whose territory it was
situated. The stone was a kind of flint, extremely
hard and capable of being made very sharp, and re-
taining its edge. Natives from far and near came
to barter for the stone with shells, and ornaments
which these inland tribes did not possess. The
method of getting out the stone was by building fires
over it, and then when it had become red-hot throwing large and small quantities of water upon it in an
amazingly dexterous way. The stone would immediately be split and riven exactly in the manner
required.

My very first discovery of gold was made in some
crevices near a big creek, which had cut its way
through deep layers of conglomerate hundreds of feet
thick. This country was an elevated plateau, inter-

sected by deeply cut creeks, which had left the various
strata quite bare, with curious concave recesses in
which the natives took shelter during the wet season.
One of the nuggets I picked up in the creek I have
just mentioned weighed several pounds, and was
three or four inches long; it was rather more than an
inch in thickness. This nugget I placed on a block
of wood and beat out with a stone, until I could
twist it easily with my fingers, when I fashioned in
into a fillet as an ornament for Yamba's hair. This
she continued to wear for many years afterwards, but
the rude golden bracelets and anklets I also made for
her she gave away to the first children we met.

In many of the rocky districts the reefs were
evidently extremely rich; but I must confess I rarely
troubled to explore them. In other regions the gold-
bearing quartz was actually a curse, our path being
covered with sharp pebbles of quartz and slate, which
made every step forward a positive agony. Wild
ranges adjoined that conglomerate country, which, as
you have probably gathered, is extremely difficult
to traverse. Certainly it would be impossible for
camels.

CHAPTER XIV

WHEN we had been on the march southwards
about nine months there came one of the
most important incidents in my life, and one which
completely changed my plans. One day we came
across a party of about eight natives—all young
fellows—who were on a punitive expedition; and as
they were going in our direction (they overtook us
going south), we walked along with them for the
sake of their company. The country through which
we were passing at that time is a dreary, undulating
expanse of spinifex desert, with a few scattered and
weird-looking palms, a little scrub, and scarcely any
signs of animal life. The further east we went, the
better grew the country; but, on the other hand,
when we went westward we got farther and farther
into the dreary wastes. At the spot I have in my
mind ranges loomed to the south—a sight which
cheered me considerably, for somehow I thought I
should soon strike civilisation.

Had not the blacks we were with taken us to some wells we would have fared very badly indeed in this region, as no water could be found except by digging. I noticed that the blacks looked for a hollow depression marked by a certain kind of palm, and then dug a hole in the gravel and sandy soil with their hands and yam-sticks. They usually came upon water a few feet down, but the distance often varied very considerably.

We were crossing the summit of a little hill, where we had rested for a breathing space, when, without the least warning, I suddenly beheld, a few hundred yards away, in the valley beneath, *four white men on horseback!* I think they had a few spare horses with them, but, of course, all that I saw were the four white men. I afterwards learned that, according to our respective routes, we would have crossed their track, but they would not have crossed ours. They were going west. They wore the regulation dress of the Australian—broad sombrero hats, flannel shirts, and rather dirty white trousers, with long riding-boots. I remember they were moving along at a wretched pace, which showed that their horses were nearly spent. Once again, notwithstanding all previous bitter lessons, my uncontrollable excitement was my undoing. "Civilisation at last!" I screamed to myself, and then, throwing discretion to the winds, I gave the war-whoop of the blacks and rushed madly forward, yelling myself hoarse, and supremely oblivious of the fantastic and savage appearance I must have presented—with my long hair flowing wildly out behind, and my skin practically indistinguishable from that of an ordinary black-fellow. My companions, I afterwards discovered, swept after me as in a furious charge, *for they thought I wanted to annihilate the white men at sight.*   Naturally, the spectacle unnerved the pioneers, and they proceeded to repel the supposed attack by firing a volley into the midst of us.   Their horses were terrified, and reared and plunged in

CIVILISATION AT LAST

a dangerous manner, thereby greatly adding to the excitement of that terrible moment.   The roar of the volley and the whizz of the shots brought me to my senses, however, and although I was not hit, I promptly dropped to the ground amidst the long grass, as also did Yamba and the other blacks.   Like a flash my

idiotic blunder came home to me, and then I was ready
to dash out again alone to explain ; but Yamba forcibly
prevented me from exposing myself to what she considered certain death.

The moment the horsemen saw us all disappear
in the long grass they wheeled round, changing
their course a little more to the south—they had
been going west, so far as I can remember—and
their caravan crawled off in a manner that suggested
that the horses were pretty well done for. On our
part, we at once made for the ranges that lay a little
to the south. Here we parted with our friends the
blacks, who made off in an east-south-easterly
direction.

The dominant feeling within me as I saw the
white men ride off was one of uncontrollable rage
and mad despair. I was apparently a pariah, with
the hand of every white man — when I met one—
against me. "Well," I thought, "if civilisation is
not prepared to receive me, I will wait until it
is." Disappointment after disappointment, coupled
with the incessant persuasions of Yamba and my
people generally, were gradually reconciling me to
savage life ; and slowly but relentlessly the thought
crept into my mind that *I was doomed never to reach
civilisation again*, and so perhaps it would be better
for me to resign myself to the inevitable, and stay
where I was. I would turn back, I thought, with
intense bitterness and heart-break, and make a home
among the tribes in the hills, where we would be safe
from the white man and his murderous weapons.
And I actually *did* turn back, accompanied, of course,
by Yamba. We did not strike due north again, as it

was our intention to find a permanent home somewhere among the ranges, at any rate for the ensuing
winter. It was out of the question to camp where
we were, because it was much too cold; and besides
Yamba had much difficulty in finding roots.

Several days later, as we were plodding steadily
along, away from the ranges that I have spoken of
as lying to the south, Yamba, whose eyes were usually
everywhere, suddenly gave a cry and stood still,
pointing to some peculiar and unmistakable footprints
in the sandy ground. These, she confidently assured
me, were those of a white man *who had lost his
reason*, and was wandering aimlessly about that fearful country. It was, of course, easy for her to know
the white man's tracks when she saw them, but I was
curious how she could be certain that the wanderer
had lost his reason. She pointed out to me that, in
the first place, the tracks had been made by some
one wearing boots, and as the footprints straggled
about in a most erratic manner, it was clearly evident
that the wearer could not be sane.

Even at this time, be it remembered, I was burning
with rage against the whites, and so I decided to
follow the tracks and find the individual who was
responsible for them. But do not be under any
misapprehension. My intentions were not philan-
thropic, but revengeful. I had become a black-fellow
myself now, and was consumed with a black-fellow's
murderous passion. At one time I thought I would
follow the whole party, and kill them in the darkness
with my stiletto when opportunity offered.

The new tracks we had come upon told me
plainly that the party had separated, and were there-

fore now in my power. I say these things because
I do not want any one to suppose I followed up
the tracks of the lost man with the intention of
rendering him any assistance.

For nearly two days Yamba and I followed the
tracks, which went in curious circles always trending
to the left. At length we began to come upon
various articles that had apparently been thrown
away by the straggler. First of all, we found part
of a letter that was addressed to some one (I think)
in Adelaide; but of this I would not be absolutely
certain. What I do remember was that the envelope
bore the postmark of Ti Tree Gully, S.A.

The writer of that letter was evidently a woman,
who, so far as I can remember, wrote congratulating
her correspondent upon the fact that he was joining an expedition which was about to traverse the
entire continent. I fancy she said she was glad
of this for his own sake, for it would no doubt
mean much to him. She wished him all kinds
of glory and prosperity, and wound up by assuring
him that none would be better pleased on his return
than she.

The country through which these tracks led us
was for the most part a mere dry, sandy waste,
covered with the formidable spinifex or porcupine
grass. Yamba walked in front peering at the tracks.

Presently she gave a little cry, and when she
turned to me I saw that she had in her hand the
sombrero hat of an Australian pioneer. A little
farther on we found a shirt, and then a pair of
trousers. We next came upon a belt and a pair
of dilapidated boots.

At length, on reaching the crest of a sandy hillock, we suddenly beheld the form of a naked white man lying face downwards in the sand below us.   As you may suppose, we simply swooped down upon him ; but on reaching him my first impression was that *he was dead!*   His face was slightly turned to the right, his arms outstretched, and his fingers dug convulsively in the sand.   I am amused now when I remember how great was our emotion on approaching this unfortunate.   My first thought in turning the man over on to his back, and ascertaining that at last he breathed, was one of great joy and thankfulness.

"Thank God," I said to myself, "I have at last found a white companion—one who will put me in touch once more with the great world outside."   The burning rage that consumed me (you know my object in following the tracks) died away in pity as I thought of the terrible privations and sufferings this poor fellow must have undergone before being reduced to this state.   My desire for revenge was forgotten, and my only thought now was to nurse back to health the unconscious man.

First of all I moistened his mouth with the water which Yamba always carried with her in a skin bag, and then I rubbed him vigorously, hoping to restore animation.   I soon exhausted the contents of the bag, however, and immediately Yamba volunteered to go off and replenish it.   She was absent an hour or more, I think, during which time I persisted in my massage treatment—although so far I saw no signs of returning consciousness on the part of my patient.

When Yamba returned with the water, I tried to make the prostrate man swallow some of it, and I even smeared him with the blood of an opossum which my thoughtful helpmate had brought back with her. But for a long time all my efforts were in vain, and then, dragging him to the foot of a grass-tree, I propped him up slightly against it, wetted his shirt with water and wound it round his throat. Meanwhile Yamba threw water on him and rubbed him vigorously.

At last he uttered a sound—half groan, half sigh (it thrilled me through and through); and I noticed that he was able to swallow a few drops of water. The gloom of night was now descending on that strange wilderness of sand and spinifex, so we prepared to stay there with our helpless charge until morning. Yamba and I took it in turns to watch over him and keep his mouth moistened. By morning he had so far revived that he opened his eyes and looked at me. How eagerly had I anticipated that look, and how bitter was my disappointment when I found that it was a mere vacant stare in which was no kind of recognition! Ever hopeful, however, I attributed the vacant look to the terrible nature of his sufferings. I was burning to ply him with all manner of questions as to who he was, where he had come from, and what news he had of the outside world; but I restrained myself by a great effort, and merely persevered in my endeavours to restore him to complete animation. When the morning was pretty well advanced the man was able to sit up; and in the course of a few days he was even able to accompany us to a water-hole, where we encamped, and stayed until he had practically re-covered—or, at any rate, was able to get about.

But, you may be asking, all this time, did the man himself say nothing? Indeed, he said much, and I hung upon every syllable that fell from his lips, but, to my indescribable chagrin, it was a mere voluble jargon of statements, which simply baffled and puzzled me and caused me pain. Our charge would stare at us stolidly, and then remark, in a vulgar Cockney voice, that he was quite *sure* we were going the wrong way. By this time, I should mention, we had re-clothed him in his trousers and shirt, for he had obviously suffered terribly from the burning sun.

Many days passed away before I would admit to myself that this unhappy creature was a hopeless imbecile. I was never absent from his side day or night, hoping and waiting for the first sane remark. Soon, however, the bitter truth was borne in upon us that, instead of having found salvation and comfort in the society of a white man, we were merely saddled with a ghastly encumbrance, and were far worse off than before.

We now set off in the direction of our old tracks, but were not able to travel very fast on account of the still feeble condition of the white stranger. Poor creature! I pitied him from the bottom of my heart. It seemed so terrible for a man to lapse into a state of imbecility after having survived the dreadful hard-ships and adventures that had befallen him. I tried over and over again to elicit sensible replies to my questions as to where he came from; but he simply gibbered and babbled like a happy baby. I coaxed; I threatened; I persuaded; but it was all in vain.   I

soon found he was a regular millstone round my neck
—particularly when we were on the "walk-about."
He would suddenly take it into his head to sit down
for hours at a stretch, and nothing would induce him
to move until he did so of his own accord.

Curiously enough, Bruno became very greatly
attached to him, and was his constant companion.
Of this I was extremely glad, because it relieved me
of much anxiety.   You will understand what I mean
when I tell you that, in spite of all our endeavours,
our mysterious companion would go off by himself
away from our track ; and at such times were it not
for Bruno—whom he would follow anywhere—we
would often have had much trouble in bringing him
back again.   Or he might have been speared before
a strange tribe could have discovered his "sacred"
(idiotic) condition.

At length we reached a large lagoon, on the shores
of which we stayed for about two years.   This lagoon
formed part of a big river at flood-time, but the
connecting stretches of water had long since dried
up for many miles both above and below it.   The
question may be asked, Why did I settle down here ?
The answer is, that our white companion had become
simply an intolerable burden.   He suffered from the
most exhausting attacks of dysentery, and was quite
helpless.   It was, of course, my intention to have
continued my march northward to my old home in
the Cambridge Gulf district, because by this time I
had quite made up my mind that, by living there
quietly, I stood a better chance of escape to civilisation by means of some vessel than I did by attempting to traverse the entire continent.   This latter idea

was now rendered impossible, on account of the poor, helpless creature I had with me. Indeed, so great an anxiety was he to me and Yamba, that we decided we could go nowhere, either north or south, until he had become more robust in health. Needless to say, I never intrusted him with a weapon.

I had found a sheath-knife belonging to him, but I afterwards gave it away to a friendly chief, who was immensely proud of it.

In making for the shores of the big lagoon we had to traverse some extremely difficult country. In the first place, we encountered a series of very broken ridges, which in parts proved so hard to travel over that I almost gave up in despair. At times there was nothing for it but to carry on my back the poor, feeble creature who, I felt, was now intrusted to my charge and keeping. I remember that native chiefs frequently suggested that I should leave him, but I never listened to this advice for a moment. Perhaps I was not altogether disinterested, because already my demented companion was looked upon as a kind of minor deity by the natives. I may here remark that I only knew two idiots during the whole of my sojourn. One of these had fallen from a tree through a branch breaking, and he was actually maintained at the expense of the tribe, revered by all, if not actually worshipped.

But the journey I was just describing was a fearful trial. Sometimes we had to traverse a wilderness of rocks which stood straight up and projected at sharp angles, presenting at a distance the appearance of a series of stony terraces which were all but impassable. For a long time our charge wore both shirt and trousers, but eventually we had to discard the latter —or perhaps it would be more correct to say, that the garment was literally torn to shreds by the spinifex. At one time I had it in my mind to make him go naked like myself, but on consideration I thought it advisable to allow him to retain his shirt, at any rate for a time, as his skin was not so inured to the burning sun as my own.

We had to provide him with food, which he accepted, of course, without gratitude.   Then Yamba had always to build him a shelter wherever we camped, so that far from being an invaluable assistance and a companion he was a burden—so great that, in moments of depression, I regretted not having left him to die.   As it was, he would often have gone to his death in the great deserts were it not for the ever-vigilant Bruno.   Still, I always thought that some day I would be able to take the man back to civilisation, and there find out who he was and whence he had come.   And I hoped that people would think I had been kind to him.   At first I thought the unfortunate man was suffering from sunstroke, and that in course of time he would regain his reason.   I knew I could do very little towards his recovery except by feeding him well.   Fortunately the natives never called upon him to demonstrate before them the extraordinary powers which I attributed to him.   Indeed his strange gestures, antics, and babblings were sufficient in themselves to convince the blacks that he was a creature to be reverenced.   The remarkable thing about him was that he never seemed to take notice of any one, whether it were myself, Yamba, or a native chief.   As a rule, his glance would "go past me," so to speak, and he was for ever wandering aimlessly about, chattering and gesticulating.

We placed no restrictions upon him, and supplied all his wants, giving him Bruno as a guide and protector. I must say that Yamba did not like the stranger, but for my sake she was wonderfully patient with him.

It was whilst living on the shores of this lagoon that I received a very extraordinary commission from a neighbouring tribe. Not long after my arrival I heard a curious legend, to the effect that away on the other side of the lagoon there was an "evil spirit" infesting the waters, which terrified the women when they went down to fill their skins. Well, naturally enough, the fame of the white man and his doings soon got abroad in that country, and I was one day invited by the tribe in question to go and rid them of the evil spirit. Accordingly, accompanied by Yamba, and leaving Bruno to look after our helpless companion, we set off in response to the invitation, and in a few days reached the camp of the blacks who had sent for me. The lagoon was here surrounded by a finely-wooded country, slightly mountainous. Perhaps I ought to have stated that I had already gleaned from the mail-men, or runners, who had been sent with the message, that the waters of the lagoon in the vicinity of the camp had long been disturbed by some huge fish or monster, whose vagaries were a constant source of terror. The dreaded creature would come quite close inshore, and then endeavour to "spear" the women with what was described as a long weapon carried in its mouth. This, then, was the evil spirit of the lagoon, and I confess it puzzled me greatly. I thought it probable that it was merely a large fish which had descended in a rain-cloud among countless millions of others of smaller species. I looked upon the commission, however, as a good opportunity for displaying my powers and impressing the natives in that country—I always had the utmost confidence in myself. Before setting out I had spent some little time in completing my preparations for the capture of the strange monster.

The very afternoon I arrived I went down to the shores of the lagoon with all the natives, and had not long to wait before I beheld what was apparently a huge fish careering wildly and erratically hither and thither in the water. On seeing it the natives appeared tremendously excited, and they danced and yelled, hoping thereby to drive the creature away. My first move was in the nature of an experiment— merely with the object of getting a better view of the monster. I endeavoured to angle for it with a hook made out of a large piece of sharpened bone. I then produced large nets made out of strips of green hide and stringy-bark rope. Placing these on the shores of the lagoon, I directed Yamba to build a little bark canoe just big enough to hold her and me.

At length we embarked and paddled out a few hundred yards, when we threw the net overboard. It had previously been weighted, and now floated so that it promptly expanded to its utmost capacity. No sooner had we done this than the invisible monster charged down upon us, making a tremendous commotion in the water. Neither Yamba nor I waited for the coming impact, but threw ourselves overboard just as the creature's white sawlike weapon showed itself close to the surface only a few yards away. We heard a crash, and then, looking backward as we swam, saw that the long snout of the fish had actually pierced both sides of the canoe, whilst his body was evidently entangled in the meshes of the net. So desperate had been the charge that our little craft was now actually a serious encumbrance to the monster. It struggled madly to free itself, leaping almost clear of the water and lashing the placid lagoon into a perfect maëlstrom.

Several times the canoe was lifted high out of the water ; and then the fish would try to drag it underneath, but was prevented by its great buoyancy. In the meantime Yamba and I swam safely ashore, and watched the struggles of the "evil spirit" from the shore, among a crowd of frantic natives.

We waited until the efforts of the fish grew feebler, and then put off in another bark canoe (the celerity with which Yamba made one was something amazing), when I easily despatched the now weakened creature with my tomahawk. I might here mention that this was actually the first time that these inland savages had seen a canoe or boat of any description, so that naturally the two I launched occasioned endless amazement.

Afterwards, by the way, I tried to describe to them what the sea was like, but had to give it up, because it only confused them, and was quite beyond their comprehension. When we dragged the monster ashore, with its elongated snout still embedded in the little canoe, I saw at a glance that the long-dreaded evil spirit of the lagoon was a huge sawfish, fully fourteen feet long, its formidable saw alone measuring nearly five feet. This interesting weapon I claimed as a trophy, and when I got back to where Bruno and his human charge were, I exhibited it to crowds of admiring blacks, who had long heard of the evil spirit. The great fish itself was cooked and eaten at one of the biggest *corroborees* I had ever seen. The blacks had no theory of their own (save the superstitious one), as to how it got into the lagoon; and the only supposition I can offer is, that it must have been brought thither, when very small and young, either by a rain-cloud or at some unusually big flood time.

So delighted were the blacks at the service I had done them, that they paid me the greatest compliment in their power by offering me a chieftainship, and inviting me to stay with them for ever. I refused the flattering offer, however, as I was quite bent on getting back to Cambridge Gulf.

On returning to my friends on the other side of the lagoon I learned for the first time that there was a half-caste girl living among them; and subsequent inquiries went to prove that her father was a white man who had penetrated into these regions and lived for some little time at least among the blacks—much as I myself was doing. My interest in the matter was first of all roused by the accidental discovery of a cairn five feet or six feet high, made of loose flat stones. My experience was such by this time that I saw at a glance this cairn was not the work of a native. Drawings and figures, and a variety of curious characters, were faintly discernible on some of the stones, but were not distinct enough to be legible.

On one, however, I distinctly traced the initials "L. L.," which had withstood the ravages of time because the stone containing them was in a protected place.

AN ACCIDENTAL DISCOVERY

Naturally the existence of this structure set me inquiring among the older natives as to whether they ever remembered seeing a white man before; and then I learned that perhaps twenty years previously

a man like myself *had* made his appearance in those
regions, and had died a few months afterwards,
before the wife who, according to custom, was allotted
to him had given birth to the half-caste baby girl,
who was now a woman before me. They never knew
the white stranger's name, nor where he had come
from. The girl, by the way, was by no means good-
looking, and her skin was decidedly more black than
white; I could tell by her hand, however, that she
was a half-caste.

On the strength of our supposed affinity, she was
offered to me as a wife, and I accepted her, more as
a help for Yamba than anything else; she was called
Luigi. Yamba, by the way, was anxious that I
should possess at least half-a-dozen wives, partly
because this circumstance would be more in keeping
with my rank; but I did not fall in with the idea.
I had quite enough to do already to maintain my
authority among the tribe at large, and did not care
to have to rule in addition half-a-dozen women in
my own establishment. This tribe always lingers
in my memory, on account of the half-caste girl,
whom I now believe to have been the daughter of
Ludwig Leichhardt, the lost Australian explorer.
Mr. Giles says: "Ludwig Leichhardt was a surgeon
and botanist, who successfully conducted an expedition from Moreton Bay to Port Essington, on the
northern coast. A military and penal settlement had
been established at Port Essington by the Government of New South Wales, to which colony the
whole territory then belonged. At this settlement—
the only point of relief after eighteen months' travel
——Leichhardt and his exhausted party arrived.

"Of Leichhardt's sad fate, in the interior of Australia, no certain tidings have ever been heard. I, who have wandered into and returned alive from the curious regions he attempted and died to explore, have unfortunately never come across a single record, nor any remains or traces of the party."

Leichhardt started on his last sad venture with a party of eight, including one or two native black-boys. They had with them about twenty head of bullocks broken in to carry pack loads. "My first and second expeditions," says Giles, "were conducted entirely with horses, but in all subsequent journeys I was accompanied by camels." His object, like that of Leichhardt, was to force his way across the thousand miles of country that lay untrodden and unknown between the Australian telegraph line and the settlements upon the Swan River. And Giles remarks that the exploration of 1000 miles in Australia is equal to at least 10,000 miles on any other part of the earth's surface—always excepting the Poles.

I continued residing on the shores of the lagoon in the hope that my patient would eventually get better, when I proposed continuing my journey north. I was still quite unable to understand his babblings, although he was for ever mentioning the names of persons and places unknown to me; and he constantly spoke about some exploring party. He never asked me questions, nor did he get into serious trouble with the natives, being privileged. He never developed any dangerous vices, but was simply childlike and imbecile.

Gradually I had noticed that, instead of becoming

stronger, he was fading away. He was constantly troubled with a most distressing complaint, and in addition to this he would be seized with fits of depression, when he would remain in his hut for days at a time without venturing out. I always knew what was the matter with him when he was not to be seen. Sometimes I would go in to try and cheer him up, but usually it was a hopeless effort on my part.

Of course he had a wife given him, and this young person seemed to consider him quite an ordinary specimen of the white man. Indeed, she was vastly flattered, rather than otherwise, by the attentions lavished upon her husband by her people. One reason for this treatment was that she was considered a privileged person to be related in any way to one whom the natives regarded as almost a demi-god. She looked after him too, and kept his hut as clean as possible. One morning something happened. The girl came running for me to go to her hut, and there lay the mysterious stranger apparently stretched out for dead. I soon realised that he was in a fit of some kind.

I now approach the momentous time when this unfortunate man recovered his senses. When he regained consciousness after the fit Yamba and I were with him, and so was his wife. I had not seen him for some days, and was much shocked at the change that had taken place. He was ghastly pale and very much emaciated. I knew that death was at hand. Just as he regained consciousness—I can see the picture now; yes, we were all around his fragrant couch of eucalyptus leaves, waiting for him to open his eyes—he gazed at me in a way that thrilled me strangely, and *I knew I was looking at a sane white man.* His first questions were "Where am I ? Who are you?" Eager and trembling I knelt down beside him and told him the long and strange story of how I had found him, and how he had now been living with me nearly two years. I pointed out to him our faithful Bruno, who had often taken him for long walks and brought him back safely, and who had so frequently driven away from him deadly snakes, and warned him when it was time to turn back. I told him he was in the centre of Australia ; and then I told in brief my own extraordinary story. I sent Yamba to our shelter for the letter I had found in his tracks, and read it aloud to him. He never told me who the writer of it was. He listened to all I had to tell him with an expression of amazement, which soon gave place to one of weariness—the weariness of utter weakness. He asked me to carry him outside into the sun, and I did so, afterwards squatting down beside him and opening up another conversation. *He then told me his name was Gibson, and that he had been a member of the Giles Expedition of* 1874. From that moment I never left him night or day. He told me much about that expedition which I can never reveal, for I do not know whether he was lying or raving. Poor, vulgar, Cockney Gibson ! He seemed to know full well that he was dying, and the thought seemed to please him rather than otherwise. He appeared to me to be too tired, too weary to live—that was the predominant symptom.

I introduced Yamba to him, and we did everything

we possibly could to cheer him, but he gradually sank
lower and lower. I would say, "Cheer up, Gibson.
Why, when you are able to walk we will make tracks
straightway for civilisation. I am sure you know the
way, for now you are as right as I am." But
nothing interested the dying man. Shortly before
the end his eyes assumed a strained look, and I
could see he was rapidly going. The thought of his
approaching end was to me a relief; it would be
untrue if I were to say otherwise. For weeks past
I had seen that the man could not live, and considering that every day brought its battle for life, you will
readily understand that this poor helpless creature
was a terrible burden to me. He had such a tender
skin that at all times I was obliged to keep him
clothed. For some little time his old shirt and
trousers did duty, but at length I was compelled to
make him a suit of skins. Of course, we had no
soap with which to wash his garments, but we used
to clean them after a fashion by dumping them down
into a kind of greasy mud and then trampling on
them, afterwards rinsing them out in water. Moreover, his feet were so tender that I always had to
keep him shod with skin sandals.

His deathbed was a dramatic scene—especially
under the circumstances. Poor Gibson! To think
that he should have escaped death after those fearful
waterless days and nights in the desert, to live for
two years with a white protector, and yet then die of
a wasting and distressing disease !

He spent the whole day in the open air, for he
was very much better when in the sun. At night
I carried him back into his hut, and laid him in

U

the hammock which I had long ago slung for him. Yamba knew he was dying even before I did, but she could do nothing.

We tried the effect of the curious herb called "pitchori," but it did not revive him. "Pitchori," by the way, is a kind of leaf which the natives chew in moments of depression; it has an exhilarating effect upon them.

On the last day I once more made up a bed of eucalyptus leaves and rugs on the floor of Gibson's hut. Surrounding him at the last were his wife—a very good and faithful girl—Yamba, myself, and Bruno—who, by the way, knew perfectly well that his friend was dying. He kept licking poor Gibson's hand and chest, and then finding no response would nestle up close to him for half-an-hour at a time. Then the affectionate creature would retire outside and set up a series of low, melancholy howls, only to run in again with hope renewed.

Poor Gibson! The women-folk were particularly attached to him because he never went out with the men, or with me, on my various excursions, but remained behind in their charge. Sometimes, however, he would follow at our heels as faithfully and instinctively as Bruno himself. For the past two years Bruno and Gibson had been inseparable, sleeping together at night, and never parting for a moment the whole day long. Indeed, I am sure Bruno became more attached to Gibson than he was to me. And so Gibson did not, as I at one time feared he would, pass away into the Great Beyond, carrying with him the secret of his identity. Looking at him as he lay back among the eucalyptus leaves, pale and emaciated, I knew the end was now very near.

I knelt beside him holding his hand, and at length, with a great effort, he turned towards me and said feebly, "Can you hear anything?" I listened intently, and at last was compelled to reply that I did not. "Well," he said, "I hear some one talking. I think the voices of my friends are calling me." I fancied that the poor fellow was wandering in his mind again, but still his eyes did not seem to have that vacant gaze I had previously noticed in them. He was looking steadily at me, and seemed to divine my thoughts, for he smiled sadly and said, "No, I know what I am saying. I can hear them singing, and they are calling me away. They have come for me at last!" His thin face brightened up with a slow, sad smile, which soon faded away, and then, giving my hand a slight pressure, he whispered almost in my ear, as I bent over him, "Good-bye, comrade, I'm off. You will come too, some day." A slight shiver, and Gibson passed peacefully away.

CHAPTER XV

AFTER the funeral his wife followed out the usual native conventions. She covered herself with pipeclay for about one month. She also mourned and howled for the prescribed three days, and gashed her head with stone knives, until the blood poured down her face. Gibson's body was not buried in the earth, but embalmed with clay and leaves, and laid on a rock-shelf in a cave.

The general belief was that Gibson had merely gone back to the Spirit Land from whence he had come, and that, as he was a great and good man, he would return to earth in the form of a bird—perhaps an ibis, which was very high indeed. I must say I never attached very much importance to what he said, even in his sane moments, because he was obviously a man of low intelligence and no culture. If I remember rightly, he told me that the expedition to which he was attached left Adelaide with the object of going overland to Fremantle. It was thoroughly well equipped, and for a long time everything went well with the party. One day, whilst some of them were off exploring on their own account, he lost himself.

He rather thought that the sun must have affected his brain even then, because he didn't try to find his companions that night, but went to sleep quite contentedly under a tree. He realised the horror of his position keenly enough the next morning, however, and rode mile after mile without halting for food or water, in the hope of quickly regaining his friends at the chief camp. But night stole down upon him once more, and he was still a lonely wanderer, half delirious with thirst; the supply he had carried with him had long since given out.

Next morning, when he roused himself, he found that his horse had wandered away and got lost. After this he had only a vague recollection of what happened. Prompted by some strange, unaccountable impulse, he set out on a hopeless search for water, and went walking on and on until all recollection faded away, and he remembered no more. How long he had been lost when I found him he could not say, because he knew absolutely nothing whatever about his rescue. So far as I remember, he was a typical specimen of the Australian pioneer—a man of fine physique, with a full beard and a frank, but unintelligent, countenance. He was perhaps five feet nine inches in height, and about thirty years of age. When I told him the story of my adventures he was full of earnest sympathy for me, and told me that if ever I intended leaving those regions for civilisation again, my best plan would be to steer more south-east, as it was in that direction that Adelaide lay.

He also informed me that the great trans-Continental telegraph wire was being constructed from north to south. This he advised me to strike and follow to civilisation.

I may be permitted a little digression here to give a few extracts from Giles's book, "Australia Twice Traversed" (Sampson Low & Company), for this contains the version of the leader of the expedition himself as to the circumstances under which Gibson

MR. ERNEST GILES

was lost. In all, it seems, Giles made five exploring expeditions into and through Central South Australia and Western Australia from 1872 to 1876. Speaking of his second expedition, Mr. Giles says: "I had informed my friend, Baron Von Mueller, by wire from the Charlotte Waters Telegraph station, of the failure and break-up of my first expedition, and he set to work and obtained new funds for me to continue my labours. I reached Adelaide late in January 1873, and got my party together. We left early in March of 1873, and journeyed leisurely up-country to Beltana, then past the Finnis Springs to the Gregory. We then journeyed up to the Peake, where we were welcomed by Messrs. Bagot at the Cattle Station, and Mr. Blood of the Telegraph Department. Here we fixed up all our packs, sold Bagot the waggon, and bought horses and other things. We now had twenty pack-horses and four riding-horses."

We next come to the introduction of Gibson. "Here a short young man accosted me, and asked me if I didn't remember him. He said he was 'Alf.' I thought I knew his face, but I thought it was at the Peake that I had seen him ; but he said, 'Oh, no! Don't you remember Alf, with Bagot's sheep at the north-west bend of the Murray? My name's Alf Gibson, and I want to go out with you.' I said, 'Well, can you shoe? Can you ride? Can you starve? Can you go without water? And how would you like to be speared by the blacks? He said he could do everything I had mentioned, and he wasn't afraid of the blacks. He was not a man I would have picked out of a mob, but men were scarce, and he seemed so anxious to come, so I agreed to take him.

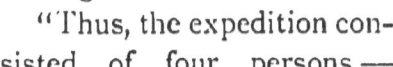

MR. W. H. TIETKINS

"Thus, the expedition consisted of four persons — myself (Ernest Giles), Mr. William Henry Tietkins, Alf Gibson, and James Andrews; with twenty-four horses and two little dogs. On Monday, 4th August, we finally left the encampment."

Now here is the passage in which Mr. Giles describes his dramatic parting with Gibson. It will be found in the chapter marked "20th April to 21st May 1874": "Gibson and I departed for the West. I rode the 'Fair Maid of Perth.' I gave Gibson the

big ambling horse, 'Badger,' and we packed the big
cob with a pair of water-bags that contained twenty
gallons.   As we rode away, I was telling Gibson
about various exploring expeditions and their fate,
and he said, 'How is it that, in all these exploring
expeditions, a lot of people go and die ? '   He said,
' I shouldn't like to die in this part of the country,
anyhow.'

   " We presently had a meal of smoked horse.   It
was late when we encamped, and the horses were
much in want of water,—especially the big cob, who
kept coming up to the camp all night and trying to
get at our water-bags.   We had one small water-
bag hung in a tree.

   "I didn't think of that until my mare came straight
up to it and took it in her teeth, forcing out the cork,
and sending the water up, which we were both dying
to drink, in a beautiful jet.   Gibson was now very
sorry he had exchanged ' Badger' for the cob, as he
found the latter very dull and heavy to get along.
There had been a hot wind from the north all day,
and the following morning (the 23rd of April), there
was a most strange dampness in the air, and I had
a vague feeling, such as must have been felt by
augurs and seers of old, who trembled as they told
events to come ; *for this was the last day on which I
ever saw Gibson.*

   " As Gibson came along after me, he called out
that his horse was going to die.   The hills to the
west were twenty-five to thirty miles away, and I
had to give up trying to reach them.   How I longed
for a camel !   Gibson's horse was now so bad as to
place both of us in a great dilemma.   We turned

back in our tracks, when the cob refused to carry his rider any farther, and tried to lie down. We drove him another mile on foot, and down he fell to die. My mare, the 'Fair Maid of Perth,' was only too willing to return, but she had now to carry Gibson's saddle and things, and away we went, walking and riding in turns of one half-hour each.

"When we got back to about thirty miles from a place which I had named 'The Kegs,' I shouted to Gibson, who was riding, to stop until I walked up to him. By this time we had hardly a pint of water left between us.

"We here finished the supply, and I then said, as I could not speak before, 'Look here, Gibson, you see we are in a most terrible fix, with only one horse. Only one can ride, and one must remain behind. I shall remain; and now listen to me. If the mare does not get water soon, she will die; therefore, ride right on; get to the Kegs, if possible, to-night, and give her water. Now that the cob is dead, there'll be all the more water for her. Early to-morrow you will sight the Rawlinson, at twenty-five miles from the Kegs. Stick to the tracks and never leave them. Leave as much water in one keg for me as you can afford, after watering the mare and filling up your own bags; and, remember, I depend upon you to bring me relief.'

"Gibson said if he had a compass he thought he could go better by night. I knew he didn't understand anything about compasses, as I had often tried to explain them to him. The one I had was a Gregory's Patent, of a totally different construction from ordinary instruments of the kind, and I was loth

to part with it, as it was the only one I had.
However, as he was so anxious for it, I gave it to
him, and away he went. I sent one final shout
after him to stick to the tracks, and he said, 'All
right!' and the mare carried him out of sight almost
instantly.

"Gibson had left me with a little over two gallons
of water, which I could have drunk in half-an-hour.
All the food I had was eleven sticks of dirty, sandy,
smoked horse, averaging about an ounce and a half
each.

"On the first of May, as I afterwards found out,
at one o'clock in the morning, I staggered into the
camp, and awoke Mr. Tietkins at daylight. He glared
at me as if I had been one risen from the dead. I
asked him if he had seen Gibson. It was nine days
since I last saw him. The next thing was to find
Gibson's remains. It was the 6th of May when we
got back to where he had left the right line. As
long as he had remained on the other horses' tracks
it was practicable enough to follow him, but the
wretched man had left them and gone away in a far
more southerly direction, having the most difficult
sand-hills to cross at right angles. We found he had
burnt a patch of spinifex where he had left the other
horses' tracks.

"Whether he had made any mistake in steering
by the compass or not it is impossible to say; but
instead of going east, as he should have done, he
actually went south, or very near it.

"I was sorry to think that the unfortunate man's
last sensible moments must have been embittered by
the thought that, as he had lost himself in the capacity

of messenger for my relief, I, too, must necessarily fall a victim to his mishap.

"I called this terrible region, lying between the Rawlinson Range and the next permanent water that may eventually be found to the north, 'Gibson's Desert,'—after this first white victim to its horrors.

"In looking over Gibson's few effects, Mr. Tietkins and I found an old pocket-book, a drinking-song, and a certificate of his marriage. He had never told us he was married."

And now to resume my own narrative. You will remember that I had settled down for a considerable time on the shores of the lagoon, where I had made everything around me as comfortable as possible. Yamba had no difficulty whatever in keeping us well supplied with roots and vegetables ; and as kangaroos, opossums, snakes, and rats abounded, we had an ample supply of meat, and the lagoon could always be relied upon to provide us with excellent fish. The country itself was beautiful in the extreme, with stately mountains, broad, fertile valleys, extensive forests, —and, above all, plenty of water. The general mode of living among the natives was much the same as that prevailing among the blacks in my own home at Cambridge Gulf,—although these latter were a vastly superior race in point of physique, war weapons, and general intelligence. The people I now found myself among were of somewhat small stature, with very low foreheads, protruding chins, high cheek-bones, and large mouths. Their most noteworthy characteristic was their extreme childishness, which was especially displayed on those occasions when I gave an acrobatic performance. My skill with the bow and arrow was, as usual, a never-ending source of astonishment. I was, in fact, credited with such remarkable powers that all my ingenuity had sometimes to be brought into play to accomplish, or to pretend to accomplish, the things expected of me. I knew that I must never fail in anything I undertook.

In the interior the natives never seemed to grow very plump, but had a more or less spare, not to say emaciated, appearance compared with the tribes near the coast. For one thing, food is not so easily obtainable, nor is it so nourishing. Moreover, the natives had to go very long distances to procure it.

Besides the low, receding forehead and protruding chin I have already hinted at as characteristic of the inland tribes, I also noticed that these people had abnormally large feet. Also, the beards of the men were not nearly so full or luxuriant as those of the blacks at Cambridge Gulf. The average height of the lagoon tribe was little more than five feet. For myself, I am about five feet seven and a half inches in height, and therefore I stalked about among them like a giant.

Now that Gibson was dead I decided to move my home farther north, and eventually settled down with my family (two children—a boy and a girl—had been born to me during my residence on the shores of the lagoon) in a beautiful mountainous and tropical region 200 or 300 miles to the north. It was my intention only to have made a temporary stay here; but other ties came, and my little ones were by no means strong enough to undertake any such formidable journey as I had in contemplation. I also made the fatal mistake of trying to bring my offspring up

differently from the other savage children. But I must
relate here an incident that happened on our journey
north. Yamba came to me one day positively quivering with excitement and terror, and said she had found
some strange tracks, apparently of some enormous
beast—a monster so fearful as to be quite beyond
her knowledge.

She took me to the spot and pointed out the
mysterious tracks, which I saw at once were those
of camels. I do not know why I decided to follow
them, because they must have been some months
old. Probably, I reflected, I might be able to pick
up something on the tracks which would be of use
to me. At any rate, we did follow the tracks for
several days—perhaps a fortnight—and found on
the way many old meat-tins, which afterwards came
in useful as water vessels. One day, however, I
pounced upon an illustrated newspaper—a copy of
the Sydney *Town and Country Journal*, bearing some
date, I think in 1875 or 1876. It was a complete
copy with the outer cover. I remember it contained
some pictures of horse-racing—I believe at Paramatta ;
but the " Long Lost Relative " column interested me
most, for the very moment I found the paper I sat
down in the bush and began to read this part with
great eagerness. I could read English fairly well by
this time, and as Yamba was also tolerably familiar
with the language, I read the paper aloud to her. I
cannot say she altogether understood what she heard,
but she saw that I was intensely interested and delighted, and so she was quite content to stay there
and listen. You will observe that in all cases, the
very fact that *I* was pleased was enough for Yamba,

who never once wavered in her fidelity and affection.
Altogether we spent some weeks following up these
tracks, but, of course, never came up with the caravan
of camels, which must have been some months ahead
of us.   Yamba at length appeared to be a good deal
wearied at my persistency in following up the tracks
in this way; but after all, was it not merely killing
time ?—a mild sort of sensation which served to
break the eternal monotony that sometimes threatened
to crush me.

How I treasured that soiled copy of the *Town and
Country*—as it is familiarly called in Sydney !   I read
and re-read it, and then read it all over again until I
think I could have repeated every line of it by heart,
even to the advertisements.   Among the latter, by
the way, was one inserted apparently by an anxious
mother seeking information concerning a long-lost
son ; and this pathetic paragraph set me wondering
about my own mother.   "Well," I thought, "she at
least has no need to advertise, and I have the satisfaction of knowing that she must by this time be
quite reconciled to my loss, and have given me up
as dead long ago."   Strangely enough, this thought
quite reconciled me to my exile.   In fact, I thanked
Providence that my disappearance had been so complete and so prolonged as to leave not the slightest
cause for doubt or hope on the part of any of my
relatives.   Had I for a moment imagined that my
mother was still cherishing hopes of seeing me again
some day, and that she was undergoing agonies of
mental suspense and worry on my behalf, I think I
would have risked everything to reach her.   But I
knew quite well that she must have heard of the loss

of the *Veielland*, and long ago resigned herself to the certainty of my death. I can never hope to describe the curious delight with which I perused my precious newspaper. I showed the pictures in it to my children and the natives, and they were more than delighted,—especially with the pictures of horses in the race at Paramatta. In the course of time the sheets of paper began to get torn, and then I made a pretty durable cover out of kangaroo hide. Thus the whole of my library consisted of my Anglo-French Testament, and the copy of the *Town and Country Journal*.

But I have purposely kept until the end the most important thing in connection with this strangely-found periodical. The very first eager and feverish reading gave me an extraordinary shock, which actually threatened my reason! In a prominent place in the Journal I came across the following passage : "*The Deputies of Alsace and Lorraine have refused to vote in the German Reichstag.*"

Now, knowing nothing whatever of the sanguinary war of 1870, or of the alterations in the map of Europe which it entailed, this passage filled me with startled amazement. I read it over and over again, getting more bewildered each time. "The Deputies of Alsace and Lorraine have refused to vote in the German Reichstag!" "But—good heavens!" I almost screamed to myself, "*what* were the Alsace and Lorraine Deputies doing in the German Parliament at all?" I turned the matter over and over in my mind, and at last, finding that I was getting worked up into a state of dangerous excitement, I threw the paper from me and walked away. I thought over the matter again, and so utterly incomprehensible did it appear to me that I thought I must be mistaken—that my eyes must have deceived me. Accordingly I ran back and picked the paper up a second time, and there, sure enough, was the same passage. In vain did I seek for any sane explanation, and at last I somehow got it into my head that the appearance of the printed characters must be due to a kind of mental obliquity, and that I must be rapidly going mad! Even Yamba could not sympathise with me, because the matter was one which I never could have made her understand. I tried to put this strange puzzle out of my head, but again and again the accursed and torturing passage would ring in my ears until I nearly went crazy. But I presently put the thing firmly from me, and resolved to think no more about it.

It is not an exaggeration to describe my mountain home in the centre of the continent as a perfect paradise. The grasses and ferns there grew to a prodigious height, and there were magnificent forests of white gum and eucalyptus. Down in the valley I built a spacious house—the largest the natives had ever seen. It was perhaps twenty feet long, sixteen feet to eighteen feet wide, and about ten feet high. The interior was decorated with ferns, war implements, the skins of various animals, and last—but by no means least—the "sword" of the great sawfish I had killed in the haunted lagoon. This house contained no fireplace, because all the cooking was done in the open air. The walls were built of rough logs, the crevices being filled in with earth taken from ant-hills. I have just said that *I* built the house.

This is, perhaps, not strictly correct. It was Yamba and the other women-folk who actually carried out the work, under my supervision. Here it is necessary to explain that I did not dare to do much manual labour, because it would have been considered undignified on my part. I really did not want the house; but, strangely enough, I felt much more comfortable when it was built and furnished, because, after all, it was a source of infinite satisfaction to me to feel that I had a *home* I could call my own. I had grown very weary of living like an animal in the bush, and lying down to sleep at night on the bare ground. It was this same consideration of "home" that induced me to build a little hut for poor Gibson.

The floor of my house was two or three feet above the ground in order to escape the ravages of the rats. There was only one storey, of course, and the whole was divided into two rooms—one as a kind of sitting-room and the other as a bedroom. The former I fitted out with home-made tables and chairs (I had become pretty expert from my experience with the girls); and each day fresh eucalyptus leaves were strewed about, partly for cleanliness, and partly because the odour kept away the mosquitoes. I also built another house about two days' tramp up the mountains, and to this we usually resorted in the very hot weather.

Now here I have a curious confession to make. As the months glided into years, and I reviewed the whole of my strange life since the days when I went pearling with Jensen, the thought began gradually to steal into my mind, " Why not wait until civilisation COMES TO YOU—as it must do in time?

X

Why weary yourself any more with incessant struggles to get back to the world—especially when you are so comfortable here?" Gradually, then, I settled down and was made absolute chief over a tribe of perhaps five hundred souls. Besides this, my fame spread abroad into the surrounding country, and at every new moon I held a sort of informal reception, which was attended by deputations of tribesmen for hundreds of miles around. My own tribe already possessed a chieftain of their own, but my position was one of even greater influence than his. Moreover, I was appointed to it without having to undergo the painful ceremonies that initiation entails. My immunity in this respect was of course owing to my supposed great powers, and the belief that I was a returned spirit. I was always present at tribal and war councils, and also had some authority over other tribes.

I adopted every device I could think of to make my dwelling home-like, and I even journeyed many miles in a NNE. direction, to procure cuttings of grape vines I had seen; but I must say that this at any rate was labour in vain, because I never improved upon the quality of the wild grapes, which had a sharp, acid flavour, that affected the throat somewhat unpleasantly until one got used to them.

When I speak of my "mountain home," it must not be supposed that I remained in one place. As a matter of fact, in accordance with my usual practice, I took long excursions in different directions extending over weeks and even months at a time. On these occasions I always took with me a kind of nut, which, when eaten, endowed one with remarkable powers of vitality and endurance.   Since my return to civilisation I have heard of the Kola nut, but cannot say whether the substance used by the Australian aboriginal is the same or not.   I remember we generally roasted ours, and ate it as we tramped along.   In the course of my numerous journeys abroad I blazed or marked a great number of trees ; my usual mark being an oval, in or underneath which I generally carved the letter " L."   I seldom met with hostile natives in this region, but when I did my mysterious bow and arrows generally sufficed to impress them.   By the way, I never introduced the bow as a weapon among the blacks, and they, on their part, never tried to imitate me.   They are a conservative race, and are perfectly satisfied with their own time-honoured weapons.

Wild geese and ducks were plentiful in those regions, and there was an infinite variety of game. From this you will gather that our daily fare was both ample and luxurious.

And we had pets ; I remember I once caught a live cockatoo, and trained him to help me in my hunting expeditions.   I taught him a few English phrases, such as " Good-morning," and " How are you ? " ; and he would perch himself on a tree and attract great numbers of his kind around him by his incessant chattering.   I would then knock over as many as I wanted by means of my bow and arrows. At this time, indeed, I had quite a menagerie of animals, including a tame kangaroo.   Naturally enough, I had ample leisure to study the ethnology of my people.   I soon made the discovery that my blacks were intensely spiritualistic ; and once a year they held a festival which, when described, will, I am afraid, tax the credulity of my readers. The festival I refer to was held "when the sun was born again,"—*i.e.*, soon after the shortest day of the year, which would be sometime in June. On these occasions the adult warriors from far and near assembled at a certain spot, and after a course of festivities, sat down to an extraordinary *séance* conducted by women—very old, wizened witches—who apparently possessed occult powers, and were held in great veneration. These witches are usually maintained at the expense of the tribe. The office, however, does not necessarily descend from mother to daughter, it being only women credited with supernatural powers who can claim the position.

After the great *corroboree* the people would squat on the ground, the old men and warriors in front, the women behind, and the children behind them. The whole congregation was arranged in the form of a crescent, in the centre of which a large fire would be set burning. Some of the warriors would then start chanting, and their monotonous sing-song would presently be taken up by the rest of the gathering, to the accompaniment of much swaying of heads and beating of hands and thighs. The young warriors then went out into the open and commenced to dance.

I may as well describe in detail the first of these extraordinary festivals which I witnessed. The men chanted and danced themselves into a perfect frenzy, which was still further increased by the appearance of three or four witches who suddenly rose up before the fire. They were very old and haggard-looking

AN EXTRAORDINARY FESTIVAL.

creatures, with skins like shrivelled parchment; they had scanty, dishevelled hair, and piercing, beady eyes. They were not ornamented in any way, and seemed more like skeletons from a tomb than human beings. After they had gyrated wildly round the fire for a short time, the chant suddenly ceased, and the witches fell prostrate upon the ground, calling out as they did so the names of some departed chiefs. A deathly silence then fell on the assembled gathering, and all eyes were turned towards the wreaths of smoke that were ascending into the evening sky. The witches presently renewed their plaintive cries and exhortations, and at length I was amazed to see strange shadowy forms shaping themselves in the smoke. At first they were not very distinct, but gradually they assumed the form of human beings, and then the blacks readily recognised them as one or other of their long-departed chiefs—estimable men always and great fighters. The baser sort never put in an appearance.

Now the first two or three times I saw this weird and fantastic ceremony, I thought the apparitions were the result of mere trickery.

But when I saw them year after year, I came to the conclusion that they must be placed in the category of those things which are beyond the ken of our philosophy. I might say that no one was allowed to approach sufficiently close to touch the "ghosts," —if such they can be termed; and probably even if permission had been granted, the blacks would have been in too great a state of terror to have availed themselves of it.

Each of these *séances* lasted twenty minutes or

half-an-hour, and were mainly conducted in silence. While the apparitions were visible, the witches remained prostrate, and the people looked on quite spellbound. Gradually the phantoms would melt away again in the smoke, and vanish from sight, after which the assembly would disperse in silence. By next morning all the invited blacks would have gone off to their respective homes. The witches, as I afterwards learnt, lived alone in caves; and that they possessed wonderful powers of prophecy was evidenced in my own case, because they told me when I came among them that I would still be many years with their people, but I would eventually return to my own kind. The warriors, too, invariably consulted these oracles before departing on hunting or fighting expeditions, and religiously followed their advice.

CHAPTER XVI

MY two children were a source of great delight to me at this time,—although of course they were half-castes, the colour of their skin being very little different from that of their mother. The whiteness of their hands and finger-nails, however, clearly indicated their origin. They were not christened in the Christian way, neither were they brought up exactly in the same way as the native children.

I taught them English. I loved them very dearly, and used to make for them a variety of gold ornaments, such as bangles and armlets. They did not participate in all the rough games of the black children, yet they were very popular, having winning manners, and being very quick to learn. I often told them about my life in other parts of the world ; but whenever I spoke of civilisation, I classed all the nations of the universe together, and referred to them as " my home," or " my country." I did not attempt to distinguish between France and Switzerland, England

and America.   Curiously enough, the subject that interested them most was the animal kingdom, and when I told them that I hoped some day to take them away with me to see my great country and the animals it contained, they were immensely delighted. Particularly they wanted to see the horse, the lion, and the elephant.   Taking a yam-stick as pointer, I would often draw roughly in the sand almost every animal in Nature.   But even when these rough designs were made for my admiring audience, I found it extremely difficult to convey an idea of the part in the economy of Nature which each creature played. I would tell them, however, that the horse was used for fighting purposes and for travel ; that the cow yielded food and drink, and that the dogs drew sledges.   It was absolutely necessary to dwell only on the utilitarian side of things.   Beasts of burden would be incomprehensible.   Both of my children were very proud of my position among and influence over the blacks.

And really I looked like a black-fellow myself at this time—not so much on account of exposure, as because my body was constantly coated with the charcoal and grease which serves as a protection from the weather and from insects.   My children, you may be interested to learn, never grasped the fact that my exile was other than quite voluntary on my part.

The children of the blacks continued to interest me as much as ever (I was always fond of children); and I never grew tired of watching them at their quaint little games.   I think they all loved me as much as I did them, and I was glad to see that their lives were one long dream of happiness. They had no school to attend, no work to perform, and no punishment to suffer. There are no children like the children of the bush for perfect contentment. They seldom or never quarrelled, and were all day long playing happily about the camp, practising throwing their reed spears; climbing the trees after the honey-pods, and indulging in a thousand and one merry pranks. Often and often I looked at those robust little rascals, and compared them sadly with my own children, who were delicate almost from birth, and who caused me so much anxiety and heartache.

When the combination of circumstances, which is now well known to my readers, caused me to settle in my mountain home, two or three hundred miles to the north of Gibson's Desert, I had no idea that I should remain there for many years.

But strangely enough, as year after year slipped by, the desire to return to civilisation seemed to leave me, and I grew quite content with my lot. Gradually I began to feel that if civilisation—represented, say, by a large caravan—were to come to me, and its leader was willing not merely to take me away, but my wife and children also, then indeed I would consent to go; but for no other consideration could I be induced to leave those who were now so near and dear to me. I may as well mention here that I had many chances of returning *alone* to civilisation, but never availed myself of them. As I spent the greater part of twenty years in my mountain home, it stands to reason that it is this part of my career which I consult for curious and remarkable incidents.

One day a great darkness suddenly came over the

face of Nature.   The sombre gloom was relieved only by a strange lurid glare, which hung on the distant horizon far away across that weird land.   The air was soon filled with fine ashes, which descended in such quantities as to cover all vegetation, and completely hide exposed water-holes and lagoons.   Even at the time I attributed the phenomenon to volcanic disturbance, and I have since found that it was most likely due to an eruption of the volcano of Krakatoa.   This visitation occasioned very great consternation among the superstitious blacks, who concluded that the spirits had been angered by some of their own misdeeds, and. were manifesting their wrath in this unpleasant way.   I did not attempt to enlighten them as to its true cause, but gave them to understand vaguely that *I* had something to do with it.   I also told them that the great spirit, whose representative I was, was burning up the land.

Another phenomenon that caused much mystification and terror was an eclipse of the sun.   Never have I seen my blacks in such a state of excitement and terror as when that intense darkness came suddenly over the world at midday.   They came crowding instinctively to me, and I stood silent among the cowering creatures, not thinking it politic for a moment to break the strange and appalling stillness that prevailed on every hand—and which extended even to the animal world.   The trembling blacks were convinced that night had suddenly descended upon them, but they had no explanation whatever to offer. They seemed quite unfamiliar with the phenomenon, and it was apparently *not* one of those many things which their forefathers wove superstitious stories around, to hand down to their children. As the great darkness continued, the natives retired to rest, without even holding the usual evening chant. I did not attempt to explain the real reason of the phenomenon, but as I had no particular end to serve, I did not tell them that it was due to my power.

Never once, you see, did I lose an opportunity of impressing the savages among whom I dwelt. On several occasions, having all the ingredients at my disposal, I attempted to make gunpowder, but truth to tell, my experiments were not attended with very great success. I had charcoal, saltpetre, and sulphur ready to my hand,—all obtainable from natural sources close by ; but the result of all my efforts (and I tried mixing the ingredients in every conceivable way) was a very coarse kind of powder with practically no explosive force, but which would go off with an absurd " puff."

Now I was very anxious to make an *explosive* powder, not merely because it would assist me in impressing the blacks, but also because I proposed carrying out certain blasting operations in order to obtain minerals and stones which I thought would be useful. The net result was that although I could not manufacture any potent explosive, yet I did succeed in arousing the intense curiosity of the blacks. My powder burnt without noise, and the natives could never quite make out where the flame came from.

As there seemed to be a never-ending eagerness on the part of the blacks to witness the wonders of the white man, I even tried my hand at making ice—a commodity which is, of course, absolutely unknown in

Central Australia. The idea came to me one day when I found myself in a very cool cave, in which there was a well of surprisingly cold water. Accordingly, I filled some opossum skins with the refreshing fluid, placed them in the coolest part of the cave, and then covered them with saltpetre, of which there was an abundance. When I tell you that the experiment was quite fruitless, you will readily understand that I did not always succeed in my rôle of wonder-worker. But whenever I was defeated, it only had the effect of making me set my wits to work to devise something still more wonderful — something which I was certain would be an assured success.

Whilst taking a stroll in the region of my mountain home one day, my eyes—which were by this time almost as highly trained as those of the blacks themselves—suddenly fastened upon a thin stream of some greenish fluid which was apparently oozing out of the rocky ground. Closer investigation proved that this was not water. I collected a quantity of it in a kangaroo skin, but this took a considerable time, because the liquid oozed very slowly.

I would not have taken this trouble were it not that I was pretty certain *I had discovered a spring of crude petroleum.* Immediately, and by a kind of instinct, it occurred to me that I might make use of this oil as yet another means of impressing the blacks with my magical powers. I told no one of my discovery—not even Yamba. First of all I constructed a sort of raft from the branches of trees, thoroughly saturating each branch with the oil. I also placed a shallow skin reservoir of oil on the upper end of the raft,

and concealed it with twigs and leaves. This done,
I launched my interesting craft on the waters of the
lagoon, having so far carried out all my preparations
in the strictest secrecy. When everything was ready
I sent out invitations by mail-men, smoke signals,
and message sticks to tribes both far and near, to come
and see me *set fire to the water!* In parentheses, I
may remark, that with regard to smoke-signals, white
smoke only is allowed to ascend in wreaths and curls ;
while black smoke is sent up in one great volume.
As by this time my fame was pretty well established,
the wonder-loving children of Nature lost no time in
responding to the summons ; and at length, when the
mystic glow of a Central Australian evening had settled
over the scene, a great gathering established itself
on the shores of the lagoon. On such occasions,
however, I always saw to it that my audience were
not too near. But anyhow there was little chance of
failure, because the blacks had long since grown to
believe in me blindly and implicitly.

With much ceremony I set fire to the raft, hoisted
a little bark sail upon it, and pushed it off. It lay
very low in the water, and as the amazed onlookers
saw it gliding across the placid waters of the lagoon
enveloped in smoke and flames, they did actually
believe that I had set fire to the water itself—
particularly when the blazing oil was seen in lurid
patches on the placid surface. They remained watching till the fire died down, when they retired to their
own homes, more convinced than ever that the white
man among them was indeed a great and powerful
spirit.

But, human nature being fundamentally the same

all the world over, it was natural enough — and, indeed, the wonder is how I escaped so long—that one or other of the tribal medicine-men should get jealous of my power and seek to overthrow me. Now, the medicine-man belonging to the tribe in my mountain home presently found himself (or fancied himself) under a cloud,—the reason, of course, being that my display of wonders far transcended anything which he himself could do.   So my rival commenced an insidious campaign against me, trying to explain away every wonderful thing that I did, and assuring the blacks that if I were a spirit at all it was certainly a spirit of evil.   He never once lost an opportunity of throwing discredit and ridicule upon me and my powers ; and at length I discerned symptoms in the tribe which rendered it imperatively necessary that I should take immediate and drastic steps to overthrow my enemy, who, by the way, had commenced trying to duplicate every one of my tricks or feats.   I gave the matter some little thought, and one day, whilst out on one of my solitary rambles, I came across a curious natural feature of the landscape, which suggested to me a novel and, I venture to say, re-markable solution of a very serious situation.

I suddenly found myself on the brink of a peculiar basin-like depression, which, from its obvious damp-ness and profusion of bush and cover, I at once recognised as the ideal abode of innumerable snakes. I marked the spot in my mind, and returned home, pondering the details of the dramatic victory I hoped to win.   Day by day I returned to this depression and caught numerous black and carpet snakes.   From each of these dangerous and poisonous reptiles I re-

moved the poison fangs only ; and then, after scoring
it with a cross by means of my stiletto, I let it go,
knowing that it would never leave a spot so ideal—
from a snake's point of view.   I operated on a great
number of the deadly reptiles in this way, but, of
course there remained many who were not so treated ;
whilst several of my queer patients died outright
under the operation.   Needless to say, I might have
met my own death in this extraordinary business had
I not been assisted by my devoted wife.   When we
had finished our work, there was absolutely nothing
in the appearance of the place to indicate that it was
any different from its state when I first cast my eyes
upon it.

Then, all being ready, I chose a specially dramatic
moment at a *corroboree* to challenge my rival in a war
song, this challenge being substantially as follows :
" You tell the people that you are as great as I—the
all-powerful white spirit-man.   Well, now, I offer you
a formal challenge to perform the feat which I shall
perform on a certain day and at a certain spot."   The
day was the very next day, and the spot, the scene
of my strange surgical operations upon the snakes.
The effect of my challenge was magical.

The jealous medicine-man, boldly and openly
challenged before the whole tribe, had no time to
make up an evasive reply, and he accepted then
and there.   Urgent messages were despatched, by
the fun-loving blacks, to all the tribes, so that we
were pretty sure of a large and attentive audience.
It was about midday when the ridge round the depression was crowded with expectant blacks, every
one of whom dearly loved a contest, or competition, of

whatever kind. I lost no time—for in love or war shilly-shallying is unknown among the blacks—but boldly leaped down into the hollow armed only with a reed whistle, which I had made for myself solely with the view of enticing the snakes from their holes. I cast a triumphant glance at my impassive rival, who, up to this moment, had not the faintest idea what the proposed ordeal was. I commenced to play as lively a tune as the limited number of notes in the whistle would allow, and before I had been playing many minutes the snakes came gliding out, swinging their heads backwards and forwards and from side to side as though they were under a spell. Selecting a huge black snake, who bore unobtrusively my safety mark, I pounced down upon him and presented my bare arm. After teasing the reptile two or three times I allowed him to strike his teeth deep into my flesh, and immediately the blood began to run. I also permitted several other fangless snakes to bite me until my arms and legs, breast and back, were covered with blood. Personally, I did not feel much the worse, as the bites were mere punctures, and I knew the selected reptiles to be quite innocuous. Several "unmarked" snakes, however, manifested an eager desire to join in the fun, and I had some difficulty in escaping their deadly attentions. I had to wave them aside with a stick.

All this time the blacks above me were yelling with excitement, and I am under the impression that several were lamenting my madness, whilst others were turning angrily upon my rival, and accusing him of having brought about my death. At a favourable moment I rushed up the ridge of the hollow and

stood before the horrified medicine-man, who, in
response to my triumphant demand to go and do
likewise, returned a feeble and tremulous negative.

A STRANGE PERFORMANCE

Even he, I think, was now sincerely convinced that
I possessed superhuman powers; but it would have

been awkward had he come along when I was laboriously and surreptitiously extracting the poison fangs from the snakes, and placing my "hall mark" upon them.

His refusal cost him his prestige, and he was forthwith driven from the tribe as a fraud, whilst my fame rose higher than ever. The blacks now wished me to take over the office of medicine-man, but I declined to do so, and nominated instead a youth I had trained for the position. It may be necessary here to remark that the blacks, under no circumstances, kill a medicine-man. My defeated rival was a man of very considerable power, and I knew quite well that if I did not get the best of him he would have *me* driven out of the tribe and perhaps speared.

Mention of the snake incident reminds me of a very peculiar and interesting sport which the blacks indulge in. I refer to fights between snakes and iguanas. These combats certainly afford very . fine sport. The two creatures are always at mortal enmity with one another, but as a rule the iguana commences the attack, no matter how much bigger the snake may be than himself; or whether it is poisonous or not. I have seen iguanas attack black snakes from six feet to ten feet in length, whilst they themselves rarely measured more than three or four feet. As a rule the iguana makes a snapping bite at the snake a few inches below its head, and the latter instantly retaliates by striking its enemy with its poisonous fangs. Then an extraordinary thing happens. The iguana will let go his hold and straightway make for a kind of fern, which he eats in considerable quantities, the object of this being to

counteract the effects of the poison.   When he thinks
he has had enough of the antidote he rushes back to
the scene of the encounter and resumes the attack ;
the snake always waits there for him.   Again and
again the snake bites the iguana, and as often the
latter has recourse to the counteracting influences of
the antidote.   The fight may last for upwards of an
hour, but eventually the iguana conquers.   The final
struggle is most exciting.   The iguana seizes hold of
the snake five or six inches below the head, and this
time refuses to let go his hold, no matter how much
the snake may struggle and enwrap him in its coils.
Over and over roll the combatants, but the grip of
the iguana is relentless ; and the struggles of the
snake grow weaker, until at length he is stretched
out dead.   Then the triumphant iguana steals slowly
away.

The spectators would never dream of killing him,—
partly on account of their admiration for his prowess,
but more particularly because his flesh is tainted with
poison from the repeated snake bites.   These curious
fights generally take place near water-holes.

I have also seen remarkable combats between
snakes of various species and sizes.   A small snake
will always respond to the challenge of a much larger
one, this challenge taking the form of rearing up and
hissing.   The little snake will then advance slowly
towards its opponent and attempt to strike, but, as
a rule, the big one crushes it before it can do any
harm.   I had often heard of the joke about two
snakes of equal size trying to swallow one another,
and was, therefore, the more interested when I came
across this identical situation in real life.   One day,

right in my track, lay two very large snakes which had evidently been engaged in a very serious encounter; and the victor had commenced swallowing his exhausted adversary. He had disposed of some three or four feet of that adversary's length when I arrived on the scene, and was evidently resting before taking in the rest. I easily made prisoners of both.

Not long after this incident a delusive hope was held out to me that I might be able to return to civilisation. News was brought one day that the tracks of some strange and hitherto unknown animals had been found to the north, and, accompanied by Yamba, I went off to inspect them. I found that they were camel tracks—for the second time; and as Yamba informed me that, from the appearance of the trail, there was no one with them, I concluded that in all probability the creatures were wild, having long ago belonged to some exploring party which had come to grief.

"Here at length," I thought, "is the means of returning to civilisation. If I can only reach these creatures—and why should I not with so much assistance at my disposal?—I will break them in, and then strike south across the deserts with my wife and family." I returned to the camp, and taking with me a party of the most intelligent tribesmen, set off after the wild camels. When we had been several days continuously tracking we came up with the beasts. There were four of them altogether, and right wild and vicious-looking brutes they were. They marched close together in a band, and never parted company. The moment I and my men tried to separate and head them off, the leader would swoop down upon us with open mouth, and the result of this appalling apparition was that my black assistants fled precipitately. Alone I followed the camels for several days in the hope of being able ultimately to drive them into some ravine, where I thought I might possibly bring them into a state of subjection by systematic starvation. But it was a vain effort on my part. They kept in the track of water-

CAMELS IN THE DESERT

holes, and wandered on from one to the other at considerable speed.

At length I abandoned hope altogether, though not without a feeling of sore disappointment, as I watched the curious, ungainly creatures disappearing over the ridge of a sand-hill. Of course I took good care not to tell any of the natives the real reason of my desire to possess a camel,—though I did try to explain to them some of the uses to which people in other parts of the world put these wonderful animals.

I never lost an opportunity of leaving records

wherever I could. As I have said before, I was constantly blazing trees and even making drawings upon them; and I would have left records in cairns had I been able to make any writing material. Talking about this, I was for a long time possessed with the desire to make myself a kind of paper, and I frequently experimented with the fibres of a certain kind of tree. This material I reduced to a pulp, and then endeavoured to roll into sheets. Here again, however, I had to confess failure. I found the ordinary sheets of bark much more suitable for my purpose.

Pens I had in thousands from the quills of the wild swan and goose; and I made ink from the juice of a certain dark-coloured berry, mixed with soot, which I collected on the bottom of my gold cooking-kettle. I also thought it advisable to make myself plates from which to eat my food—not because of any fastidiousness on my part, but from that ever-present desire to impress the blacks, which was now my strongest instinct. In the course of my ramblings in the northern regions I came across quantities of silver-lead, which I smelted with the object of obtaining lead to beat out into plates. I also went some hundreds of miles for the sake of getting copper, and found great quantities of ores of different kinds in the Kimberley district.

A very strange experience befell Yamba not long after I had settled down among the blacks in my mountain home; and it serves to illustrate the strictness with which the laws against poaching are observed. The incident I am about to relate concerned me very nearly, and might have cost me my life as well as my wife. Well, it happened that Yamba

and I were one day returning from one of the many
"walk-abouts" which we were constantly undertaking
alone and with natives, and which sometimes extended over several weeks and even months. We
had pitched our camp for the afternoon, and Yamba
went off, as usual, in search of roots and game for
the evening meal. She had been gone some little
time when I suddenly heard her well-known "coo-
eey" and knowing that she must be in trouble of some
kind, I immediately grasped my weapons and went
off to her rescue, guiding myself by her tracks.

A quarter of a mile away I came upon a scene
that filled me with amazement. There was Yamba
—surely the most devoted wife a man, civilised or
savage, ever had—struggling in the midst of quite
a crowd of blacks, who were yelling and trying
forcibly to drag her away. At once I saw what
had happened. Yamba had been hunting for roots
over the boundary of territory belonging to a tribe
with whom we had not yet made friends ; and as she
had plainly been guilty of the great crime of trespass,
she was, according to inviolable native law, confiscated by those who had detected her. I rushed up
to the blacks' and began to remonstrate with them
in their own tongue, but they were both trucu-
lent and obstinate, and refused to release my now
weeping and terrified Yamba. At last we effected
a compromise,—I agreeing to accompany the party,
with their captive, back to their encampment, and
there have the matter settled by the chief. Fortunately we had not many miles to march, but, as I
anticipated, the chief took the side of his own warriors,
and promptly declared that he would appropriate

Yamba for himself. I explained to him, but in vain, that my wife's trespass was committed all unknowingly, and that had I known his tribe were encamped in the district, I would have come immediately and stayed with them a few nights.

As showing what a remarkable person I was, I went through part of my acrobatic repertoire; and even my poor eager Bruno, who evidently scented trouble, began on his own account to give a hurried and imperfect show. He stood on his head and tumbled backwards and forwards in a lamentably loose and unscientific manner, barking and yelling all the time.

I do not know whether the wily chief had made up his mind to see more of us or not; but at any rate he looked at me very fiercely as though determined to carry his point, and then replied that there was but one law—which was that Yamba should be confiscated for poaching, whether the crime was intentional on her part or not. So emphatically was this said that I began to think I had really lost my faithful companion for ever. As this awful thought grew upon me, and I pondered over the terrible past, I made up my mind that if necessary I would lose my own life in her defence, and to this end I adopted a very haughty attitude, which caused the chief suddenly to discover a kind of by-law to the effect that in such cases as this one the nearest relative of the prisoner might win her back by fighting for her. This, of course, was what I wanted, above all things—particularly as the old chief had not as yet seen me use my wonderful weapons. And as I felt certain he would choose throwing spears, I knew that victory was mine.

He selected, with a critical eye, three well-made spears, whilst I chose three arrows, which I purposely brandished aloft, so as to give my opponent the impression that they were actually small spears, and were to be thrown, as such, javelin-fashion. The old chief and his blacks laughed heartily and pityingly at this exhibition, and ridiculed the idea that I could do any damage with such toy weapons.

The demeanour of the chief himself was eloquent of the good-humoured contempt in which he held me as an antagonist ; and a distance of twenty paces having been measured out, we took our places and prepared for the dramatic encounter, upon which depended something more precious to me than even my own life. Although outwardly cool and even haughty, I was really in a state of most terrible anxiety. I fixed my eyes intently upon the spare but sinewy chief, and without moving a muscle allowed him to throw his spears first. The formidable weapons came whizzing through the air with extraordinary rapidity one after the other ; but long experience of the weapon and my own nimbleness enabled me to avoid them. But no sooner had I stepped back into position for the third time than, with lightning dexterity, I unslung my bow and let fly an arrow at my antagonist which I had purposely made heavier than usual by weighting it with fully an ounce of gold. Naturally he failed to see the little feathered shaft approach, and it pierced him right in the fleshy part of the left thigh—exactly where I intended. The chief leaped from the ground more in surprise than pain, as though suddenly possessed by an evil spirit. His warriors, too, were vastly impressed. As blood was drawn in this way, honour and the law were alike supposed to be satisfied, so Yamba was immediately restored to me, trembling and half afraid to credit her own joyful senses.

My readers will, perhaps, wonder why these cannibal savages did not go back on their bargain and refuse to give her up, even after I had vanquished their chief in fair fight; but the honourable course they adopted is attributable solely to their own innate sense of fair-play, and their admiration for superior prowess and skill.

Why, when the chief had recovered from his astonishment he came up to me, and greeted me warmly, without even taking the trouble to remove my arrow from his bleeding thigh! We became the very best of friends; and Yamba and I stayed with him for some days as his guests. When at length we were obliged to leave, he gave me quite an imposing escort, as though I were a powerful friendly chief who had done him a great service!

CHAPTER XVII

I MUST say I was not very much troubled with
mosquitoes in my mountain home, and as I had endured dreadful torments from these insects whilst at
Port Essington and other swampy places, I had good
reason to congratulate myself. Whilst crossing some
low country on one occasion I was attacked by these
wretched pests, whose bite penetrated even the clay
covering that protected my skin. Even the blacks
suffered terribly, particularly about the eyes. I,
however, had taken the precaution to protect my eyes
by means of leaves and twigs. At Port Essington the
mosquitoes were remarkably large, and of a greyish
colour. They flew about literally in clouds, and it was
practically impossible to keep clear of them.

The natives treated the bites with an ointment made
from a kind of penny-royal herb and powdered charcoal. Talking about pests, in some parts the ants
were even more terrible than the mosquitoes, and I
have known one variety—a reddish-brown monster, an
inch long—to swarm over and actually kill children by

stinging them. Another pest was the leech. It was
rather dangerous to bathe in some of the lagoons on
account of the leeches that infested the waters. Often
in crossing a swamp I would feel a slight tickling sensation about the legs, and on looking down would
find my nether limbs simply coated with these loathsome creatures. The remarkable thing was, that
whilst the blacks readily knew when leeches attacked
them, I would be ignorant for quite a long time, until
I had grown positively faint from loss of blood.
Furthermore, the blacks seemed to think nothing of
their attacks, but would simply crush them on their
persons in the most nonchalant manner. Sometimes
they scorch them off their bodies by means of a lighted
stick—a kind office which Yamba performed for me.
The blacks had very few real cures for ailments, and
such as they had were distinctly curious. One cure for
rheumatism was to roll in the black, odourless mud
at the edge of a lagoon, and then bask in the blazing
sun until the mud became quite caked upon the
person.

The question may be asked whether I ever tried to
tell my cannibals about the outside world. My answer
is, that I only told them just so much as I thought
their childish imaginations would grasp. Had I told
them more, I would simply have puzzled them, and
what they do not understand they are apt to suspect.

Thus, when I showed them pictures of horse-races
and sheep farms in the copy of the Sydney *Town and
Country Journal* which I had picked up, I was obliged
to tell them that horses were used only in warfare, whilst sheep were used only as food. Had
I spoken about horses as beasts of burden, and told

them what was done with the wool of the sheep, they would have been quite unable to grasp my meaning, and so I should have done myself more harm than good. They had ideas of their own about astronomy ; the fundamental "fact" being that the earth was perfectly flat, the sky being propped up by poles placed at the edges, and kept upright by the spirits of the departed—who, so the medicine-man said, were constantly being sent offerings of food and drink. The Milky Way was a kind of Paradise of souls ; whilst the sun was the centre of the whole creation.

I had often puzzled my brain for some method whereby I could convey to these savages some idea of the magnitude of the British Empire. I always had the *British* Empire in my mind, not only because my sympathies inclined that way, but also because I knew that the first friends to receive me on my return to civilisation must necessarily be British. Over and over again did I tell the childish savages grouped around me what a mighty ruler was the Sovereign of the British Empire, which covered the whole world. Also how that Sovereign *had sent me as a special ambassador*, to describe to them the greatness of the nation of which they formed part. Thus you will observe I never let my blacks suspect I was a mere unfortunate, cast into their midst by a series of strange chances. I mentioned the whole world because nothing less than this would have done. Had I endeavoured to distinguish between the British Empire and, say, the German, I should have again got beyond my hearers' depth, so to speak, and involved myself in difficulties.

Half instinctively, but without motive, I refrained

from mentioning that the ruler of the British Empire was *a woman*, but this admission dropped from me accidentally one day, and then—what a falling off was there! I instantly recognised the mistake I had made from the contemptuous glances of my blacks. And although I hastened to say that she was a mighty chieftainess, upon whose dominions the sun never set; and that she was actually the direct ruler of the blacks themselves, they repudiated her with scorn, and contemned me for singing the praises of a mere woman. I had to let this unfortunate matter drop for a time, but the subject was ever present in my mind, and I wondered how I could retrieve my position (and her Majesty's) without eating my words. At length one day Yamba and I came across a curious rugged limestone region, which was full of caves. Whilst exploring these we came upon a huge, flat, precipitous surface of rock, and then—how or why, I know not—the idea suddenly occurred to me *to draw a gigantic portrait of her Most Gracious Majesty Queen Victoria!* At this period, I should mention, I was a recognised chief, and periodically—once every new moon—I gave a kind of reception to my people, and also to the neighbouring tribes. At this interesting function I would always contrive to have some new wonder to unfold. My visitors never outstayed their welcome, and I always managed to have an abundance of food for them.

Well, I came upon the cave region a few weeks after my unfortunate blunder about the Queen; and I determined to have my great portrait ready for the next reception day. Taking some blocks of stone of handy size, I first wetted the surface of the rock and

AN EXTRAORDINARY PORTRAIT

then commenced to rub it, until I had a pretty smooth face to work upon. This took some time, but whilst I was doing it Yamba got ready the necessary charcoal sticks and pigments such as the blacks decorate themselves with at *corroborees*. I had a slight knowledge of drawing, and climbing up on some projecting stones I commenced to draw in bold, sweeping outline, what I venture to describe as the most extraordinary portrait of Queen Victoria on record. The figure, which was in profile, was perhaps seven feet or eight feet high, and of more than equally extravagant proportions in other respects. Of course, the figure had to be represented entirely without clothing, otherwise the blacks would simply have been puzzled. Now to describe the portrait as much in detail as I dare. The crown was composed of rare feathers such as only a redoubtable and cunning hunter could obtain ; and it included feathers of the lyre-bird and emu. The sceptre was a stupendous gnarled waddy or club, such as could be used with fearful execution amongst one's enemies. The nose was very large, because this among the blacks indicates great endurance ; whilst the biceps were abnormally developed. In fact, I gave her Majesty as much muscle as would serve for half-a-dozen professional pugilists or " strong men." The stomach was much distended, and when I state this fact I am sure it will excite much curiosity as to the reason why.

Well, as the stomach is practically the greatest deity these savages know, and as food is often very hard to obtain, they argue that a person with a very full stomach must necessarily be a daring and skilful hunter, otherwise he would not be able to get much food to put into it.

This extraordinary portrait was finally daubed and decorated with brilliant pigments and glaring splashes of yellow, red, and blue. I also used a kind of vivid red dye obtained from the sap of a certain creeper which was bruised between heavy stones. I spent perhaps a week or a fortnight on this drawing (I could not give all day to it, of course); and the only persons who knew of its existence were my own children and women-folk. After the completion of the great portrait, I went away, and waited impatiently for my next reception day. When the wonder-loving blacks were again before me I told them that I had a remarkable picture of the great British Queen to show them, and then, full of anticipation and childish delight, they trooped after me to the spot where I had drawn the great picture on the rocks. It is no exaggeration to say that the crowd of cannibals stood and squatted in front of my handiwork simply speechless with amazement. Eventually they burst out into cries of wonderment, making curious guttural sounds with their lips, and smacking their thighs in token of their appreciation. I pointed out every detail—the immense size of the great Queen, and the various emblems of her power; and at last, stepping back from the rock, I sang " God save the Queen," the beautiful national hymn of Great Britain, which I had learned from the two ill-fated girls, and which, you will remember, has the same air as that of a Swiss song.

The general effect not merely removed any bad impression that might have been created with regard to my damaging admission about the sex of the great ruler; it more than re-established me in my old position, and I followed up my success by assuring them

that her Majesty included in her retinue of servants
a greater number of persons than was represented in
the whole tribe before me. Furthermore, I assured
them that whilst the mountain home I had built was
very large (judged by their standard), the house of
Queen Victoria was big enough to hold a whole
nation of blacks.

In order to give you some idea of the nervous
horror I had of losing prestige, I may tell you that,
far from being satisfied with what I had done to
vindicate the great Sovereign whose special ambassador I was supposed to be, I soon decided to give
yet another demonstration which should impress even
those who were inclined to cavil—if any such existed.
I pointed out that whilst the Queen, great and powerful and beloved ruler though she was, could not
lead her warriors into battle in person, yet she was
represented in war time by her eldest son, who was a
most redoubtable warrior and spear-thrower, and acted
on behalf of his illustrious mother on all occasions
when she could not appear. But as mention of the
Prince of Wales called for a demonstration of *his*
personality also, I determined to make another experiment in portraiture,—this time in the direction
of sculpture. I think it was having come across a
very damp country, abounding in plastic clay, that
put this idea into my head. First of all, then, I cut
down a stout young sapling, which, propped up in the
ground, served as the mainstay of my statue; and
from it I fastened projecting branches for the arms
and legs.

Round this framework I built up my figure with
blocks of clay; and at length, after, perhaps, three or

four weeks' industrious modelling, I completed a statue of his Royal Highness which measured about seven feet six inches in height. The body and limbs were of abnormal development, much on the lines of my representation of his august mother. Fuller details would be interesting, but hardly edifying. This statue I "unveiled" at another of my monthly receptions, and, judged by its effect, it was even a greater success than the colossal portrait of the Queen. A monster *corroboree* was held alongside the Prince of Wales's statue, but, unfortunately, he went to pieces in a day or two, when the fierce sun beat down upon the clay, and cracked it. This gradual disintegration of the great ruler's deputy vastly amused the blacks, and I eventually had to hasten the Prince's end, lest their mirth should compromise my dignity.

You will hardly be surprised when I tell you that the blacks looked to me for everything. I was judge, wonder-worker, and arbitrator. Often they would pick up one of my possessions, and, whilst not exactly coveting it, they would ask for one like it.

Take, for example, the reed flutes which, when played by me, were such a source of joy to the blacks and their children. Well, I was soon called upon to make flutes for the natives, which I did out of long reeds; but these instruments only had two holes in them at first, as the blacks could not play them when other holes were added. The great drawback to these flutes was that the reed dried very quickly and became useless for musical purposes; so I was kept pretty busy, more especially as I did not want to create jealousy by refusing some and gratifying others.

Although the immediate country in which I established my home was fertile and extremely rich in tropical vegetation, the adjoining ranges were in striking contrast to it ; many districts being rugged and slaty and painfully difficult to traverse on foot. There were, however, many interesting natural curiosities which beguiled the time in travelling.

Once I came across a certain kind of spider, whose web was so strong and thick that it only broke under considerable pressure from the finger. The spider itself was fully two inches or three inches long, and had formidable claws. Inland fishing, too, I found extremely interesting. Of course, the inland blacks have a very different method of fishing from that adopted by the coast tribes. Often the inland people would build a fire on the banks of the lagoon, and throw something into the water to attract the fish to the surface. When the fish rose they would promptly be speared. Some of them weighed as much as ten pounds, and proved excellent eating. The blacks themselves never inquired how the fish came into these inland holes ; it was enough for them to know they were there and were good eating. The usual fish-hooks were of bone ; and although I experimented with hooks of gold and copper I found them practically useless, and, in the long run, reverted to articles of native manufacture. In a certain limestone country, which I struck in the course of my wanderings, I discovered some extraordinary caves with water-holes, in which blind fish existed. They certainly had indications of eyes, but these were hidden beneath a kind of permanent skin covering. In any case they would have had no use for eyes, because the water-holes were situated in the most profound darkness. In other caves I discovered quantities of extraordinary animal-bones, probably of prehistoric origin.

If I have omitted to mention Bruno in connection with every incident related in these pages, it must not be supposed that my faithful companion did not play an important part in my daily life.

He was always with me; but it must be remembered that he was now growing old, and the natives around me were by no means so keen to possess him as the tribes of Carpentaria had been in the days gone by.

All kinds of extraordinary incidents befell me whilst on the "walk-about." Many a time have I been deceived by mirage. One most complete deception befell me one day whilst Yamba and I were tramping over a stretch of low, sandy country. Suddenly I fancied I descried the boundless ocean in the distance, and with my usual impetuosity rushed frantically forward in the firm belief that at last we had reached the coast. Yamba explained that it was only a mirage, but I would not stay to listen, and must have gone miles before I gave up in disgust and returned to my patient wife. This brings me to another and perhaps still more extraordinary illusion. One day whilst Yamba and I were passing through one of those eternal regions of sand-hills and spinifex which are the despair of the Australian explorer, I suddenly saw in the distance what I was certain was a *flock of sheep*. There they were apparently—scores of them, browsing calmly in a depression in a fertile patch where most probably water existed.

In an instant the old desire to return to civilisation, which I had thought buried long ago, reasserted itself, and I dashed forward at full speed yelling back to Yamba, "Sheep, sheep—where sheep are, men are. Civilisation at last!" When at length I had got near enough for the creatures to notice me, you may imagine my disgust and disappointment when quite a little forest of tall heads went high into the air, and a *flock of emus* raced off across the country at full speed. These huge birds had had their heads down feeding, and not unnaturally, in the distance, I had mistaken them for sheep.

I think every one is aware that prolonged droughts are of very common occurrence in Central Australia, and are mainly responsible for the migratory habits of the aborigines—particularly those of the remote deserts in the interior. The most terrible drought I myself experienced whilst in my mountain home was one that extended over three years, when even the lagoon in front of my dwelling, which I had thought practically inexhaustible, dried up, with the most appalling results. Just think—never a drop of rain falling for over three long years, with a scorching sun darting down its rays almost every day! During this terrible period the only moisture the parched earth received was in the form of the heavy dews that descended in the night. Even these, however, only benefited the vegetation where any continued to exist, and did not contribute in the slightest degree to the natural water supply so necessary for the sustenance of human and animal life. The results were terrible to witness. Kangaroos and snakes; emus and cockatoos; lizards and rats—all lay about either dead or dying ; and in the case of animals who had survived, they seemed no longer to fear their natural enemy, man.

Day by day as I saw my lagoon grow gradually smaller, I felt that unless I took some steps to ensure a more permanent supply, my people must inevitably perish, and I with them. Naturally enough, they looked to me to do something for them, and provide some relief from the effects of the most terrible drought which even they had ever experienced. Almost daily discouraging reports were brought to me regarding the drying up of all the better-known water-holes all round the country, and I was at length obliged to invite all and sundry to use my own all but exhausted lagoon. At length things became so threatening that I decided to sink a well. Choosing a likely spot near the foot of a precipitous hill, I set to work with only Yamba as my assistant. Confidently anticipating the best results, I erected a crude kind of windlass, and fitted it with a green-hide rope and a bucket made by scooping out a section of a tree. My digging implements consisted solely of a home-made wooden spade and a stone pick. Yamba manipulated the windlass, lowering and raising the bucket and disposing of the gravel which I sent to the surface, with the dexterity of a practised navvy. What with the heat, the scarcity of water, and the fact that not one of the natives could be relied upon to do an hour's work, it was a terribly slow and wearying business ; but Yamba and I stuck to it doggedly day after day.

At the end of a week I had sunk a narrow shaft to a depth of twelve or fourteen feet, and then to

A WATER FAMINE

my infinite satisfaction saw every indication that
water was to be found a little lower down. In the
course of the following week I hit upon a spring, and
then I felt amply rewarded for all the trouble I had
taken. Even when the lagoon was perfectly dry, and
only its parched sandy bed to be seen, the supply
from our little well continued undiminished; and it
proved more than enough for our wants during the
whole of the drought. I even ventured to provide
the distressed birds and animals with some means
of quenching their insupportable thirst. A few yards
from the well I constructed a large wooden trough,
which I kept filled with water; and each day it was
visited by the most extraordinary flocks of birds of
every size and variety of plumage—from emus down
to what looked like humming-birds. Huge snakes,
ten and fifteen feet long, hustled the kangaroos
away from the life-giving trough; and occasionally
the crowd would be so excessive that some of the
poor creatures would have to wait hours before their
thirst was satisfied,—and even die on the outer fringe
of the waiting throng. I remember that even at the
time the scene struck me as an amazing and unprecedented one, for there was I doing my best to regulate
the traffic, so to speak, sending away the birds and
animals and reptiles whose wants had been satisfied,
and bringing skins full of water to those who had
fallen down from exhaustion, and were in a fair
way to die. As a rule, the creatures took no
notice whatever of me, but seemed to realise in
some instinctive way that I was their benefactor.
Of course I had to cover over the top of the
well itself, otherwise it would have been simply

swamped with the carcasses of eager animals and birds.

But, it may be asked, why did I take the trouble to supply everything that walked and flew and crawled with water when water was so precious? A moment's thought will furnish the answer. If I suffered all the animals, birds, and reptiles to die, I myself would be without food, and then my last state would be considerably worse than the first.

I think the snakes were the most ungrateful creatures of all. Sometimes they would deliberately coil themselves up in the trough itself, and so prevent the birds from approaching. I always knew when something of this kind had happened, because of the frightful screeching and general uproar set up by the indignant birds—that is to say, such as had the power to screech left. I would hurry to the spot and drag out the cause of the trouble with a forked stick. I never killed him, because there were already enough of his kind dead on every side. The very trees and grass died; and in this originated another almost equally terrible peril — the bush fires, of which more hereafter. Talking about snakes, one day I had a narrow escape from one of these ungrateful reptiles. A number of baby snakes had swarmed into the trough, and I was in the very act of angrily removing them when I heard a shout of horror from Yamba. I swung round, instinctively leaping sideways as I did so, and there, rearing itself high in the air, was an enormous snake, fully twenty feet long. Yamba, without a moment's hesitation, aimed a tremendous blow at it and smashed its head.

The drought was productive of all kinds of curious

and remarkable incidents. The emus came in great flocks to the drinking-trough, and some of them were so far gone that they fell dead only a few yards from the fount of life. I picked up a great number of these huge birds, and made their skins into useful bed coverings, rugs, and even articles of clothing. When this terrible visitation was at its height Yamba made a curious suggestion to me. Addressing me gravely one night she said, "You have often told me of the Great Spirit whom your people worship; He can do all things and grant all prayers. Can you not appeal to Him now to send us water?" It was a little bit awkward for me, but as I had often chatted to my wife about the Deity, and told her of His omnipotence and His great goodness to mankind, I was more or less obliged to adopt this suggestion. Accordingly she and I knelt down together one night in our dwelling, and offered up an earnest prayer to God that He would send water to the afflicted country. Next morning that which seemed to me a miracle had been wrought. Incredible though it may appear, all the creeks, which until the previous night had been mere dry watercourses for an untold number of months, were rippling and running with the much-needed water, and we were saved all further anxiety, at any rate for the time. There may be, however, some scientific explanation of this extraordinary occurrence.

No sooner had we recovered from the delight caused by this phenomenally sudden change than the rain came—*such* rain ! and the tremendous tropical down-pour lasted for several weeks. The country soon reverted to something like its normal appearance.

The bush fires were extinguished, and even my lagoon came into existence again.

Talking about bush fires, we often saw them raging madly and sublimely in the mountains. They would burn for weeks at a stretch, and devastate hundreds of miles of country. For ourselves, we always prepared for such emergencies by "ringing" our dwelling —that is to say, laying bare a certain stretch of country in a perfect circle around us. Often we were almost choked by the intense heat which the wind occasionally wafted to us, and which, combined with the blazing sun and scarcity of water, rendered life positively intolerable.

I now wish to say a few words about Bruno—a few last sorrowful words—because at this period he was growing feeble, and, indeed, had never been the same since the death of Gibson. Still, I was constantly making use of his sagacity to impress the blacks. My usual custom was to hide some article (such as my tomahawk), near the house in Bruno's presence, and then start off on a tramp accompanied by the blacks.

After we had gone a few miles I would suddenly call a halt, and pretend to my companions that I had forgotten something. Then I would order Bruno to go back and fetch it, with many mysterious whisperings. The dear, sagacious brute always understood what I wanted him to do, and in the course of perhaps an hour or two he would come and lay the article at my feet, and accept the flattering adulation of my black companions with the utmost calmness and indifference. Bruno never forgot what was required of him when we encountered a new tribe of blacks. He would always look to me for his cue, and when he saw me commence my acrobatic feats, he too would go through his little repertoire, barking and tumbling and rolling about with wonderful energy.

His quaint little ways had so endeared him to me that I could not bear to think of anything happening to him. On one occasion, when going through a burning, sandy desert, both he and I suffered terribly from the hot, loose sand which poured between our toes and caused us great suffering. Poor Bruno protested in the only way he could, which was by stopping from time to time and giving vent to the most mournful howls. Besides, I could tell from the gingerly way he put his feet down that the burning sand would soon make it impossible for him to go any farther. I therefore made him a set of moccasins out of kangaroo skin, and tied them on his feet. These he always wore afterwards when traversing similar deserts, and eventually he became so accustomed to them that as soon as we reached the sand he would come to me and put up his paws appealingly to have his " boots " put on !

But now age began to tell upon him ; he was getting stiff in his limbs, and seldom accompanied me on hunting expeditions. He seemed only to want to sleep and drowse away the day. He had been a splendid kangaroo hunter, and took quite an extraordinary amount of pleasure in this pursuit. He would run down the biggest kangaroo and " bail him up " unerringly under a tree ; and whenever the doomed animal tried to get away Bruno would immediately go for his tail, and compel him to stand at bay once more until I came up to give the *coup de grâce*.

Of course, Bruno received a nasty kick sometimes and occasionally a bite from a snake, poisonous and otherwise. He was not a young dog when I had him first; and I had now made up my mind that he could not live much longer. He paid but little attention in these days to either Yamba or myself, and in this condition he lingered on for a year or more.

One morning I went into the second hut— which we still

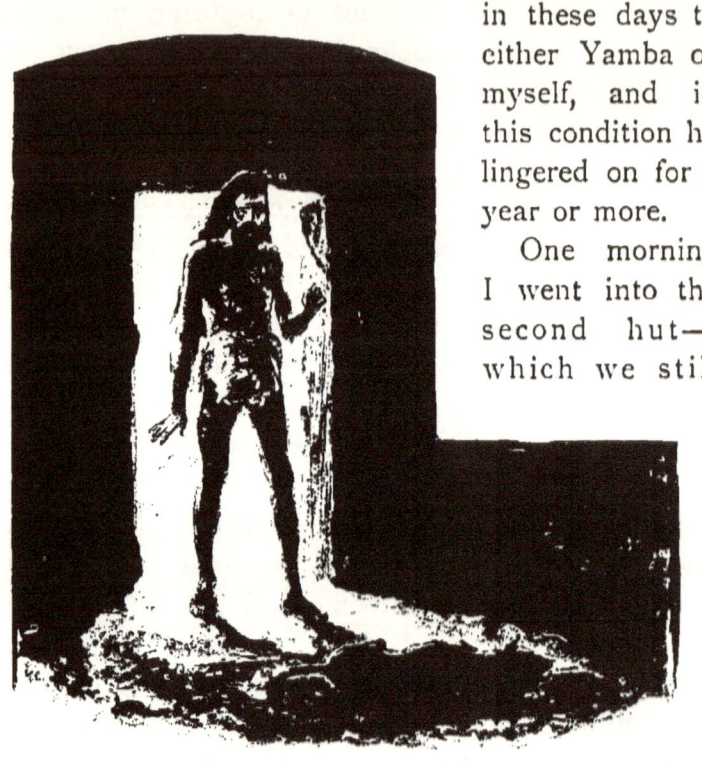

DEATH OF BRUNO

called Gibson's, by the way, although he had never lived there—when to my dismay and horror (notwithstanding that I was prepared for the event), I beheld my poor Bruno laid out stiff and stark on the little skin rug that Gibson had originally made for him. I do not think I knew how much I loved him until he was gone. As I stood there, with the tears coursing down my cheeks, all the strange events of my wondrous career seemed to rise before my mind—events in which poor dead Bruno always took an active part. He was with me on the wreck; he was with me on the island; he was with me in all my wanderings and through all my sufferings and triumphs. He got me out of many a scrape, and his curious little eccentricities, likes, and dislikes afforded me never-ending delight. But now he was gone the way of all flesh; and although I had expected this blow for many months, I do not think this mitigated my poignant grief. Yamba, too, was terribly grieved at his death, for she had become most devotedly attached to him and he to her. I rolled the body of the faithful creature in a kind of preservative earth and then in an outer covering of bark. This done I laid him on a shelf in one of the caves where the wild dogs could not get at him, and where the body of Gibson, similarly treated, had also been placed.

CHAPTER XVIII

I ALWAYS felt instinctively that any attempt at missionary enterprise on my part would be dangerous, and might besides afford jealous medicine-men and other possible enemies an excellent opportunity of undermining my influence.

Sometimes, however, when all the tribe was gathered together, I would bring up the subject of cannibalism, and tell them that the Great Spirit they feared so much had left with me a written message forbidding all feasting off the bodies of human beings. The " written message " I referred to on these occasions was my old Bible. Of course the blacks failed to understand its purport as a book, having no written language of their own ; but my manner and words served to impress them.

My natives seemed ever to manifest the keenest interest in the accounts I gave them of the wonderful resources of civilisation ; but experience showed that I must adapt my descriptions to the intellect of my

372

hearers. For example, I used to tell them that in the great cities ("camps" I called them) there was never any real darkness if men chose, because there were other lights at command which could be turned off and on at will. The most effective analogy in this respect was the twinkling of the stars in the heavens; but my hearers were greatly amazed to think that such lights could be under the command of man.

The blacks had long since put me down as a great spirit come to visit them, and they even located by common consent a certain star in the heavens which they decided was at one time my home, and to which I should eventually return. Every time I made a false step, I had to devise some new "miracle" by way of counterblast.

On one occasion I actually made a perambulator for the conveyance of children! It was the very first time that these primitive savages had seen the principle of the wheel applied to locomotion, and it passed their comprehension altogether. With childish delight and an uproar that baffles all description, both men and women almost fought with one another for the honour of pushing the crude little conveyance about. The perambulator was made out of logs, and was a four-wheeled vehicle; the rims of the wheels being cut from a hollow tree. My blacks were also much amazed at the great size of my mountain home; but their wonderment increased greatly when I explained to them that some of the buildings in the great "camps" of the white man were as large as the hills, and much more numerous.

Elsewhere I have spoken of the extraordinary system of telegraphy that exists among the blacks. Well,

in the early eighties news began to reach me that
numbers of white men had appeared in the north;
and in one of my many long tramps I one day came
upon a party of white men engaged in prospecting.
I speak of this remarkable meeting thus abruptly
because their tent met my gaze in the most abrupt
manner possible.   It is ever so in the Australian bush.

THE PERAMBULATOR

I found that this party was by no means an isolated
one, and I actually stayed in various camps for a few
days, before returning to my mountain home.   I
need hardly remark that the white men were far more
astonished to see me than I was at meeting them.   Of
course I could have joined them and gone back to
civilisation, but this I would not do without my native
wife and family.   It was in the Kimberley district that
I met these parties of prospectors; and I may here

remark that I had for some time been aware of the existence of this auriferous region. I learned afterwards that the Kimberley was geographically the nearest point I might have made for in order to reach civilisation.

When I settled down again in my mountain home I soon fell into my old way of living, which was practically identical with that of the blacks, save that I did not always accompany them when they shifted camp. Parties of natives were constantly calling upon me, and would stay perhaps three or four days at a time. I encouraged these visits, and invariably prepared some entertainment for my guests,—even going to the extent of providing them with wives, according to native custom. But, you will ask, where did I get wives to hand round in this convenient fashion? A very interesting question this, and one which requires a somewhat lengthy answer. Now, the blacks do not look upon the advent of a female child with any favour; on the contrary, they frequently get rid of it at once in order to save themselves the trouble of taking it with them when on the walk-about.

As I was always very fond of children, I decided to try and put a stop to this dreadful habit of child-murder, so I made it known far and wide that parents could pass their girl-babies on to me, and I would rear and look after them. The result of this widely-advertised offer was that I soon had quite an orphan asylum established—an institution which was valuable to me in many ways. Quite apart from the satisfaction I derived from knowing I had saved these children from a terrible death, I was looked upon as a kind of prospective father-in-law on a gigantic scale, and young men came from all parts to treat with me for wives.

As I have said before, my regular reception days were held at the new moon.

My visitors, as well as my own people, gradually grew to have quite a reverence for the Bible; but I am afraid it was not on account of the sacredness of the book, but rather owing to the wonderful things it contained, and which were interpreted by me in such a way as would appeal directly to the primitive minds of these people.

Oftentimes I made mistakes. For instance, what seemed to interest them enormously was the story of how Moses struck the rock and obtained a miraculous supply of water. Anything in the way of fresh water procured in the desert interested them keenly. Only, unfortunately, they floored me by asking me to accomplish a similar miracle !

Another Bible story which brought me some discomfiture was about Balaam and his ass. Now, when I decided to tell the story of Balaam, I knew from experience that if I mentioned an "ass," that animal would require all kinds of tedious explanation, which would probably result in needless mystification and consequent suspicion ; so I boldly plunged into the story of *Balaam and his* KANGAROO ! But what staggered the blacks altogether was that Balaam's kangaroo should be able to speak. Now, it seems that a talking animal is the greatest possible joke known to the blacks, and so my narrative was greeted with uproarious mirth ; and my "impossible" story even spread from tribe to tribe. I found it was no use telling the blacks anything they could not readily comprehend.

One day I told them about the destruction of Sodom and Gomorrah by fire and brimstone, and this again landed me in disaster, for I was promptly asked how could any one, Great Spirit or other, burn up *the stones* of which the houses were composed? And, of course, each instance of this kind would be pounced upon by a tribal medicine-man or some other jealous enemy, and used to discredit me. A few days after telling the Sodom and Gomorrah story, I was on a walk-about with Yamba in my mountain region, when I suddenly discovered that shale existed in very considerable quantities, and I thereupon conceived the idea of demonstrating to the blacks that, not only was the Bible narrative a true one, but that it was quite possible to ignite stone; *and I would even show them how it was done!*

Aided by Yamba and other members of my family, I constructed an immense shaft-like cairn, mainly composed of loose pieces of shale intermixed with sandstone. I put in the sandstone and other stones, partly in order that the blacks might not notice the uniform construction of the cairn; and partly also because I knew that when the ordinary stones were heated, they would probably burst or explode with a loud sound, and so terrify the superstitious onlookers. The cairn was about fifteen feet high, with an opening at the summit and other small openings at the sides in order to ensure a good draught. At the base I left an opening sufficiently large for me to crawl through. Then I placed inside a quantity of inflammable material—such as wood and dry bark;—and as all these preparations went forward in a very leisurely manner, my monthly reception was quite due when everything was ready. Wishing to have an exceptionally large gathering, I sent out invitations to all the surrounding tribes to come and see my wonderful performance at which I would "set fire to the rocks and stones."

A perfectly enormous crowd assembled at the time appointed, for my previous achievements had led the black-fellows to suppose I had some marvellous manifestation in store for them. Never can I forget the keenness with which that great assembly anticipated the entertainment in store for them. And remember, they were growing pretty *blasé* by this time, having witnessed so many miracles.

In the twilight of the evening, when the murmur of the multitude was hushed, I crawled cautiously into the cairn (I should have been buried alive had it collapsed), and at once commenced operations with the flint and steel and tinder which I had taken care to leave there. In another minute I had set fire to the wood and dry material that filled the bottom of the shaft. When I was satisfied that it was thoroughly alight, I discreetly withdrew and joined the wondering crowd, which I had forbidden to approach too close. Dense clouds of smoke were now rolling from the apertures of the great cairn, and in a short time the shaft was a fierce and raging furnace, with the ordinary stones red hot and occasionally bursting with loud explosions, which threw showers of glowing slag high into the air.

The blacks were almost paralysed with fear, and many of them threw themselves prostrate on the ground, ignoring the hail of stones that fell upon their naked bodies. I stalked about majestically

SETTING FIRE TO ROCKS AND STONES

among them, exulting in my power and the success
of my manifestation. The big cairn burnt for many
days more fiercely than even a stack of coal would do ;
and I never ceased to wonder that the blacks themselves had not long ago found out the inflammable
nature of the " stone."

By this time Yamba could speak English tolerably
well, but we did not invariably use that language.

Gradually and half unconsciously I fell into the
habit of speaking the native tongue, until I suddenly
found that the practice was obtaining such a firm hold
upon me that I was forgetting French altogether ;
whilst it was only with difficulty that I could form
grammatical sentences in English. I soon came to
the conclusion, therefore, that it was necessary for me
to hold much more converse in English than I had
hitherto done ; and from the moment that this curious
" scare " suggested itself to my mind, Yamba and I and
our children spoke nothing but English when we were
by ourselves in the evening. I cultivated my knowledge of English in preference to any other language,
because I knew that if ever we should reach civilisation, English and not French would be the language
spoken. It may be interesting also to mention that
one of the first indications I had that I was losing my
English was an inability to *think* in that language.

In general appearance I was now absolutely like a
black, and wore only an apron of emu skin as a protection against the scrub I encountered when on the
walk-about. In the ordinary way I never had any
marks upon me with the exception of these scratches.
Of course, on festive occasions, I was gaily painted and
decorated, and no doubt I would have been initiated

into manhood, and borne the tribal and other marks, were it not for the fact that I was a man when I came among the blacks.

It is obviously impossible for me to record minutely the happenings of every day, mainly because only the salient incidents stand out in my mind. Besides, I have already dealt with the daily routine, and have probably repeated myself in minor details.

A constant source of grief to me was the weakly condition of my two children, who I knew could never attain mature age. And knowing they were doomed, I think I loved them all the more.

Yet so incomprehensible is human nature that I often found myself speculating on what I should do after they—and Yamba—were gone; because by this time my faithful helpmate was growing ominously feeble. You must remember that when I first met her on the desert island she was an oldish woman, judged by the native standard; that is to say, she was about thirty.

The death-bed of my boy is a scene I can never forget. He called me to him, and said he was very glad he was dying, because he felt he would never have been strong enough to fight his way through life, and endure daily what the other black boys endured. Therefore, he argued wistfully, and half inquiringly, he would only be a burden to me. He was a very affectionate and considerate little fellow, with an intelligence far beyond that of the ordinary aboriginal child. He spoke in English, because I had taught both him and his sister that language. At the last I learned— for the first time—that it was always worrying him, and almost breaking his little heart, that he could never compete with the black boys in their games of strength and skill; and no doubt he would have become an outcast were it not that he was my son.

Almost his last whispered words to me were that he would be able to assist me more in the Spirit-land than ever he could hope to do in the flesh. He was perfectly conscious to the last, and as I knelt down by his couch of fragrant eucalyptus leaves, and stooped low to catch his whispered message, he told me he seemed to be entering a beautiful new country, where the birds always sang and the flowers bloomed for ever. Spirit voices kept calling him, he said, and he felt himself being irresistibly drawn away from me.

Upon my own feelings I do not wish to dwell. All I will say is I kissed my boy on the eyes and mouth, and then, with a soft "Good-bye, they have come for me," he closed his eyes for ever.

I felt it was to be. A few days afterwards the little girl, my remaining child, was taken ill, and so feeble was she, that she soon joined her brother in the better land. I seemed to be overwhelmed with misfortunes, but the greatest of all was yet to come. I have hinted that Yamba was beginning to show signs of infirmity through advancing years. I could not help noticing, with a vague feeling of helpless horror and sickening foreboding, that she had lost her high spirits and keen perception—to say nothing about the elasticity of her tread and her wonderful physical endurance generally. She was no longer able to accompany me on the long and interesting tramps which we had now taken together for so many years. Her skin began to wither and wrinkle, and she gradually took on the appearance of a very old woman. The result of this

was I began to have fits of frightful depression and
acute misery.   I stayed at home a good deal now,
partly because I knew the country thoroughly and no
longer cared to explore, and partly also because I
missed the companionship and invaluable assistance
of my devoted wife.   I constantly buoyed myself up
with the hope that Yamba was only ailing temporarily,
and that her enfeebled condition had been brought on
mainly by the misfortunes that had befallen us of late.
But she grew more and more feeble, and both she and
I knew that the end was not far off.   Never once,
however, did we allude to such a catastrophe; and
whenever I fixed my eyes earnestly upon her in the
vain hope of discerning some more favourable symptom,
she would pretend not to notice me.

I would sometimes take her for a long walk, which
was really much beyond her strength, solely in order
that we might delude ourselves with vain hopes.   And
she, poor creature, would tax herself far beyond her
strength in order to afford me a happiness which the
real state of things did not justify.

For instance, she would run and leap and jump in
order to show that she was as young as ever; but after
these strange and pathetic demonstrations she would
endeavour to conceal her great exhaustion.

Very soon my poor Yamba was obliged to remain
at home altogether; and as she grew more and more
infirm, she plucked up courage to tell me that she knew
she was going to die, and was rather glad than otherwise, because then I would be able to return to civilisation—that goal for which I had yearned through so
many years.   She pointed out to me that it would not
be so difficult now, as I had already been brought into

contact with parties of white men; and, besides, we had long ago had news brought to us about the construction of the Trans-Continental Telegraph Line from Adelaide to Port Darwin. No sooner had she spoken of death than I broke down again altogether. The thought that she should be taken from me was so cruel that its contemplation was quite insupportable, and I

AS YOUNG AS EVER

threw myself down beside her in a perfect agony of grief and dread.

I told her I did not mind how long I remained among the blacks so long as she was with me; and I tried to persuade her, with all the eloquence I could muster, that, far from dying, she would return to civilisation with me, so that I might spread abroad to the whole

2 D

world the story of her devotion and her virtues.   As
she continued merely to smile pityingly, I changed my
tone and dwelt upon the past. I went through the whole
story of my life, from the time she was cast upon the
desert island in the Sea of Timor, and at the recital of
all the hardships and dangers, joys and troubles, which
we had passed through together, she broke down also,
and we wept long and bitterly in one another's arms.

By this time she had become a convert to Christianity,
but this was entirely a matter of her own seeking.   She
had such implicit belief in my wisdom and knowledge,
that she begged me to tell her all about my religion
in order that she might adopt it as her own.   Like
most converts, she was filled with fiery zeal and
enthusiasm, and tried to soften the approaching terror
by telling me she was quite happy at the thought of
going, because she would be able to look after me even
more than in the past.   "How different it would have
been with me," she used to say, "had I remained with
my old tribe.   I should still be under the belief that
when I died my highest state would be to be turned
into an animal; but now I know that a glorious future
awaits us, and that in due time you will join me in
heaven."

Yamba did not suffer any physical pain, nor was she
actually confined to her bed until four days before her
death.   As the various tribes knew the love and
admiration I had for her, the fact that she lay dying
spread rapidly, and crowds of natives flocked to my
mountain home.

Widespread sympathy was expressed for me; and
all kinds of tender consideration were evinced by these
savages.   All day long an incessant stream of women-

folk kept coming to the hut and inquiring after my dying wife.

It seemed to be Yamba's sole anxiety that I should be well equipped for the journey back to civilisation. She would rehearse with me for hours the various methods adopted by the black-fellows to find water; and she reminded me that my course at first was to be in a southerly direction until I came to a region where the trees were blazed, and then I was to follow the

" GOOD-BYE, MY HUSBAND, I AM GOING "

track that led westward. She had elicited this information for me from the blacks with remarkable acuteness.

These last days seemed to pass very quickly, and one night the dying woman had a serious relapse. Hitherto she had always addressed me as "Master," but now that she stood in the Valley of the Shadow she would throw her arms about my neck and whisper softly, "Good-bye, *my husband.*

Good-bye, I am going—going—going. I will wait for you—there."

For myself I could not seem to realise it. Sometimes I would rise up with the sole intention of finding out whether this frightful thing was or was not a ghastly dream. Then my memory would go back over the long years, and every little instance of unselfishness and devotion would rise before my mind. As I looked at the prostrate and attenuated form that lay silent on the couch of eucalyptus leaves, I felt that life was merely the acutest agony, and that I must immediately seek oblivion in some form or the other, or lose my reason. It seemed, I say, impossible that Yamba could cease to be. It seemed the cruellest and most preposterous thing that she could be taken from me.

Frantically I put my arms around her and actually tried to lift her on to her feet, begging of her to show how robust she was as in the days of yore. I whispered into her ears all the memories of the past, and the poor creature would endeavour to respond with a series of feeble efforts, after which she sank back suddenly and breathed a last pitiful sigh.

Language is utterly futile to describe my horror—my distraction. I felt as I imagined a man would feel after amputation of all his members, leaving only the quivering and bleeding trunk. I felt that life held no more joy, no more hope; and gladly would I have welcomed death itself as a happy release from the wretchedness of living. In my delirium of grief I often besought the repulsive savages about me to spear me where I stood.

Upon this subject I can dwell no more, because of what followed I have only the vaguest recollection.

For days I seemed to live in a kind of dream, and was not even sure that the people I met day by day were real beings.   As to my awful loss, I am sure I did not realise it.   What I did realise, however, was the necessity for immediate action.   Like a dream to me also is the memory of the sincere grief of my blacks and their well-meant endeavours to console me.   The women kept up a mournful howl, which nearly drove me crazy, and only strengthened my resolve to get away from that frightful place.   So dazed did I become, that the blacks concluded some strange spirit must have entered into me.

They seemed to take it for granted that I left all arrangements for the funeral to them; the sole idea that possessed me being to complete my arrangements for the great journey I had before me.   I told the natives frankly of my intention, and immediately forty of them volunteered to accompany me on my travels as far as I chose to permit them to come.   I readily accepted the kindly offer, partly because I knew that alone I should have gone mad; and partly also because I instinctively realised that with such a bodyguard I would have nothing to fear either from human foes or the tortures of thirst.

I left everything.   I cut off my long hair with my stiletto and distributed it among the natives to be made into bracelets, necklaces, and other souvenirs; and then I departed with little ceremony from the place where I had spent so many years of weird and strange exile.   Most of my belongings I gave away, and I think I turned my back upon my mountain home with little or no regret.   My dress consisted solely of the usual covering of emu skin; whilst attached to a

belt round my waist were my tomahawk and stiletto.
My bow and arrows were slung over my shoulder.
Day after day we marched steadily on, precisely as
though we were on a walk-about.   The conditions of
the country were constantly changing, and I came
across many evidences of its natural richness in
minerals—more particularly gold.

One day as we were all resting near the base of a
rock, which was a kind of huge outcrop from the plain,
I began idly to chip the stone with my tomahawk.
Suddenly the edge glanced aside, revealing a bright,
shining, yellow metal.   I sprang to my feet in astonishment, and realised in a moment that this great mass
of rock was auriferous to an enormous degree, and
there was one gigantic nugget, spread out tentacle-
wise in it, which if removed would, I am sure, be as
much as a couple of men could carry.

Week after week passed by, and still we continued
our southward march.   In time, of course, my companions returned to their own country ; but so leisurely
had our progress been that I had ample time thoroughly
to ingratiate myself with other tribes,—so that, as usual,
I went from tribe to tribe practically armed only with
my own knowledge of the savages and my invaluable
repertoire of tricks.   In the course of months I came
upon the blazed or marked trees, and then struck due
west.

Very few incidents worth recording befell me, and I
kept steadily on my way for eight or nine months.   At
last—at last—I came upon unmistakable signs of the
proximity of "civilisation"; for strewn along the track
we were now following were such things as rusty meat-
tins ; old papers ; discarded and very much ant-eaten

clothing; tent-pegs; and numerous other evidences of pioneer life. One day, about noon, I espied an en-campment of tents 500 or 600 yards ahead of me, and I promptly brought my men to a halt whilst I went forward a little to reconnoitre. Curiously enough, the sight of these tents did not cause me any great emotion. You see, I had met prospectors before in the Kimberley region, and besides, I had been looking for these tents so long from the time I first came across the evidences of civilisation aforesaid, that my only surprise was I had not reached them before. Walking about were Europeans in the usual dress of the Australian pro-spector. Suddenly a strange feeling of shyness and hesitancy came over me. Almost stark naked and darkened as I was—a veritable savage, in fact—I realised I could not go and introduce myself to these men without proper clothing. I knew the value of caution in approaching so-called civilised men, having had bitter experience with the Giles expedition. Re-turning to my blacks, I told them that at last I had come up with my own people, but did not want to join them for some little time yet. Then I selected a couple of my companions, and explained to them that I wanted some white man's clothing.

I instructed them to creep quietly into the camp, take a pair of trousers and shirt that were hanging outside one of the tents, and bring back these articles to me. They undertook the commission with evident delight, but when they returned in the course of a few minutes they brought only the shirt with them; the trousers, it seemed having been removed no doubt by the owner, a few minutes before they arrived. My blacks were intensely amused when I donned the shirt; and con-

sidering that this was practically the only article of
wearing apparel I possessed, I have no doubt I did cut
a very ludicrous figure. Then came another difficulty.
I reflected I could not possibly go and show myself
among these white men wearing one of their own shirts.
Finally I decided to bid farewell then and there to my
escort, and continue my march alone until I reached
another encampment.

In the course of another day or so I reached a second
camp. Into this I decided to venture and explain who
I was. Before taking this step, however, I rubbed off
all the clayey coating on my skin, trimmed my hair and
beard to a respectable length by means of a firestick,
and threw away my bow, which was now my only
remaining weapon; then I marched boldly into the
camp. Some five or six bronzed prospectors were
seated at supper round the fire in front of the tent as I
approached; and when they caught sight of me they
stared, astounded for the moment, and then burst into
laughter, under the impression that I was one of their
own black servants playing some joke upon them.
When I was but a few yards away, however, I called
out in English—

"Halloa, boys! have you room for me?"

They were too much taken aback to reply immediately, and then one of them said—

"Oh yes; come and sit down."

As I seated myself among them they asked—

"Have you been out prospecting?"

"Yes," I said quietly, "and I have been away a
very long time."

"And where did you leave your mates?" was the
next question.

"I had no mates," I told them. "I undertook my wanderings practically alone.

They looked at one another, winked, and smiled incredulously at this. Then one of them asked me if I had found any gold.

"HALLOA, BOYS! HAVE YOU ROOM FOR ME?"

I said, "Oh yes, plenty of gold," and then the next query—a most natural one—was, "Well, why have you not brought some of the stuff back with you? How far have you travelled?"

I told them I had been tramping through the heart of the Continent for eight or nine months, and that I had no means of carrying nuggets and quartz about with me.   But this explanation only served to renew their merriment, which reached its climax when, in an unguarded moment, I put a question which I had been burning to ask—

"What year is this?"

"This is Bellamy's 'Looking Backward' with a vengeance," cried one of the prospectors—a sally that was heartily appreciated by the whole of the company, with the exception of myself.   I began to think that if this was the reception civilisation had for me, it were better for me to have remained among my faithful savages.

But in a few minutes the men's demeanour changed, and it was obvious that they looked upon me as a harmless lunatic just emerged from the bush.   I was assured that this conclusion was correct when I saw the diggers looking at one another significantly and tapping their foreheads.   I resolved to tell them nothing further about myself, well knowing that the more I told them the more convinced they would be that I was a wandering lunatic.   I learned that these men were a party of decent young fellows from Coolgardie.   They offered me a meal of tea and damper, and pressed me to stay the night with them, but I declined their hospitality.   I gratefully accepted a pair of trousers, but declined the offer of a pair of boots, feeling certain that I could not yet bear these on my feet.   My rough benefactors told me that I should find many other camps to the south and west; so I wandered off into the bush again and spent the night alone.

My next move was in the direction of Mount Margaret; and along the road which I traversed I came across an interesting variety of picks, shovels, and other mining tools, which had evidently been discarded by disappointed prospectors. I decided not to enter this town but to go round it; then I continued my tramp alone towards Coolgardie and thence to Southern Cross.

After working for some time in the last-named town (my impressions of "civilisation" would make another whole book), I made my way to Perth, the capital of Western Australia. In Perth I was advised that it would be better for me to go to Melbourne, as I would stand a much better chance there of getting a ship on which I might work my passage to Europe. Accordingly I proceeded to Melbourne as soon as I could, and the only noteworthy incident there was my humorous interview with the French Consul. I addressed that dignified functionary in execrable French, telling him that I was a French subject and wanted to be sent back to Europe. I bungled a great deal, and when my French failed I helped myself out with English. The Consul waited patiently till I had finished, stroking his beard the while, and looking at me in the most suspicious manner.

"You claim this because you are a Frenchman?" he said.

"That is so," I replied, involuntarily relapsing into English once more.

"Well," he said coldly, as he turned away, "the next time you say you are a Frenchman you had better not use any English at all, because you speak that language better than I do."

I tried to argue the point with him, and told him I had been shipwrecked, but when I went on to explain how long ago that shipwreck was, he smiled in spite of himself, and I came away.   From Melbourne I went to Sydney, and from Sydney to Brisbane.

About May 1897, I found myself in Wellington, New Zealand, where I was advised I stood an excellent chance of getting a ship to take me to England.   I sailed in the New Zealand Shipping Company's *Waikato*, and landed in London in March 1898.

THE END

Printed by BALLANTYNE, HANSON & Co.
Edinburgh & London

www.ingramcontent.com/pod-product-compliance
Lightning Source LLC
Chambersburg PA
CBHW030825110726
47900CB00006B/1742